A MOST
Civil PROPOSAL

C. P. ODOM

Meryton Press

Oysterville, WA

A MOST CIVIL PROPOSAL

ISBN: 978-1-936009-21-3

Graphic design by Ellen Pickels

*To my wife, Jeanine, who lit up my life
and gave me the reason to write.*

*And to my first two reviewers, Carol and tJean,
who helped me learn and made me look better than I was.*

Prologue

"Will that be all for tonight, Mr. Darcy?"

Fitzwilliam Darcy, lost in the turmoil of his thoughts, turned from the window to find that his valet had completed preparations for the morrow.

"Yes, Jennings," replied Darcy absently, "thank you. That will be all, and I wish you good night."

"Will you be rising as usual tomorrow?"

"Yes. As usual." Darcy turned back to the window.

"Then I wish you good night also, sir," said his valet, and the click of the closing door followed shortly.

Darcy again tried to concentrate. He was coming to the conclusion that it was nigh impossible to determine just how his well-ordered and well-planned life had descended into the tumult and uncertainty that plagued him at present. As recently as the previous day, he had been firm in the belief that his emotions were well in hand, that his detachment was still in place, that he was...safe. Safe from the bewitchment of Elizabeth Bennet, secure in his position in society, and fixed in his confidence as the master of his own fate.

And now? Now he knew that safety had been only an illusion and that he had actually stepped well over the edge of the precipice before being fully aware of the danger. At what point had it happened? Was it during his walk with her in Rosings park the day before? Perhaps — or perhaps not; it did not matter. He knew only that his present resolve to speak to Miss Bennet on the morrow was as real as his previous resolve to ignore her had been imaginary.

He snorted. Speak to her? No, it was much more significant than that. He would make an offer of marriage to her despite the humiliation and strife that would result. He, the master of Pemberley, and she, the daughter of a country gentleman of small fortune and no connections! But it did not matter any more, and he could not determine when that point had been reached.

The mistress of Rosings, his aunt Lady Catherine de Bourgh would not be pleased. The thwarting of her long-held ambition to align himself with his cousin Anne de Bourgh and to join Pemberley with Rosings would not make her temperate. She was well used to having her own way, and he had walked carefully in past visits, remaining noncommittal without overtly contradicting her oft-expressed plans. Indeed, he and Anne had derived considerable amusement as he deftly sidestepped her mother's blunt suggestions. It had seemed harmless fun then since neither of them had any wish to marry. In fact, Anne had told him many times that she knew her health never would allow any kind of marriage, and she would be happy to live out her life quietly in a modest country estate rather than Rosings. But Anne's wishes were meaningless to his aunt, and when Lady Catherine learned of his engagement to Elizabeth Bennet, she would be outraged beyond measure.

"It will not do," he said aloud, picturing Elizabeth's face crumpling under the onslaught of her ladyship's disdain. Then he snorted again, this time in amusement. Miss Bennet had already demonstrated her ability to stand up to his aunt — never retreating yet never quite offering offence. Impertinence it might be called, but courage it could also be named, and he cherished that quality as he imagined her at his side, one eyebrow arched in amusement while Lady Catherine thundered and raged ineffectually.

While his aunt's reaction boded to be extreme and predictable, Darcy was none too sure about the rest of his family and friends. He well knew his uncle Lord Matlock would not be pleased, but just exactly what his response might be was not certain. He took his position as the head of the family seriously, and he would not be happy about a match between the Darcy name and fortune and a country girl with little to bring to the marriage.

His jaw clenched, and his brows knit together in determination; for the thought of Miss Bennet being abused—of his allowing her to be abused—was too painful to consider. "I will not allow *any* mistreatment from my relations," he pledged aloud. *"None!"*

Now the subject that had gripped his thoughts all evening returned anew. How would he address her? He planned to take the opportunity the next day since his aunt's parson and Elizabeth's cousin, Mr. Collins, and his guests were invited to take tea at Rosings. His cousin Colonel Richard Fitzwilliam had urged the invitation, noting it would be the last chance before their departure on Saturday. Darcy could not determine whether his cousin suspected his attachment to Miss Bennet, but Fitzwilliam's amiable attentions to her had played no small part in forming Darcy's resolve. Despite Richard's need to pay at least some notice to money when he married, Darcy was decidedly uncomfortable both with Richard's ease with the lady and with her own response. He wished again that, just once, he could conduct a conversation with her without saying something he did not intend and often did not mean. Much as he enjoyed her verbal repartee, it made him more than a little uncomfortable that many of their exchanges resulted from statements that he never would have previously believed could fall from his lips. Unwillingly, his own words echoed in his mind: *"But pride—where there is a real superiority of mind, pride will be always under good regulation."*

"Idiot!" he groaned in mortification. Even though he could not fault the sense of the statement, how could he have made such an immodest declaration aloud and in company? He had always despised such boasting by other men, and he remembered the night at Netherfield as those words tumbled from his mouth without thought. He cringed inwardly as he also remembered her turning away to hide her smile—yet another joust won by Miss Bennet.

At least it will be finished after tomorrow! Then he could speak of emotions and thoughts that could not be talked of until he declared himself. Fleetingly, he wondered whether he should proceed with more caution, perhaps a simple statement of his esteem and desire to court her in the usual manner, but his inner tumult was such that he rejected the idea almost before it presented itself to his mind. Her wits were much too quick for such discretion; she, of course, must know of his regard for her. He would not disappoint her with a tepid request for courtship when his own fervent love asserted, nay *required*, a clear declaration of intent. *After tomorrow, all will be complete.*

Remembrance of earlier missteps, however, now added to his discontent.

This was too important to leave to chance. He could not afford to make a hash of the fundamental step of proposing marriage when he had, on previous occasions, so oft been unable to manage even simple conversation. A plan of action was called for. Pacing in agitation in front of the fireplace, he imagined himself facing Elizabeth after suggesting a walk through the formal gardens after tea. After seating her on one of the benches in the garden, he was facing her...he was opening his mouth...

In vain have I struggled. It will not do. My feelings will not be repressed. You must allow me—

He stopped short and groaned as the words sounded in his mind. He could almost see Miss Bennet looking up, first in surprise at his usual inability to speak clearly and then in disbelief as he testified to his inward struggles. Why could he not simply say he loved her beyond measure instead of starting out by saying he did not *want* to love her? Such explanations were unnecessary and, though true, could be construed as insulting since she was as cognizant of the disparity between their stations as he. His attraction to her was clear, and she must also be aware that those distinctions no longer mattered.

He resumed pacing, increasingly convinced that he would be unable to speak to her at all. His agitation increased as a sudden vision came to mind: he struggled to speak, he could not, and he turned to flee the garden, leaving Elizabeth behind in growing distress at being abandoned.

He closed his eyes. *I must do this right!*

As he paced, his eyes swept over the writing desk and the sheets of stationery upon it, and he halted, struck by the memory of his time at Cambridge. Then, too, he had faced difficulties in presenting the results of his studies in the presence of his more easily spoken fellows. But he had been driven to overcome this perceived inadequacy on his part, and he had learned to compensate by preparing himself before his verbal addresses, marshalling his thoughts by committing them to paper, and subjecting them to rigorous analysis before giving them voice. He had not had to perform similar preparation since completing his studies, but the scheme appeared fitting to deal with his present apprehension.

He lost no time in taking the candle to the desk and seating himself.

Selecting a pen and pulling a sheet of stationery in front of him, he opened the inkwell, dipped his pen, and began:

Miss Bennet, you must allow me to tell you how ardently I admire and love you...

DARCY LEANED BACK, MASSAGING HIS shoulders to work out the cramps after long hours spent in intense concentration. His feet were chilled as the fire had long ago died down, but he regarded the many pages before him with a measure of satisfaction. The scores of corrections and even the sentences that were entirely marked through did not cause him embarrassment; he actually felt relief at having properly set down his first thoughts and then subjecting them to intense scrutiny. He had spoken them aloud, judging their impact on the only audience that really mattered — Miss Bennet — and made his changes ruthlessly. Several crumpled pages littered the top of the desk when entire passages were rejected in favour of copying the one or two worthy sentences to a new sheet. He could not imagine the mortification that would have resulted had he delivered his sentiments with no preparation. Though it could have no impact, of course, on her acceptance, the embarrassment of presenting himself in such a manner was not to be considered.

Gathering the pages into order, he pulled out a fresh sheet of stationery. The only remaining task was to make a fair copy of the written thoughts and then to burn the offending sheets before trying to get a bit of sleep before dawn...

Chapter 1

When Elizabeth returned to the Parsonage after walking with Colonel Fitzwilliam, she went directly to her room as soon as the colonel left them. There she could think without interruption of all he had told her, and she soon found her anger rising as Mr. Darcy's interference between her sister Jane and Darcy's friend Mr. Bingley became more apparent. She had heretofore attributed the principal design and arrangement of separating them to Miss Bingley, but Colonel Fitzwilliam's disclosures now pointed to Mr. Darcy as the offending conspirator. When she thought of how his pride, caprice, and arrogance had destroyed the chance for happiness of the most affectionate and generous heart in the world, she felt the tears sting her eyes. Further consideration of the matter brought on a headache, which worsened so towards evening that she determined not to attend the cousins at Rosings, where they were engaged to drink tea. Her friend Charlotte Collins, seeing that she was quite unwell, did not press her to go and, to the extent possible, prevented her parson husband from prevailing on her to attend even though he could not conceal his apprehension of Lady Catherine's being rather displeased by her staying at home.

When they were gone, Elizabeth, as if intending to exasperate herself as much as possible against Mr. Darcy, chose for her employment the examination of all the letters Jane had written to her since her being in Kent. They contained no actual complaint, nor was there any revival of past occurrences or any communication of present suffering. But in all and in almost every line of each, there was a want of that cheerfulness which had used to characterize her style and which, proceeding from the serenity of a mind at ease with itself and kindly disposed towards every one, had scarcely ever been clouded. Elizabeth noticed every sentence conveying the idea of uneasiness with an attention that it had hardly received on the first perusal. Mr. Darcy's shameful boast to his cousin of what misery he had been able to inflict gave her a keener sense of her sister's sufferings. It was some consolation to think that his visit to Rosings was to end on the day after next and a still greater consolation that she would be with Jane in less than a fortnight, able to contribute to the recovery of her spirits by all that affection could do.

She could not think of Darcy's leaving Kent without remembering that his cousin was to go with him, but Colonel Fitzwilliam had made it clear that he had no intentions toward her at all, and agreeable as he was, she did not mean to be unhappy about him.

While settling this point, she was suddenly roused by the sound of the doorbell, and her spirits were a little fluttered by the idea of its being Colonel Fitzwilliam himself, who had once before called late in the evening and might now have come to inquire particularly after her. But this idea was soon banished, and her spirits were very differently affected when, to her utter amazement, she saw Mr. Darcy walk into the room.

Darcy had been surprised, nay he had been shocked, to discover that Elizabeth was not with the Parsonage party when they arrived for tea that evening. His preparations had been made, he had reviewed them in his mind, and he was comfortable with his planned approach. Now she had not attended, and he was thrown into disarray.

He wondered at her absence. She knew there was but one day before his departure. Could she truly be ill?

Sudden concern over her well-being replaced his anxiety, and he made an excuse to leave the room as soon as was practicable. He saw Fitzwilliam's eyes raised in question, and he knew without having to look that her ladyship was not happy. In fact, he heard her loudly questioning his cousin as he exited the room: "Fitzwilliam! Where does my nephew go? Has he forgotten his duty to our guests?"

Any response that the colonel made was lost on Darcy as he went up the stairs and strode down the hallway to his room, surprising Jennings as he was laying out bedclothes and preparing for the morning.

"Mr. Darcy?"

"My hat and coat, Jennings," Darcy demanded abruptly. The valet was clearly puzzled but said nothing as he quickly retrieved the coat and helped his master into it. He picked up a whisk, prepared to brush off the shoulders as usual, but Darcy was too impatient to wait. He waved Jennings off, snatched his gloves and hat from the bed, and turned for the door.

"Mr. Darcy, sir!" his valet exclaimed in distress.

"Yes?" he responded sharply, and Jennings swallowed at the impatient look on his face.

"Where shall you be if there are inquiries, sir?"

Darcy forced himself to calmness. Jennings could not know his intentions, but he had been with him too long not to recognize his employer's uncharacteristic behaviour.

"If Lady Catherine asks, tell her that I am unwell and sought fresh air to alleviate my distress," he said finally, his thoughts in such chaos that he found concentration nigh impossible.

"And if anyone else asks, sir?"

"Tell them whatever you please!"

The door closed abruptly as his footsteps echoed down the hall. Jennings remained standing, his mouth open in consternation as he stared after his departed employer, trying in vain to determine what could have brought about this agitated behaviour.

Even afterwards, Darcy could remember little of the rapid journey to the Parsonage until he rang the doorbell.

"Miss Bennet," he told the surprised girl who answered the door. His stomach quivered in anticipation as she dropped a quick curtsey and then led him to the drawing room where the ladies habitually sat. Removing his hat and gloves while he followed, Darcy breathed deeply, trying to calm himself as he stepped into the room.

Miss Bennet looked up, the utmost surprise on her face, then stood to render a curtsey, and he was instantly lost. He had prepared himself, he knew what to say, and he knew how to say it, but suddenly his tongue cleaved to the roof of his mouth, and he could speak not a word. His admiration for her threatened to choke him, and he chastised himself savagely— *Talk, you fool! Say something!*

"Miss Bennet," he finally forced out. "Mrs. Collins said you were feeling unwell. I thought...I thought to inquire whether you were feeling better."

"I thank you for your concern, sir, and I have indeed improved," she said in a tone of cold civility, and Darcy's stomach tried to turn over at the tone of her voice.

Why is she so cold? he asked himself. *Can she not see why I have come? Does she have no suspicion?*

Darcy sat down, but he was still unable to speak. Suddenly, he could not remember any of what he had so carefully prepared, and he raged inwardly at being struck as dumb as the veriest dullard!

He stood and walked to the side of the room, to the window, and then back to his seat, his agitation increasing. Miss Bennet watched him silently, waiting and saying nothing. Abruptly, he remembered the papers in his pocket. As a student, his written preparations, placed carefully in a coat pocket, had served to give him the confidence to speak, but he had never needed to consult those notes. Their mere presence on his person had been sufficient, but in this instance, he suddenly knew that he required more as-surance, and he at once pulled the papers from his coat and unfolded them.

As he looked at his written words, he felt a wave of calm sweep through his body. He closed his eyes in relief, and then, wasting no time, he began—

"MISS BENNET."

Elizabeth looked up in renewed surprise at his words, but even more at his tone. Mr. Darcy had spoken her name with unaccustomed gentleness, almost as if he were caressing the words. She could not understand...

"Miss Bennet," he continued as gently as before, "you must allow me to tell you how ardently I admire and love you."

Elizabeth's astonishment was beyond expression. She stared at him in shock and felt a blush mount her cheeks. She could not account for his words and said nothing in return, a fact that evidently provided sufficient encouragement, for he continued.

"From the earliest moments of our acquaintance..."

Elizabeth looked down demurely, staring at her hands in her lap.

"I was impressed by your lively spirits, your warm heart, and your ease with all you meet. The more I saw, the more I was attracted, especially as these attributes are so lacking in my own person. I was soon bewitched and utterly lost though I did not realize it at first. I remember when you first came to Netherfield to tend your sister, your petticoats stained with mud but your cheeks bright with exertion and your hair windblown and enticing."

Darcy watched Elizabeth keenly as she sat with a blush on her cheeks, unable to meet his gaze.

"I must confess I first wondered — and almost hoped — that you had come because of me, but I was soon disabused of that base thought as your concern for your sister showed your true merit. I was so used to being the object of all manner of plots and artifice by almost every unmarried girl and their ambitious mothers that I was unprepared for your artless devotion to your sister. Your actions proved me utterly wrong then and not for the last time. But I also was deeply impressed by your wit and your spirit, and I quite enjoyed crossing verbal lances with you at Netherfield and again here at Rosings. Even though," he said wryly, "I was more often forced to retire from the field in defeat than otherwise."

He consulted his notes again and continued, "I cannot fix on the time or the place when I knew I loved you. I was in the middle before I knew that I had begun. But I soon began to imagine you every place I was wont to go: in my carriage, in my house in London, by my side at the theatre, and most especially at my home at Pemberley. When I saw you on your walks, I envisioned you on the many pathways at Pemberley. I saw you with Georgiana, being the sister that she never had, providing the advice and the example that I was not able to supply. I grew to realize that we could fit together well, that your liveliness would balance my reserved nature, and my knowledge and experience of the world, garnered over years of managing my own affairs, would work to your benefit.

"I know that I have not been able to speak clearly before now. Indeed, I have usually found myself so stricken in your presence that I have said what I did not intend and did not mean, and I have not been able to say that which I fully meant to say." He frowned somewhat and then reddened slightly, looking again at his papers. "I have never been in love before — never even felt attraction before — and I know I have not presented myself to best effect. As you can see" — he waved his papers at her — "I was as speechless as ever until I retrieved my prepared notes. I have no skill at casual discourse, a talent so many others seem to exhibit with as little effort as breathing, a talent that I hope to improve upon in the future under your excellent tutelage. "

Elizabeth looked up at that moment and felt a shock run through her as Mr. Darcy fixed her with an intense gaze that she suddenly realized had never been a glare of disapproval at all but the exact opposite. "I should have said more," he continued, "but I can only say that a man who felt less might have done so."

Taking a deep breath, he turned to the last page and continued, "There will be some who will raise objections to our match, who will make reference to the difference in our situations, to your lack of fortune, to your country origins. Some may come from my family," and Elizabeth, looking up, was surprised by the fierceness of his expression. But he continued, his face softening, "and some may come from society in general. I cannot say at this time. But these objections are meaningless to me, and I will permit no one to abuse you in any way. I am my own master and need neither approval nor advice from my family in choosing whom I marry. I cannot pretend never to have entertained similar objections myself; I wish I could. But I have since confronted them and rejected them utterly. I cannot conceive of any woman more worthy to be at my side, more intelligent, witty, lively, courageous, and caring, and I know I can never love another as I love you. I beg you, Miss Bennet, to relieve my present distress and do me the honour of accepting my hand in marriage."

Elizabeth was in a state beyond amazement. She had never imagined receiving a proposal of marriage in such a heartfelt, open, and touching manner from any man, and she was quite unable to explain having received it from Mr. Darcy. She could see that he had no doubt of a favourable answer; he spoke of apprehension and anxiety, but his countenance expressed real security, and though her intentions did not vary for an instant, she was sorry for the pain he was to receive. In spite of her deeply rooted dislike, as well as her smouldering anger due to his interference between Jane and Mr. Bingley, she could not be insensible to the compliment of such a man's affection and could not respond with anything less than civility equal to his own. Composing herself, Elizabeth rejected several openings, before finally speaking.

"I must confess, sir, that I am most completely surprised at your sentiments."

"Surprised?" He was clearly startled.

"Indeed, quite surprised." She looked up and continued, "In cases such as these, it is, I believe, the established mode to express a sense of obligation for the feelings avowed, however unequally they may be returned."

Darcy, leaning against the mantelpiece, stiffened and felt his calm composure shatter as the meaning of her words sent a thrill of disquiet through his chest. *However unequally they may be returned?* he thought in confusion. *Dear God, what could she mean? She could not refuse me, could she?*

"I do indeed feel a profound sense of gratitude at the sincerity and the emotion expressed in your declaration, and I am complimented by your assurances. I never expected to hear so eloquent a statement, and I am quite sincerely sorry to offer pain to anyone. But, sir," she dropped her eyes back to her lap, "I am afraid that I must refuse your offer. I do fear that I cannot match your feelings, and I am convinced that a marriage occasioned by such unequal affections would render both parties unhappy in the extreme."

Elizabeth could not bear to look up. He had shown a depth of feeling that she had never deemed possible, and she feared that the sight of pain on his face might well shake her resolve. Nevertheless, she was determined neither to yield nor to give vent to either anger or venom in light of his civilities though she would not waver in the light of *her* objections.

For his part, Darcy listened with a sense of confusion and of bleak despair; indeed, the anguish that rocked him was beyond anything he had ever experienced. The constricting sensation in his chest and throat increased as she spoke until it was difficult for him to draw even a ragged breath. Other emotions followed close behind—disbelief, shock, and then anger. He turned away, trying to find the reserve that had served him for so long, attempting to don the mask of indifference he had crafted over the years, but he found to his consternation that he could not resurrect what he had given up.

She refused me! He repeated the shocking words to himself again and yet again. After everything he had told her and everything she meant to him, she refused him and dismissed him with no explanation. It was not to be borne!

He opened his mouth in rage, but the rustling of the papers still in his hand distracted him. He looked at them, and his anger dissolved. At no time in his preparations had he anticipated failure, certainly not failure this extreme. He had imagined that he held all the advantages—that once he overcame his scruples and knew himself, all was finished and done. Several moments passed as he struggled to find composure.

Elizabeth sat in anxious anticipation, glancing up at Mr. Darcy's rigid figure as he stared out the window in silence. She dreaded what was surely to come—the anger and recriminations that were the natural emotion of such a proud, arrogant man at meeting so cavalier a refusal. She opened her mouth to beg leave to return to her room, but before she could speak, he turned back to her. He had evidently regained some degree of equanimity, and he was able to continue with a measure of civility at odds with the anguish of his face.

"I beg leave to inquire as to the particulars of your refusal, Miss Bennet," he offered, his voice as soft as before but no longer tender. Oh, no, not even a little tender. Raw pain was in that voice—pain, suppressed anger, and raging emotions held tightly in check. "I referred to my many mistakes in my addresses. If you might enlighten me as to the details behind your sentiments, I would be deeply obliged."

Elizabeth bit her lip. She did not want to provide specifics that could only add to his distress, but she did not want to deceive him either. "I think it would be best to leave matters where they are, Mr. Darcy," she said quietly. "I have no wish to continue a conversation that could only lead to intemperate displays by both parties. I truly believe it would be better to disengage and go our separate ways."

He stared at her grimly, his mouth compressed to a thin line by the emotions raging behind his expression. "I do not agree, madam," he said with an edge to his voice that he was unable fully to conceal. "I would rather know how I have offended the woman with whom I hoped to share the rest of my life than to slink off in fear that I might suffer *intemperance*. Again, I beg you would enlighten me on the reasons for this summary dismissal of my petition!"

Elizabeth looked up, her eyes flashing at the challenge, and her determination to rein in her anger disappeared as she stood up to face him. Very well, she had given him the chance to withdraw, and he had rejected it. Let the result be on *his* head!

"Then if you so wish it, I will tell you," she said fiercely. "I have provocations, sir—provocations based on the ruined hopes of a most beloved sister! Can you deny you played a part in most arrogantly separating Mr. Bingley and my sister Jane? Can you deny it?"

Darcy stared at her in dismay, struggling for words. Was this to be the cause of his destroyed hopes? Was the effort he made on behalf of a valued friend the grievance that would divide them forever?

Miss Bennet refused to drop her gaze as he stared down at her, and he could not help but admire her spirit even as disaster washed over him. She hardly came to his shoulder—he towered over her—and yet she met his eye unflinchingly. At length, he sighed and was the first to avert his eyes.

"Is this what you think of me, then?" he asked, in sadness as much as anger. "That I blast the hopes of others due to arrogance? That I disarrange their lives because they are below my station in life?"

"Can you deny it?"

"I will not try to deny I played a part in separating your sister from Bingley, but I *will* deny that I did so out of mean or base motives," Darcy said at last. He turned toward the window, his back to the room. He could not endure the sight of those beautiful eyes glaring at him with such anger.

How can I make her see how it seemed to me? he asked himself in desolation; then, his anger rising at being so treated, he wondered, *And do I even want to try?* But of course he must make the attempt. Surely if he explained himself, she would understand his motivations.

Despite the fact that his hopes had turned to dust in his mouth—or perhaps even because of it—he found that he was no longer strangled into incoherence. He turned to face her.

"Miss Bennet, my actions were based on affection and concern for my friend, much as your anger is raised by your concern for your sister. And until this moment, when you spoke of your sister's ruined hopes, I believed that I had acted for the best."

"For the best, Mr. Darcy?" Elizabeth retorted. "What incredible arrogance! I fail to see how it was your part to interfere in any way! You can have no defence to this!"

"You may not give credence to what I have to say," he responded with some heat, "but I do have an explanation for my actions. Will you hear me out?"

"I again suggest that you leave, sir. This conversation can have no significance."

"What if your sister had Bingley's fortune and Bingley had nothing?" Darcy snapped. "Would you not at least feel justified in trying to determine whether his feelings for your sister were true and honourable? And how would you do that?"

Despite her anger, Elizabeth could not help but accept the justice of this statement, and she bit her lip in frustration. *Intolerable man!*

"Will you hear my defence, Miss Bennet?" Darcy asked again.

Elizabeth struggled to calm herself and at length resumed her seat. "Proceed, sir."

Darcy again faced the window as misery gripped his heart and he groped to gain control of his emotions. However, he must at least explain himself, slight though the chances of any reduction in her disapproval might be.

"I seek your justice, Miss Bennet, and I ask you to apply that justice to the account I shall give. Some parts of it may pain you, and I beg your pardon for any injury to your feelings. But here is the central point: you charge that I detached Bingley from your sister, and there is some truth in that. However, the issue is more complicated. When visiting with Bingley in Hertfordshire, I soon saw that he preferred your eldest sister to any other lady that we met there. But I had often seen him in love, and I did not at first consider his attachment anything beyond what I had seen before. Then, when I had the honour of dancing with you during the ball at Netherfield, Sir William Lucas unintentionally revealed to me that Bingley's steady attentions to your sister had led to a general anticipation of their marriage. He spoke of it as a settled fact with only the timing of the event being yet in doubt."

He turned from the window and looked directly at her. "That was the point at which I decided to act on behalf of my friend. I began to observe him, and I quickly determined that his partiality for your sister was beyond what I had ever previously witnessed. But here is the point at issue: I also observed your sister throughout the length of that evening. I noted that her look and manners were as open, friendly, and engaging as ever, and that she obviously received his attentions with pleasure. But, though I looked most carefully, I could detect no affection on her part to match that of my friend."

"Jane's feelings were as fervent as Mr. Bingley's, however unable you were to discern them!" Elizabeth burst out. "Simply because she does not display them for the amusement of society does not mean that she does not suffer!"

"I must bow," Darcy said, with a slight inclination of his head, "to your superior knowledge of your sister and admit the possibility—indeed, the likelihood—that I was in error and that your resentment is not entirely unreasonable. But, in my defence, I must tell you that your sister's countenance and air were so serene that an impartial observer would likely conclude that that her heart was not touched in this affair. While I will admit that I was desirous of believing your sister indifferent, I must state most adamantly that I do not usually allow my hopes or fears to influence my investigations and decisions. I did not believe your sister to be indifferent because I wished to believe it; I believed it because of impartial conviction."

Darcy paused to collect and organize his thoughts. The next assertions were going to be difficult, perhaps even disastrous, but he had achieved a certain detachment as he crafted his explanations, even as he felt his heart's desire melting away. After saying too little up to this point, he was now determined to disclose every aspect and consideration, whether it inclined to his benefit or the opposite. He would conceal nothing.

"Another objection to my friend's attachment to your sister was your family's lack of connections. But this would be less of a problem for him than it was for myself, and just as I overcame this obstacle, Bingley likely would have done the same. But there was an even greater impediment that remained—both for Bingley and for myself—and that is the lack of propriety displayed by your family."

Darcy winced as Elizabeth's expression suddenly darkened. What he would say next could only make it worse, but it was far too late to stop. "I fear this will only increase your resentment, but it must be said. It was the total lack of propriety that your mother and your three younger sisters displayed in almost every public situation that concerned me greatly, for I feared that your mother would influence your sister towards Bingley because of his fortune. I can see that you are angered, and it pains me to offend you, but I said that I would explain myself fully, and I will do so. However, I would like to add that the censure just mentioned in no way applies to you or your eldest sister, for you have behaved at all times with the utmost decorum and civility. I will only add that, based on my observations that evening, I determined to preserve my friend from what I had concluded to be a most unhappy connection. He left Netherfield for London on the following day but with the clear intention of soon returning, and I travelled shortly after to change that intention."

Darcy glanced at Elizabeth and groaned inwardly as she sat white-lipped in anger. He knew well her fierce devotion to those she loved, and he had just delivered a challenge that could not have been better crafted to inspire her protective instincts.

"I come now to the part in which I acted. Bingley's sisters were as opposed to the match as myself—although, perhaps, not for all the same reasons—and they joined me in an attempt to detach him from your sister. When we joined him in London, we lost no time in pressing our point. I endeavoured to advise my friend on the evils of such a choice and was able to describe my doubts and argue them pointedly. However much my assurances may have affected his determination, I do not believe it would have been sufficient to prevent the marriage had I not, in all earnestness, assured him of your sister's indifference. He had before believed her to return his affection with sincere, if not with equal, regard. But Bingley has great natural modesty with a stronger dependence on my judgment than on his own, and it was not unduly difficult to convince him that he had deceived himself. Once that was achieved, it was but the work of a moment to persuade him against returning to Netherfield. Until tonight, I never had reason to blame myself for having made these efforts on his behalf. I may have erred, but it was not done with malice."

Darcy could not determine the effect of his words. She was no longer gripped with the same anger as before, but her face disclosed no hint of her feelings as she watched him without expression. He was embarrassed, nay mortified, at what he had yet to relate, but he did not hesitate. His situation could hardly be worse.

"There is one part of my conduct in this affair over which I am truly pained, for it does not flow from an honest mistake. That part is that I aided Miss Bingley in concealing from her brother that your sister was in Town. I did not see her, but I knew of it, and Bingley is even yet ignorant of it. It is possible that they could have met without ill consequence, but I judged that his affection for her was not extinguished enough for there to be no danger, so I did what I did and believed it to be for the best at the time. This is the part I have played in the affair, Miss Bennet. It was certainly not my best moment, but I acted to protect my friend on the basis of honest conviction, and though you tell me I erred in my judgment, I did not do so out of any attempt to inflict wanton harm on those involved."

Darcy was at an end. Exhaustion and despair overwhelmed him as waited to discover the impact of his confessions. He was afraid even to allow himself to hope, but he was incapable of discerning her present feelings as she sat completely silent and still, her head bowed and her hands motionless in her lap. He believed that her rage had dissolved, but what she might be thinking was beyond his abilities to determine.

Chapter 2

In truth, Elizabeth's feelings could not have been in greater turmoil. She had been offended and enraged beyond measure by the arrogance of Mr. Darcy's statements, but the whole of his disclosure began to affect her as it continued. She desperately wanted to retain that high state of indignation that she found so pleasurable, but recollections of her own started to affect her composure, and now, as her emotions warred against her judgment, she struggled to resolve the conflicting aspects of his account.

Unwillingly, she considered Darcy's statement that he had been convinced of Jane's indifference, and she could not help remembering Charlotte's opinion that Jane ought to make her partiality known. She was forced to admit that, though Jane's feelings might be fervent, there was some justice in his assertion that she did not often display them openly.

But how dare he act so when he could not know her true feelings! she told herself angrily, but then she remembered his demand that she consider the situation if the tables were turned—if Jane were rich and Bingley were not. She could not help but admit the justice of that. She was so confused!

After some minutes of silence, Elizabeth finally responded, her voice flat and emotionless. "I confess, sir, that certain points of your...explanation...do indeed make me question some of my previous opinions."

Darcy stiffened as a momentary thrill of hope went through him at Elizabeth's words, but her chin came up sharply as she looked directly back at him, "But I do have considerable trouble lending your explanations sufficient credence when there are yet other matters that give me cause to question your character."

"And those matters are...?" Darcy said, more sharply than he had intended, wounded and angered that she would somehow doubt his character and his honour.

"One of those matters we have touched on before, Mr. Darcy," Elizabeth said with growing heat, "and that is your treatment of Mr. Wickham. Many months ago, he unfolded your character in his recital of the misfortunes, which have been by your infliction. On this subject, what can you have to say?" She could have continued, but she stopped herself, shocked by the sudden look of fury on Mr. Darcy's formerly impassive countenance. She watched in horrified fascination as his fists clenched and unclenched, his arms quivering as all his muscles convulsed in a frenzy of emotion and the obvious struggle to gain control of himself.

Wickham again! he raged. *I know not what he has told her, but how could she believe him? How could she have been so deceived?* And then he remembered Wickham's skill at presenting himself, the easy grace of his manners, the way in which he had almost convinced Georgiana to—

Enough! He was tempted to turn and leave the room immediately, and several minutes went by while he debated furiously in his mind. Surely, in this matter he could defend himself, but should he? *It will do no good; she will not listen; she has been poisoned against me!* But the part that still loved Elizabeth cried out, *You cannot let Wickham do this, for then his revenge will be complete!*

He turned around finally, at least outwardly composed, and he found that Elizabeth had retreated to the other side of the room. He was dismayed by the look on her face. It was fear.

The realization that she was afraid stunned and mortified him, but it was enough to force him to settle his mind. No matter what happened, he must make her understand about George Wickham.

"Miss Bennet, I am greatly sorry," he said gently. She watched him, ready to flee the room if he so much as moved. "I am sorry that I have frightened you. Events of today have sorely tested my self-control, and I let my rage against George Wickham show. Please forgive me."

She nodded, but whether in forgiveness or acknowledgement, he could not tell. He sighed. "Madam, I would have wished never to have reason to remember again what I am about to tell you, but the present situation leaves me no choice. It is not only for my justification but also for your protection that I must inform you of what lies between George Wickham and me. May I sit?" he asked, and she jerkily nodded her head.

He pulled out a chair. "Well, at least you have not yet fled the room," he said dryly.

His attempt at humour, feeble as it was, seemed to break the spell that had held Elizabeth frozen, and she moved to seat herself. "I considered it, sir," she said coolly.

"I daresay. My sister has commented that sometimes, and I quote her: 'Your towering presence is quite intimidating.' I had thought she merely teased me, but now I fear it must true, and I am sorry you took fright."

Darcy inhaled deeply. "I do not know what George Wickham has told you about me, Miss Bennet, though I could probably guess based on what you have said tonight and previously at the Netherfield ball. I suspect he claimed that I have ruined his prosperity and denied him his inheritance?"

"He did."

"Further, I would imagine that I stand accused of wilfully and wantonly throwing off the companion of my youth, the favourite of my father, a young man who had every expectation of profiting by the patronage of my family only to see it cruelly denied. Would that be a fair summary of what Wickham has laid at my feet?"

"It would."

"Do you believe this?"

"I have been given no reason to doubt Mr. Wickham's word," she said defensively.

"I see," he said. "These actions would undeniably be unpardonable, Miss Bennet"—he paused—"were they true."

Elizabeth looked at him fiercely. "Do you deny it?"

"I do indeed, madam. Most strenuously and in every particular, I do deny it.

"In order to refute these charges, I will lay before you the whole of Wickham's connection with my family. I do not know the particular details of what he has accused me, but I will present everything, and unlike him, I can provide testament to the truth of what I am about to relate by providing a witness of undoubted veracity, my cousin Colonel Fitzwilliam. He is acquainted with all the pertinent details and will corroborate everything I am about to relate."

This last staggered Elizabeth completely. She had believed Mr. Darcy incapable of defending himself against the detailed charges provided by Mr. Wickham, and now he had shaken that belief by offering immediate authentication from a source of whom she thought well and who, moreover, would be privy to the private affairs of the Darcy family. She suddenly felt completely unsure of that which she, only moments before, had believed unshakable.

"As you probably know, George Wickham is the son of my father's steward, a good and loyal man who for many years managed all of the Pemberley estates for my family. The elder Wickham was so faithful in his duties that he earned the obligation of my father, who not only made George his godson but also supported him at school and later at Cambridge. George's own father could not have afforded to give him a gentleman's education since his own wife kept the family poor by her extravagances. My father was fond of Wickham's society due to his engaging manners, and he planned to reward that opinion by providing him a living in the church." He looked at Elizabeth. "Does this correspond with what you have heard, Miss Bennet?"

At her nod, he continued, "I, however, have had quite a different opinion of George Wickham for some years. I was witness to his behaviour in a manner that my father was not, since Wickham could not conceal his vicious propensities and his want of principal from me, a young man of nearly the same age. I had too many opportunities to see him in unguarded moments, which my father could not have."

Elizabeth remembered Mr. Wickham's countenance as he described the offences against his person with a convincing charm and ease. In contrast, Mr. Darcy showed grimness rather than charm and intensity rather than ease. He looked like a man faced with an unwelcome task that could not be avoided, and she felt her already uncertain understanding weaken even further.

Darcy continued speaking even as she thought. "What I have to relate may cause you pain since I do not know to what degree Wickham may have engaged your sentiments. But even if you do have some partiality for him, it shall no longer prevent me from unfolding his real character. It only increases my determination, for you would not be the first young lady whose affections he has toyed with as you will shortly hear."

To this, Elizabeth could not help but remember how amiably Mr. Wickham had engaged her, even when it had been obvious to her that his intentions could not be serious due to her lack of fortune. She also remembered the warning from her Aunt Gardiner about having affection where the want of fortune would make it imprudent. It was with a decided sinking sensation in her stomach that she listened to Mr. Darcy's account.

"My father died five years ago, and he remained attached to Mr. Wickham to the last. In his will, he left him a legacy of one thousand pounds, and he also particularly recommended that I support Wickham's advancement in whatever profession he chose. He especially favoured the church, and if Wickham did choose to take orders, he desired that he receive a valuable family living when it became vacant. Wickham's own father died shortly after that, and within a year he wrote to inform me that he had resolved against taking orders. He mentioned his intention of studying law and suggested that he receive an immediate pecuniary reward in lieu of the family living since his legacy of one thousand pounds would not provide an income to support his study. I wished, rather than believed, him to be sincere, but I was quite prepared to agree to his request since I knew he should not be a clergyman.

"We soon settled the business, and Wickham received the sum of three thousand pounds in return for resigning all claim to assistance, whether the living became available or not. All connection between us was now broken since I thought too ill of him to desire his acquaintance. I heard little of him for three years. I believe he stayed mainly in town, living a life of idleness and dissipation since he evidently had never intended to study the law. But when the family living became available, Wickham again wrote me asking for the presentation of the living. He wrote that his circumstances were exceedingly bad, which I could well believe, and he now stated that he was resolved to take orders. He seemed to have little doubt that I would present the living, and he reminded me of my father's desires.

"I trust you can hardly blame me, Miss Bennet, for refusing to comply with this request and for rejecting the subsequent repetitions of it. His resentment was violent in his reproaches to me, and he doubtless was equally abusive of me to others. After that, I had no contact with him and do not know how he lived."

Darcy sat straight in his chair with his eyes focused far away as he continued his account. "But Wickham was not done with my family. Last summer, he again intruded into my life in a manner which is the most painful I have ever experienced, and his prey this time was the sweetest, the most innocent heart in the land. I speak of my dear sister, Georgiana."

"Oh, no," Elizabeth moaned, closing her eyes in disbelief. She had reason to know that, whatever else she had believed of Mr. Darcy, his affection for his sister was apparent and sincere. A single tear slid down her cheek as she stared in dismay at Mr. Darcy's frozen visage. If his face had been grim before, it was chiselled in granite now.

"Miss Bennet, I must ask your secrecy on this matter, for until this moment, no other mortal knew of these events except the participants and Colonel Fitzwilliam." Elizabeth managed to nod, for she could not talk, and he continued.

"My sister is very precious to me, for I lost my mother in my youth and now lately my father. She is more than ten years my junior, and I share her guardianship with my cousin Fitzwilliam. Last summer, Georgiana travelled to Ramsgate with a Mrs. Younge, who was in charge of the establishment formed for her in London. We were quite deceived in the character of Mrs. Younge, who proved to have a prior acquaintance with George Wickham. The two evidently had conspired since she allowed Wickham, who also travelled to Ramsgate, to meet with my sister. Georgiana has a most affectionate heart and could not have been suspicious since she still retained a strong impression of his kindness to her as a child."

Darcy's dark eyes flashed with remembered fury. "With the aid of Mrs. Younge, Wickham recommended himself to Georgiana to such an extent that he was able to persuade her that she was in love and to convince her to agree to an elopement."

Elizabeth could not stand the look of raw pain on Mr. Darcy's face, regardless of any previous opinion of him, and she cried out, "Sir, enough! I do not need to know more, I do not doubt the truth of your report!"

Darcy heard her, but he was committed to a full accounting.

"Georgiana was then but fifteen, Miss Bennet! Fifteen!" He stopped for a moment before continuing remorselessly, "Her youth, of course, is her excuse, and additionally, she herself disclosed this plan to me when I joined her unexpectedly a few days before the intended elopement. She has always looked up to me almost as a father, and she could not face the grief and offence of such an action. She acknowledged the whole to me, and I acted instantly. I wrote to Wickham, who left the place immediately, and Mrs.

Younge was, of course, instantly discharged."

This last was too much, and Elizabeth wept openly, her handkerchief clutched to her mouth.

"Wickham's chief object," Darcy said, "was unquestionably my sister's fortune of thirty thousand pounds, but I am convinced that he hoped also to revenge himself on me. Had he succeeded, his vengeance would have been complete indeed. The thought of what a marriage to such a man would have done to Georgiana's tender spirit makes my blood run cold to this day."

Darcy's smile was savage as he reflected, "Not that such an event would have long transpired, Miss Bennet. If you thought my temper was extreme earlier, you have not seen that of Colonel Fitzwilliam. He would have called out Wickham immediately, and, if he would not fight, he would have killed him as he stood. It took all my powers of persuasion to dissuade him from that course after Wickham's plans were thwarted. Had they succeeded, Wickham's life would have been measured by the length of time it took Fitzwilliam to find him. A man who has faced Bonaparte's armies on the continent could not be frightened by the likes of George Wickham.

"This is the end of my report, madam. I had not seen Wickham again until that day in Meryton when I met you on the street with him. My reaction to him you saw, but you could not know the history between us that led me to act as I did. Perhaps I should have made my knowledge of him available at that time, but I did not want to chance any possibility of harm to my sister. Perhaps that is a fault of my nature. It has certainly not played to my advantage with you. But I hope that this faithful narrative will at least acquit me of the charge of cruelty towards George Wickham. As testimony to the truthfulness of my account, I repeat that I can appeal to Colonel Fitzwilliam, and I urge you to consult with him on any particulars about which you still have questions. I will charge him to give full and complete disclosure, since I already have your assurance of confidence in this matter."

Darcy was silent. He was spent, exhausted, and he had no idea what the result of his assurances would be. That he had affected Miss Bennet was obvious; her tears attested to that. But she would not look at him, and he could make no estimate of whether he had improved or harmed himself in her regard—except that her opinion of him could hardly have gotten worse.

In truth, Elizabeth was not considering her opinion of Mr. Darcy at all; her concern was with her own foolishness, and her growing dismay at

Darcy's revelations had translated to a feeling of definite nausea. She wanted to flee the drawing room, not in fear but to take herself to her own room to let loose the tears that threatened to spring from her eyes.

Mr. Wickham did not deceive me as much as I deceived myself, she thought miserably. *I allowed my dislike of Mr. Darcy to affect me so much that I eagerly listened to Mr. Wickham's tales—nay his slanders. And Colonel Fitzwilliam can attest to this? Surely, Mr. Darcy would not offer such if that assurance was not easily at hand. Oh, foolish, foolish girl!* She could not remember ever being as mortified in her life as she was at the present moment.

She sat in agitated reflection for upwards of fifteen minutes while Darcy remained motionless in his chair. Her tears died away, and she tried to pull her thoughts together, but as she struggled to determine *what* she could possibly say, the sound of Lady Catherine's carriage announced the return of the party from Rosings.

"Please , sir, I beg leave to go to my room," she said in agitation.

"Miss Bennet—"

"Please do not, sir," Elizabeth said in desperation. "I cannot speak of this; I must have time to think!"

"Will you walk with me in the morning?" Darcy asked. He could not believe the pleading tone in his voice. He had never uttered such in his life before that moment, and it stung his pride, but after the intensity of the past hour, he could not leave the matter unresolved. "Can we not talk further then after you have refreshed your spirit by rest?"

Elizabeth did indeed need the healing balm of sleep; however, her inner turmoil was so great that she feared sleep would not come early that night if at all. Nevertheless, in desperation to quit the room, she nodded in agreement though the tears again flowed from her eyes.

At that moment, the door to the parlour opened to admit Mr. Collins, followed by his wife. Both Darcy and Elizabeth jumped to their feet, and Mr. Collins's mouth gaped in shock as he beheld the two distressed occupants in the room. Two servants were also visible in the hall, peering through the doorway. Mr. Collins looked from Elizabeth's tearful face to Darcy's grim, stony expression, and he was completely at a loss of what to say. Elizabeth, unequal to face any further observations, whether by her cousin or her friend, uttered a low, "Please excuse me," and hurried away to her room.

Darcy bowed stiffly. "Mrs. Collins, Mr. Collins, I must beg your pardon.

I had not realized how long I had stayed. I must bid you good evening," and, bowing once more, he quickly departed.

Mr. Collins looked at his wife in confusion. He did not know what to say, but he did know what to do. He would ask for Lady Catherine's advice on the morrow.

Chapter 3

After reaching the sanctuary of her room, Elizabeth cried for a full half-hour, sobbing out the emotions that had been loosed by Mr. Darcy's proposal and its aftermath. She did not try to think; what she had experienced had been too emotionally charged to bear any scrutiny just yet. Instead, she gave vent to all the feelings that threatened to strangle her, instinctively letting the poisons drain out. She had finally cried herself out, and she was sitting up in her bed, her eyes still puffy and reddened, when there came a soft knock at the door. When she did not respond, the knock was repeated, and this time the door opened and Charlotte peered inside.

"Lizzy?" she asked, the concern in her voice evident, "Are you ill? Is your headache worse? Can I be of help?"

"No, Charlotte," Elizabeth said, "I am not ill, though my headache is not gone. I am just distressed. I will be well after I have a chance to rest."

Entering the room, Charlotte closed the door and crossed to sit on the bed by Elizabeth. "Lizzy, you have been crying. What is the matter? Did you quarrel with Mr. Darcy?"

"There was a quarrel, right enough, Charlotte," Elizabeth laughed bitterly, "but it was not quarrelling that has made me cry; my own foolishness and stupidity are the source of my tears."

"Are you sure, Lizzy? Mr. Collins is very upset. The servants were quite disturbed when we arrived home. They reported loud voices and crying from the parlour, but none dared to enter to see whether anything was wrong. And Lady Catherine was most displeased with Mr. Darcy's sudden departure from Rosings. She would not stop speaking of it, and then we find him here in my drawing room with you."

Charlotte paused, looking carefully at her friend before leaning forward and taking her hand. "My husband," she said in a low voice, "fears that Mr. Darcy must have made advances to you and reduced you to tears."

Elizabeth could not stop a sharp, bitter laugh. "My cousin has once again displayed his unerring instinct for reaching the wrong conclusion, Charlotte. Mr. Darcy made no improper advances of any kind. His behaviour was most correct."

"Then what, Lizzy? What could have upset you so?"

Seeing that there was no avoiding Charlotte's question, Elizabeth decided she could not lie to her oldest and best friend.

"Charlotte, will you promise to keep what I tell you secret — not even to tell your husband? I know that is much to ask, but I cannot talk of this if there is a chance it might spread beyond the two of us."

Charlotte was troubled, but at length she agreed, and Elizabeth looked down at the bed.

"Mr. Darcy came to . . . to make me an offer of marriage."

"See, I told you, Lizzy," Charlotte said happily, squeezing her friend's hand.

"You were right, Charlotte," Elizabeth said wryly, "but not in the way you think. Congratulations are not in order. I do not want to marry Mr. Darcy. I refused him."

"You did not!" Charlotte exclaimed in horror.

"But I did. Oh, his proposal was really most moving, almost poetic, in fact. It caught me completely by surprise, but my previous opinion was completely against him, both because of his arrogant behaviour, because of Jane, and because of his abuse of Wickham. I quite definitely refused him."

"And that was what made you cry?"

"No, what made me cry was what came after that, after he pressed me for the reasons for my refusal. I tried to avoid answering, but when he persisted, I was more than happy to provide the details of my objections. I challenged him to defend himself as I was sure he could not, but I was wrong. He spoke long in his defence, and it was hard to listen at first; I was so angry. But I

32

did listen to him, and then…then I found that my very clever assignment of blame was based more on my own mistaken prejudice than on real cause. His previous behaviour may have been arrogant, but his proposal was most civil. I wholly misunderstood his actions on Bingley's behalf, and his supposed abuse of Wickham was a complete deception, in which I played a part. I am now convinced that the truth of the matter is the exact opposite, with Mr. Darcy being the innocent party and Mr. Wickham being the villain of the piece. In fact, not only was Wickham actually the source of severe affronts to Mr. Darcy rather than the reverse, but he also engaged in a campaign to destroy Mr. Darcy's character in Hertfordshire, with me and my so-called unerring judgment as his most willing accomplice!"

She laughed in bitter self-condemnation. "I have accused Mr. Darcy of being proud, arrogant, conceited, and disdainful of the feeling of others. How much of that may be accurate is unclear to me at the moment, but am I any better? I quail inside as I remember how I prided myself on my discernment and valued my own abilities! Even worse, I remember that I often disparaged Jane's generous candour and gratified my vanity in useless or blamable distrust!"

A tear ran down Elizabeth's cheek, and she brushed it away. "How I am humiliated by this discovery, Charlotte. Had I been in love, I could not have been more wretchedly blind. I have been so misled by my vanity that I could not detect Mr. Wickham's deceit or Mr. Darcy's innocence. I allowed his effrontery and neglect, occasioned at the beginning of our acquaintance, to drive reason away. Until this moment," she said dully, "I never knew myself."

Charlotte was distressed greatly by Elizabeth's account—distressed by everything, from her unbelievable refusal of a man of Mr. Darcy's value to her cruel words about herself.

"You are convinced of his innocence of what Mr. Wickham said?" she asked.

"Yes," Elizabeth nodded. "I cannot speak of the particulars, for it concerns affairs private to the Darcy family, but he offered a trustworthy witness of his account. Yes, I am now convinced of Mr. Darcy's innocence in this, at least."

"And what of Jane?" asked Charlotte. "Do you believe him innocent in that affair also?"

"No, not innocent," said Elizabeth slowly, "but not as guilty as I previously affirmed. Since I believe his assertions in regard to Wickham, I must give credence to those in regard to Jane. And there, I am forced to concede, while he was wrong in some aspects, he was not maliciously wrong. And in some others," she whispered, "especially concerning my family, I do fear that he is more correct than not. He is arrogant, to be sure, and I do resent the opinions he expressed, but I fear that Jane's disappointment has been as much the work of her own relations as otherwise."

She broke down in sobs again "I have grown so used to the impropriety of my mother and my young sisters that I did not see it until his cruel words showed me how they appeared in another's eyes."

At length, Charlotte said softly, "And what of his pride and arrogance, Lizzy?"

Elizabeth wiped her tears away. "On that we did not speak. And although the tone of his proposal softened the harsh words that might otherwise have come to mind, I have no reason to change my opinion of him. . . except that my opinion has been so dreadfully wrong about everything else!"

"I see," said Charlotte. "So he may not be as arrogant as you thought?"

"Well . . . perhaps," Elizabeth granted unwillingly.

"So after his explanation, were you tempted to amend your refusal?"

"Oh, no, Charlotte. He did not renew his proposal, so I had no cause to reconsider my refusal. But, in truth, even after everything I have learned, at heart I still believe he is the last man in the world I could be prevailed on to marry."

Charlotte was saddened but contented herself with a brief embrace before departing.

Chapter 4

Darcy's thoughts were still whirling in confusion and shock when he arrived back at Rosings, to the extent that he had no clear memory of passing through the park. He was, however, fortunate enough to reach his room without seeing his aunt. His good fortune came to an end at that point, for he did not even have time to ring for Jennings before a visitor knocked at his door. Darcy rolled his eyes in frustration, but there was no other recourse than to answer, and he was not surprised to find his cousin Fitzwilliam with his eyebrows arched in a look of sardonic mischief with which Darcy was so familiar.

"I heard you come back just now," his cousin said easily, "and I thought you might wish to get thrashed at billiards before retiring." Darcy was tempted to decline, but he saw Fitzwilliam's expression sharpen as he recognized Darcy's discomfiture. He sighed in surrender, for he also perceived the dedicated look that Fitzwilliam assumed when he was determined to accomplish some task. Just now, he suspected that Richard's task was to quiz his dear cousin Darcy about his odd behaviour this day, and there being no way to avoid the inquisition, he accepted the invitation. He would have to talk to Richard at some time or other, for his cousin was relentless when he was in that mood. In any event, he had a favour to request. He knew that Richard might discuss some generalities regarding Wickham if Miss Bennet did indeed apply to him for confirmation, but he was too loyal and dutiful to make the slightest comment about the affair at Ramsgate.

When they entered the billiard room and Darcy uncharacteristically closed the door behind them, Fitzwilliam's eyebrows rose again. Wordlessly he watched as Darcy removed his coat and began to examine the cues. Neither spoke as Fitzwilliam prepared the table. Darcy silently selected a cue and applied chalk to the tip. Fitzwilliam finished racking the balls and chalked his own cue. Eventually, as Darcy settled into position, Fitzwilliam's patience reached an end.

"Darcy, do you want to tell me what in blazes is going on with you?" he burst out, but Darcy only stroked his cue, breaking the balls smartly. One ball made a corner pocket with a satisfying sound, and he again chalked his cue while his cousin fumed.

"What do you mean?" Darcy said finally as he lined up his first shot. "Are you referring to tea? I left the house because I did not feel well and decided to take a walk." He stroked the cue smoothly and landed a ball in the side pocket, leaving the cue ball perfectly positioned for a shot on the corner.

"So you say!" Fitzwilliam responded. "But this is only the latest incident. You have been acting quite the strange one for the past week. First, you put off our departure, when in past years you would have been as eager as I to escape from Rosings. Then you hardly had a word to say to me all week, you cannot refrain from quarrelling with Miss Bennet whenever she visits, and you just stare out the window or hold a book in your lap without turning the page. Then tonight you disappear when my aunt has guests, leaving me to try to explain your unprecedented breach of manners. Did you know Lady Catherine wanted to send the servants out to search for you and drag you back? If I was a wagering man, I would place a month's pay that you had finally been smitten by one of the stylish ladies in town who have been scheming to become Georgiana's sister for these several years now."

Darcy could not help smiling. Close, but yet not close.

"Little chance of that," he murmured as he lined up and took his next shot.

"Then what? I will not let up, you understand. I *will* have a proper answer, or we shall be here all night."

Darcy looked at his cousin intently. "Richard, I need a favour," he said after a few moments.

"You will not get so much as a kind word until you tell your dear cousin why he has to allow himself to be battered about the ears by his aunt while you disappear at will."

Darcy frowned. "I am serious. I need your help, but I also need for you to put a muzzle on your curiosity—at least for now."

Fitzwilliam looked at him in exasperation. "Let me see if I have this straight. You want me to refrain from asking why you have been wandering around with a dazed look for more than a week, but at the same time you want me to do you a favour?"

"That about sums it up."

"And you will not tell me what is troubling you?"

"I cannot. At least not right now. Maybe sometime, but not now."

Fitzwilliam threw up his hands in disgust. "Oh, all right! Why should I expect anything else?"

"Thank you."

"Now, what favour do you need?" Fitzwilliam said disgustedly. He had thought to at least disconcert Darcy and affect his game, but it appeared that whatever afflicted him did not affect his skill at billiards. He was in for another merciless drubbing.

"Your comment about Miss Bennet," Darcy, suddenly tongue-tied, ventured eventually. "We did have a . . . quarrel."

Fitzwilliam just raised his eyebrows. Darcy took a breath as he lined up another shot. "In the course of a rather . . . heated . . . discussion, I was forced to reveal to her the whole of my history with Wickham."

That truly shocked Fitzwilliam. He well knew Darcy's nearly obsessive urge for privacy.

"You did not include the part about Georgiana, did you?"

"Yes."

Fitzwilliam was silent as he watched Darcy put yet another ball in the pocket. Darcy stood up and looked at him. "What I need, Richard, is . . . well, Miss Bennet may seek to confirm the . . . truth . . . of what I told her. What I would like is for you simply to answer her questions if she asks them. Just tell her what happened."

Fitzwilliam stared, suspicion growing as his mind quickly put together the pieces of this most intriguing puzzle.

"You trust her that much?"

Darcy bent over his next shot. "I do."

That was the last piece needed to resolve the question.

"Then, of course." His smile gleamed suddenly in his tanned face. "If she asks, I will answer her fully. That is no problem, Darcy. No problem at all."

He watched Darcy prepare for his next shot; then, as his cousin pulled the cue back, he said softly, "Impulsive as always, I see."

Darcy missed the shot—badly.

"What did you say?" Darcy's expression was dark as he rose from the table.

"Oh, nothing." Fitzwilliam cheerfully moved to take his first shot. Quickly he lined it up. "Previously, there were just the three of us who knew what transpired at Ramsgate—except for Wickham, long may he rot…" His first shot sank a ball in the side pocket.

"And now, suddenly, Miss Bennet will make a fourth…" He sank this shot in a corner pocket.

"Plus there is the famous impulsiveness of the Darcys…" Darcy's face was stony, but his cheeks were flushed as another ball rattled home.

"And of *course*, there is little chance of a stylish lady *from town* bewitching my famously taciturn cousin…" The last ball slammed home in a corner pocket, clearing the table.

"So, of course I will be pleased to alleviate any concerns of the lovely Miss Bennet, who, after all, hails *from the country*, not from town. It will be my pleasure, Darcy." Fitzwilliam laughed out loud at his cousin's glowering expression.

"Ah, the Darcy Stare of Displeasure. It is not nearly as good as the Major General's, mind you, but it is almost as good as Father's. Will you rack the balls, Cousin?"

After several seconds, Darcy could see that he was not going to dim the spirits of his irrepressible cousin, and his glare faded into a rueful smile while he prepared the table.

"Shall I mention the legend of the impulsive Darcys when I see Miss Bennet?" Fitzwilliam drawled.

"Richard," Darcy said seriously, "just do what I asked. The situation is not yet one that inclines me to humour."

"Of course, Cousin." Fitzwilliam patted him on the shoulder. "But I laughed in Spain when we were down to our last ten rounds and then the bayonet, so I daresay I can find a chuckle in your situation."

"Someday, Richard, *someday*!" Darcy growled.

"You have said that before, you know," Fitzwilliam said in delight as he broke the rack. Two balls rattled home, and Darcy groaned.

WHEN JENNINGS MADE HIS EXIT at long last, Darcy gave a sigh of relief. He settled before the fire, feet outstretched to catch the warmth. His relatively good humour from earlier had dissipated, and now depression closed in. He had held it at bay while playing with Fitzwilliam, but it returned now in full force.

She refused me, he thought again. The sense of astonishment still remained, even beyond the pain of the words. The previous night and the certainty that she would soon be his betrothed seemed an age past, so distant that not even a hint of that memory still remained.

How did everything go so wrong, he thought despondently. *How could I have thought she perceived my intentions and awaited my addresses when she so clearly perceived nothing of the sort? Instead, she thought I despised her!*

Then, when he tried to explain how he had acted to separate Bingley from her sister, he insulted her family as if to prove her opinion right. Could he not have found a better way to express himself? Yes, her mother was completely insensitive to the customary manners of society, but did he have to call it a 'total lack of propriety?' And how pitiful was his attempt to lessen the sting by saying that she and her eldest sister were different from their mother!

And the saddest memory of that terrible night—he had frightened her! He groaned aloud as that terrible look on her face would not leave his memory. That cursed Wickham! Would he never be free of his evil influence? First his sister and then the woman he loved! Out of the whole, blasted country, how could he surface in Hertfordshire?

As if these doleful thoughts were not enough to depress him, the more he pondered the actions he had taken to separate Bingley and Miss Bennet, the more he was disturbed by what he had done. He had acted in certitude and with no thought that the parties involved would suffer anything more than transitory pain. Yet Miss Elizabeth had informed him that her sister still suffered from thwarted hopes, and he could not doubt her sincerity. Given that opinion—especially after tasting the bitterness of rejection himself—he could not view his interference with any satisfaction whatever. He winced at the thought of the unhappiness he had caused.

Does Jane Bennet feel the same stabbing pain that I do? he wondered miserably. *From her point of view, Bingley deserted her just when she had every right to expect that he would formally declare himself. If she feels the same as I, how can I pretend that I am not responsible? And what of Bingley? Does he feel the misery I feel at this moment? Does he still harbour love for a woman who, he believes, does not love him in return?* The thought that he could have inflicted such pain struck at his good opinion of himself, and he quailed under a bitter lash of ruthless self-examination such as he had never before endured.

Darcy put his face in his hands. Even though he was relatively satisfied with his explanation of his conduct, he still could not escape the conviction that he had acted wrongly, despite his good intentions. Could he make amends for what he had done? Would Miss Bennet give him the chance? Would she meet him in the morning as she had agreed?

The uncaring fire that danced merrily in the fireplace had no answers, and Fitzwilliam Darcy had no one in whom to confide. He considered his cousin but rejected him. Surely, he had already retired; he was usually up before the sun — the result of years of military life — so Darcy had no one to debate with but himself. He most assuredly did not have the confidence of the one woman in the world with whom he most wished to talk.

Even if Miss Bennet will never see me again, he resolved, *I cannot bear the thought of Bingley and Jane Bennet being in the same misery as myself. I must try to repair my fault on their behalf, no matter what else comes.*

Chapter 5

Breakfast at Rosings was a dreadful affair for Darcy since he was anxious to be out of the house to the park. His aunt was as strident as always, but this time her attention was focused on him, and she spent half the meal chastising him for his disappearance the previous evening. He ignored her for the most part, restricting himself to a few responses as his cousin Fitzwilliam watched in some enjoyment but added no comment. At last, Darcy was able to excuse himself and leave the table. Fitzwilliam looked as if he might join him, but at Darcy's slight shake of the head, he settled back in his chair. Shortly afterward, Darcy strode from the house toward the area of the park where he hoped to encounter Miss Bennet. He was anxious in two regards: whether she had already been up and out before breakfast, or even more alarming, whether she had decided against coming at all.

For her part, after a restless night, Elizabeth had awoken dreading the meeting she had agreed to with Mr. Darcy, for she had not yet recovered from the emotional tension of the previous evening. Soon after breakfast, she told Charlotte of her intent to indulge herself in air and exercise, and though Charlotte raised her eyebrows, she said nothing. As soon as Elizabeth exited the Parsonage, she could not help being cheered by the fresh air and sunshine, but all too soon, she caught a glimpse of a gentleman standing in the distance. Mr. Darcy stepped forward with eagerness as soon as he saw her, and shortly they met.

"Good morning, Miss Bennet," he said with a bow as she curtseyed in response. "It was good of you to come." Darcy could easily discern her agitation, but agitated or not, his heart swelled at the sight of her. He was distressed by the dark circles under her eyes though he knew his own eyes were red from lack of sleep.

"Good morning, Mr. Darcy." Her voice was so soft as to be almost inaudible. "I have come as I agreed last night, sir, though little do I know what you wish to gain by it."

"Perhaps you would care to simply walk for the moment? It is a lovely morning."

"As you please, sir."

Darcy did not offer his arm since he was uncertain whether it would be accepted, and they began to walk at a steady pace that gradually had an effect. Soon, despite her worry, Elizabeth's spirits began to rise. Part of it was the joy of walking one of her favourite paths in the Park, but another part was due to the completely different light in which she viewed her companion. On their previous walks when he had intercepted her, their time together had been marked by uncertainty and tenseness where each had been unaware of the true nature of the other's feelings. On this morning, at least, that was no longer the case. The intensity of the previous evening had dispelled those misconceptions.

They proceeded in cordial silence for upwards of fifteen minutes, and it was Darcy who first spoke.

"Miss Bennet, I informed Colonel Fitzwilliam that you might make enquiries of him regarding my association with George Wickham. He will accompany me when we call to take our leave later this afternoon and will make himself available to you if you have any questions yet to ask."

Elizabeth flushed slightly. "Truly, sir, I have no questions for the colonel. Once you forced me to open my eyes, I soon remembered any number of ways in which Mr. Wickham rather effortlessly convinced me to deceive myself." She looked down at the ground, suddenly angry that tears were again threatening to flow, and she needed several moments before she could again speak. Her voice was low, and Darcy was unable to see her eyes behind her bonnet. "I must apologize, sir, for the harshness of my accusations last evening regarding Mr. Wickham and for my own prejudice which previously prevented me from seeing what was most clearly apparent to me last night."

"Do not distress yourself on that account," Darcy said. "George Wickham has a talent for deception that is most dangerous to those who, like yourself and my sister, do not tend to the kind of suspicion that is likely to perceive his true nature. He has deceived, I am sure, countless others as a matter of course. I would wager that he has amassed a sizable string of creditors in Meryton already. It has been so everywhere he goes."

Elizabeth did not say anything to this, and they walked on for several minutes more before Darcy spoke again. "I had much to think on last night as well, and there is one topic especially on which I dwelt with considerable discomfort. That is the affair of your sister and my friend."

Darcy looked over at her, but he still could not see her face or judge the impact of his words on her. "I do not seek your sympathy, Miss Bennet, when I tell you that I felt extremely disheartened last evening. It is only the simple truth and is, I hope, easily understandable. But in the midst of my own disappointments, I also came to realize that your sister and very possibly my friend might, at that same instant, be feeling similar emotions. It was a thought that gave me considerable pain.

"I will not attempt to pretend that I do not wish for a chance to change your opinion of me. But whether you grant me that chance or whether you send me away, I realized last night that I must attempt to repair the harm wrought by my interference. I will call on Bingley as soon as possible after I return to London and acquaint him both with my knowledge of the true state of your sister's affections and of the disagreeable part I played in the matter." Darcy's face was grim, because he was well aware of the hazards to his friendship with Bingley at such a confession. "I cannot foretell the outcome of my efforts, for that will be up to Bingley and your sister, but I am determined to make the effort."

Elizabeth still said nothing, and at length Darcy, with great trepidation, ventured, "Miss Bennet, you have not spoken, and yet I confess that I cannot keep from wondering whether the content of our later conversation last evening and this morning has in any way altered those sentiments which led to your refusal of my suit."

Darcy was now in such a heightened state of emotion that he could hardly bear to look at her, and yet he could not look away as she at last stopped walking and raised her face to him. His heart sank as he read her expression, for it showed only grim determination.

"Mr. Darcy," she said quietly, "I do admit that my opinion of you as regards Mr. Wickham was completely in error. I will even admit that some part of your interference between your friend and my sister was due to honest error rather than callous disregard for their feelings though the end result still remains painful to both parties. And I do appreciate your willingness to correct your error."

Elizabeth now came to the difficult part of what she had to say. "But even given my altered opinion in these matters," she continued, "I cannot give a different answer than I gave last evening. I do not *know* you, Mr. Darcy. The nature of your proposal was completely at variance with the cold, proud, and indifferent manner you have displayed from our first acquaintance in Hertfordshire, and I am in complete confusion in trying to appraise your character."

Darcy was stunned at her words, for he thought he had managed an adequate defence of his character the previous night. Since his father's death had forced him to assume a number of responsibilities at an early age, he had laboured mightily to make himself into the man the world expected him to be. He had always been known among his friends and associates for his honesty, for his discernment, and for his obedience to the dictates of society; others often sought his advice in difficult matters. In no small measure, his relationship with Bingley had begun when he came to the aid of the younger man in just such a situation. Miss Bennet may have been correct that he had acted wrongly to separate Bingley and her sister, but that mistake did not condemn the whole of his character. Could she not see that his proposal was as much a part of him as was the correctness of his manners?

"I have always tried to conduct myself as a gentleman ought, both in my public and private affairs," he said defensively. "I find myself at a loss to understand your claim of my being, as you say, cold, proud, and indifferent."

"Mr. Darcy, do you not *see*?" she retorted in exasperation. "How can the man who professed such a tender regard for me just last evening be the same man who sat by poor, silly Mrs. Long for a full half-hour without saying a word? Who never deigned to even attempt conversation with any of the country savages and who rebuffed every friendly entreaty by those who sought to simply engage you in ordinary pleasantries?" She sighed at the shocked look on his face, and she concluded tiredly, "Mr. Bingley told Jane that you were remarkably agreeable among your intimate acquaintances, but until last night, the only impression I had of you was one of arrogant disdain for the feelings of others who were not of that group. How can I be blamed for forming an opinion of you that was only inflamed by Mr. Wickham's vile utterances?"

Darcy was stricken to silence when she finished, and now he could no longer meet *her* eyes. Conflicting emotions warred within his breast, fierce anger at the unfairness of her charges, challenged by the sudden insight of those scenes she mentioned as they must have appeared to her.

Could she be right? Was this truly how he was seen by others, as cold, proud, indifferent, and arrogant? His mind was a whirl, and he tried to make sense of the contradictory thoughts and emotions flashing through his memory. *I need time*, he told himself numbly. *Time to sort all this out, to determine what is real and what is not.*

But he did not have time. He was leaving the next morning, and in his arrogance, he had thought to leave with everything resolved between himself and Elizabeth. Instead, matters were more convoluted than they were before.

He heard Elizabeth sigh and tried to focus on her. "I believe I must return, Mr. Darcy," she said tiredly. "My headache grows worse, and I cannot believe there is anything to be gained by continuing this discussion."

As she turned back toward the Parsonage, Darcy automatically turned along with her. He was conscious of her glancing up at him in confusion at his continued presence, but he knew only that he could not let her go with this barrier still between them. It was obvious that even with her altered opinion of his actions, she still looked upon him with real dislike, and the pain from that drew both sharp anger and even sharper despair.

He forced himself to put aside his conflicting emotions, and after some minutes of silent walking and rather desperate thought on his part, he made his determination. "Miss Bennet," he began, "I now find myself in a similar state of confusion as you earlier related. It is tempting for me to withdraw in order to sort out the truth of what we have both discussed, but I find that approach has one intolerable drawback. That is, that I might well leave this place tomorrow with no chance to change your opinion of me and with no assurance that I will ever see you again. So, despite the confusion of my feelings, I have rejected that alternative."

Elizabeth glanced at Darcy in some apprehension. Surely he was not going to renew his proposal yet again?

"The dictum of our society is rather simple," he pressed on, "in the situation where a man develops an attraction towards a woman who is not aware of that attraction or who has insufficient knowledge of the suitor on which to make a decision. That social practice, Miss Bennet, is a courtship."

Elizabeth halted, her thoughts suddenly even more confused. Darcy said softly, "Miss Bennet, after I see Bingley in London, may I call on you at your uncle's house?"

He looked down at her as she remained silent, her bonnet lowered so that he could not see her face. At length, after she made no response, he tried again. "Miss Bennet—"

"Oh, have done, sir!" she burst out. She could not master her own thoughts; they were in such turmoil, and she wanted nothing more than to be away from him and safe in her own room. Her emotions threatened to overwhelm her—anger at Mr. Darcy for all he had expressed and related the previous night, distress mixed with hope for her sister, mortification for her own errors of judgment, exasperation with the man beside her. They combined to make her forget all politeness. But almost as soon as the words were said, she realized her unfairness and sighed.

"Please forgive me, sir," she said shortly, and though what she really wanted was simple silence, she added, "Pray continue."

"I was asking whether I might call on you after your return to London."

"Why do you persist in this quest?" she demanded. "Have I not made clear that I do not return your affections?" She made an effort to calm herself. "While I do admit that I have been in error about many aspects of your character, I have not yet been able to consider and think on all I have learned. I do not yet know if I even *like* you! We have not had, in the whole of our acquaintance, a single civil conversation, and now you ask my leave to call on me—to court me?"

"I do, Miss Bennet. Once I see Bingley."

"Yes," she sighed, "Mr. Bingley."

"I will see Bingley directly I return to London," said Darcy. "I will tell him what I have learned. I believe he will be receptive."

Elizabeth thought of those letters from Jane, wondering whether Mr. Darcy's mission might result in healing her sister's pain. Realizing what that effort might cost him in terms of his pride and that he had pledged to make the attempt even if she still rejected him utterly, she was suddenly ashamed of her outburst. She could not in good faith remain so unyielding in the face of his good intentions.

"Oh, very well, sir. Repair your error with Mr. Bingley first," she said, taking a deep breath, "and then you may call."

"Thank you." he said, daring for the first time to hope just a little. Her manner remained unyielding, but she had not denied him the chance to rectify his situation.

"In truth, sir," she replied, "I cannot give you any encouragement. I will not renege on my agreement, but I fail to see any hope in your efforts."

Darcy pondered this for a moment. *She still holds her ground against me, but it could be ever so much worse.* A slight smile softened the severity of his features. "I believe I will chance it, Miss Bennet."

"As you wish then, Mr. Darcy," she said coolly.

"Then perhaps you will give me the name of your relations in London so that I might know *where* to call," Darcy suggested.

Elizabeth's chin came up. "My Uncle and Aunt Gardiner live in Gracechurch Street. My uncle Gardiner is the one in trade, you know. It is my Uncle Philips who is the country lawyer in Meryton."

Darcy winced visibly at her sarcasm; nevertheless, he thanked her.

Once again, Elizabeth was mortified by her rudeness. She could not seem able to control herself, and she was instantly contrite. "I must again ask your forgiveness, Mr. Darcy. That was cruelly said, and I apologize."

"I quite understand, Miss Bennet. It has indeed been a day to strain anyone's civility." He gestured down the path. "Shall we return?"

They walked in silence under the trees, and gradually the tension subsided. Darcy felt, if not joyous, at least hopeful. And Elizabeth, while still upset, was thankful that the moments she had dreaded the most in their conversation were over. She felt her spirits lighten as the bright sunshine and the crisp air worked to bring her to good cheer.

At one point, Darcy was surprised to hear soft laughter, and he looked down to see a slight smile on her lips and the familiar sparkle to her eyes.

"I am cheered to see you laugh again, Miss Elizabeth," he ventured cautiously.

"Oh, I am not made for dreary thoughts, sir," she said. "At least not for long. I was just contemplating the reaction of certain people at the thought of your calling on me. I did tell you once, if you remember, that I am diverted by follies and nonsense, whims and inconsistencies?"

Elizabeth looked up with one eyebrow arched, a circumstance Darcy knew from experience presaged a flashing of her wit. "I do remember," he said, immediately on his guard, yet relieved that she might yet jest with him after the high emotion of the past days.

"Oh, yes, sir. There are any number of our neighbours who will be shocked that you call on a lady who is *only tolerable*."

Darcy groaned aloud. "You heard."

"Oh, yes," she said wickedly. "It was most incautiously said."

Darcy groaned again, "Is every misspoken word I have ever uttered going to come back to haunt me?"

Elizabeth lowered her head to hide her smile, but in truth, Darcy was not overly unhappy. He would far rather be teased, even with a slight edge of malice, than to be ignored or rejected.

"I did not know you heard me," he said, "but I suspected." He considered his words. "I should have apologized."

"It might have made some things easier," she agreed.

"No doubt." But this time it was he who chuckled, at which Elizabeth raised an eyebrow in query. "I was just thinking," he said with a small smile, "that this will make a good tale to tell our children."

"Mr. Darcy, you presume too much!" Elizabeth was instantly irritated by his presumption.

"Yes, you are correct. I am sorry; I spoke without thinking."

But as they walked on, Darcy's spirits would not be repressed, and he smiled again. "I should warn you, Miss Bennet, before we call later, that my cousin Fitzwilliam seems to have deduced my inclination toward you. When I informed him that you might consult with him, he seems to have taken that information and to have made some rather shrewd conjectures—rather close to the mark, I am afraid to say—so you might prepare for some teasing from him. He is much better at it than I am, you know."

"Indeed," Elizabeth said, as the Parsonage came into sight. "Did you confirm his suspicions, Mr. Darcy?"

"Oh, no, but I did not have to. I was taking a shot at billiards and was thus not prepared for his challenge, and my reaction confirmed the accuracy of his speculation."

Darcy was silent for several steps and then continued, "Richard did mention that his concern first arose because I had been behaving rather oddly of late." The thought seemed to amuse him, Elizabeth noted with some surprise, because she was firmly of the opinion that he had no sense of humour.

But she said nothing, and they soon reached the Parsonage.

"Goodbye, Miss Bennet," Darcy said, taking her hand. "My cousin and I will call on your party in the afternoon."

At first Elizabeth worried that he was going to kiss her hand, but he contented himself with a bow, his eyes fixed on hers as they darkened in a most disturbing manner. She now knew that gaze to be motivated, not by displeasure, but by esteem, and this thought was at last too much. Without replying, Elizabeth turned and hurried through the gate.

Chapter 6

Friday, April 10, 1812

At first, Darcy was relieved when Lady Catherine did not continue her harangue during luncheon. However, little more than halfway through the meal, his relief was supplanted, first by curiosity and then by alarm. Her ladyship always dominated the conversation, especially at table, and her present silence, broken only by the clink of silverware and the occasional short comment, was, while welcome to his personal tastes, not at all normal. No more than a few moments' observation confirmed that something was amiss. His aunt's pinched mouth, flared nostrils, and silent focus on her plate convinced him that she was coldly furious—at him. While his own experiences over the past two days had been distinctly unnerving, he could not recall having done anything to provoke this singular behaviour in his aunt.

Upon returning to his room afterwards, he noted another odd occurrence. As he approached his door, two maids at the end of the hall abruptly ceased their conversation, busying themselves with the folded bedding that one of them carried. They stole a glance at him as he paused at the door and then leaned their heads together, whispering, as he entered. He wondered at the unusual behaviour, but he did not bother himself overmuch since his aunt's household had never been one in which he felt comfortable. Unlike his own household, Rosings was not composed of long-term, often lifetime, employees who frequently represented more than one generation of service to the Darcy family.

Since he and Fitzwilliam planned to take their leave of the Collinses and their visitors that afternoon, he immediately rang for Jennings and soon was descending the stairs to find his cousin waiting for him. To Darcy's discomfort, Fitzwilliam was in high good humour, remarking several times as they walked on the *impulsiveness* of the Darcys and the *disappointment* of the ladies in town, and his cheerfulness was affected not a jot by Darcy's cold replies and growing irritation. Blessedly, at last they reached the Parsonage.

They found the women sewing in the front parlour, and Fitzwilliam was at his charming best as he bowed over the hand of Mrs. Collins, thanking her for the many delightful visits during the past weeks. He then moved to Miss Lucas, who was as silent and unable to respond as ever. As Darcy also thanked Mrs. Collins, he noted her husband's entry into the room. However, when the parson turned to greet him, Darcy was surprised to receive only an uncomfortable bow rather than the man's normal obsequious performance. Collins said not a word, but the sudden discomfort and embarrassment of his wife could only be attributed to the parson's uncharacteristic behaviour.

After Darcy paid his respects to Miss Lucas, he crossed to Elizabeth, who was already in conversation with his cousin. She turned to him as he approached, her expression guarded.

"Miss Bennet," he said, "it was most pleasant to have the opportunity to renew our acquaintance." Darcy could not help falling into that formal tone of voice he used in public, especially when he saw the easy manner in which his cousin conversed with her. Her reply was only a nod and a quiet, "Thank you, Mr. Darcy."

"Please accept my best wishes for a safe and pleasant journey home to your family," he continued. "I believe you will be stopping in town to visit with your relations?"

"Yes, Mr. Darcy. I leave Saturday week."

"And you will be staying there before continuing on to your home?"

"For at least some few days. I will be joining my eldest sister, and my aunt has several events planned."

"I trust you will find your sister in good spirits when you return."

For the first time, Elizabeth met his eyes, and she could not restrain the surge of hope inside her. *He really will do as he promised,* she thought excitedly then chastised herself. Of course, he would do as he pledged. Even if he was disagreeable, he had always been honest and honourable. Bingley certainly affirmed it.

"I hope I shall, Mr. Darcy," she said aloud.

"Then I shall take my leave, Miss Bennet, and leave you to the capable conversation of my cousin." With a bow, he turned to go.

"Most *impulsive*, Darcy," Fitzwilliam interjected quietly, earning a curious look from Elizabeth and a glare from Darcy. Fitzwilliam chuckled under his breath before turning back to Elizabeth.

Darcy again noted Collins's agitated behaviour as he thanked the man for his hospitality. The pathetic man was actually sweating, and he obviously wished the gentlemen gone immediately. There being nothing left to say, Darcy finished with a cold bow and turned to leave. As he did, he observed his cousin again in conversation with Elizabeth, who appeared uncertain and uncomfortable, and he knew that Richard was engaged in a bit of subtle teasing.

Well, I warned her, he thought, with a certain degree of satisfaction, and made his departure.

Lady Catherine's earlier manner at Rosings, coupled with Mr. Collins's odd behaviour at the Parsonage were enough on his mind that, upon returning to his room, Darcy rang for Jennings. One glance at the discomfort on the valet's usually calm visage convinced him that something was seriously amiss.

"All right, man, I can see that my suspicions are warranted," he said. "Out with it!"

"Mr. Darcy, sir, this is most distressing," Jennings began uncomfortably, "but I have heard some quite unseemly talk among the staff. I have pointedly attempted to correct such gossiping, but my efforts have been ignored." He sniffed in disapproval and then continued, "The comments involve your person, Mr. Darcy, and they also concern a friend of Mrs. Collins, a Miss Bennet."

Darcy cursed under his breath and then collected himself. "And what do they say?"

"I do not know for sure, Mr. Darcy, since I left the room when my advice to avoid gossip was ignored."

Darcy sighed. "I am afraid that this is what you should expect when the household staff changes as often as occurs here, but there is no help for it now. Jennings, I need to know what is being said below stairs. I hate to ask this of you, but I must know. Please endeavour to find out whatever you can and give me a report after supper."

"Very good, sir," said Jennings, and he quietly left the room.

DARCY STAYED IN THE LIBRARY reading until supper, which was a repeat of luncheon, and even Fitzwilliam and Anne noticed Lady Catherine's cold behaviour. He ate quickly and, ignoring Fitzwilliam's raised eyebrows, made his exit as soon as possible to return to his room. There, he quickly summoned Jennings. As soon as the man entered, Darcy could tell that he did not bring good news. He did not think he had ever seen his valet quite this upset and angry.

"Have a seat, Jennings. This appears as if it may take some time."

"Indeed it may, sir. I have been busy listening to a variety of different accounts from the staff, and none of them seems to see even the slightest impropriety in indulging in such talk! It is all quite upsetting, sir!"

"I daresay," said Darcy. "Well, let me have all the particulars. Omit nothing, for I need complete information so I know how to proceed."

"Very well, sir," said Jennings. "First"—and he ticked off the point on his finger—"the Parsonage servants, who appear to be almost as ill-behaved as those here at Rosings, have evidently spread a report that you visited the Parsonage last evening and there spent several hours alone with Miss Bennet in the parlour."

Darcy struggled to control his sudden fury, and it was several moments before he felt himself under sufficient control to respond to Jennings report.

"I see," he said at length, and motioned to his valet to continue.

Jennings well understood his employer's anger and shrugged helplessly. "I am sorry, sir, but the staff, as I say—"

"I know, I know, Jennings. Pray continue."

"As I say, the Parsonage staff was all excited about this as a most improper and indeed, compromising, situation, especially since it is the house of a clergyman. Next"—he ticked off another finger—"the Rosings staff has taken that bit of gossip and added to it that you and Miss Bennet have several times been seen walking in the park and that you have other times ventured to meet Miss Bennet alone at the Parsonage. They are talking of other assignations beyond that of last evening.

"Next," he continued, "Mr. Collins was incautious enough this morning to speak to Lady Catherine in front of one of the servants. He not only repeated what was being said already but also added his own estimation, which is—and please pardon me for saying it, sir—that you made improper advances toward Miss Bennet last evening, which she rejected. He believes you tried to force yourself on her, which resulted in Miss Bennet fleeing the parlour in tears."

This brought Darcy to his feet in anger. "That idiot! That he would spread such filth about his own cousin is completely intolerable! And that the servants would then gossip about it! Can they not see how harmful this type of talk can be to the family? Is there no one in charge below stairs at either household?"

"There does not appear to be, sir. The previous housekeeper left over two months ago, and she has not been replaced. The butler ought to step in, but it appears that he is rather fond of the bottle and will not be bothered to control the staff."

"Well, is that all?" asked Darcy, calming himself and resuming his seat.

"Not quite, sir. And this last is the most disturbing of the lot. One of the kitchen maids, who appears quite the ringleader, has ventured that the parson's opinion regarding improper advances could not have been accurate, since she saw you just this morning walking with Miss Bennet. Your conversation, seen from a distance, could not be discerned but it was clear that both parties were at times upset. She ventured to suggest that you must have seduced Miss Bennet and her tears last night resulted from her attempts to induce you to marry her followed by your flat refusal."

This last brought a groan from Darcy, but Jennings continued. "I thought I overheard her saying that she had written to her sister of this story, but when I confronted her, she would not confirm the truth of it. I did check, but the afternoon post had been picked up already."

Darcy's face was stony though his thoughts were in turmoil as Jennings concluded. "That is the last of what I could learn, sir. I am sorry to be the bearer of bad tidings. I have never been subjected to such ill-bred associates. They would never be tolerated in a decent household."

Darcy thanked him for his efforts and dismissed him for the evening, but after more than an hour of deep contemplation, he was interrupted by a knock at the door.

"Come," called Darcy, startled out of his concentration, and he was surprised to see Fitzwilliam enter. The worry was evident on his cousin's normally pleasant face.

"Darcy," he said without preamble, "my man, Sergeant Henderson, has just told me of some most disturbing news that he picked up in the kitchen."

"I can guess," Darcy groaned. "I spoke with Jennings earlier."

"What!" exclaimed Fitzwilliam, looking sharply at Darcy. "Cousin, they are saying you have seduced Miss Bennet!"

"Among other things," growled Darcy. "What an unholy muddle!" Seeing the look of concern still on his cousin's face, he burst out, "It is not true, Richard! Nothing improper has passed between Elizabeth and me!"

"Elizabeth, is it?" Fitzwilliam said with some heat. "She did not look as if she would have welcomed your calling her by her Christian name this afternoon. What exactly *has* passed between you, Darcy?"

Darcy realized that, once his cousin's protective nature was aroused, nothing less than the full account would do, and he resignedly set himself to it.

"Will you pour two brandies? I shall explain everything, but it may take some time."

Darcy then told his cousin of all that had transpired between himself and Elizabeth, from their meeting in Hertfordshire, to his abortive proposal, to that night's unwelcome report from Jennings. By the time he was finished, their glasses had been refilled and were once again half-drained.

"What a bunch of gossiping old hens!" Fitzwilliam remarked. He took a sip of his brandy. "At least that explains her ladyship's behaviour at dinner."

"Too right. But as angry as she must be, she will never bring it up to me for fear that I might be forced to defend Miss Bennet's honour by offering marriage."

"Do you think she has any inkling of your true feelings?"

Darcy shook his head. "I would be quite surprised. But more important is the question of what I should do." He ran his hand through his hair as he considered the situation. "I am inclined to think that the best course is to simply ignore it," he said at last. "Almost anything I might do would only lend credence to these pernicious rumours."

Fitzwilliam considered this a moment. "The thought has its attractions, but I am concerned about the letter written by one of the kitchen staff. Did

Jennings have any idea where it was sent?" Darcy shook his head, and Fitzwilliam sighed. "That makes it more difficult. What if this gossip should make its way to London?"

"That would not be pleasant," Darcy agreed. "But how bad could it be? Why could I not simply ignore it, even if it did become a topic of conversation?"

"Because you, my dear cousin, are a supremely eligible bachelor and are therefore a figure of prominence in London society. If the gossip makes it to the scandal sheets, it *will* be published, and it *will* be noticed."

"Even so, it has happened before, and I have successfully ignored it."

"Yes, but those were trifling mentions, seeking to connect you to this or that available young woman. This involves more than yourself. *You* might successfully ignore it even if it were published in the *Chronicle*, and you might well escape with barely a singe. But not Miss Bennet," he said quietly. "What will merely singe you could completely ruin her. If you do not want the girl hurt, you have to do something."

Darcy grimaced at the truth of Fitzwilliam's observation. "There is only one response acceptable in a situation such as this, and that is an offer of marriage. But that has already been attempted with the dismal results I have mentioned."

"Then your offer will have to be renewed, and Miss Bennet must be prepared to accept or face the consequences. It does seem as if she may have acquitted you of the worst of her opinions, and this additional information may convince her of the wisdom of this course."

Darcy considered this, but the problem was that he believed he understood Elizabeth better than his cousin did—for all his superior skill in conversation. Richard had not seen the manner in which Elizabeth had stood up to him, and he believed that even this disturbing news would not move her from her course. It might be different if the gossip actually were published and talked about, for then Elizabeth would have little choice if she wished to prevent scandal from damaging her or her family. However, she had that morning given him a chance to continue their acquaintance, and he would prefer to keep to that course.

"I will acquaint Miss Bennet with this distressing news," Darcy said slowly, "but I believe that any renewal of my offer would be rejected." Fitzwilliam opened his mouth to protest, but Darcy held up his hand. "Trust me on this, Richard. She would be outraged by any attempt to force her to accept marriage due to household gossip that we both know has no foundation. Yet she must be informed. We are scheduled to depart in the morning at nine, and I will attempt to see her in private if she walks early. But what if she does not walk? Perhaps we should delay until the afternoon or even the following day."

Fitzwilliam was not wholly in accord with Darcy's refusal to renew his offer, but he submitted to his cousin's better understanding of Miss Bennet. On the subject of their departure, however, his opinion was fixed.

"There are two points against delaying our departure, as I see it," he said firmly. "One is that a letter has already been dispatched, so time lost may be time needed. Second is the disgraceful state of the staff here. With the arrangements already in place, changing our plans at the last minute will likely give rise to further whispers, such as 'Mr. Darcy is unable to leave his mistress,' and *that* news will shortly be included in some other post." He paused thoughtfully, looking at his cousin. "I still believe that you should renew your offer or possibly take this to Miss Bennet's father."

"It will not work, Richard. That eventuality may come, but I am convinced that she will reject any offer I might make now. And even if I saw her father and he agreed with me, I doubt that he would force her to marry against her will."

"Possibly you are correct" — Fitzwilliam sighed — "yet I do not wish to see Miss Bennet hurt."

"Nor do I," he answered, running his hand through his hair again. "What if I cannot see her before we leave? If she does not walk, I will have no chance to notify her."

Fitzwilliam brightened at a sudden thought. "Write her a letter, Darcy. If you do not see her in the morning, take it to her at the Parsonage."

"She will not accept a letter from me. And even if she did, as you pointed out, the staff would then gossip about *that*."

"Ummm," said Fitzwilliam in reluctant agreement, then brightened again. "What about Anne?" he suggested. "I know she corresponds with Mrs. Collins; I have seen several notes left to be delivered. Perhaps she could take your letter and enclose it inside one of her own?"

Darcy nodded slowly. "That would work. I know Anne relishes the opportunity to circumvent Lady Catherine whenever possible to do so without being discovered."

"Yes, she will not oppose her openly," Fitzwilliam said sadly. "Still, I do not know whether either of us would be any braver if we had to live in her ladyship's household and under her authority."

"Too true."

"It ought to be a *good* letter to Miss Bennet, Cousin." Fitzwilliam smiled.

"At least I *write* better than I *speak*," he jested in return.

The two men then made one final toast, draining their glasses before Fitzwilliam excused himself for the evening and Darcy sat down to write. For the third night in a row, he would get little sleep, and it was past three in the morning before he at last finished. He addressed his letter to 'Miss Elizabeth Bennet,' sealed it, and stamped it with the Darcy family crest. Lastly, before retiring, he enclosed it in a plain sheet of stationery.

Chapter 7

"**G**ood morning, Anne," Darcy said in greeting the next morning. "Thank you for admitting me on such short notice."

His cousin was sitting by the window, looking outdoors with a wistful expression. He suddenly felt guilty for his robust health and his errand when this young woman was so hindered by her own frail body that she was unable to share in the beauties of the world upon which she gazed.

"It is no trouble," she responded, turning to him at last. "I have been awake for hours."

Darcy nodded in sad understanding of his cousin's frailties before mentally shrugging off his sympathy and focusing on his purpose. "We are ready to go" he began, and she nodded, for he had taken leave of her the previous evening. "But I wish to solicit your aid in an urgent matter. It is," he said, looking her in the eye, "one that needs to be kept from your mother's notice."

"It is, is it?" she said with more interest than before. "And what do you need my help with, Cousin Darcy?"

"I need your aid to get a letter to Miss Elizabeth Bennet at the Parsonage."

"Ah, the valiant Miss Bennet," she said with a slight smile. "That *does* explain some of the oddities I have noted on this visit."

Her discerning gaze made Darcy uncomfortable. Anne might have inherited her physical frailty from her father, but she had also inherited his incisive mind.

"For obvious reasons, I cannot simply hand my letter to her. I thought you might enclose it in one of your own to Mrs. Collins, which I could then deliver to her before we leave," he told her, taking out his letter and setting it on the table.

Anne looked at it with interest but did not reach to take it, instead fixing him with an inquisitive stare.

"I must inform Miss Bennet of some very urgent matters, Anne," he said haltingly. "She must be made aware—and quickly, I might add—of vital information that affects her personally."

"Ah, the gossip," Anne said quietly but with a twinkle in her eye.

Darcy did not ask how she knew. The rest of her mother's staff might be undeserving of employment in a household of note, but her own maid, Margaret, had served Anne de Bourgh all her short life, and the older woman was fiercely loyal to her mistress.

"Yes, the gossip," Darcy confirmed, "none of which is true, by the way."

"I never doubted it." Anne's eyes brightened as she reached for the letter. "I like Miss Bennet very much," she said mildly though Darcy could read the interest in her expression. "You could not have made a wiser choice—or one so calculated to drive my mother into an absolute passion! Therefore, I will be pleased to assist you in this endeavour."

"Yes, well," Darcy stammered as an empty feeling in the pit of his stomach threatened his equanimity. "There is nothing settled yet, Anne, but I thank you for your assistance. There is one further request—when you write to Mrs. Collins, would you ask that she urge Miss Bennet to read the letter? Miss Bennet is, ah... very independent minded... and might well refuse to either receive or read it."

"Why is that?" Anne was confused. "Does she not know of your intentions? Do not tell me that you have not the courage to declare yourself to her."

"She knows," said Darcy uncomfortably. "The question is not my intentions but her reception of them."

"Oho!" chortled Anne. "Do not tell me she rejected you! Oh, this is too much. Our Miss Bennet is truly a gem among women."

"Do you have to enjoy it so much?" Darcy grumbled, wondering whether all of his acquaintances would soon know what he would have much rather kept a dark secret. "We *are* cousins, you know. You might at least have a little consideration for my feelings!"

"Oh, by all means, I should," said Anne with absolutely no contrition whatever. "But do you desire my consideration or my aid?"

"Your aid, of course. Will you give it?"

"Do you have to ask? To outmanoeuvre my mother while helping to foster a match between you and the lovely Miss Bennet—how could I not help you in this?"

"Thank you. Please have Margaret deliver it to Jennings, and I will leave it at the Parsonage," Darcy said quietly. "I hope to have the opportunity to talk to Miss Bennet this morning in private. But if I am unsuccessful, I will trust in your letter. Thank you for your help. I hope that our next meeting will see you improved in health."

"As do I, Cousin," she sighed as he bent to kiss her hand. "As do I."

She was already moving toward her writing desk as he left the room.

ELIZABETH WAS ALONE WITH CHARLOTTE in the drawing room when she was surprised to see the door open and Mr. Darcy's tall figure stride into the room. His dark eyes brightened as he saw her, and she had to look down. She felt her cheeks redden, for even after another long night of thought, she remained as confused about him as ever. Needing more time to examine her feelings, she had deliberately stayed indoors in order to avoid any possibility of another meeting along the paths of Rosings. Oh, how she looked forward to being with Jane, with whom she might discuss all that had passed in the last several days!

"Please excuse the interruption, Mrs. Collins," she heard him say, "but when I took leave of my cousin Anne this morning, she mentioned that she had a note for you, which I offered to deliver." Elizabeth looked up as he handed the letter to Charlotte, and for the first time since she had known him, she was struck by how handsome he truly was. Always before, she had seen him through the eyes of amusement and dislike. But now, knowing his attraction to her, her viewpoint was altered, and she could not help but be impressed by his attractive features, his stature, and his well-built frame. As he made his farewell to Charlotte and turned to her, she recognized the open admiration in his eyes, and she had the feeling that he was fixing her in his memory, trying to store a recollection to be examined at a later time. The feeling of being so scrutinized was, surprisingly, not wholly unpleasant, and when he gave a small bow and bid her goodbye, she inclined her head in return. As he turned to the door, she caught one last look from him, and he was gone.

Elizabeth was lost in contemplation of this brief but unsettling encounter and did not see her friend frowning at the packet she held, wondering at its being so thick. However, when Charlotte opened it, she found a brief note from Miss de Bourgh wrapped around what appeared to be another letter.

Charlotte's frown grew deeper as she read the note, and Elizabeth, who had returned to her sewing, peered at her in curiosity. She was surprised when Charlotte finally looked up from her perusal of the note and shoved a letter, folded and sealed, but with no writing on either side, along the table to her, saying, "It seems that this one is for you, Lizzy. Miss de Bourgh says that it is from Mr. Darcy and asks me to pass it on to you."

"Mr. Darcy!"

"It appears so," said Charlotte. Then, as Elizabeth showed no inclination to pick it up, she asked, "Are you not going to open it, Lizzy?"

"It is not proper for Mr. Darcy to send me a letter, Charlotte," Elizabeth said slowly. "Especially after what I shared with you earlier. No, I shall not open it," she concluded firmly.

Charlotte was troubled by this response. She knew her friend was right about the proprieties, but she was so firmly decided that Elizabeth and Mr. Darcy would make a splendid match that she was determined to advance the prospect if at all possible. Finally, she decided to share Miss de Bourgh's specific urging that Elizabeth accept the letter as the best way to convince her.

Elizabeth listened with considerable astonishment. The idea that the quiet, sickly Anne de Bourgh could not only take amusement in thwarting her mother and could even have conspired with her cousin was not at all what she had envisioned. When Charlotte had finished, she once again urged Elizabeth to take Mr. Darcy's letter, and eventually, Elizabeth yielded—partly to Charlotte's opinion and partly to her own curiosity.

Rosings, 10 o'clock of the evening, April 10

Miss Elizabeth Bennet,

Please forgive the mode of delivery of this note, but I was forced to resort to desperate stratagems in order to appraise you of distressing news that has come to me, news that concerns us both. Briefly, the situation is thus…

Elizabeth read the explanation of the unwelcome rumours with consternation and growing concern, well aware how slight an error could cause irreparable harm to a young lady's reputation, damaging her chance of making a good marriage or of even being recognized in polite society.

The question now to be addressed concerns what is to be done in light of this situation. At this time, my cousin Fitzwilliam and I believe the greatest hazard is that this rumour may spread into open scandal, possibly among London society. If it were just your family, the salacious tales might die a well-deserved death, but my prominence in society, unwelcome as it is, makes such a fortunate conclusion less likely. The simplest and most convenient course of action to mitigate the damage of such an occurrence would be, of course, for you to reconsider my offer of marriage, but I believe I know you well enough to be assured that you are resolute in your refusal. Therefore, I have decided the best course is to inform you of what I have learned and to hope that the worst may be avoided.

I will journey today to London and visit Bingley on the morrow, after which I will wait to hear that you have joined your sister, remaining watchful as to whether this story spreads. If it does so, I will inform you immediately either by riding to Kent or by sending an express, for by that point, no delay may be risked, and any breach of propriety must be ignored. In case there might be any doubt in your mind, let me assure you that even open scandal would not affect my course. My affections and wishes are unchanged, and my offer of marriage remains open; I urge you to consider what I have related and also to consider your response should events take an unfortunate path.

I know this situation cannot be to your liking, nor is it to mine. I intend, if you are still willing to grant me the chance, to conduct a more traditional courtship in the hope of changing your opinion of me. I do not wish to have you come unwillingly to marriage, even though it would result in my union with one whom I hold most dear, but in the event that the more fortunate event becomes unfeasible, I hope that you will see the sense of it. In that event, and assuming your agreement, please be assured that you will never in the future have reason to doubt your financial security nor my love and my respect of you and our future family.

I remain, your most ardent and respectful admirer,
F. Darcy

Charlotte watched in distress as Elizabeth rose from her seat and changed colour as she read the letter with increasing agitation. She paced about the room, silently mouthing the words until she finally threw herself back into the chair with a muttered, "What an insufferable, arrogant man! The very nerve of him, to…to…oh, I am so very angry!"

At length, Elizabeth calmed down enough to read the letter through once more while Charlotte put her sewing aside and simply sat waiting for her to regain the ability to converse. When she judged that point had been reached, she ventured, "Then the letter *was* from Mr. Darcy?"

"Oh, yes, Charlotte. There could not be a more prideful, conceited man in the entirety of England than Mr. oh-so-proud Darcy!"

But as calm slowly returned, Elizabeth grew more concerned with the problem Mr. Darcy related rather than his solution to it. Could he be mistaken?

"Charlotte, Mr. Darcy makes mention of some…rumours…among the staff here and at Rosings concerning Mr. Darcy and myself. Have you heard of any such?"

When Charlotte would not meet her eye, Elizabeth's stomach roiled. At last, Charlotte said, "Lizzy, I cannot talk of it. My husband has absolutely forbidden me to speak on the matter."

Elizabeth reached over and took her hand consolingly, for Charlotte was quite distraught. "Mr. Darcy believes that Lady Catherine, still hoping to accomplish a marriage between her daughter and nephew, wishes to prevent the rumours from escaping beyond the bounds of Rosings. Has her ladyship commanded Mr. Collins to order your silence?" She could see the answer in the misery on Charlotte's features, and she continued wryly, "It seems that, from what Mr. Darcy writes, Lady Catherine's efforts may well be too late."

Charlotte twisted her hands in anxiety for her friend. "Can I help, Lizzy? I would not go against my husband's wishes, but if there is anything I can do that does not conflict with his orders, please tell me."

Elizabeth sighed and tried to force a smile. "I am not sure anyone can do anything, but here is what Mr. Darcy relates," and she quickly acquainted her friend with the outline of Darcy's letter.

Charlotte's spirits were lifted immeasurably. "It is not so very bad, is it, Lizzy? I must admit to a feeling of vindication that his regard for you is as I predicted. And now he desires to court you openly while assuring that you will not be ruined by scandal. Surely, you must see how fortunate is the solution he suggests? If he did not care, he could simply endure the embarrassment to himself instead of renewing his offer of marriage."

"But that is the core of the problem, Charlotte," Elizabeth said angrily. "*He* plots the course, *he* makes the decisions, *he* commands—and *I* must do as he wishes or else expose my sisters and my family to the humiliation of scandal! It is altogether intolerable!"

"But Lizzy, does he not say how much he loves you?" Charlotte tried to mollify her friend's anger with rational advice. "Does he not say how he will ensure the future for you and your children? And does he not say that you will never doubt his love and respect for you? Do you have reason to doubt his sincerity in these regards? Are not these assurances beyond the realm of what most young women are presented when considering marriage? Oh, Lizzy, you must give some thought to the realities of life and not give over everything to your romantic notions! Does not Mr. Darcy express enough romance for any dozen impractical young men?"

Elizabeth was taken aback by the vehemence of Charlotte's arguments, and she finally confessed that she did not doubt Mr. Darcy's sincerity. She flushed in embarrassment as she continued, "I must admit that I have no present reason to believe him unprincipled or unjust. I have rejected my previous opinion of his character based on—I am embarrassed to admit—the vile charges made by Mr. Wickham. Even though his manners are proud and repulsive, I must accede that you are partly right."

Charlotte was pleased at the concession. Elizabeth was so independent of mind that she was more than capable of defending her points against all arguments, but there were other thoughts she wished Elizabeth to consider.

"Lizzy, I want you to listen to me now," she said, as she leaned forward to take Elizabeth's hand. "I have never thought Mr. Darcy to be as prideful as you believe, but put that aside for now. I want you to consider that he is not the same as the young men we saw in Hertfordshire. He is not even the same as his friend, Mr. Bingley. Mr. Darcy has had many weighty responsibilities thrust upon him at an age when other young men think only of dances with the prettiest girls at the next ball. He has had the responsibility of managing a great estate in the country as well as maintaining a household in town. He has even had the care of a much younger sister. In all of these, he has acquitted himself admirably, even while being betrayed by his boyhood friend and pursued by every mother with an unmarried daughter in both town and country. Then, you tell me he was so inarticulate when he made his proposal that he had to pull out written pages to settle himself! If you would have my opinion, I think what you have been calling pride and conceit is more a mask of protective reserve to put on in uncomfortable social situations. Oh, I am sure that he does need to amend his manners in some regards, but that is a task that a good wife could accomplish."

This last statement made Elizabeth blush; the idea that she might have the power to soften his manner was not without attraction.

"And," Charlotte continued, "I cannot comment on the reason for his letter because of my husband's wishes, but you must give credence to the logic of his arguments. Perhaps he is too quick to make decisions for others, but after all, he has been doing it for some time now for those under his care—his sister, his staff and his tenants, even his friend Mr. Bingley, and now you. I urge you to consider carefully before you reject him again. It could not only prove harmful to your reputation and that of your family, but you may also be rejecting a man who, with his own talents and disposition, in many ways could be the best match for you in terms of your own character. Do promise me that you will try to think very carefully on this."

While Elizabeth could agree with the logic, Charlotte's rational advice clashed greatly with her feelings. However, she knew that certain of her beliefs could not bear close examination, considering the faulty basis on which they had been formed. Finally, she sighed, "You have given me much to think on, Charlotte. I feel grieved that I continue to make hasty and faulty assumptions regarding Mr. Darcy. I still do not know whether I can accept him as the man with whom I will spend the rest of my life, but I do know that I must consider it. But for now"—she sighed—"I feel in the need for a long, long walk and some time by myself."

Elizabeth spent much time walking and thinking without forming any conclusions by the time she returned to the house. She could not rid herself of the memory of Mr. Darcy's tenderness of voice when he made his proposal, nor could she forget his words, *'You must allow me to tell you how ardently I admire and love you.'* The very memory sent a shiver down her spine, and she hugged herself in her room as she tried to convince herself that she never wanted to hear that caressing tone from him again.

There was again no invitation to Rosings though Mr. Collins did call on Lady Catherine in the afternoon, and Elizabeth was now quite anxious to return to London. After a supper at the Parsonage marked by little conversation and no amity, Elizabeth retired early to her room with many thoughts to occupy her.

Chapter 8

Sunday, April 12, 1812

When Darcy arrived in Town the previous evening, he sent a note to Bingley asking whether his friend was available to receive a visit the following afternoon, and an affirmative response in Bingley's untidy scrawl was delivered after dinner. Thus, following church in the morning and luncheon with his sister afterwards, at the stroke of one o'clock he left his sister, Georgiana, to her music and Mrs. Annesley's companionship and boarded his coach to take him to Bingley's townhouse. The butler escorted him to the parlour where he found Bingley and his sister sitting on opposite couches. Miss Bingley was engaged in ignoring the book in her lap and talking to her brother while her brother was obviously ignoring her and everything else as he stared silently out the window.

Bingley turned as Darcy was announced, but his sister was quick to jump to her feet and interpose herself between them before he could say a word.

"Mr. Darcy," she exclaimed with a smile as bright as it was artificial, "We were not informed you had returned from Kent. How went your visit with your aunt?"

"It has, at least, concluded, Miss Bingley," Darcy replied stiffly. "Bingley, there is a matter of some importance I must discuss with you in your study."

His shortness stopped Caroline Bingley in her tracks. Would this man ever come to see her rather than Charles?

"Yes, of course, Darcy," Bingley replied indifferently and gestured to the door, leaving his sister staring after them, wondering with some anxiety what could bring Mr. Darcy there in such urgency and abruptness.

In his study, Bingley dropped with a loose-boned collapse into the upholstered depths of an armchair while Darcy seated himself with more care before the hearth. The younger man stared into the fireplace, and Darcy was distressed to see that he was in worse shape than he had been before the trip to Kent. He shook his head, determined to get the painful interview behind him though not at all sure how to do it correctly.

"Bingley," he opened, "as you know, Colonel Fitzwilliam and I have been in Kent these past weeks." Bingley listened politely but without particular interest though his awareness quickened with Darcy's next statement.

"When we arrived, I was informed that my aunt's parson, Mr. Collins, was newly married to a young lady that we were introduced to in Hertfordshire, a Miss Charlotte Lucas, the elder daughter of Sir William Lucas."

"Mr. Collins?" Bingley inquired, his brow furrowing in remembrance.

"You may remember him from the ball at Netherfield when he attempted to dance with Miss Elizabeth Bennet."

"I seem to recall the man..." Bingley said

"Probably not," Darcy said dryly, "since your eyes hardly left those of Miss Jane Bennet the entire night."

Bingley flushed and looked away, saddened at the memory and upset at being reminded of it.

Darcy continued, "I was surprised to find that Mrs. Collins had a visitor — Miss Elizabeth Bennet — and my cousin and I attended Mrs. Collins and her friend a number of times during our stay."

Bingley was curious but not excessively interested until Darcy's next statement, "While there, Miss Elizabeth had occasion to question my opinion regarding the sentiments of her sister toward you. In fact, Charles, she forced me to the conclusion that my belief in her sister's indifference was in error."

This news drew Bingley upright as the words penetrated his depression. Agitated, he jumped to his feet. "I do not understand. What do you mean, 'the sentiments of her sister toward me'? I assume you mean Miss Bennet?"

At Darcy's nod, he leaned forward in urgent emotion. "Speak clearly, Darcy! What *exactly* does that mean?"

Darcy swallowed. This was going worse than he feared, but he had no choice but to continue. "To speak clearly then, I now know that I was entirely mistaken when I assured you in November that Miss Bennet did not care for you. In truth, Miss Elizabeth informed me that her sister's regard was sincere and deep, and that she was quite heartbroken when you departed Netherfield and did not return."

"What!" Bingley exclaimed. "Miss Bennet was heartbroken? Oh, my God, what have I done?" He collapsed in his chair. Darcy was stricken as Bingley rocked back and forth, pressing his face into his hands, not saying a word but presenting a picture of such misery as to threaten to tear his heart out.

"What must she think of me?" he groaned in despair. "I left her to the derision of the neighbourhood when she loved me! What a hideous, thoughtless monster I am!"

Darcy closed his eyes in pain. Obviously, Bingley's attraction to Jane Bennet was as deep as hers was to him. He arose and clasped his friend's shoulder.

"Bingley," he said slowly, "you were not completely at fault in this matter. It was I who assured you of Miss Bennet's indifference. I stressed the disparity of your situations, and that was arrogance on my part, for which I most heartily apologize. I believed that Miss Bennet's mother would have forced her daughter to marry against her wishes because of your fortune, and I have now been informed that also was wrong, for Miss Bennet was—and is—determined to marry for love."

Bingley looked up in anger. "How can you *know* all this, Darcy? Miss Elizabeth would tell you of such? *That* I find hard to believe!"

Darcy swallowed and looked away, unable to face the accusation in his eyes. "Miss Elizabeth and I...well, we had a rather heated confrontation, and this...all this information came out."

"I see," Bingley said coldly, barely mollified.

"Bingley, there are two other pieces of information you need—or rather three, now that I think of it. First is that Miss Bennet is at this moment visiting her aunt and uncle in London and has been for these three months."

This brought Bingley to his feet in agitation. "Here? In London? Could it be possible? But would she even see me? How could I blame her if she did not? After abandoning her as I did, why would she want to? Oh, what shall I do?"

"Second," Darcy continued, "and this part pains me greatly, much more

70

than my honest error in estimating Miss Bennet's regard. I must tell you that your sister received Miss Bennet here when you were out and then returned the visit at her uncle's home before severing the relationship. Miss Bingley told me of this, and to my discredit, I did not inform you."

If Bingley had looked angry before, his present expression could only be termed cold fury. "Caroline did *what*? She did not tell me? Severed the relationship? And you did not tell me?" He paused to collect his thoughts, and at length, he fixed Darcy with a fierce glare. "I thought better of you, Darcy—much better!"

"I thought better of myself, Charles, and I must beg your forgiveness for my arrogant interference."

Bingley said nothing—just stared at Darcy with that same glare. After several endless minutes, while Darcy resumed his seat but could not meet his friend's eyes, Bingley ground out between gritted teeth, "I am too angry to think just now, Darcy. I think it best you leave before I say something I may later regret."

Darcy got to his feet and turned to go. "As you wish, Bingley. I cannot blame you for being disgusted with me, for I am quite disgusted with myself." He turned back before leaving, saying, "There was a third item. Miss Bennet's uncle's name is Gardiner, and he lives in Gracechurch Street. And I would strongly advise you to go there immediately since I have reason to believe the situation is not beyond repair."

Darcy bowed to his friend and exited the room. On his way out, he was accosted by Miss Bingley as he passed by the door to the parlour; she urged him to join her for a private conversation, but he had no time for her or her attempt to ensnare him into further conspiracy.

"Please excuse me, madam," he said with a bow, "but I must be on my way. Your brother has commanded me to leave his house."

Caroline had never been so shocked in her life. "Charles? He did what?"

"Caroline!" Bingley demanded harshly from his study. "I will see you in here *immediately*!"

Caroline started to turn to Darcy, but he had already proceeded down the hall.

"*Immediately!*" her brother commanded again with an icy sternness she had not even dreamed he possessed.

Before Darcy could retrieve his hat, gloves, and stick from the butler, he heard raised voices issuing from the study. He shook his head in sadness as he left, even feeling a touch of compassion for Caroline Bingley. Not only had he never seen Bingley this angry, he had not believed he could *be* this angry. He did not know if his friend would ever forgive him, and he bitterly wondered whether he could have made a worse muddle of his private life if he had set out with that objective firmly in mind.

IT WAS MID-AFTERNOON WHEN MRS. Gardiner heard the front bell ring. Jane sat on the couch, reading to her two oldest cousins when the sitting room door opened and the maid brought in a card on a tray. Mrs. Gardiner was surprised to read, 'Charles Bingley, Esq.' on the front. On the back, scrawled untidily, was 'Miss Jane Bennet.'

She looked over and caught her niece's attention. "It seems that Mr. Bingley has come to call on you, Jane."

Jane's cheeks reddened; a look of anxiety and desperate hope in equal measure washed across her face before she managed to compose herself.

"Shall I ask him to come up, dear?" asked Mrs. Gardiner quietly, and Jane could only nod. Mrs. Gardiner turned to the maid and instructed her to show the gentleman in.

A moment later, Bingley was shown into the sitting room. His eyes were immediately drawn to Jane, and Mrs. Gardiner noted with interest that Jane sought his gaze with equal intensity but could not hold it. Her cheeks flushed again, and she had to look down.

"Miss Bennet," Bingley said earnestly with an eager bow, "I am so happy to find you in town. I just learned of your presence this very morning from Mr. Darcy, and I lost no time coming to call. I hope I find you in good health?"

Jane answered softly in the affirmative and then remembered her manners. "Mr. Bingley, may I introduce my aunt, Mrs. Edward Gardiner?"

Bingley turned to her and bowed over her hand, "Mrs. Gardiner, I am pleased to make your acquaintance."

"And I yours, Mr. Bingley. Would you care for some tea?"

"Perhaps later, Mrs. Gardiner. What I would very much like is some time with your niece. Mr. Darcy informed me of something this morning—something quite surprising to me—and I very much need to discuss it with Miss Bennet."

Mrs. Gardiner looked at the young man in surprise and disapproval. "This is not a proper request, Mr. Bingley," she said sternly. "While I understand that you are acquainted with my niece from Hertfordshire, I also understand that you have done nothing to warrant such a petition."

Bingley hung his head in shame. "I quite understand your attitude, Mrs. Gardiner, but, unless I am misinformed by my friend, I believe that Miss Bennet will not be opposed to hearing what I have to say."

Mrs. Gardiner looked over at Jane, and it was immediately obvious that Jane did indeed wish to talk with him. And he did appear most earnest…

"Jane," she told her niece, "would you be so good as to take your cousins to their room while I have a word with Mr. Bingley?"

"Of course, Aunt," agreed Jane, standing and offering her hands to each of her cousins, and the three of them left the room, closing the hall door behind them.

Mrs. Gardiner turned back to Bingley and looked at him with an intensity that made him swallow in sudden discomposure.

"You will pardon me if I speak frankly, sir," she said sternly, her eyes maintaining her fixed gaze. "I am familiar with your former acquaintance with my niece, and I do *not* wish to see her hurt further. You quitted Hertfordshire last autumn with no warning to her, no notes or letters, and from what I am told, at a point where all concerned had reason to expect a declaration regarding your intentions. The mortification of such treatment was, as you may well imagine, extreme. I must warn you that I will *not* have you again toy with my niece's affections, Mr. Bingley!"

"I assure you that my intentions were and remain honourable," Bingley said earnestly. "But mistakes have been made—most of them mine—and I am determined to right them. I beg you for the chance to do so."

Mrs. Gardiner gazed at him silently for several moments, and his evident earnestness finally convinced her.

"Very well, Mr. Bingley, I will agree because I see that Jane also wishes to talk with you. But I will be in the next room, and I will leave the door open."

"Thank you," Bingley said in relief. He had known it was not going to be easy. If he had just come to call and talk of the weather and other trivialities, he would not have had to go through this, but he was finished with caution.

After Mrs. Gardiner sent for Jane to return, she stayed long enough to see Bingley seated in a chair across from her niece before exiting the room. For her part, Jane felt a surge of anticipation rise inside her opposed by dread that her hopes might again be dashed. Bingley's words and manner had been uncommonly direct and forceful, and yet she was afraid to even have wishes.

"Miss Bennet," he began, "I received a visit this morning that has completely overturned everything I thought I knew about our time in Hertfordshire. Before I get into that, however, I must confess that the primary mistake has been mine. When I left Netherfield in the autumn and did not return, I did so because I had allowed myself to be convinced of your indifference towards me."

He saw Jane's startled reaction and continued, "Yes, I see that this surprises you. And my mistake was that I was not firm enough to listen to my own counsel and allowed myself to be influenced by others. They talked to me of prudence, and to my shame, I listened and allowed myself to be convinced."

He stood up suddenly in agitation. "But I was miserable, Miss Bennet, for I thought I loved one who did not return my love. Only this morning did I learn from Mr. Darcy that I was not alone in my misery—that you shared it."

Jane was confused. "Mr. Darcy? How could he know anything about my feelings?"

"He had it from your sister, Miss Elizabeth, whom he met while visiting in Kent. I confess," he said with a frown, "I do not quite understand how she came to tell him of this, but he assures me that it is true. It was he who acquainted me of your presence in London these months. I was completely unaware of it. He also told me you had called on my sister Caroline and that she returned the visit. I also knew nothing of that."

He came to a stop in front of her. It seemed the most natural thing in the world to sink down to one knee in before her and take her hand.

"Miss Bennet, I have been counselled of prudence, and I have listened to that counsel, and I have been miserable. I will have no more of prudence! Your aunt said that I had made no declaration of my feeling in Hertfordshire; that is true, and it was my mistake. I am done with that also. Miss Bennet, I must tell you that I love you, I loved you in Hertfordshire, and I love you even more after these months of misery. When I entered this room and saw you, I knew I could never live without you. I would be the happiest man in the world if you would agree to be my wife."

Jane was filled with overflowing joy, both by his declaration of love and by the overwhelming suddenness of it all, but she was unable to say a word as he continued, "I can well understand if you could not forgive me for my mistakes, for they are grievous. I allowed myself to be swayed by the arguments of others rather than listening to my own heart, and that failing has caused us both pain. But I will do my best to make amends. I will start, if you cannot accept me at this point, by returning to Netherfield and asking your father for permission to court you in the hope of convincing you of my steadfastness, for I do dearly love you, and..."

Jane tried to get his attention, but though he held her hand, he could not hold her eye as he continued to tell her of what he would do to win her love in the future. At last, she put out her other hand and placed her fingers over his mouth. "Please stop," she said, and when she had his attention, she simply said, "Yes."

"Yes?" he asked in surprise and incredulity.

"Yes," she confirmed with a smile.

At that, Bingley, who had been so full of words just moments before, was struck dumb. Jane squeezed his fingers, the gentle, happy smile remaining on her face, and said, "Perhaps we should go to my aunt."

Chapter 9

J ust after noon on Monday, Darcy was working on his correspondence in his study when he heard a knock at the front door of his townhouse. Shortly, Stevens came to the study door. "Mr. Bingley asks for a moment of your time, sir."

Darcy looked up in surprise. "Please show him in." Before he could rise to his feet, he heard rapid footsteps in the hall, and Bingley literally burst through the door. Gone was the grim, baleful man of the previous day and returned was the effusive, amiable Bingley of yore, smiling widely, if somewhat sheepishly, as he approached his friend.

"Darcy, I have the pleasure to inform you that both our missions have been successful and I am engaged to be married! In fact, I am just back from asking Mr. Bennet for his consent."

Darcy's eyebrows rose in surprise. "That was fast work." He cocked his head at his friend, whose smile had just grown wider if possible. "In fact, it is *most* unlike the Bingley I have known for these past years." Darcy held out his hand. "Congratulations, Charles."

Bingley pumped the proffered hand enthusiastically.

As Darcy gestured Bingley to a chair, he ventured, "Do I dare hope that I am forgiven?"

Bingley could not help but laugh. "Certainly Darcy, certainly. For a while there, I do not quite know what came over me. I cannot remember ever being that angry before."

"I am certain that I deserved every jot of your anger. I should not have presumed to interfere."

"Never mind that. You made your mistake and then owned up to it when you discovered your error. Caroline, however..."

Darcy saw a cloud of anger descend on Bingley again, and he continued, "Caroline tried to keep lying to me, and I banished her to the charity of the Hursts. Until I am satisfied that she understands the gravity of what she did and affirms that she will not repeat her mistake, especially in her treatment of Jane, she can stay there." He smiled wickedly. "I also suspended her allowance, and I am afraid she has already overspent her income for the quarter."

"That is quite singular, Charles." Darcy was surprised and pleased at Bingley's newfound determination. "I am impressed. But now, may I invite my sister to join us? She will be most excited by your news."

At his nod, Darcy rang for a servant, and when Georgiana knocked softly on the door, Darcy invited her to sit on the couch beside him. "Georgie," he said with a smile, "Mr. Bingley has an announcement."

Georgiana looked over at Bingley expectantly.

"Miss Darcy, I am engaged to be married!"

Georgiana sat forward in surprise. "That is most happy news, Mr. Bingley!"

She felt considerable relief since she had been made uncomfortable for some time by Miss Bingley's obvious attempts to match her brother with herself. This news would certainly bring a halt to *that*. Now if it were equally possible to achieve a similar result for her brother...

"But you have not said who you are marrying," she chided.

"Miss Jane Bennet. Your brother and I became acquainted with the Bennet family when we were at my estate in Hertfordshire."

"She is a very nice young lady, Georgie," said Darcy. "She is almost as amiable as Charles, if that can be believed."

"I am on my way to her uncle's house right now, Darcy. Would you care to join me?"

Darcy immediately accepted. As Mr. Gardiner was Mrs. Bennet's brother, it might be well to be acquainted with what he would have to bear with equanimity when he came to call on Elizabeth. It would not do to react to her relations here in town as he had previously done with her immediate family in Hertfordshire.

"May I come also?" asked Georgiana softly. "I should like to meet Mr. Bingley's intended."

Darcy was surprised and somewhat apprehensive at exposing his sister to the society in Cheapside, but he could see that she very much wanted to come, and Jane Bennet was an appropriate acquaintance for his sister, even if her relations might not be of the finest calibre. Georgiana had so few friends, and he would much prefer she looked to the Miss Bennets as examples rather than to Miss Bingley, so he agreed quickly to her request.

MRS. GARDINER WAS NOT SURPRISED to hear that Bingley was at her door, but she was astonished to find that Mr. Darcy had accompanied him since, by Elizabeth's previous account, there was an aversion on his part to the match. She was equally unprepared to learn that Miss Darcy has accompanied them, given Mr. Wickham's information that she was exceedingly proud.

The gentlemen stood as she entered the sitting room, and she greeted Mr. Bingley warmly, giving no hint of concern regarding his companions, whom he immediately sought leave to introduce to her.

Mrs. Gardiner politely invited them all to sit down and then rang for tea. "I am sorry that Jane has not returned from her walk in the park with the children," she told him, "but I do expect her back momentarily."

Bingley was obviously disappointed, but she could see he was overflowing with good cheer, which he was quick to share.

"I have just returned from Longbourn," he told her, "and Mr. Bennet has given his consent. He asked me to deliver this letter to your husband informing him of the arrangements."

Mrs. Gardiner glanced at the letter then put it aside. "I will give it to Mr. Gardiner when he returns. Now, tell me all about your visit. I know Jane will be equally interested in all the arrangements, but you will just have to repeat yourself when she comes home, for I cannot wait!"

Bingley was more than willing to accommodate and happily related the details of his talk with Jane's father.

"We have not settled on a firm date though we discussed the possibility of late May or early June before it gets too warm. But Mr. Bennet said that Mrs. Bennet might have another opinion when she arrives. Did I mention that? He suggested that Jane might remain here for several weeks more, which would allow Mrs. Bennet to assist her in shopping for wedding clothes."

"I am sure that will be acceptable to all concerned," Mrs. Gardiner smiled. "We have enjoyed Jane's company these past months, and she is quite the favourite with my children. In addition, Jane's sister Elizabeth will be returning from her visit in Kent this Saturday, and I am sure she will be most pleased to stay and help with the preparations."

The conversation continued, but Darcy's heart leapt at the thought that he might have more time with Elizabeth than he had previously imagined. He was unclear just how long she planned to stay before returning to Hertfordshire, but he thought it might have been as little as a few days. Several weeks would be much better.

Further, Darcy was thoroughly ashamed of himself for once again making hasty assumptions. Whatever he had expected to find here in Cheapside, he had not expected to find this household, and given his already mistaken assumptions regarding the wife, he determined that he would withhold any opinions of her husband until he met him.

For there his mistake had been early evident. While Mrs. Gardiner had been most charming and amiable as she conversed with Bingley and himself, she must have quickly recognized Georgiana's painful shyness. Darcy observed how skilfully the older woman had, from the start, managed to include his sister in the conversation without demanding more participation from her than she was able to give. Their hostess was a charming and elegant lady, whatever her husband did in life, and Darcy was eager to meet him. Calling on Elizabeth in such a convivial environment exceeded his original expectations, and he very much looked forward to it.

"I wonder what can be keeping Jane," Mrs. Gardiner said eventually. "I am afraid that the children may have taken advantage of her good nature to convince her to stay just a little longer. If they are not returned soon, I will send Hannah to the park to look for them. Mr. Bingley, we anticipated that you might again join us for supper. Do you think your companions might also be interested?"

Darcy looked at Georgiana. She usually was uncomfortable in formal social situations, but Mrs. Gardiner had made her feel most at ease, and she gave him a small smile and a nod. Turning to Mrs. Gardiner, Darcy said, "We have no engagements for the day, Mrs. Gardiner. We would be pleased to accept."

Mrs. Gardiner watched the small interaction with interest. She had not found Mr. Darcy as intimidating as she had been led to believe, and she was now convinced that the opinion she had received of the sister was completely wrong, for the girl was perfectly charming and polite, just so shy that she could barely respond beyond a few words. Certainly, Darcy was a most solicitous brother, for he had not even considered accepting or rejecting the invitation without first gaining her thoughts. She would have to speak with Elizabeth about Mr. Wickham and his information, for her suspicions of *that* man were now aroused.

At that moment, the sounds of voices floated up the stairwell, and a moment later the two older Gardiner children burst into the room, followed by Jane. Both gentlemen rose to their feet, and Jane's face lit up with happiness when she saw Bingley. She did not have to be told the result of his errand; she could see it in his wide smile as he crossed the room to take her hand. As he raised it to his lips, he confirmed, "Your father has given us his consent, dear heart."

"I never doubted it, sir," she told him quietly, filled with a sublime joy that now her dreams were brought to fruition, and there were no more impediments.

Darcy waited until Bingley had delivered his news. "Miss Bennet," he said, with an earnestness that surprised her, "Please accept my sincere congratulations and my best wishes for your future happiness." And, to her further surprise, he also took her hand and bent to kiss her fingers lightly.

Unsure of the cause of this excess of civility from this reserved and distant gentleman, Jane could only nod and thank him quietly.

"Miss Bennet," Darcy continued, turning toward his sister, "allow me to introduce my sister, Miss Georgiana Darcy. Georgiana, Miss Jane Bennet." Jane was rather surprised to finally meet Darcy's sister, and she was further surprised to see that the girl appeared so retiring that she kept her eyes cast downward as she returned Jane's curtsey.

"Miss Bennet," Georgiana said hesitantly, forcing herself to speak, "I am very pleased to meet you. I hope you and Mr. Bingley will be most happy."

Jane thanked her and then escorted Georgiana to a small couch with just room for them both to sit. Bingley contented himself with sitting in a comfortable chair beside them.

Meanwhile, Darcy walked over to Mrs. Gardiner and the two attractive children sitting politely beside her. That he clearly desired an introduction could not fail to please a loving mother. "Mr. Darcy, this is my oldest child, Benjamin, and my daughter, Felicia. Benjamin is eight years old, and Felicia will be six next month."

Darcy offered his hand to the boy, an action that gratified the boy at being greeted as an adult. Darcy then bowed to kiss the hand of the young girl, causing her to blush and giggle as she attempted a curtsey. Then, introductions complete, Mrs. Gardiner directed them both to the nursery to prepare for supper and turned to Darcy with a pleased smile.

"You have certainly won the hearts of at least two of the Gardiner household, Mr. Darcy."

Darcy returned her smile, but then his expression grew sober. "I do have some experience with smaller children, Mrs. Gardiner, though I would wish it otherwise. My sister was about the same age as your Felicia when my mother died, and though more than ten years older, I often struggled to comfort her when she was so confused and saddened. And I have had almost the sole care of her since I buried my father beside my mother five years later. I cannot see a young child without remembering my many experiences with Georgiana."

Mrs. Gardiner looked at Darcy with even greater respect. "That was a considerable responsibility for a young man to assume," she said quietly.

Darcy nodded his head in acknowledgment, and thankfully the conversation then moved to happier subjects. He was soon surprised to discover that Mrs. Gardiner had spent many years at Lambton, near Pemberley, and they were able to find a number of interesting topics to canvass. When Elizabeth's name came up, Mrs. Gardiner was surprised to find that Darcy had spent considerable time with her in Kent. Elizabeth had, of course, mentioned that Mr. Darcy was visiting his aunt while she stayed with Charlotte, but she could not recall more than a passing reference to meeting the man. Yet he made several comments that indicated Elizabeth had dined at Rosings a number of times while he was there and had at other times been in company with him and his cousin Colonel Fitzwilliam.

Her curiosity being aroused, Mrs. Gardiner ventured to inquire further, asking how Elizabeth found her ladyship and whether he believed that she was enjoying her visit. To this, Darcy replied in a positive but noncommittal manner that was in contrast to his earlier easy and forthright conversation.

To the question as to whether he himself had a pleasant stay, he replied that he had, though he ventured nothing more. Having heard enough to interest her but not enough to warrant further inquiry, Mrs. Gardener passed on to other topics until Mr. Gardiner returned home.

After introductions were made, Darcy regarded the man with intense curiosity but soon established that the husband measured up to his wife's politeness and civility in every regard, and he soon found himself once again engaged in pleasant conversation. He had been cheerfully describing the beauties of Pemberley and the work required to manage it for some time before he became aware of the skilful manner in which Mr. Gardiner guided the conversation with sage questions and comments that kept him expounding on one of his favourite topics until dinnertime.

Dinner was an equally pleasant, though thoroughly informal, affair. Seating was not by cards but by chance, and he selected a seat with Jane on one side and Mr. Gardiner on the other while Georgiana sat across from him. Mr. Gardiner proved quite adroit at conversing with his sister, though his host had to do much of the talking until he discovered her love for music and engaged her by soliciting her opinion of various composers and whether she had visited the opera or philharmonic.

As dinner concluded, Bingley ventured, "Mr. Gardiner, I must apologize that I am not able to return your hospitality by tendering an invitation to dine at my house. My sister is at present staying with my other sister, Mrs. Hurst, and is unable to act as hostess."

"That is quite understandable, sir. There will be other occasions, I am sure."

"Charles," Darcy said, "since you are inconvenienced at the moment, perhaps I could offer the hospitality of my own table in your stead?"

"That would be most welcome, Darcy!" he replied with pleasure—and no little surprise.

Darcy turned to Mr. Gardiner. "Then perhaps your family might join us—and Mr. Bingley—for the evening meal, sir? On Wednesday?"

Mr. Gardiner quickly responded affirmatively, and a time was agreed on. Later, when the Darcys and Bingley were in the carriage back to Darcy's house, Georgiana was open in her praise toward Bingley's intended.

"Miss Bennet is very nice and kind, Mr. Bingley," she told him. "I do hope that you will be very happy."

"I am sure we shall," Bingley beamed, his eyes distracted in memory.

Georgiana turned to her brother. "William, I invited Miss Bennet to spend the morning with me tomorrow. I meant to ask your permission, but I quite forgot."

Darcy smiled, pleased to see that Georgiana had indeed gotten on with Jane Bennet as well as it had appeared. "It is of no significance, dearest. I quite approve, but soon you shall be choosing your own friends, whether I approve or not."

The reference to her coming out into society caused her to worry rather than to celebrate, and she passed the rest of the ride home in silence while Darcy and Bingley conversed.

Chapter 10

Wednesday, April 15, 1812

When the maid brought the mail on Wednesday afternoon, Elizabeth felt a small thrill of excitement when she saw that it included a letter from Jane. She thought that it might contain good news, but not even her most optimistic feelings could have prepared her for the contents:

Dearest Lizzy,

I have the most wonderful news! Dear sister, Mr. Bingley has called to-day most unexpectedly and did not wait even a half-hour before he professed his love for me and asked me to marry him! Is it not too unbelievable?"

Elizabeth intently read Jane's detailed and excited description of events, with her sister quick to excuse and forgive all of Mr. Bingley's faults and missteps. She smiled often as she pictured the scene in her mind, and the only thing tempering her happiness at the news was the predictable ending of the letter:

I must admit that I was puzzled by what Mr. Bingley said about Mr. Darcy, but Charles confirmed that his information did indeed come from Mr. Darcy and that you were the source of that knowledge. Though I am certainly

84

grateful, you must write and tell me how you ever could have told this to
someone you had previously disliked so!

But that puzzle can be solved in time. I am so full of joy at the thought of
how happy my mother and the rest of my family will be, but most especially
am I overjoyed by knowing how this news will be received by you, my dearest
sister. You cannot know how much your love and care have meant to me
these many months. But now I must close and write to my mother. I am, as I
always will be,

Your most loving sister,
Jane

Elizabeth was unaware that she had sprung to her feet and exclaimed aloud at the most happy news in Jane's letter until Charlotte was at last able to attract her attention.

"Lizzy, what is it?" Charlotte asked. "I know it is not bad news, for you look as if you are about to burst out laughing, but you must not keep us in suspense!"

"Oh, Charlotte," Elizabeth said gaily, leaning over and embracing her friend. "It is the most wonderful news! Jane writes that she is engaged to Mr. Bingley!"

Both Charlotte and her sister were thrilled by the news and demanded all the details. Elizabeth consulted the letter to tell them what she could, but she did not mention what Bingley had said of Darcy, and Charlotte was left to wonder if what she had learned earlier from her friend was related to this blissful news.

Thursday, April 16, 1812
ELIZABETH RECEIVED ANOTHER LETTER FROM Jane on the following day, just after she had returned from a very long walk. The tension in the Parsonage house was worse than ever, with Maria lamenting that there had been no invitations to Rosings, though she was at a loss to explain why. Both Charlotte and Elizabeth were well aware of the reason they were being shunned by Lady Catherine, and Elizabeth was relieved to avoid the company of that formidable woman. Her cousin also shunned her, and she would have ended her visit early except that her uncle had already arranged to send a

servant and a coach to meet them on Saturday. But hearing from Jane so soon after the previous happy letter cheered her immensely, and she excused herself to read it in her room. It began with the expected news that Bingley had obtained their father's consent; then it moved to more surprising news:

When Mr. Bingley arrived, he brought Mr. Darcy and his sister with him. Mr. Darcy was very gracious in congratulating me on my engagement, and I am still wondering how you came to talk of me to him. Do not think that you will be able to use your cleverness to keep from telling me, Lizzy! You are being very sly about something, for you hardly mentioned him in your letters, yet you had taken him into your confidence. I will know everything, sister, and you shall not sleep until I do!

Elizabeth eagerly read Jane's long description of the visit with both interest and amusement until she came to the joyous conclusion:

I am happy that you will be joining me in less than a week; we have so much to talk of. Is it possible that, only three days ago, I was so downhearted and unhappy? So much has happened in so little time! Hurry home, Lizzy! Until then, I am,

Your most loving and curious sister,
Jane

Elizabeth smiled at the renewed image of Jane's happy state and at her jesting—but still serious—threat to know the truth about Mr. Darcy. And she was surprised, nay astonished, to hear that he had gone to Gracechurch Street and had evidently enjoyed himself when there. Previously, she would have thought that his pride would have prevented either, and she could not but wonder if this moderation in his manners was due to her. The thought was certainly gratifying, but she could not forget the arrogance behind his distant and haughty behaviour in Hertfordshire. It remained a barrier between them, though perhaps it was not the impassable obstacle that she once believed, and she was in good humour as she reread the letter. This time, Jane's description of Miss Darcy provided a renewed sense of astonishment. It did seem that every single thing Mr. Wickham had related concerning the Darcy family was the most arrant falsehood. She could recall his words perfectly—*It gives me pain to speak ill of a Darcy. But she is too much like her brother—very, very proud*—and she was again most heartily ashamed of having allowed herself to be so misled.

I shall have to start completely over with Mr. Darcy, she thought, *for I can be sure of nothing. His manners are distant and coldly polite except when he is with his own circle, and I have judged that to be from excessive pride. But if his sister is so shy, could he also be?* She shook her head at such puzzling thoughts and turned again to her letter, this time concentrating on Jane's happiness.

That night in her room, Elizabeth read both of Jane's letters again, and when she considered all that had happened in the last week, her mind was in such a whirl that she knew she would be unable to sleep. She had tried the previous night to write a reply to Jane, but after two attempts at explaining how she had come to provide Mr. Darcy with such private information, she had given up. Her own opinions of that most infuriating man were in such a confused state that she could not even begin to acquaint Jane with the details of what had occurred until she first resolved some of the more contradictory areas herself.

Previously, when she considered all that had happened, she had settled it in her mind by thinking: *If he does what he promised—to reveal his interference with Bingley—then perhaps I might be able to think more on his other assurances.* That decision prevented her from moving on to consider other pieces of the puzzle that was Fitzwilliam Darcy. But now he had not only done as he had promised, but the most fortunate result had come to pass with stunning swiftness, and she no longer had an excuse. She *must* consider the vexing dilemma of Mr. Darcy and face those problems that had proven so difficult to address previously.

Her primary problems, as she saw them, were twofold. Firstly, what would she do when Mr. Darcy called on her in London? She had no doubt he would call now that he had accomplished his mission with Bingley with such stunning success. Such a man never would have suffered the mortification he had undertaken only to fail to follow through on his intention.

Her second problem was more troubling—could she bring herself to marry him if the worst happened and scandal threatened to utterly ruin her family and herself? The thought of her name being openly rumoured as the mistress of *any* man was enough to make her ill, yet she had avoided think-ing of it too long already; she *must* consider the vexing dilemma facing her.

But was the threat of scandal really as serious as Mr. Darcy had indi-cated? Could he be in error or exaggerating? Elizabeth pulled out his letter again—though she was near to knowing it by heart—and upon re-reading, had to reluctantly agree with his assessment. First was the fact that she now believed him to be an honest and honourable man. Second—his experi-ence in the world was significantly greater than her own, giving his opinion weight. And third—Colonel Fitzwilliam believed it too.

And I do know how seriously a lady's reputation can be tarnished by the mere perception of improper behaviour, she thought. *It is intolerable that I might be ensnarled when I have done nothing wrong!*

Well, to be fair, neither had Mr. Darcy, but it was so unfair that the overwhelming damage would be to *her* reputation. *And the reputation of all my family. Even Jane.* That last was a sobering realization, especially con-sidering the happy news just received. What cruelty that Jane's happiness might be marred, or even shattered, by these unfair slanders! She was again roused to anger against Mr. Darcy, blaming him for the unpleasantness that threatened, only to be almost immediately forced by her own conscience to question the fairness of that thought. Had he not written of the disparity of the repercussions himself? Furthermore, he was adamant that his offer of marriage was not affected by any threat of scandal, though that considera-tion only served to irritate her more. His preferred solution allowed him to achieve what he had been unable to obtain otherwise: the marriage she had so forcefully rejected!

But then she remembered that her refusal had been based partly on an entirely mistaken belief in the probity of Mr. Wickham and the wickedness of Mr. Darcy. Something had gone much awry with those two young men who shared so much in common and should have turned out similarly; one appeared to have all the goodness while the other had only the appearance of it! She was beginning to wonder just how important amiability was in the assessment of a man's character, a question she never would have asked herself one short week earlier!

But who *was* this most perplexing man? Elizabeth paced about her room. Untangling the confusion in her own mind looked as if it might take even longer than she had feared, especially when her disloyal memory kept playing those haunting words, *'You must allow me to tell you how ardently I admire and love you.'* The predictable shiver she experienced at the memory only increased her agitation as she tried to concentrate.

IT TOOK A CONSIDERABLE TIME and was well past midnight before Elizabeth finally finished her pacing and thinking. She had wrestled long, attempting to find a balance between her emotions and her reason, between the recommendations of others and her own wounded pride and vanity. As she sat in bed, resting her head on her knees, she found it hard to believe that, after a long evening of intense thought, she had arrived at the conclusions she had.

At the beginning of the evening, she had been firmly of the opinion that, while she might be forced to accept Mr. Darcy in order to preserve her sister's happiness, she would have much preferred to completely reject his offer. So it came as some surprise, as the evening progressed and she considered every fault of this most baffling and complex man, that she found her reservations dwindling as the cold light of reason dispelled each obstacle she could name.

"He is altogether too cold and aloof," she declared at first, thinking he might be the same as a husband.

But when she examined whether she really thought he would be a cold and distant husband, she concluded that, despite her previously firm opinion, she could no longer believe it. His expressions of love and respect, both in his original proposal and afterwards, had been altogether convincing, and it was unlikely that the man could be at the same time both affectionate and unfeeling. She was forced to reluctantly discard her first objection.

"But what about children?"

Elizabeth dearly looked forward to having a family, and she briefly worried that Mr. Darcy would not be desirous of the same. Then she considered the manner in which he had cared for his sister and the assurances he had made in his letter. *'Our* children,' he had phrased it. Despite her irritation with him for his presumption, that was not the expression of a man who did not want a family, and that argument was also reluctantly abandoned.

One after the other, all her objections were evaluated and rejected. She had even considered the intimacies of the marriage bed, but while she did not know enough to form a firm opinion, she at length concluded it could not be *too* repulsive. Mr. Darcy was certainly handsome enough in a physical sense, tall and fit with attractive features, dark, curly hair, and those dark, expressive eyes. *He* would certainly not be a husband similar to Mr. Hurst, attentive to his plate and his port but largely indifferent to his wife. It was no surprise *that* couple had no children!

No, she now knew those intense looks that he had so often directed at her did not indicate disdain and disapproval but rather admiration and regard. They were also — she had only tonight come to realize with a thrill both alarming and pleasant — indicative of something more: *desire* — the physical desire a man feels for a woman. The very idea brought sudden warmth to her cheeks as she pondered the idea that a man, who evidently was subject to a considerable measure of passion, so much that he was struck inarticulate in her presence, might bring that same passion to the marriage bed. Even with her negligible experience, she could not believe it a fault for a husband to feel such for a wife, though she was certain her mother would not agree.

In any event, the mistress of Pemberley would have her own chambers and surely would not be called on to submit to her husband every night. Elizabeth remembered the sly comments she had overheard her mother and her friends make in low voices, that *headache* was so very useful as a defence against an overly passionate husband. She did not believe that she could ever resort to such subterfuge herself, at least not against a husband such as Mr. Darcy. That thought also made her cheeks flame, especially when she remembered the tender, caressing tones of his proposal, and the prospect of his addressing her in those same tones in the privacy of her bedchamber spread the blush from her cheeks over her whole face and down her neck.

In the end, her objections diminished to a single question, and that was whether she could ever feel true affection and love for such a man. Despite her declaration that she did not *know* him, Elizabeth admitted that she had by now formed a goodly measure of respect for his character and capabilities. Even if she was not so sure of his manner, her belief in Mr. Darcy's total lack of amiability must be in error since Bingley had attested to his ease and cordiality within his own circle. So, despite her misgivings, Elizabeth could only conclude that, surprising as it was, there were reasons to hope for a degree of felicity in a marriage with Mr. Darcy.

"But I do not love him!" she protested aloud, knowing that she did not feel the same ardent love Mr. Darcy professed to her — the love that made him willing to risk the censure of his friends, family, and society in order to marry her.

But what did she mean when she spoke of love? As she examined the idea more deeply, she realized that a woman's definition of love — at least a woman such as herself, already fortunate enough to be a gentleman's daughter — likely varied substantially from that of a man, especially one like Mr. Darcy. What she truly feared was marriage to a husband who would not treat her with the consideration and enduring respect necessary to ensure a contented home life and the security that she, as a mother and wife, would need in order to bear and nurture children. She was well aware that, to most of society, social advancement, wealth, and security were the greatest considerations when contemplating marriage, not the impractical sentiments that were written of in romantic novels. While she disagreed with such cold-blooded calculation as the sole basis for entering a marriage, she could not completely disregard such considerations. Certainly, she had not thought before of the security her children would enjoy with Mr. Darcy as a father, but the advantages could not be ignored, not when added to all else that she had considered that night.

After long hours of pacing and arguing aloud, she found herself arriving at the same conclusion as had her friend Charlotte, though for not always the same reasons: From any rational point of view, it made no sense to refuse a proposal of marriage from Fitzwilliam Darcy!

The shock of these reasoned conclusions was profound, and Elizabeth was dazed as she sat in bed. Her *feelings* had not changed materially. She still did not *know* him — not truly — not like Jane knew Bingley, certainly. No, she and Mr. Darcy were certainly not similar in their character or temperament, but she was forced to admit that they *were* well suited in the manner of intellect and capabilities. The fact that she could now contemplate a future as Mrs. Elizabeth Darcy with perfect equanimity was most astonishing! She was well aware that the arguments in Darcy's favour were all matters of logic and rationality and that she did not feel the same for him that he did for her. But her debate that evening had, for the first time, kindled a kind regard toward him and his admitted goal of a formal courtship, and she now found herself looking forward to renewing their acquaintance. Indeed, the prospect no longer aroused any opposition but rather engendered a surprising feeling of cheerful anticipation.

He had shown himself to be more than worthy of her respect, and the dreaded possibility of being trapped in a loveless marriage did not appear to threaten since she believed in the sincerity of his affections. If they *did* marry, it appeared that at least *she* would be loved. In this regard, he surely had more to lose than she since she could give no absolute guarantee that she could learn to love him. Surely he must understand that. Nevertheless, he had been mistaken with regard to her feelings before, so she must be sure that he did understand. She would speak with him, to affirm that he was not deceived as to her feelings before matters proceeded further. But, if the future turned out as it now appeared that it might, she felt comfortable that she could be a good wife to him with every possibility of contentment and happiness for herself and the children she hoped to bear.

It was at least a start, and with that thought in mind, though she knew it must be nearing dawn, she was at last able to sleep.

Chapter 11

At last the day of her departure arrived, and on Saturday morning Elizabeth awakened early. She was just placing the last of her things in the trunk when she heard a soft knock at the door, and Charlotte entered the room. After the two friends secured Elizabeth's trunks, Charlotte took her hand and pulled her to the bed to sit down.

"Lizzy," she said earnestly, "I do want to apologize to you for the manner in which you have been slighted by Mr. Collins and Lady Catherine. She has been abominably rude to you since the night Mr. Darcy visited, and I am grieved for the pain that you have suffered."

Elizabeth embraced her friend. "Her ladyship's ability to pain me was never very great, Charlotte, and it will surely end with my departure. I can hardly wait to see Jane and share her joy now that she is engaged."

"It is indeed wonderful how matters have arranged themselves after the unhappiness Jane suffered in the winter," Charlotte said, "but it is you that I am worried about. After Mr. Darcy left his letter, you promised me that you would at least consider what we discussed, yet you have not mentioned it, and I did not wish to intrude. But now you are almost ready to leave — I must know that you will approach this matter most carefully."

"What you really are asking is whether I have rejected my foolish romantic sentiments that kept me from accepting Mr. Darcy's offer of marriage, is it not?"

Charlotte blushed, but Elizabeth only laughed and squeezed her friend's hand fondly. "I have indeed considered your arguments, and you will, I hope, be gratified to know that I found them quite persuasive. I cannot predict the future, but if Mr. Darcy does renew his offer, I can assure you that 'impractical romantic sentiments' will not determine my response. At least, they will not be my *only* considerations. Beyond that, you will have to trust me."

Charlotte was well-satisfied, for she was all too aware of the firmness of Elizabeth's convictions, and if she had been moved to alter her opinion that much, she felt she could safely trust her friend's reasoned honesty.

"I think that is a wise choice, Lizzy, and I do wish you every happiness. In a union with Mr. Darcy, I think you have an excellent chance to be very happy indeed."

"If it does come to pass, I very much hope you are correct in your prediction," she laughed. "Surprisingly, I am rather looking forward to seeing Mr. Darcy again, though I am still mortified at the way I took Mr. Wickham's side against him. But I am at least certain that he is not nearly as wicked as he was described, and I believe that I have a fair chance to improve his humour if nothing else, for I shall not hesitate to tease him at every opportunity!"

Charlotte smiled at her friend's irrepressible spirits and summoned a servant to carry the trunks downstairs.

AFTER THE THREE LADIES FINISHED breakfast, Anne de Bourgh's phaeton stopped at the front gate, and Charlotte went out to meet her. However, she was back shortly to inform Elizabeth that Miss de Bourgh desired to speak with her. Elizabeth got her shawl and went out to meet the young lady, who was nearly swallowed by the large bonnet intended to protect her from the morning sun and air. But Miss de Bourgh's eyes shone bright and friendly from beneath the brim as she greeted Elizabeth.

"I understand that you will be leaving us this morning, Miss Bennet," she stated cheerfully, "and I thought it best to call on you to make my good-byes since my mother has seen fit to banish you from our table. I wanted you to know that you will be missed by at least one of the de Bourgh line."

Elizabeth was startled to see a side of her that she had never seen when visiting Rosings. Miss de Bourgh had never shown this much spirit before.

94

"I thank you, Miss de Bourgh," she said with a smile. "And I must apologize for not having taken the opportunity to further our acquaintance during our earlier meetings. I seem to have been so busy responding to the conversation of your mother and cousins that I have quite neglected you. It appears now that I have missed an opportunity."

"Please do not distress yourself," Anne said carefully. "My mother is quite used to having her own way, and my cousins and I have developed different methods of dealing with her. For myself, I tend to retreat into my inner thoughts."

"Perhaps we will have an opportunity in the future to repair this error," Elizabeth replied with equal care.

"I also wish that, Miss Bennet," said Anne. Then she looked at Elizabeth closely, with a twinkle in her eyes as she asked blandly, "Is it true, then, that you refused my Cousin Darcy's offer of marriage?"

Elizabeth started at this unexpected question and could only look at her in confusion. Anne laughed. "Do not think that my excessively reticent cousin disclosed such a private matter, but I guessed it when he asked me to help deliver his letter to you. I must offer you my congratulations on standing up to him since he dearly needed to learn a little humility."

Elizabeth had to smile at this saucy comment, which further amused Anne. Her smile faded, however, as Miss De Bourgh turned to a more serious topic. "I presume that your absence from our parlour this past week is related to the decidedly improper gossip circulating among the staff at Rosings, Miss Bennet, and for that I must also apologize." Elizabeth's furious blush confirmed the accuracy of her estimate, and Anne continued, "I am most sorry for the pain it must have caused you."

"It was painful, Miss de Bourgh, but I anticipate a great degree of relief once I am on my way home."

"No doubt," said Anne dryly and then added, "I do hope that you and Darcy will be very happy together."

Elizabeth was again taken aback, and she could not believe that such an intelligent, lively, even impertinent girl had been so completely concealed beneath the drab exterior she had always exhibited. Impulsively, she reached out to squeeze Anne's hand.

"Miss de Bourgh, if you ever feel the need to spend some time away from...Rosings, I would be delighted if you might consent to visit me."

"That might be a very good idea," Anne said, as she gathered up the reins and urged the phaeton into motion. "After the honeymoon, of course," she chortled, leaving Elizabeth speechless.

AFTER THE VISIT, ELIZABETH WAS more anxious than ever to be away. At length the chaise arrived, the trunks were fastened on, the parcels placed within, and it was pronounced to be ready. While Maria went to her room to make sure she had forgotten nothing, Charlotte and Elizabeth descended the stairs to the chaise. As Elizabeth embraced Charlotte and made her farewell outside by the carriage, she could not help feeling melancholic to be leaving her friend to such society as Mr. Collins and Rosings.

But Charlotte had chosen her situation with her eyes open, and while it was obvious that she was sorry to see Elizabeth leave, especially in such an unsettled situation, she did not seem to desire compassion for herself. Her home and her housekeeping, her parish, her poultry, and all their dependent concerns had not yet lost their charms.

No sooner had she thought of Mr. Collins than that worthy deigned to leave his study to see his guests off. After he bade his cousin a distant and cool farewell, he handed her into the carriage. Maria followed, the door was closed, and the carriage drove off.

"Good gracious!" cried Maria, after a few minutes silence, "I am glad to be going home. Our visit was so agreeable at first, but the last week has been so boring. And though we dined six times at Rosings and drank tea there twice, we had not a single invitation this past week!"

"I do believe you are correct," said her companion with a sigh.

"But still," said Maria, becoming more cheerful, "the first part of the visit *was* most agreeable! How much I shall have to tell!"

Elizabeth privately added under her breath, "And how much I shall have to conceal."

Their journey was accomplished without much conversation or any alarm, and within four hours of their leaving Hunsford, they reached Gracechurch Street. As the coach pulled up in front of the Gardiner home, Elizabeth looked up to the windows of the sitting room above and was delighted to see Jane leaning out with a large and joyous smile, waving vigorously to her. Then she ducked back inside the window and disappeared. By the time Elizabeth exited the coach, the front door flew open, and her sister ran forward to embrace her. The tumultuous events of the past week, combined with the arrival of her dearest sister, were unexpectedly too much for Jane, and she tightened her embrace of Elizabeth, shedding tears of joy and emotional release. Elizabeth held her usually reserved older sister, overcome herself by the emotion that led Jane to such an unusual public display, but Jane was able to quickly recover herself and release her embrace.

By this time, her aunt and uncle, along with a beaming Mr. Bingley had also exited the house, and she greeted each in turn, concluding with Bingley as he bowed over her hand and accepted her congratulations. The trunks of the two passengers were quickly unloaded and taken inside, and Elizabeth and Maria entered the house with the rest of the party. Her uncle briefly informed her that he would like a few words with her in his study as soon as she was refreshed, and the two young ladies departed to their rooms to clean up after the journey.

"You wished to speak to me, Uncle?" Elizabeth asked as she entered his study.

"Yes, I did, Lizzy," replied Mr. Gardiner, putting down the book he was reading. "Please, take a seat. I trust you are refreshed from your journey?"

"Yes, I am," she smiled, "but you really do not have to go through all the civilities before coming to the point. I believe I have a good idea of what you wish to discuss."

Mr. Gardiner smiled. "Then you can imagine how surprised I was yesterday afternoon when Mr. Darcy paid me a visit and wished to speak to me regarding one of my favourite nieces."

"I daresay," Elizabeth murmured, trying to stifle a smile.

"Perhaps 'surprised' is not a strong enough word," he continued. "I think 'astonished' would more accurately describe my emotions when he asked my permission not only to call on you when you returned to London but to formally court you."

Elizabeth had to stifle more than a smile at her uncle's droll manner, and she arched an eyebrow as she asked, "And did you grant your permission, sir?"

Her uncle was serious now. "I told him that I would first need to talk to you and would then have to discuss it with my brother. He informed me that you were aware of his intention and had given him permission when you were in Kent."

"That is correct."

"Lizzy, now you must be serious. I have been firmly of the belief that your opinion of Mr. Darcy was most decidedly negative. Since I have made his acquaintance, I have come to the completely opposite conclusion, and both your aunt and I quite like him. But how did *your* opinion change so dramatically—dramatically enough that you agreed to a formal courtship?"

"Because I was wrong in my opinions," she said carefully. "In fact, I was so completely in error regarding Mr. Darcy that it is quite embarrassing to remember the things I said about him." She paused to compose her thoughts. She did not want to share every aspect of her conversations with Mr. Darcy, but there were some things she must share. "Perhaps the most significant error I made will serve as an example. You will remember, I hope, the good opinion I had of Mr. Wickham in Hertfordshire and how egregious I found Mr. Darcy's offences against him?" Her uncle nodded gravely.

"Then, sir, I must tell you that the truth is the complete opposite. I have every reason to believe Mr. Darcy to be an honourable man, and I have the certain knowledge that Mr. Wickham is not only no gentleman but is a quite wicked man besides. You can imagine the shock to my pride and vanity when it became obvious on what false pretences I had based my opinions. And further examination of other circumstances only proved more embarrassing. When Mr. Darcy asked permission to attempt to change my bad opinion of him, I could not in good conscience refuse."

"I see," said Mr. Gardiner thoughtfully. After some thought, he asked, "And has your opinion changed enough that you would consider marriage? Assuming he asks, of course."

Elizabeth smiled. "He has already asked once. I have no doubt that he will ask again. Mr. Darcy is a most determined man."

"Again?"

Elizabeth nodded.

"You refused him?"

She nodded again.

Mr. Gardiner sat back and tried to organize his dazed thoughts. At length, he smiled.

"Then I shall certainly not keep such a determined young man from seeing my most surprising niece, at least until I can write to my brother Bennet." He thought for a minute and then said, "Perhaps we could invite him to dinner next Saturday?" When he saw her distressed look, he continued blandly, "Or I *could* invite him to dine with us tonight." He picked up a note from his desk and handed it to Elizabeth. "Perhaps you would give that to the groom to deliver?"

The folded note was addressed to 'Mr. Fitzwilliam Darcy, Esq,' and Elizabeth realized he was teasing her. "Uncle!" she responded in mock sternness, "You are being most vexing!" This only drew a laugh from him, and she had to smile as well. On her way out the door, she paused.

"Uncle, I know it is highly unusual, but if the opportunity presents itself... might I ask for the loan of your study for a time tonight?" Elizabeth asked. He raised his eyebrows at her in query, and she blushed slightly. "There remain a number of questions between Mr. Darcy and myself that still need to be resolved," she said simply, and after a slight hesitation, he agreed to her request.

"Thank you, Uncle," she said gratefully, going around his desk to embrace him briefly before leaving with the note in hand.

Chapter 12

Darcy was in his study, engaged in pleasant thoughts of the coming evening with Elizabeth and quite neglecting his correspondence when his butler, Stevens, knocked at the door and showed Colonel Fitzwilliam into the room. When he saw his cousin, still wearing his regimental uniform, stride into the room with a bleak look on his face, sudden worry clutched at his stomach.

As soon as they were alone, Fitzwilliam immediately pulled a slip of paper from his uniform pocket and handed it to Darcy. It read:

We are recently informed that a certain bachelor from Derbyshire, well-known as one of the most eligible young men of fashionable society, has apparently taken a mistress, a comely but unknown country lass. Shockingly, he is flaunting his new light o' love under the nose of his own relations, keeping her in, of all places, the nearby home of a churchman.

"Oh, wonderful," Darcy groaned.

"It was published on Thursday, but I did not learn of it until today. You know the *Chronicle*. There is just so much garbage in it that I did not come upon it until now."

"This is disgusting," Darcy growled. "Even after your warnings, I still did not expect it to really occur. But how can they get away with publishing this kind of faradiddle? How are those responsible not called out on a regular basis?"

"Darcy, you do not understand how clever they are. They name no names, do they? If you tried to make this an affair of honour, your accusations would be denied. It would always be someone else. Meanwhile, they report your objection, which only serves to identify you more directly. Then, after having milked the scandal of all interest, they move on to another topic. By then, the society gossips will have taken up the story and do the rest of the work, leaving you tarnished and Miss Elizabeth Bennet ruined."

Darcy sat back in his chair, shaking his head. Fitzwilliam was right; blast it! There was no physical enemy to contend with, no reality to attach to this vaporous threat. Fifteen minutes earlier, he had been enjoying the thought of an evening spent in pleasant company, imagining a successful step forward in his pursuit of Elizabeth, and the eventual possibility of inviting the Gardiners to visit the two of them at Pemberley and partake of the fishing and other beauties. At least this was not published earlier while Elizabeth was still at Hunsford and the chance of the matter turning out disastrously was much greater. Still, it would certainly force her to make a decision earlier than he desired, and he could only hope that she and the Gardiners could forgive his clumsy attentions now that scandal threatened her reputation. He sighed helplessly. The situation was what it was, and he must face it and hope that Elizabeth could manage the same.

"I have been invited to dine at the Gardiner's tonight, and I will have to make her aware of this."

Fitzwilliam nodded gloomily in agreement. Darcy ran his hand through his hair in frustration. "I had hoped for some calmer moments with Elizabeth here in London," he continued, "and now this arises!"

"Truly, it may not be as bad as you think, Darcy." Fitzwilliam brightened. "Surely a young lady as fair-minded as Miss Bennet will understand that this is not your fault and that you have her best interests at heart."

"I can only hope you are correct, Richard," said Darcy, with a certain degree of trepidation.

ELIZABETH WAS UNCOMMONLY ANXIOUS AS she awaited Mr. Darcy's arrival, and the sly smiles her aunt and uncle exchanged at her discomposure only made everything worse. Maria Lucas seemed content to simply sit in a corner chair and work on her sewing, and Bingley was happily seated by Jane, both of them conversing in low tones, leaving her alone with her thoughts. At least Elizabeth could enjoy the radiant happiness so obvious on Jane's face. The frank adoration on Bingley's open countenance was equally striking, and though she was conscious of the lack of similar strong feelings herself for Mr. Darcy, she was far from indifferent to the man coming to call on her. She smiled inwardly. Mr. Darcy had provoked many reactions in her, but *indifference* had never been one of them! Thus, she was perhaps more anxious to please than was her normal aspiration, and she naturally feared that every power of pleasing would fail her in that situation. When she heard a carriage arrive, a quick glance out the window confirmed that it was Mr. Darcy's coach, and the gentleman himself was even then stepping to the ground. The bell rang almost immediately, and in moments he was shown into the sitting room.

As he bowed in introduction to the various members of the party, she noticed his gaze repeatedly returned to her. Self-consciously, she rose and crossed the room to greet him.

"Miss Elizabeth," he said softly as he bowed over her hand, lightly brushing his lips over her fingers.

"Mr. Darcy," she said in reply, unable to keep the twinkle out of her eyes and the slight smile off her lips as she unconsciously reacted to his gallantry.

Darcy was pleasantly surprised by the unexpected warmth of her welcome. He, too, had been feeling unsettled—there were so many things between them that had not even been discussed, much less resolved, and he was cheered at the reception. Her manner was open and friendly, and he could not help but note the difference between this meeting and all the others in Kent and Hertfordshire.

How could I possibly have believed that she greeted me with expectation then? he thought. *Those were greetings of cold politeness, and I had not the wit to even recognize it.*

His discomposure must have shown in his face, for she suddenly looked uneasy. "Is something wrong, Mr. Darcy?" she asked quietly. They were standing alone some paces from the others after their initial greeting and thus had a small measure of privacy.

"No, nothing at all," he responded, forcing a smile. "I just had occasion

102

to remember some of my mistaken assumptions in the past, and the recollection was not pleasing."

She cocked an eyebrow at him. "You must learn my philosophy, Mr. Darcy, and think only of the past as its remembrance gives you pleasure."

He laughed. Oh, how he enjoyed their jousting! "I think your philosophy stems from a different root, Miss Elizabeth. Your retrospections must be free of that which might cause reproach, so your contentment is not based on ignoring that which would cause embarrassment but rather on its absence. But I am not so fortunate. I have painful memories though I would not change them, for how else would I learn?"

He sobered suddenly. "A matter has arisen that must be addressed immediately. I will speak to your uncle and request the opportunity to talk with you privately as soon as may be."

Elizabeth was troubled by the stormy expression that came and went over his face. "I had already approached my uncle regarding this as I have some items of my own I should like to discuss. He has agreed to the use of his study. However, you should still ask him."

Darcy nodded, and he reluctantly left her to approach her aunt and uncle. Elizabeth turned to see Jane staring at her in both surprise and confusion. She had not had a moment of privacy in which to inform Jane of any of what had occurred in Kent, though her sister had made one sly remark that Elizabeth had best prepare for a *long* talk before bed. Bingley, too, sat with his mouth open in astonishment, looking back and forth between herself and his friend, the light of comprehension only just beginning to dawn in his eyes.

Maria Lucas still attended to her sewing but with a hint of a smile on her face. To Elizabeth, that smile intimated that Maria was not as surprised by Darcy's greeting of her as she ought to have been, which led to the further thought that Charlotte had likely confided at least some aspects of the events in Kent to her sister before they left the Parsonage. Mr. Gardiner had offered his carriage to take Miss Lucas on to Hertfordshire on the morrow, and Maria was eager to accept. She had not only the news of her stay at Hunsford to share around the neighbourhood, but she had the infinitely more attractive information of the fortunate union secured by the eldest Bennet girl and possibly the second eldest as well.

Well, Elizabeth thought ruefully as she walked over to sit by Jane, *there is no chance of evasion or disguise now; the cat is well and truly out of the bag!*

It was not long before Elizabeth saw Mr. Darcy and her uncle rise and leave the room, and she was accordingly not surprised when, a few minutes later, the maid approached to say that her uncle desired her presence in his study. As she excused herself, Elizabeth was aware, even without seeing, of the calculating look that Jane and Bingley exchanged. They either were, or soon would be, adding their sums and reaching an uncomfortably accurate conclusion. Her aunt was, as usual, several steps ahead of everyone else, and she sent Elizabeth a smile that betrayed a considerable amount of self-satisfaction. Elizabeth shook her head in amusement, thinking of how pitilessly she was going to be interrogated later by them both.

When she entered her uncle's study, the men rose politely, and Mr. Gardiner said, "Please take a seat, Lizzy. Mr. Darcy has asked for some time to speak with you privately, and as your guardian while you stay with us, I have felt compelled to set the usual conditions, little though I believe it is necessary for either of you. But I will remind you," he smiled, "that you need not settle everything tonight since we dine at seven." Darcy darkened slightly, Elizabeth flushed more, and Mr. Gardiner chuckled to himself as he left the room, closing the door behind him.

Once they were alone, they at first sat silently with so much to say that neither could venture a word. At last, Darcy sighed. "Where shall we start, Miss Bennet?"

Elizabeth smiled. "*I* shall start by thanking you for your efforts with Mr. Bingley. I know it could not have been easy."

Darcy squirmed in his seat with remembrance. "Yes, it was difficult. I have never seen Bingley so angry. I had not believed he could *get* that angry. Did you know he ordered me from his house?"

"He did?" Elizabeth stared at him in astonishment. "That is remarkable!"

Darcy nodded. "Most assuredly he did, though he did stop by my townhouse the next afternoon after he spoke to your father, and he then very generously forgave me. He was quite exuberant by that time and invited me to accompany him to your uncle's house."

"Jane did not say a word of Mr. Bingley's being angry," Elizabeth said, shaking her head in amusement, "though she did write that you had called. I have to wonder if he has yet told her of it. Jane and I have not had a chance to speak privately since I returned. However, based on the looks I received when I left the sitting room, I believe that she and Mr. Bingley are probably discussing us quite extensively right now."

He smiled briefly and then sobered. "May I assume that you do not know about his sister?" When Elizabeth shook her head, he continued, "He banished her to the Hurst's home after he found out about her deceptions, and then he suspended her allowance. He will not allow her to return, and possibly more significantly, he will not even discuss the matter with me. Though," he smiled wickedly, "I have not pressed him very hard."

Darcy continued thoughtfully, "I suspect that Charles may not need nearly as much advice from me in the future. But, since that was the goal I was trying to guide him toward in any event, one good result is that he is much closer to being his own man than he would have been otherwise. Not," he said wryly, "that I would recommend the way in which events shaped themselves if I could do it over again."

"I daresay," said Elizabeth with a slight smile. "Now I believe it is your turn, Mr. Darcy."

Darcy looked uncomfortable as he took the torn section of newsprint from his pocket and handed it to Elizabeth. Her brow crinkled as she read it, and he tried to prepare himself for her anger and hurt as she was confronted with proof of her unfair entanglement in this noxious affair.

What he was not prepared for was the tinkling sound of laughter.

Shocked, he could only stare at her as she looked at the section again in amusement before handing it back to him with a smile on her face. "I . . . I expected you to be upset," he said haltingly.

"If you only knew, sir," she said with an impertinent smile, "how many hours I have spent trying to puzzle out the riddle of your character, arriving at conclusions only after long and difficult struggle, and now I find it was all for naught. One can only laugh or cry when faced with such irony, and I would much rather laugh."

Darcy could only look at her in confusion and stammer, "I am sorry . . . I do not believe I understand . . ."

Elizabeth sighed. "Sometimes I do not understand myself either, Mr. Darcy."

"I do want you to know that I meant what I said in my letter, and my offer of marriage remains open."

"I never doubted it, sir. You have, if nothing else, impressed me with your determination." But then her expression sobered, and she continued, "But before I answer, there are certain things that I must tell you, and I must apologize in advance because some of what I have to say may pain you."

Darcy nodded silently, his chest tight.

"First," she began, "there is the letter that you wrote me at Hunsford and the whole situation that caused it. I must tell you that I was infuriated when I first read it, both at being involved so unfairly and at the manner in which you stated that your intentions and affections remained unchanged. I considered it a measure of your arrogance and your presumption that you would say what you did, but after I talked with Charlotte and calmed down, I could see the sense of what you wrote and even understand the reason that you offered to renew your proposal."

Darcy winced. "I feared that the letter would upset you, but Fitzwilliam and I could see no other way to apprise you of what we had discovered, nor did we believe that we could delay our departure without making the situation worse. I did walk in the park, hoping to talk to you in person, but I did not meet you."

"After our confrontation the previous day, I purposely stayed inside." With a sigh, she added, "Perhaps it would have been better to have followed my usual custom. As to your assessment of the situation, you and your cousin were likely correct. Certainly, Charlotte energetically defended you, pointing out the logic of your arguments and demanding of me why I was so offended when you were being so generous to defend my reputation." She smiled in remembrance and continued, "After my anger cooled, I even allowed that she might not be completely in error."

"I am sorry to have been the cause of such turmoil," he said carefully. "And you need not apologize for your anger on receiving my letter—I suspected as much—and your reaction to it was not unreasonable." He ran his fingers through his hair in the manner that, Elizabeth was beginning to understand, betrayed his inner agitation, and she waited to see if he had more to add before she continued.

"But your letter and our conversations before you left did give me many things to think about," she said, "even though I am forced to admit that I was not able to fully consider them until I received Jane's letter announcing her engagement to Bingley. I knew then that you were, truly, a man of your word, and I was at last able to think deeply on all the matters that were at issue between us." She coloured slightly. "You cannot know how mortified I was when I understood the manner in which I let myself be deceived by Mr. Wickham. No, Mr. Darcy," she said, as he started to interject a comment, "I know you are going to say that I must not be so hard on myself, because he has deceived others, but that is not the issue here. What I had to admit is that if I had been so very wrong in my judgment of Mr. Wickham, then I might have been wrong about other things as well. I went back to the very beginning of our acquaintance to consider how I might have deceived myself and drawn other wrong conclusions. It took a very long time to think through everything, and the conclusions I came to were quite surprising to me."

Elizabeth met Darcy's eyes firmly. "When I at length ended my deliberations, I was shocked to discover that I could no longer find any sound reason, after all, to refuse your proposal." She noted the manner in which he suddenly sat up straighter, and his gaze on her was intent. "I was almost as surprised by my conclusions as I was by your unexpected declaration. We both know that just over a week ago, I had no knowledge of your true feelings. I believed that you despised me, and I was resolved to despise you in turn. Then, as I sat thinking that night, I realized I had just concluded that you were right in at least one of your assertions, and we indeed were well matched. It was a staggering reversal, and I was quite discomfited as I tried to deal with it."

Elizabeth could not look away from Mr. Darcy as his eyes were fixed on hers with an intent look that could only remind her of the strength of his love for her. She struggled to continue.

"You must know how deeply I regret the manner in which I was wrong about your character. Hopefully, we have both improved in understanding since that evening at the Parsonage. But that leads to the matter that you must know before I can give you an answer: my conclusions were based on logic and reasoning—matters of the head rather than matters of the heart. I know of your feelings for me; as surprised as I was by your declaration, I can have no doubt of your love, and it is still a marvel to me. But I must tell you that it is too much to expect that I could return your love in such a short time when this is the first time I have seen you since you left Rosings. And today is the first chance we have had to talk with a complete understanding of each other. So, just as you have been honest with me, I will not attempt to profess feelings that are not my own. I have come to believe in your honour and your honesty, and I already know many things to admire in you, but at this moment there is an inequality in our feelings for one another, and the imbalance favours my comfort more than yours, for I know I am loved and you have no corresponding assurance."

"Is that all?" he asked softly.

"Is it not enough, sir? Truly, I will understand if you now wish to withdraw your offer."

"Nonsense!" he stated firmly. Elizabeth looked confused, and he had to laugh softly. "If you think that I am going to be frightened off by a little honesty on your part, Miss Elizabeth Bennet, then you have not yet measured the extent of my determination!

"Now," he leaned forward in his chair, fixing his eyes on her, "there was a mention of an *answer*, now that I have been suitably warned."

Elizabeth smiled slowly, her spirits rising. "But sir, an answer requires a *question*, and as I think back, I can only remember a *statement*." She leaned forward as well, one lovely eyebrow arched, as she asked softly, "Was there not a *question* that you had for me, Mr. Darcy?"

Darcy gave a sharp bark of laughter at her impudent comment, and then grinned hugely, suddenly feeling better than he had for months.

"Miss Elizabeth Bennet," he said forcefully, cheered by the smile that she shared with him, "will you do me the honour of taking my hand in marriage?"

"Well, sir," she said demurely, "it does seem that I have no choice but to accept your kind offer, so the answer is yes, I will marry you. But now you know the reason that I laughed at that rancid piece of gossip. Since I had already demolished all my previous objections to you, all it did was change the timing and not the result. Assuming," she said with a smile, "that you did not simply drop me as a bad business."

"Little chance of that," Darcy growled as he took her hand possessively.

"Though, I *am* sorry to miss the lengthy courtship you promised me," she teased. "After I spent so many hours in thought and found myself having to change so many of my opinions of you, I was quite looking forward to my return to London." She smiled softly and squeezed his hand. "I have not been courted before, and I found that the idea had gained an attraction that caught me completely by surprise."

He smiled back at her, his happiness somewhat tempered by her honest sentiments. *What more could I have expected?* he told himself firmly. *A sudden profession of love at such a time would not be in her character. Honesty flows both ways, and if she can trust me enough to warn me of her feelings, then I am well satisfied.*

Elizabeth was serious as she continued. "Now you turn out to have been right about the threat of scandal. We truly must marry, and now that we are engaged, let me put your mind at rest. Do not worry that my reservations will make me unhappy. Please believe me when I tell you that I am not disposed to melancholy, and the assurance of your esteem has given me confidence in our future life. I have complete trust in your pledge that I will be treated with respect and consideration, and many wives never have such a hope. And I will do my utmost to be a good wife, to care for you and our children, and to always work for your contentment and satisfaction. I feel gratified that you have chosen me despite the unkind things I have said about you."

Darcy was moved by the strength of her assurances, and her words were balm to the pains that he had earlier felt. Suddenly he rose to his feet, and Elizabeth looked up as he towered over her, so tall and imposing, yet with more warmth and sympathetic understanding on his face than she would have believed possible before. He reached out to her, and her hands went to his almost without conscious thought, and she found herself being pulled to her feet and then being pulled to his chest. She did not resist as his arms enfolded her into an embrace

The experience of being held by any man was a novel one for her, and she found that the sensation of Mr. Darcy's arms around her gave rise to unfamiliar and unexpected feelings. She felt a contentment that she had never known and had not even been aware of missing. More, she felt a protection and security that was equally unprecedented. She could not put into words why it was, but had she been disposed to examine how her character had been formed while growing up in a household exemplified by chaos and lack of direction, she might have had an inkling. She had never had anyone to lean on except Jane, and the support they provided each other was different from what she now felt in Darcy's arms. She could not put a name on it, but she knew that she did not want it to end.

Yet end it must, and eventually she was stirred to find her handkerchief and dry the few tears that had somehow run down her cheeks, due not to anguish but rather to the release of emotions she had been holding strictly in check. As she dabbed her eyes, Darcy raised her chin to look her in the face. "Elizabeth," he said intently, wanting to make sure she understood and believed him, "you have made me happier tonight than I have ever been in my life." His eyes darkened in that familiar way as he looked at her, and he said simply, "I do not believe I could live without you, and I cannot believe the desperately small margin by which I avoided that fate. Do not worry about what you termed reservations. I understand, believe me, and I could not expect more given the turbulent nature of our acquaintance. But from this point on, you may be secure in my love as my mother was in my father's love all the days of her life. I admit that some of what you said pained me, but I know that your words were honest and truthful, and I would always have it that way between us. I am satisfied and content that we shall be friends at the least and hopefully more in time."

He suddenly smiled. "If you would have me adopt some of your philosophy, then you should adopt some of mine. I have been saying to myself very many times these past days, that it could have been *ever* so much worse!"

That did amuse Elizabeth as she stood with his arms still about her. "It could indeed, Mr. Darcy," she said with a light laugh, "it could indeed."

"Then do you not think it is time to stop calling me 'Mr. Darcy'?" he said with a smile.

"Then what shall I call you, sir?" she asked with a raise of her eyebrow. "Shall I call you Fitzwilliam?"

Darcy winced. "No one calls me Fitzwilliam, Elizabeth."

"But is it not your Christian name, Mr. Darcy?" she teased.

"My parents named me Fitzwilliam, but my friends simply call me 'Darcy.' My mother called me William when I was young, as does Georgiana now, and I would have you do the same."

"Then I shall do so, William," she said easily. "Except when I am angry, when 'Fitzwilliam' might slip out!"

He laughed and looked down at her lovely face. "Thank you, Elizabeth," he said, kissing her on the forehead. "Perhaps we should join the others so that dinner is not delayed on our account."

Elizabeth tucked her head back into his chest and nestled closer to him. "I find that I like being held, William. I had not expected it, but I find that I like it very much."

"Then I shall hold you often, my dearest, but we will have to join them at some point."

"Yes, I know," she said regretfully, finally pulling free of Darcy's embrace. "And now would be a good time, for I am beginning to feel quite hungry."

They met Mr. Gardiner when they left his study, and he looked worried as he recognized a mix of emotions on his niece's face, Elizabeth smiled at his concern. "Do not be troubled, Uncle. William and I had much to discuss but we had no harsh words, believe me. We have both made mistakes in our acquaintance, and some items needed to be resolved to put those mistakes behind us."

"To be sure," he said, though he was not sure that he did see, but her use of Darcy's Christian name did not escape him or the way that Darcy looked on her with the deepest affection. So he was not unduly surprised when Elizabeth said with a teasing smile, "Perhaps we might join the others now, for we have a small announcement to make before dinner."

"Ah," he answered in the same mode as his niece. "A *short* courtship then, I presume?"

"Long enough, Uncle," she responded, looking up at Darcy with her eyes twinkling. "Long enough."

Elizabeth had her hand on Darcy's arm as they joined the others, and the warmth of their expressions was sufficient to alert Mrs. Gardiner, and she was not surprised when Mr. Gardiner announced that his niece had something to say before the meal began. Bingley and Jane stared at them in rapt fascination.

"Mr. Bingley, Jane, Aunt, Uncle, Maria," Elizabeth said, forcing herself to break free of Darcy's gaze to meet the eyes of the others in the room, "I would like you to be the first to know that Mr. Darcy has made me a proposal of marriage, which I have accepted. We are engaged to be married."

Jane stared at her in stunned astonishment at actually hearing the words spoken, despite the suspicion she and Bingley had shared before dinner. Bingley recovered more quickly, suddenly understanding how Darcy had come to know of Jane's true state of mind. Mr. and Mrs. Gardiner suffered no similar level of surprise, however, and they lost no time in offering their congratulations. Bingley followed some seconds later, but a full thirty seconds went by before Jane could stir from her chair. When she did, she made up for her earlier frozen state by the strength of her embrace, and the tears she shed were assumed to be tears of joy though Jane herself was not

---

so sure. Knowing of Elizabeth's intense dislike of Mr. Darcy, she was stuck by a horrified suspicion that her sister might have agreed to marry Darcy in order to secure her own happiness with Bingley. The thought that Elizabeth might sacrifice herself for her sake could not be dispelled from her mind as she wept in her sister's embrace.

Chapter 13

Saturday, April 18, 1812

That night in their bedroom after preparing for bed, Elizabeth and Jane were both awash in questions, but Elizabeth was adamant in being first to query Jane on every aspect of her engagement.

"Leave out not the smallest detail, Jane!" Elizabeth laughed merrily. "I want to know all!"

But Jane was too disturbed to begin. "Lizzy," she said slowly, "I cannot talk of my own happiness when I am so upset for fear of your own."

Elizabeth's brow wrinkled in confusion. "Why, whatever do you mean? I am happy enough — perhaps not as happy as you, but I do not understand your concern."

"But how can you be engaged to Mr. Darcy? I know how much you dislike him."

"That is all in the past." Elizabeth smiled. "I have been sorely mistaken in my previous opinion of Mr. Darcy, but in cases such as these, a good memory is unpardonable. This is the last time I shall ever remember it myself."

"My dearest sister, now do be serious! I want to talk plainly. I am very worried over how Mr. Darcy came to know of my feelings for Bingley and how he came to tell his friend. I am sure that somehow his regard for you was involved, but I cannot fathom how it came to be."

"Worried? Why should you be worried?"

Jane would not meet her eye. "I am afraid that you have agreed to marry Mr. Darcy in order to secure his help on my behalf, and I would be mortified if I achieved my own happiness at the expense of yours."

Elizabeth was at first too confused to understand her meaning, but when she puzzled it out, she gave a short laugh. "Jane, Jane, Jane," she said as she embraced her sister, "how can you suspect that? No, do not fear that. Mr. Darcy determined to go to his friend on his own. It is a long and complicated story, and you shall know of it, but *not* until you have told me yours."

Jane at first would not be mollified, but the solemn assurances of her sister at length had the desired effect, and Jane's spirits rose until she finally yielded to her sister's entreaties for information. Elizabeth listened with great delight until Jane came to the Darcy's visit to Gracechurch Street.

"I was quite surprised at how agreeable Mr. Darcy was when he visited, and I found Miss Darcy simply delightful though she was so terribly shy at first. They stayed the afternoon and then for dinner, and Miss Darcy invited me to visit the next day and spend the morning. I had a wonderful time, and I often found myself wondering how Mr. Wickham could have thought she was so cold and proud."

"That is because that … *that man* … is not a gentleman!" Elizabeth said in a voice colder than Jane had ever heard, "and nothing he said regarding Mr. Darcy or his sister can be trusted." Jane was stunned, knowing of her sister's favourable impression of him, but she was even more surprised when Elizabeth related the whole of her experiences at Hunsford. Her astonishment at Mr. Darcy's proposal was lessened by the strong sisterly partiality, which made any admiration of Elizabeth appear perfectly natural, but she was soon shocked to her core by Wickham's history with the Darcy family. She would not previously have believed that so much wickedness existed in the whole race of mankind as was here collected in one individual. At first, her natural inclination to find good in everyone motivated her to labour to prove the possibility of error, but further reflection on the near disaster that had almost struck her new friend forced her to cease the effort.

"I do not know when I have been more shocked," she said. "That Wickham should be so very bad is almost past belief, but consider what poor Miss Darcy must have suffered! And suffers still! It is no wonder that she is so shy; she must be afraid that everything she might do will turn out as wrong as her experience with Wickham. Oh, what a wicked, wicked man!"

Elizabeth had to smile at this; she did not think she had ever heard Jane speak so harshly. But her sister's ire with Wickham could not last long given her nature, and she was soon inclined to sympathy with Mr. Darcy. Knowing how taciturn he had appeared in Hertfordshire, she was impressed by the eloquence with which he had delivered his sentiments. She could only feel them justified in that Elizabeth deserved such, but she was grieved for the unhappiness that her sister's refusal must have given him.

"Poor Mr. Darcy. After expressing himself so well and so tenderly, consider how extreme must have been his disappointment."

Elizabeth had to laugh at the memory. "He *was* quite well-spoken, but he did not start that way. When he first entered the room, he could say nothing; he paced, he stood, but no words came out. Only when he took the papers from his coat was he able to find a means of expression. Indeed, I was quite astonished at first, for I had never heard him speak so gently." She sobered in contemplation. "I once challenged him that he did not present himself well to others because he could not be troubled, and I considered that I had scored a point against him. But I begin to think that I simply never bothered to look, for he appears to be exceedingly uncomfortable in social situations with people he does not know."

"Was that when you changed your mind, Lizzy—after he explained about Wickham?"

"Not exactly." Elizabeth smiled. "I was still incensed over his part in separating you and Bingley even if he was not as much in error as I first thought. But he convinced me to walk with him the next morning, and it was then he pledged that he would try to amend his error."

"And that is how Bingley knew," exclaimed Jane. "Oh, now I understand! Once I wrote that Bingley and I were engaged, that is when you agreed to marry Mr. Darcy."

"Not exactly," Elizabeth repeated. "I only agreed to receive him when—and if!—he came to call."

"And allow him to court you."

"Well, yes."

"It was not a very long courtship!" said Jane teasingly. But she was again grieved when Elizabeth related the manner in which the gossip and threat of scandal had necessitated her early decision to accept Mr. Darcy's suit rather than risk ruin to herself and damage to her family.

"You know how little a thing can lead to the destruction of a girl's reputation, Jane, no matter how innocent she may be. And I had you and the rest of my family to think of, so I had to think deeply and clearly about Mr. Darcy rather than simply giving way to my irritation with him."

"Oh, Elizabeth! To be forced into agreement by such pressures! It is terribly distressing that such vile gossip and whispers could cause such harm!"

"Jane, calm yourself!" Elizabeth laughed. "I had already discarded almost all the objections I had even before tonight, so you must consider that this merely changes the timing. And, as Charlotte would say, it is not so very bad! You agreed that Mr. Darcy has been most cordial and civil since returning from Kent, and from what you have said of Miss Darcy, I appear to be most fortunate in my future sister. Much more fortunate than you, for you shall be sisters with Miss Bingley and Mrs. Hurst!"

They both had to laugh.

"But are you certain—" Jane hesitated. "Forgive the question, but are you certain that you can be happy with him? I do not want to see you forced into a marriage with a man you cannot love, no matter how advantageous the match!"

Elizabeth was warmed by the devotion and concern in her eyes. She smiled and squeezed Jane's hand.

"Do you remember how I used to laugh when Charlotte told me that I was too romantic and I should be more practical? Can you believe that I finally listened, at least a little, to her advice? For that is surely true; after the news that you were engaged to Mr. Bingley, I forced myself to sit down with Mr. Darcy's letter and made myself forget my anger at his arrogance and presumption, and I actually tried to consider the situation with dispassion. And by the time I was done, I found that all but one of my objections could not stand up to the bright light of reason."

"And what was your last objection?" Jane asked quietly, for this was a new Elizabeth to her—much more sober, more reflective. Her sister had always possessed a sparkling wit and an intelligent and lively disposition, but she was so quick of mind that she seldom paused to reconsider a matter.

"My only objection was that I do not return the love that Mr. Darcy holds for me, and I was concerned that it could in time prove to make marriage unendurable," said Elizabeth quietly. "But we discussed that tonight, and I believe my fears are put to rest. We shall be friends at least, and I believe we

116

share a mutual respect that will prevent a marriage such as our parents have."

Jane was saddened at this; though she loved her parents, she could not deny the truth of Elizabeth's statement.

"I do think that you and Mr. Darcy will make a good match," she said quietly. "I have never shared your opinion of him, and he was most sincere and gracious when he called to congratulate me."

"I am sure you are right," said Elizabeth with a sudden smile. "In any case, I did not desire to spend my whole life with my family at Longbourn! Eventually, I should have settled for someone who was easy of manner and would be kind to me, for I do so want children. So why not Mr. Darcy? After all, he is *not* Mr. Collins!"

This drew a laugh, then Jane slyly interjected, imitating her mother's tones, "And he *does* have *ten thousand a year*!" This time, the sisters laughed until they had tears running down their cheeks.

When they recovered, Elizabeth asked, "Jane, has Mr. Bingley told you that when Mr. Darcy confessed his interference, Mr. Bingley was so angry that he ordered Mr. Darcy from his home."

"No! Charles has not said a word of this!"

"Yet it is true. William told me of it tonight, though he has since been forgiven. But Mr. Bingley also banished Miss Bingley to the Hurst town-house and suspended her allowance."

"He banished Caroline? Oh dear … but that does explain why she is not at his house."

"It is indeed singular behaviour for him," said Elizabeth in considerable satisfaction. "Perhaps this is a new Bingley! I begin to think that he has grown quite protective of you."

Jane blushed. She desired to avoid confrontation as much as possible, but the idea of Bingley being incensed on her behalf could not but please her. "But I wonder that he has not forgiven his sister as he has his friend."

"Jane, do you not see the difference? Mr. Darcy did what he did for what he believed was Mr. Bingley's own good, and when I forced him to acknowledge that he was mistaken, he made his confession and tried to right the wrong. And he must have done so knowing that it might cost him Mr. Bingley's friendship. Yes, I know he did it partly for my sake, but I do believe that he would have done so in any case. But Miss Bingley is a different matter. I daresay she continued to try to mislead her brother and very likely refuses to ask for forgiveness."

"Perhaps that is true," said Jane sadly.

"Then it is up to Miss Bingley," Elizabeth said. "I believe that Mr. Bingley will not tolerate any disrespect to you, even by his sister, and he will not allow her back until she forsakes her duplicity and promises to treat you as a true sister. So it is not up to Mr. Bingley or you, Jane. It is up to her."

Jane's distress at having to think ill of Caroline Bingley was soon over-shadowed by the joy of confidences shared by the two sisters. For her part, Elizabeth was relieved by having unburdened herself of all the secrets weighing on her since that eventful night at the Parsonage. She was certain of a willing listener in Jane whenever she might wish to talk on the issue again, but for now, she forgot about those concerns in her delight at being once more with her sister, and they talked far into the night.

Chapter 14

Sitting in his shaving chair the next morning with a hot towel wrapped about his face while Jennings stropped his razor, Darcy was busy mulling over the events of the previous days and the tasks ahead of him. He knew that he ought to feel more outrage at the way the insidious scandal had forced the hand of all parties, but in reality, his overriding emotion was one of relief—relief that he and Elizabeth would wed, relief that he could now introduce her to Georgiana, relief that so many uncertainties were now settled. Facing her father later that day could quite possibly be unpleasant, to be sure, and the reaction from Mrs. Bennet would likely be in accord with her usual lack of decorum, but neither presented any serious challenge compared with what he had already overcome.

He remained similarly preoccupied during church, struggling to pay attention to the sermon as best he could, but he was quite relieved when he finally returned home with Georgiana.

"Georgiana, I must ask you to take your meal with Mrs. Annesley today without me," he said as Stevens accepted their coats. "I have an important errand to attend to right away."

"Of course," Georgiana answered, curious about what could be taking her brother out on a Sunday. He usually stayed at home after church except for an occasional ride, though that was much less common in town than it was at Pemberley.

"Thank you, dearest," he said, kissing her cheek. "When I return in the late afternoon, we will be paying a visit to the Gardiners."

"Oh, good," said Georgiana. "I will be glad to see Miss Bennet again. And Mr. Bingley, of course," she said with a smile, "since he seldom seems far from her side."

"Quite true." Darcy smiled.

"In any case, I will not be completely alone. Richard sent a note saying he would be stopping by this morning."

"Excellent," Darcy said, excusing himself to change into riding clothes.

His horse was ready for him when he walked out to the small stable behind his townhouse, and he took a deep breath of the refreshing air as he emerged from his gate and turned north. It was a cool, spring day, and Darcy was glad for his greatcoat as he urged his mount into a ground-eating trot. Almost without requiring thought, he easily fell into a familiar rhythm, rising and falling with the horse's stride to soften the harsh gait. His mind was busy with other problems, such as planning where and when he and Elizabeth might be wed. If the choice were solely his, with no other issues to be considered, he would prefer the chapel at Pemberley, for it was at Pemberley that he was most truly at home. He hoped that Elizabeth would be of like mind, but he knew that they still faced a number of difficulties associated with their irregular and decidedly conflicted courtship. Those problems had first to be resolved before she could feel truly comfortable at either Pemberley or here in town. But he cheered himself, thinking: *It could have been so much worse!* He grinned at what had become almost a refrain in his mind of late.

Darcy did not push the pace, but it was still short of noon when he arrived at Longbourn, where a lad ran out from the stable to take the reins when he dismounted.

"Let him walk for at least a quarter-hour before stabling him," he instructed the young boy, who bobbed his head in acknowledgement before leading the horse away. He pulled a card from his pocket and handed it to the housekeeper who answered the door. "Mr. Bennet, please," he said, and the housekeeper bobbed in courtesy. He removed his gloves, hat, and greatcoat, giving them to a younger maid who took them away.

A head popped out beyond the door immediately to his right, to be quickly joined by another, both obviously belonging to the younger Bennet sisters. Lydia was the first one's name, he suddenly remembered, and the other one was called Kitty. The two girls began to giggle and then retreated back into the room. He shook his head at their unseemly behaviour, marvelling that Elizabeth and Jane had successfully avoided growing up into similarly silly girls.

The housekeeper was back in less than a minute. "Mr. Bennet will see you in the library," she said, showing him into Mr. Bennet's private room. Books overflowed every available place—shelves, tables, even chairs. The gentleman himself was just lowering the volume he was holding and rose to greet him.

"Mr. Darcy," he said politely, inclining his head.

"Mr. Bennet." Darcy gave the older man a bow befitting his state as master of the house, Darcy's elder, and Elizabeth's father.

Motioning Darcy to a chair, Mr. Bennet resumed his seat and regarded the young man with an unreadable expression. "I have been expecting to see you, Mr. Darcy, but I am surprised that you came to me, rather than the other way around," he said, leaning back in his chair and folding his arms over his chest. "But I am forgetting my manners. How may I be of service?"

Darcy was confused by the remark, but he settled himself and began, "The purpose of my mission today is simple. I have been fortunate enough to receive the agreement of your daughter, Miss Elizabeth, to my proposal of marriage, and I have come to request your consent and blessing."

"I see," Mr. Bennet said softly, and Darcy was surprised that his reply was so mild and unconcerned. As the man continued to look at him, he grew uncomfortable. He did not know Elizabeth's father at all, but this behaviour was not at all what he had expected.

At length, Mr. Bennet bestirred himself to continue. "Your request comes as rather a surprise, Mr. Darcy. I just received a request for the hand of my eldest daughter, Jane, earlier in the week from your friend Mr. Bingley, but I confess that I had not been aware of any regard on your part that might have warned me of your intentions toward my Lizzy. In fact, I was not aware that you have had any contact with my daughter since your departure from Netherfield last autumn."

"I renewed my acquaintance with Miss Elizabeth when she was visiting her friend Mrs. Collins. I was visiting my aunt Lady Catherine de Bourgh at her estate in Kent at the same time. I believe that you know that Mr. Collins is Lady Catherine's parson?" At Mr. Bennet's nod, he continued, "At the end of my visit, I asked if I might call on her when she returned to London, and she agreed. I was introduced to her uncle, Mr. Gardiner, when I called with Bingley to congratulate Miss Bennet on her engagement, and the day before Miss Elizabeth returned, I informed him of my wishes. He gave his permission, pending his correspondence with you."

"Which I have not yet received, it being only Sunday."

Darcy was still unable to decipher Mr. Bennet's manner as he continued, "I was invited to dine with the family, and Mr. Gardiner was kind enough to permit me some moments of privacy with your daughter. I then made her an offer of marriage which she accepted, and this is what occasioned my visit this morning."

Mr. Bennet was silent for a minute or so before he finally sighed. He picked up a letter from his desk. "I was not completely forthright with you, Mr. Darcy. This is not my first information of your interest in my daughter," he said in a decidedly unfriendly tone. "I have received a letter from my cousin, Mr. Collins. Normally, much as I abominate writing, I cannot help but value the correspondence of Mr. Collins, for the absurdities he usually expresses are so often diverting. On this occasion, sir, I was *not* diverted. In this letter he warns me of the most dire threats to the virtue and reputation of my daughter Elizabeth."

Darcy could hardly believe that foolish man had taken it upon himself to inform Mr. Bennet of his absurd imaginings. It was certain that Lady Catherine could not have been aware of his writing, since the news it contained would effectively force a marriage between Elizabeth and himself.

"And I am to believe that you took what your cousin related seriously?"

"How could I not, sir, when he writes that the whole estate is in an uproar due to you first attempting to force your attentions on her, and then later making her your mistress!" responded Mr. Bennet angrily.

"I find it difficult to believe that you would credit anything Mr. Collins claims," responded Darcy with some heat, "knowing, as you must, how foolish that man is. In addition, I find it equally incomprehensible that you would think your daughter would actually be a party to such a scheme. But, in any event, even if everything that Mr. Collins related were true, it would not signify, since the repair of such transgressions is to force either marriage or disgrace on the parties involved, and I am here seeking your consent to our marriage. I will further inform you, sir, that, neither Miss Bennet nor I have acted improperly. I love her too dearly to ever do anything so dishonourable. I feel incredibly fortunate and honoured to have received her acceptance of my hand."

"What concerns me is the manner in which this engagement occurred!" said Mr. Bennet grimly, "For this also was brought to my attention," and he picked up a newspaper that Darcy easily recognized as the *Chronicle.*

"Both Elizabeth and I are already aware of that vile gossip," Darcy retorted, "but unlike you, we know how such misinformation came to be distributed and published."

"Then pray share such information with me, Mr. Darcy," said Mr. Bennet sarcastically. "I cannot wait to be informed by what manner my Lizzy was embroiled in such a sordid affair."

"Due to gossip among the inept staff at the Hunsford Parsonage," responded Darcy icily, "which was taken up and bandied about by the even more ill-disciplined servants of my aunt's household. Evidently, the information was spread to London by those parties and thence into the scandal sheets. But I repeat, nothing untoward occurred between Elizabeth and myself, sir. She has behaved at all times with the utmost propriety — as have I."

"But now she has been involved in this disgusting business, regardless, has she not? I must insist on a full account of the situation in which you have placed my daughter, sir," he demanded coldly.

Darcy then proceeded to provide a summary of the events that had led to that point, from his first attraction to Elizabeth to meeting her again at Hunsford, emphasizing that nothing improper had occurred beyond spending several hours in private conversation. He briefly reviewed the situation of Mr. Wickham, but he did not speak of the attempted elopement with his sister, because the man's attitude disposed him against sharing such private matters. For one thing, it was ironic in the extreme that Mr. Bennet was now attempting to assume the role as a protective father, when he had previously abdicated his role as the head of his family and allowed all the girls to grow up essentially unrestrained, leading to the two younger girls' unseemly behaviour just exhibited in the hall.

Mr. Bennet listened to Darcy's account without saying anything, his elbows on the desk and his chin resting on his clasped fingers. When he finished, Mr. Bennet finally stirred

"It is an interesting tale you have woven for me, but I have yet to hear a reason why I should allow my favourite daughter to marry you."

Darcy was appalled at this response. "Do you want to see her ruined?" he blurted out.

Mr. Bennet made no reply, so Darcy continued. "You must understand how dearly I love your daughter, sir. I admire her intelligence, her kindness, her understanding, her strength and courage. Even before we knew of this gossip, I had secured her agreement for a courtship, and I had every hope of improving her opinion of me. And she informed me last night that the gossip did not signify to her, since it only changed the timing of her answer and not the outcome."

"Is it the custom in the society that you keep, to court a young lady without her father's permission?" said Mr. Bennet sarcastically.

Darcy flushed at the biting tone of the older man's voice but maintained control of his temper. "As I mentioned, I spoke to her uncle as her guardian and planned to speak with you when she returned home. But when the despicable gossip was actually printed, our hands were forced and events were accelerated, leading to her acceptance last evening."

"Ah. The gossip. Most convenient for your plans, was it not?"

"I do not comprehend your meaning, sir!" said Darcy heatedly.

"It is easy enough to understand, sir. You propose to my daughter, she refuses you, and then the conveniently ill-behaved servants manage to spread gossip about the countryside until it shows up in the paper, forcing my Lizzy to now consent to your proposals. Would she ever have married you otherwise, Mr. Darcy? One wonders whether your aunt's staff had some encouragement for their behaviour."

Darcy was appalled. In fact, he was infuriated. He would be within his rights to call the man out if he said as much in the company of others, and it took several moments before he could trust himself to speak.

"Sir, I told you of what your daughter said—that the gossip only changed the timing of her acceptance of my proposal, not the acceptance itself. Yes, she would have agreed to marry me to avoid the utter ruin of herself and her family, but she has stated that she is actually unconcerned with the gossip and is perfectly happy with our arrangement. By what stretch of the imagination do you disbelieve what I have told you when you have only to ask your daughter?"

Mr. Bennet once again astounded Darcy by commenting sadly, "I can only conclude that Lizzy must have been greatly influenced by your fortune and the attendant benefits associated with marrying such a well-found man."

"That is completely without sense, sir!" Darcy snapped. "Evidently, for all your professed regard for your daughter's nature, you have no true estimation of her character at all. Did you not hear me say that she refused me most decidedly? If she was influenced by my fortune, that would have been the moment to demonstrate it. How could she know that I would be so persistent? Many would not, and you know this if you would but turn your mind to it! She not only challenged me on behalf of her sister, she supported Wickham against me. No, sir, it will not do. She had ample opportunity to demonstrate her greed and did not do so. It was only after I convinced her that she had been misled that she even agreed to allow me to call on her in London."

Elizabeth's father was taken aback by the vehemence of Darcy's response, but he still could not abide the man and looked at him with dislike. "Whether you or Mr. Wickham have the right of it is not as clear to me as you say it is to my daughter. Elizabeth's opinion of you, as well as my own, was influenced by that man's account of his misfortunes at your hand. You say that she has changed her mind about Wickham because of your proofs, but I have to question whether her judgment may have been equally affected by the transference of Mr. Wickham's attentions to Miss King. No, I cannot so easily give way to your version of the facts, sir."

By this time, Darcy was fast losing what respect he had previously possessed for the man, and was completely set against sharing any further family information with Mr. Bennet in an attempt to correct his opinion. He was also at the ragged edge of his temper, and he leaned forward on the desk, his fists resting on the surface.

"By what right, sir, do you dare question my character in this matter?" he said, enunciating each word carefully. "What report of my dishonesty has been publicly acknowledged? What tradesmen have I defrauded? On my word, sir, you might bestir yourself from this room and solicit the opinion of the merchants in Meryton regarding Mr. Wickham! You will find, I am sure, many unpaid accounts. I know this well, sir; you may rely on it. It has been ever thus, and I have several times assumed his debts in Derbyshire and at Cambridge. So I must be insistent, sir. I demand to know what personal knowledge you have to so defame me."

Mr. Bennet seemed reluctant to answer, but eventually he said, "Perhaps I was too hasty. I cannot speak of any personal knowledge."

"Then I might further point out that Mr. Bingley, whom you have given your consent and blessing to marry your eldest daughter, has several times testified to my character and honesty, yet you and others seem inclined to believe the slanders spread by Wickham simply because he is fair spoken although there are no such favourable witnesses for that man. I might also point out that your brother Gardiner seems favourably disposed toward me since he not only dined with me but twice invited me to dine with his family. In addition, he gave his conditional approval to call on his niece, an event unlikely to have occurred if he had reason to question my character."

Darcy stood up straight. "I will speak plainly, sir. I can see that any further efforts to convince you would be fruitless, so I will simply ask, do I have your consent to marry your daughter, Elizabeth? Or would you prefer to see her ruined through no fault of her own due to your dislike of me?"

Mr. Bennet glared at Darcy, but he knew that he was well and truly without recourse. "Well, well, of course you must marry, after everything that has occurred. I will not withhold my consent, but I will not give my blessing, sir."

"Does this mean you do not desire to see your daughter married from Longbourn?"

"I will not ask the reverend of Longbourn Chapel to perform a ceremony that I cannot bless."

Darcy nodded coldly. "I will take the necessary steps then. Will any of your family be in attendance at our wedding, sir?"

"I will not forbid my wife and daughters to attend, but I will on no account be present myself."

"If you would be so kind as to put your sentiments in writing, I will deliver them to Elizabeth."

Mr. Bennet was offended by hearing this man's use of his daughter's Christian name, but he could hardly forbid it at that point. He only nodded. Darcy bowed stiffly and excused himself.

As Darcy stood waiting in the hall, Lydia and Kitty again peeked around the edge of the doorway and giggled when out of sight. Soon he heard Mrs.

Bennet approach to determine what was distracting her daughters. She stood, astonished, to find him in the hall. Darcy greeted her politely, and found that his view of her had changed. After contending with the wilful self-deception of her husband, he could feel considerably more sympathy toward a woman who was merely silly.

"I did not know you were come to call, Mr. Darcy. Are you here with your friend, Mr. Bingley?"

"No, madam. I came here to speak with your husband."

Lack of sensibility or not, Mrs. Bennet's instincts were more than sufficient to detect the sudden advantage of such a visit.

"Would you care to step into the parlour and sit with us for the moment?"

"Thank you, but no, madam. I am but waiting on a letter that Mr. Bennet is preparing to be delivered to Elizabeth. When he is finished, I must be on the road immediately."

Mrs. Bennet was equally up to the task of recognizing the possible meaning of Darcy's unconscious use of Elizabeth's name. And he had been talking with her husband...

Her conjectures were interrupted when Hill approached the door to the library. She was inside the room only momentarily before returning with two letters, which she gave to Darcy. He looked at them; Mr. Bennet had prepared one for his daughter and one for his brother Gardiner. Nodding and thanking the housemaid, he then bid Mrs. Bennet a polite farewell, leaving that bemused woman in contemplation of the possible advantage to her family of this visit. As he walked through the door, he heard her piercing voice immediately demanding answers to her many questions from her husband.

Darcy went straight to the stable, meeting the lad leading his horse partway. Thanking the boy, he quickly mounted, eager to be gone. As soon as he could manage, he urged the horse into a gallop, still seething in anger and desperate to be home—and to see Elizabeth as soon as might be arranged.

He groaned as he thought of how saddened she would be by her dear father's response. That thought acted to quell his anger, and he gradually eased his horse back to an easy walk. He spent the remainder of the journey reviewing what he still wanted to accomplish that day.

Chapter 15

Sunday, April 19, 1812

No sooner had he sighted the rear gate to his townhouse than it swung open, and Darcy turned into the stable area. Johnson, the head groom, along with two apprentices, was already waiting for him, and Darcy dismounted quickly. He was exceedingly eager to put that morning's disastrous errand behind him and move on with the other tasks he had to accomplish that day.

Darker tasks than I thought I would have when I left here in such good spirits this morning, he thought sourly as one of the apprentices took the reins.

"Welcome back, sir," the groom said, assessing the condition of Darcy's horse with a single look. "Looks as if Ned got a fair workout, sir," he said. As the lad began to lead the horse away, Johnson called after him, "Walk him for a full half-hour, now, before he touches even a drop of water."

"I am afraid I was eager to get back to town," said Darcy as he removed his gloves. "I certainly worked him harder coming back than I did going out."

"Ned's a good 'un, sir," said Johnson, "so long as he gets cooled down good before he gets to the water."

"If you would be so good as to provide a couple of your lads with transportation, I have some notes to write for delivery to my solicitor's office and then to the *Times*. I will be going out after I clean up, so please have my carriage ready in two hours."

128

"Very good, sir."

"Thank you. Meanwhile, I have a number of tasks to accomplish and too few hours left to do them."

"Aye, sir," said Johnson as he turned back to his beloved stables, "you've the right of it there!"

Darcy handed his coat, hat, and gloves to the footman who ran up as he approached the rear entrance, and his butler met him as he entered the door. "Welcome back, Mr. Darcy," he said. "I trust that your journey was pleasant?"

"Pleasant enough, thank you," said Darcy, returning Stevens's smile. There was no need to let Mr. Bennet's disagreeable and reluctant consent cast any further damper on the joy of this day. The primary concern was settled, and he and Elizabeth *would* marry, displeasure of her father or no. "Do you know where my sister and cousin are?"

"Miss Georgiana is in the music room, and Colonel Fitzwilliam left the house on an errand about a half hour ago."

"I have some notes to prepare for immediate delivery, and then I must wash the road dust off. Please inform Miss Darcy that I will wait on her in about an hour."

"Very good, sir," said the elderly man.

"Please have tea sent to my study, Stevens," Darcy called over his shoulder. "My throat is caked with road dust."

"At once, sir."

Darcy proceeded to his desk, though he would have preferred the bath first. He composed a note to his solicitor, informing that capable man of his forthcoming marriage and instructing him to secure a marriage license as soon as practicable. He included the fact that his prospective bride was not yet of age but that her father had consented to the marriage, though he did not mention Mr. Bennet's refusal to bless the union since it did not matter from a legal point of view. He also asked for a rough draft of marriage agreements, setting down the important points he had worked out in his head during the ride back from Longbourn, requesting a rough draft by the following afternoon if at all possible, otherwise first thing on the morning next. He wanted to review at least the outline of the agreement with Elizabeth before he took it to her father to sign.

He frowned at the thought of so soon having to confront Mr. Bennet again, but his mood was lightened by the arrival of a tray with tea and sweet cakes. After the first cup of tea, he devoured two of the cakes, since he had skipped the noon meal while travelling to Longbourn and back. The drafting of a brief announcement to be placed in the 'Engagements' section of the *Times* took only a moment, and the note to his Uncle and Aunt Matlock requesting to call on them on Monday afternoon took scarce longer. However, he spent considerably more thought on the letter to Lady Catherine before ringing for Stevens. When the butler entered, he handed him the notes and letters for delivery.

The bath was as refreshing as he had anticipated, and he arose from the tub with a feeling that he was leaving the gloomy events of the morning in the same bathwater as the road dust. Jennings had caught his master's mood, and he was brisk as he helped him dress. Within fifteen minutes, Darcy was heading down the stairs smartly, having to restrain himself from descending the steps two at a time. The sounds of Mozart drifted down the hall, and he entered the music room quietly to be rewarded with the sight of his sister concentrating completely on her playing. She could not see him from where she sat at the pianoforte, and he enjoyed the skill and the feeling she put into her presentation.

There were better practitioners from a technical point of view, he thought, but there were few who could better express their love for the music. In that respect, though Georgiana had the greater skill and technical execution, she and Elizabeth were similar in the warmth of their performance.

When she finished, he gave her a brisk round of applause as he walked toward the instrument. The unexpected sound caused Georgiana to turn and rise from the bench.

"William!" she exclaimed as she came towards him with both hands outstretched. "You have certainly been gone long enough. I knew you went riding, but I anticipated your return before now."

Darcy clasped her hands and leaned forward to kiss her on the check. "It has been a most eventful day, dearest, and we need to talk. I have important news."

At her raised eyebrows, he repeated, "Very important. Please, have a seat here beside me."

Georgiana seated herself beside her brother and looked inquisitively at him.

Darcy chose his words with care. He was anxious about breaking this news to his sister since she had no forewarning of his attachment or his intentions to Elizabeth. He smiled grimly to himself. *I did not have much forewarning myself,* he thought reproachfully. *Perhaps Richard is right about this impulsiveness business!*

Georgiana watched her brother wrestle with his thoughts. He ran his hand through his hair as he often did when he pondered how best to phrase something delicate. Finally, he leaned forward and took one of her hands in his. "Dearest, I know this is going to come as a surprise, perhaps even a shock to you, because it has taken place with great suddenness." He drew a breath and said, "Georgiana, I am to be married."

Georgiana at first could not understand what he had said. Whatever she expected, it had not been that! William had seemed distracted in the past months, but he had not been seeing any young woman that she knew of, except those within his normal circle...

A sudden fear struck her. She could not meet her brother's eyes, so she did not see the delight that danced in them as he stared at a vision of Elizabeth that only he could see. Instead, she stayed focused on her hands as she asked in trepidation, "I am confused, William, and, yes, very surprised. Are you really engaged?"

Darcy laughed. "Yes, quite engaged, dearest."

Georgiana's fear now began to choke her. She was baffled, and had to struggle to continue. "Who are you to marry, William? Is it... is it Miss Bingley?" she said so softly that Darcy had to strain to hear.

"Miss Bingley?" He threw back his head with a roar of laughter, which alleviated at least some of Georgiana's anxiety. "No, no, Georgiana. I have been aware of Miss Bingley's machinations since first meeting her and would have gone to my grave a bachelor before embarking on such a perilous adventure as forming an attachment with her!"

Darcy noted the look of relief in his sister's eyes and squeezed her hand. "No, Georgiana, the young lady is no one you know—at least, not directly. You remember Mr. Bingley's intended, Miss Bennet?"

"Of course, William. She is very nice, and I like her very much."

"I am engaged to her sister, Miss Elizabeth Bennet."

Georgiana's eyes opened wide in amazement. Her brother was usually so very dependable that surprises were uncommon, but he had certainly sprung one on this occasion! She stammered, "How...I mean, when...?"

He explained their brief acquaintance in Hertfordshire and subsequent meeting in Kent.

"This is amazing, William," she said with growing excitement. Surely, the sister to Miss Bennet could not be anything similar to Miss Bingley, could she? Perhaps she would at last have a sister who could also be a friend! "But why have you been so secretive? I cannot recall a single time when her name has come up in conversation. I do remember hearing Miss Bingley mention Miss Jane Bennet in the winter, though I do not believe she cared much for her."

"No, she did not," her brother recalled with some embarrassment, "and she did not like Miss Elizabeth Bennet at all. If you remember her ever making a derisive remark at my attraction to 'a fine pair of eyes,' she was referring to Miss Elizabeth."

"So Miss Bingley does not care for Miss Elizabeth?" Georgiana smiled. "I must admit to feeling a certain inclination in her direction already!"

Darcy chuckled at her show of spirit. He was heartened to think that Elizabeth would provide a much more valuable example for Georgiana during the next few important years as she entered society than any of her other acquaintances would have done. "I believe that you will take to Elizabeth easily, though she is quite lively and witty. She is also," he said with a smile, "a lady of exemplary fortitude. For example, she refused to be intimidated by Lady Catherine's usual unending stream of suggestions and instructions, disputing her with considerably more spirit than I have ever been able to show."

"Lady Catherine?" Georgiana was completely intimidated by her formidable aunt, and she did not see how anyone could successfully stand against her when even her brother avoided open conflict.

"Indeed. And she did so in such a skilful manner that her ladyship did not even realize that Miss Elizabeth was being impertinent. She was actually quite taken with her, at least at first. We spent much time together at Rosings, and that is where I got to know her better and found myself completely lost."

Georgiana smiled at her brother. "It sounds so romantic. And it also sounds very unlike you, William!"

Darcy laughed, feeling the thrill once again of finally having things settled between Elizabeth and himself—or at least, most things settled, he reminded himself. He still needed to give her the unpleasant news of his visit with her father, which he knew would distress her. There was also the matter of that repulsive gossip printed in the *Chronicle*.

"Richard says that it is completely like me and only to be expected, considering the usual Darcy impulsiveness!" Darcy said with a chuckle.

"He does enjoy teasing you about that."

"What do I enjoy teasing my too beloved cousin about, Georgie?" a voice said from the door.

Darcy and Georgiana looked behind them to see Colonel Fitzwilliam in his scarlet uniform, just entering the room.

"At trying to provide a model of socially acceptable behaviour to a totally disreputable relation," said Darcy.

"At being impulsive," said Georgiana.

Fitzwilliam gave a big grin as he came around to seat himself in a comfortable chair in front of them. "Has Darcy been confessing to his recent activities, Georgie?"

"Actually," said Georgiana slyly, "I believe he has been confessing to providing you the source for a complete new story, Richard!"

"What is this, Darcy? Do I dare believe that you have already met with the delightful Miss Elizabeth Bennet? And that the lady has accepted you?"

"The answer," said Darcy, "is 'yes' and 'yes.'" He made a quieting motion to his cousin, lest Richard start recounting the entire eventful but embarrassing story of what had taken place in Kent. Fitzwilliam grinned at him in glee, but had no more desire than Darcy to reveal the details of that lively episode—at least not yet!

"Well, well, well," said Fitzwilliam. "This does appear to contain the seeds of yet another Darcy tale."

"Georgie was expressing the fear that I might have connected myself with Miss Bingley," Darcy said, trying to change the subject by teasing Georgiana, and he did succeed in drawing a blush from her.

Fitzwilliam shuddered at the thought. "Dear Heavens, no, though I quite understand your concern in that area, Georgie. Miss Elizabeth is delightful and is in no way similar to the many fashionable society ladies—and their mothers!—who have been pursuing your brother with scant success these many years." This thought cheered Georgiana considerably as he continued. "Georgie, we must share with Miss Elizabeth the story of your parents' courtship. It should provide considerable insight into her new husband's character!"

"You will not have the chance, Richard," Darcy said with an attempt at dignity. "I have resolved to share that with Elizabeth at the first opportunity in the hope of salvaging at least some semblance of respectability!"

Fitzwilliam laughed heartily and turned back to Georgiana. "Miss Elizabeth is intelligent, lively, witty, and truly compassionate, Georgie. She will make a wonderful sister for you. In fact, if circumstances had been different—had I not been a younger son, or had Miss Elizabeth's fortune been greater—I might have jousted with your brother for her favour!"

That earned a glare from Darcy, which amused him greatly. But then he noticed the sudden look of concern on Georgiana's face. He immediately reached forward and took her hand.

"Do not distress yourself, Georgie," the colonel told her gently. "Miss Bennet is not a fortune hunter. No, no, I can see your concern, but trust me on this. I cannot speak of just how I know, but I do indeed have definite knowledge that she is not. Your brother has connected himself with a most worthy young lady."

Having been serious long enough, however, Fitzwilliam continued. "Though he has connected himself with a young lady of inestimable spirit who faced up to both Lady Catherine and your fearsome brother."

"Indeed?" Georgiana said with a smile, both at his assurances and his jest. "She stood up to William too?"

"Aye, she did, Georgie. Faced him down and quite broke him to her will."

"It sounds as if I will enjoy meeting this fearless young woman."

"Fitzwilliam!" Darcy said in warning.

"And after she finishes instructing you in how to deal with imperious family members, Georgie, I would wager that the direction of the Darcy family affairs may pass to new and more capable hands!"

"Fitzwilliam!" Darcy said in heat, glaring at his irrepressible cousin in exasperation.

Fitzwilliam's answer was a peal of laughter and a handshake of hearty congratulation that mollified Darcy somewhat but did not make him any less wary of what his cousin might plan for the future. But, at that instant, he had a more immediate concern.

"Georgiana, I will be calling on Elizabeth directly. If you are available, I would dearly wish for you to accompany me."

"See what I mean, Georgie?" said Fitzwilliam in a stage whisper. "Your brother is smitten, I say. Smitten!" He looked back at Darcy's glare blandly.

"I believe that I also shall accompany you to offer my own congratulations, Darcy."

"I might have missed it," said Darcy, "but I somehow do not remember issuing an invitation."

Fitzwilliam dismissed Darcy's comment with a flip of his hand. "You are much too well bred to be uncivil, Darcy. It is one of the things that makes you so endearing to your poorer relations."

"Then perhaps you might be of at least some service, Richard, and accompany me to visit your parents tomorrow afternoon? I wish to inform them in person rather than sending a letter."

"Of course."

Darcy stood to leave. "The carriage will be ready in a quarter hour. If you could entertain Georgiana until then without any further damage to my character, Cousin, I have some business to attend to before we leave."

As Darcy left the room, he heard Fitzwilliam say behind him, "Had you not noticed Darcy's rather odd behaviour of late, Georgie? That should have warned you that something unprecedented was in the wind!"

Darcy heard the tinkling of Georgiana's laughter behind him, and he did not have to look back to know that Fitzwilliam was completely ignoring his admonition against further damage to his character. He could only shake his head as he closed the door.

DARCY LOOKED UP AT THE knock on the door to his study, and his butler entered.

"Your carriage is ready, sir."

"Very good," said Darcy, putting down his pen. "Oh, Stevens," he said to his butler, who had turned to leave.

"Sir?"

"You may make a small announcement to the staff, telling them that I am soon to be married."

His butler first looked at his master quizzically since Darcy's wide smile at first made him wonder whether the younger man was jesting. But his look told him that his master's smile was a smile of delight, not of humour.

"Truly, sir?" he asked, still not certain that he was reading his employer correctly.

"Truly, Stevens," he replied.

"Then I believe congratulations are in order, sir," Stevens said with a smile. "It would do this heart good to see a mistress in the house again. And children, too, of course. Indeed it would, sir."

"I think so too," Darcy said cheerfully, "but now I have to depart."

Stevens smiled to himself as the master strode off, almost bouncing from exuberance. He had held his position for most of Darcy's life, and he was quite fond of his young master. It would be good so see him well settled before his own time came, and perhaps there might even be time for children before then.

Chapter 16

Elizabeth was reading to her cousins in the sitting room with Jane and Bingley when she heard the sound of a coach on the street below. She closed her book and looked out the window to see the familiar, red-coated figure of Colonel Fitzwilliam handing down a tall young lady from the carriage steps. It could only be Mr. Darcy's sister, whom Jane had described so admiringly. She cringed inwardly as she remembered how easily she had believed Mr. Wickham's description of Miss Darcy's exceedingly proud manners. She dispatched her cousins to the nursery and informed her aunt that their guests had arrived.

She reached the sitting room moments before the visitors were announced, and this time she was more prepared when Darcy's eyes instantly found her as he stepped into the room. She returned his smile and crossed the room to greet him, surprised and gratified to feel an honest pleasure at his arrival. Of course, it did not hurt that his eyes darkened in intensity when he first caught sight of her or that his gallantry continued as he bent to kiss her hand before turning to his sister.

"Elizabeth, may I present my sister, Miss Georgiana Darcy? Georgiana, this is my betrothed, Miss Elizabeth Bennet."

Georgiana and Elizabeth made their curtsies.

"I am pleased to meet you, Miss Elizabeth. My brother has told me much of you," Georgiana ventured in a voice so soft that Elizabeth had to strain to hear.

"And he has told me much of you also," Elizabeth responded with a smile. She turned to greet Colonel Fitzwilliam, pleased to again see his friendly face.

"My dear Miss Bennet," he exclaimed, "it is wonderful to see you again! Darcy told me the good news, and I invited myself along to give you my most sincere congratulations."

"Thank you, Colonel, but I must correct you. The title of Miss Bennet belongs to my elder sister, Jane." She gestured to her sister, who was standing close at hand, and made the introductions.

The Colonel bowed deeply. "I am most pleased to meet you, Miss Bennet. Please accept my abject apologies, and allow me to offer you my congratulations on your own recent engagement." Jane was pleased at his gentle manners and nodded her head in acceptance.

While Darcy introduced Colonel Fitzwilliam to her aunt and uncle, Elizabeth took Miss Darcy's arm, tucking it in hers before giving Darcy one of her impish smiles that he loved so much.

"If I might be allowed to borrow your sister for a few minutes, sir?" she asked archly. "I believe everyone else except for Colonel Fitzwilliam is well acquainted, and I have no doubt that both of you may adequately entertain my aunt." Then she took Georgiana over to a couch, and the two girls sat down together while Darcy and his cousin sat down near Mrs. Gardiner. Fitzwilliam and Mrs. Gardiner easily fell into conversation, and Bingley, of course, needed no entertainment, as he had his Jane. For his part, Darcy was content just to watch Elizabeth and Georgiana.

Though she was forced to do the greater share of the talking at first, Elizabeth quickly determined that Jane was indeed correct in her assessment of Miss Darcy. She was possessed of both sense and good humour, with manners that were perfectly unassuming and gentle, and she was truly as shy as Jane had described, though she was clearly trying hard to uphold her end of the conversation.

Elizabeth several times glanced over at Mr. Darcy who seemed content to leave his cousin Fitzwilliam to attend to her aunt. His expression was one with which she was very familiar, though it was not the look of imperious reserve she had so often seen before. It was instead that dark look of interest, and she found it almost overwhelming to be the complete focus of those penetrating eyes. She had to force herself back to her conversation with Georgiana.

Georgiana had tried her best to prepare herself for meeting the unknown lady who was destined to become her new sister, but not even her brother's lavish praise of Miss Elizabeth Bennet could offset the deep anxiety that had gripped her when the coach stopped before the house on Gracechurch Street. Despite the fact that she already had met Miss Jane Bennet, she was still afraid that she might be confronted with a sophisticated, if less imposing, version of Miss Bingley.

Her concerns were immediately put to rest by Elizabeth's warm affection in conjunction with her lively wit and her understanding of Georgiana's qualms. But the quelling of her fears did not bring ease of conversation to the younger girl, though she desperately wished to reciprocate Elizabeth's attempts to draw her into conversation. It was only when Elizabeth steered the topic to that of music that Georgiana began to lose some of her timidity.

"Your brother says that you practice your music most diligently, Miss Darcy," Elizabeth said, "and he also says that you are quite proficient."

Georgiana looked up with a shy smile. "William is much too kind to me, Miss Elizabeth." It was her longest sentence so far.

"I am sure he is only telling the truth. He has told me that deceit of any kind is his abhorrence!" she said, with a sly glance at Darcy, who only raised an eyebrow in return. "He is *your* brother, you know. He would never say it if it was not so, would you not agree?"

"Well, yes," Georgiana said softly, dropping her head in embarrassment at the compliment. Then she looked up in sudden triumph, "He also told me that he very much enjoyed hearing *you* sing and play, and that must be true as well!"

Elizabeth coloured slightly at the further evidence that Mr. Darcy had been watching avidly when she had not suspected any regard at all.

"Well, we shall have many chances to play together in the future, and you can make up your own mind," she said cheerfully, "though I will strive to only play duets with you so that you can cover for my deficiencies!"

Georgiana managed a giggle, and she impulsively reached over and squeezed Elizabeth's hand, "I am so glad we will be sisters, Miss Elizabeth."

"As am I, Miss Darcy," Elizabeth said warmly. But then she cocked her eye at the younger girl. "However, if we are to be sisters, we cannot continue to call each other Miss Elizabeth and Miss Darcy. You must call me Elizabeth or Lizzy, which is what my sisters call me."

"Oh, I could not!" Georgiana exclaimed in embarrassment.

"But you must!" Elizabeth replied with a laugh, "For others will find it strange if I call you Georgiana while you still refer to me as Miss Elizabeth or Miss Bennet. We would not," she said with a wink, "want anyone to think we are quarrelling!"

"Oh, I could never quarrel with you, Miss Elizabeth!" Georgiana cried in dismay.

Elizabeth raised her eyebrow at her, and waited expectantly.

At length Georgiana relented. "Elizabeth."

"That is much better," she said. "Now, do you prefer Georgiana?"

"Well," she said shyly, "I have not had a chance to make many friends of my own yet. William and Mrs. Annesley call me Georgiana, except that sometimes William calls me Georgie when he teases me. And cousin Fitzwilliam always calls me Georgie, but he teases me all the time, and calls me other names at times."

"Georgiana is a lovely name, so I will call you that, if you please. But what is this about your brother teasing you?" She glanced over at Darcy as he sat watching her intently with a bemused expression. "We shall have to tease him right back!"

"Oh, no! I do not think I could tease William. He has been so good to me, and he has so many concerns to deal with." This last thought caused a cloud to pass over Georgiana's face, and Elizabeth immediately realized that memories of Ramsgate and Mr. Wickham had just intruded into the younger girl's mind. A quick look at her brother showed his concern as well.

She reached over and squeezed Georgiana's hand, before leaning close with a twinkle in her eye and whispering to her, "Then I shall have to tease him for both of us! Then you can laugh with me without having to be so bold yourself." This last seemed to relieve Georgiana's sudden discomposure. Elizabeth glanced again at Darcy and gave him an encouraging smile. Darcy immediately smiled back, and Elizabeth was surprised at how it dispelled his solemn demeanour and gave him an unexpected boyish exuberance. She turned back to Georgiana with yet another item to add to the catalogue of Fitzwilliam Darcy.

Georgiana had also witnessed her brother's expression, and she covered

Elizabeth's hand with her own, "I have never seen William so happy, Elizabeth. I am so pleased that he has found you. I had begun to despair that he would ever marry."

Elizabeth was also conscious of her good fortune; there were many things that she and Mr. Darcy still had to learn about each other, but she had already decided that she could not have been more fortunate in her new sister.

Mr. Gardiner arrived about a quarter-hour later. Darcy immediately rose to greet him, and drawing close, he asked quietly whether he might see him privately as soon as may be. From his stiffness of manner, Mr. Gardiner instantly perceived that the man was decidedly unhappy. He agreed, and the two men left the room so quietly that their absence was not at first noticed.

"Thank you for seeing me so quickly," Darcy began as Mr. Gardiner closed the door behind him.

"It is quite all right. Am I correct in my assumption that you need to discuss your visit with my brother Bennet?" asked the older gentleman, offering his hand. Darcy clasped it, grateful that at least one of Elizabeth's relations was eminently sensible and polite. Recounting the particulars of the morning's encounter to one of less understanding would have been truly mortifying.

"You are quite correct, sir, and I must tell you that my journey was not an unqualified success," he answered, pulling out the two letters Mr. Bennet had given him. "In fact, while he felt himself compelled to give his consent, he has taken a decided dislike to me and was quite emphatic in withholding his blessing to our marriage. I believe he will be more forthcoming in his letter to you."

That Mr. Gardiner was upset by this news was obvious by the look he gave the two envelopes. Putting the note to Elizabeth aside for the moment, he held the other in his hand. "Before I read this, would you care for tea or coffee, Mr. Darcy?"

"Coffee would be preferable to my taste, sir, but I would be happy with tea as well."

Mr. Gardiner nodded and ordered coffee for both of them before he broke the seal on his letter. He said nothing as he read, but Darcy could discern that he was quite uncomfortable with its contents. As he finished reading the several pages, the coffee was brought into the study, and he put the letter aside in order to serve.

"I see that you were not wide of the mark when you described your interview with my brother," he said when they had both settled back in their chairs. "I am surprised. He is usually more sensible than this. However, I will not comment beyond that. I believe that our time would be better spent in consideration of what we should do and the plans we should make."

Darcy nodded in agreement, understanding that the other man would not criticize his brother directly. Since Mr. Bennet had not forbidden the marriage, his dislike of Darcy was of no real significance; it would make the planning more difficult, to be sure, but it would not prevent it.

"My brother has authorized me to act for him in all respects of this matter," Mr. Gardiner continued, and again Darcy nodded since this was in line with Mr. Bennet's character. He had washed his hands of a distasteful task in order to return to his beloved books, and Darcy struggled to conceal his distaste for the man's indolence and indifference to his daughter's feelings at such an emotional time.

"As soon as I returned, I drafted a note for my solicitor instructing him to obtain a license so that Elizabeth and I may be married in whatever place meets with her approval."

"That seems a prudent move," said Mr. Gardiner, "but we should consult with Lizzy and my wife for their opinions."

"Perhaps you might invite Mrs. Gardiner to join us now before we inform Elizabeth of this."

"Thank you, I shall do so. I am accustomed to discussing even my business matters with her; she is a woman of considerable insight." Mr. Gardiner quickly excused himself and returned shortly with his wife who was not, however, as effective as her husband in concealing her feelings at Mr. Bennet's reaction.

"This is not at all fitting, Mr. Gardiner!" she exclaimed. "Lizzy would no doubt prefer to be married from Longbourn, and he is denying that without any justification other than personal aversion!"

"Perhaps so, Madeline, but he is her father and is within his rights. And he did not refuse consent, which is the situation with which we must deal. The question now is: how shall we advise Lizzy when we break this news to her?"

"With respect to a site, I might suggest my family's chapel in town, St. ———, or else the chapel at Pemberley," said Darcy. "Either would be agreeable to me, but I would not force a choice on Elizabeth; I am amenable to her wishes."

"And I would further suggest our own church, St. ———, which Lizzy has often attended when visiting us. But we shall have to wait to see what Elizabeth thinks," said Mrs. Gardiner. "She will not be pleased at having to make this choice — not at all."

"It is not as bad as it might be, Madeline," said her husband. "While my brother is adamant in his own disapproval, he will not forbid either her mother or her sisters from attending."

"That is something," agreed his wife. "Perhaps Elizabeth will have another opinion. Now, what about her wedding clothes? I know my sister will wish to help both her daughters with their shopping."

Mr. Gardiner was not able to contain his uneasiness, and he was forced to disclose that Mr. Bennet was completely set against any purchase of wedding clothes for Elizabeth. Mrs. Gardiner was so outraged at this that she simply sat in silence, knowing that any further outburst on her part would be inappropriate.

But when I have some privacy with Edward, she thought, *just wait!*

However, in this matter, Darcy was dismissive. "This is of no consequence, Mrs. Gardiner. I will provide for whatever Elizabeth should require out of my own funds; she shall not be forced to do without."

"That is most generous, sir, but hardly necessary," objected Mr. Gardiner. "We will be more than happy to provide for any purchases my niece may need to make."

Darcy only smiled. "Do you remember the part of the marriage ceremony in which the husband vows to endow his wife with all his worldly goods? I would not have you support such unexpected expenditures simply to uphold a social custom regarding the wedding clothes. Consider, sir, that if I am run down in the street by a runaway coach on our way out of the church, Elizabeth would soon have the use of my entire fortune!"

And with this good-natured jest, Mr. Gardiner gave way. "I will contest no further, sir," he said with a smile. "Now we need to apprise Lizzy of this unfortunate news."

"There is one other thing, sir. I also instructed my solicitor to prepare the marriage agreements, and he should have a rough draft in a day or two. I will bring these to you when they are ready since you will now be acting for Mr. Bennet in this matter."

"Quite correct, Mr. Darcy. Now, we had better bring Lizzy into this conversation. Madeline, would you ask her to come here while you entertain our guests?"

When Elizabeth entered the study, she was sobered by the grim expressions on the faces of both men, but she was not long left in doubt as to the reason.

"Lizzy," her uncle began, "I dislike having to tell you this, but Mr. Darcy's meeting with your father this morning did not go well at all. My brother has written a letter to me, and the upshot is that he has given his consent to your marriage, but he has withheld his blessing." Elizabeth was both puzzled and distressed by this unexpected news, and her uncle gave her the letter that her father had addressed to her. After she broke the seal and began to read, she was shocked at the vituperative tone of the letter. It was completely unlike him! She paled as she read the abusive terms in which he described Darcy and the accusation that he had trapped her into marriage. However, he was equally abusive toward her that she had accepted him. He seemed to believe that she should have found some way to avoid allowing the scandal to tarnish herself and her family while still refusing Darcy. It was most unfair and uncharitable, and she could not stop the tears that stung the corners of her eyes.

Darcy wanted nothing more than to comfort her, but he restrained himself as she finished the letter. When she finally folded it and put it aside, her uncle said gently, "Lizzy, would you care to withdraw to compose yourself? Mr. Darcy and I have many things to discuss, and it certainly would be understandable if you need some time by yourself."

"No, uncle," she said quietly, taking the handkerchief that Darcy handed her and drying her tears. "It is just that I have never known my father to express himself in such a manner."

"Nor have I," replied Mr. Gardiner, unable to fully conceal his irritation. "As I said to Mr. Darcy, my brother is usually more sensible than this." He sighed unhappily and continued, "In his letter to me, your father authorized me to make all the arrangements, since he refuses to be involved in any manner." It obviously pained him to have to disclose this last revelation.

"I will not speak of my own letter, Uncle, other than to say that I absolutely deny that his charges have any validity at all."

A MOST CIVIL PROPOSAL

"I never doubted it, Lizzy," said Mr. Gardiner softly. He was embarrassed for the decided dislike that Mr. Bennet had formed for Darcy, but the man in question appeared little concerned on his own behalf. *His* eyes were full of concern for Elizabeth.

Elizabeth saw this, and his sympathy and worry warmed her. She could only imagine what his interview with her father must have been like—to be accused of what her father had accused him in his letter. Impulsively, she reached over and squeezed his hand, which comforted him. When she started to draw her hand back, he resisted, and she allowed it to remain clasped within his.

"We had best start, then," her uncle said, "for we have many things to discuss. One of the first things to settle is a location for the wedding. Mr. Darcy has suggested London, either in our church or his own. Alternatively, he also suggested the chapel at his estate in Derbyshire."

At the reminder that she could not be married from Longbourn, Elizabeth was stirred to anger at her father for his lack of concern, as well as his dismissive and abusive accusations of Darcy—and of herself, for that matter. It took some moments for her to quell that anger and concentrate on the question her uncle raised.

This, at least, is easily addressed, she thought.

"It will be much easier for my mother and sisters, as well as my Aunt and Uncle Philips, to attend in London than in Derbyshire. Beyond that, I have no preference." She looked her uncle in the eye. "There appears to be little cause to delay the ceremony unless Mr. Darcy has reasons of his own for waiting."

Mr. Gardiner looked at Darcy, who shrugged. "I am willing to do whatever Elizabeth desires, whether next month or tomorrow."

"There is no need to be in a rush, Lizzy," Mr. Gardiner offered gently.

Elizabeth's smile was brittle. "I do not think you take my point, uncle. After my father's letter, it would be a useless exercise to go back to Longbourn. For better or worse, my home henceforth will be with Mr. Darcy, and I see no reason not to begin my life there as soon as practicable."

Mr. Gardiner was silent as he digested that. "I had not thought of it from that point of view, Elizabeth. But I am reluctantly forced to agree with you." Darcy nodded in agreement.

"I see no reason why we should not be married in a week," she continued.

"Are you sure that you wish to be so hasty, Elizabeth?" Darcy said in surprise. "Surely you will want a wedding gown, which will have to be made and fitted. Your mother will, I am sure, wish to be involved with the selection of that and an appropriate wardrobe."

Mr. Gardiner was embarrassed as he said to Elizabeth, "I would guess your father informed you that he will allow no money for wedding clothes?" She nodded, and her uncle continued, "Mr. Darcy earlier offered to fund whatever purchases are required, Lizzy."

Elizabeth smiled sadly at Darcy. "That was generous of you, sir, and well meant, but it is hardly necessary. We both know that most brides are married in their Sunday best, and I could certainly do the same. There will be time for any additional purchases later, and I truly do not wish to delay the ceremony. While I love both my uncle and aunt, I have no desire to be a guest in their home for months with too much time to dwell on wrongs, both real and imagined. I would much prefer to be settled in my new home as soon as possible."

"Then it shall be as you wish, Elizabeth," Darcy said, understanding and sympathizing with her reasoning. "But I believe that a wedding gown can be made and fitted even within the week. Mr. Gardiner," he said, turning to her uncle, "might your wife assist my sister in helping Elizabeth? With knowledge of the right shops, I feel sure that her gown, and possibly other items, may be acquired within the set time."

"Certainly, Mr. Darcy. I am sure she will be pleased to assist."

"Thank you. Elizabeth," he said, turning to her, "as you are familiar with your uncle's church, would you feel comfortable being married there?"

"Oh, certainly. It is not a large church, but it is quite agreeable in appearance without being overly ornate. And Reverend Jackson would do very well to conduct the ceremony."

"Then I suggest we consider the location as settled. Might you make the arrangements, Mr. Gardiner? I assume a day or two's delay would not be objectionable in the case of a conflict. In addition, I shall change the instructions to my solicitor and have him arrange for a special license from the Archbishop, so that we may then be married whenever suitable preparations have been made."

All being agreeable, Mrs. Gardiner was sent for once again and was perfectly willing to assist her niece, but she did tell her that a single week was not realistic. "I believe that two to three weeks at least would be required, Lizzy. For example, it will take at least two weeks to sew and fit a wedding gown. Many items, like bonnets and gloves, would not have to be specially fitted, but the gowns certainly would be."

"But could they not be delivered after the wedding took place?" Elizabeth asked.

"Surely, my dear, but—"

"Aunt, I am really quite determined on this. I am caught in-between now—no longer a daughter and not yet a wife. Please understand—I want to go to *my* home as soon as may be. Whether I am married in my Sunday best or a brand new gown is of no import to me and, I suspect, of little import to Mr. Darcy." He nodded in agreement, squeezing her hand, which still remained clasped within his.

"Then perhaps we can agree on next Saturday unless there is a problem with the church?" said Elizabeth, and her aunt and uncle reluctantly consented. It was also arranged that Mrs. Gardiner would accompany Elizabeth to start her shopping the next afternoon, while her uncle would see to the church and Darcy would see to the legal requirements. Darcy also issued an invitation to dine at his house on Tuesday evening, which was quickly accepted.

After Mrs. Gardiner excused herself to return to her guests, Elizabeth and Darcy remained holding hands, sitting quietly together. Mr. Gardiner silently rose and left the room, closing the door gently behind him.

Elizabeth did not resist as Darcy gently pulled her arm toward him. She allowed herself to be drawn so that she sat on his lap while he folded her head to his chest. She welcomed the comfort of his arms as they wrapped around her, feeling the strength as they both held and consoled her.

"I am sorry about today, Elizabeth. I keep trying to think of something I could have said that might have changed your father's mind, but no explanation appeared to be enough. He seemed determined to thwart me at every turn."

"Let us forget about it, William," she said softly. "From what he wrote, my father already had his mind made up before you called. Just hold me for a while."

Darcy was well content as he held Elizabeth, his chin resting on top of her dark curls. But at the same time, he was quite frustrated since he had to struggle to keep his hands still on her back. He could feel her soft warmth beneath his fingers, and he longed to move one hand down her spine to her slim waist and the other up to her lovely, slender neck.

You can wait, he commanded himself, *in less than a week we will be married*. But another part of him asked, *And what then? Will you take this young bride to your marriage bed as if she desired the marriage as much as you? Will you ravish her when she does not even know what being a wife entails? Are you a beast or are you a man?* Darcy did not have a good answer for those inner voices, but he could control them. He would not hurt Elizabeth. He could wait.

He hoped.

After several minutes of silence, Darcy informed her that he had sent an announcement of their engagement to the *Times*. "It should ensure that the gossip goes no further. After our engagement is published, interest will die."

"It is so unfair," Elizabeth said. "What if it had not been you? What if you had not acted honourably? My reputation, indeed my life, might easily have been damaged forever!"

Darcy nodded. "I agree; it is not fair. In affairs such as these, women are far more vulnerable than are men. A scandal that might hardly affect a man can completely destroy a young woman's reputation. It is not fair, but it is the world we live in."

After a minute or so, Elizabeth had reason to think on some of what she had said today, and one part gave her pause. "William," she ventured tentatively, "I wonder now whether I was thinking clearly when I was so forceful in recommending a mere week before our marriage. Now I am wondering whether that will cause a problem because it is so quick."

Darcy chuckled. "Do not worry about that, Elizabeth. I shall simply tell the truth and say that I desired to be married as quickly as possible, else I should have carried you off to Gretna Green!"

Elizabeth giggled, though her cheeks turned red, for she knew that often the groom was most anxious to take his bride to his bed and therefore insistent on a brief period of time between receiving a girl's acceptance and having her in the church. She knew that Darcy desired the same, for she could almost feel the rigid self-control as she sat on his lap. Though she did not want to be totally rigid in forbidding him any liberties at all, she was grateful that he did not force her to decide on where and what to limit.

"Thank you, William," she said softly. "I really do desire to have things settled as soon as possible. The problem with my father was simply the last straw, which, when added to all the other turmoils of our acquaintance, makes me simply want to retreat to the safety and comfort of my home. But the home that I have always known can no longer offer me what I seek. I just want to retire to the security of our own family party as soon as I can, and if you were to suggest Gretna Green again, I should not protest very much!"

Neither of them said anything for several minutes, but eventually Elizabeth pushed herself up and got to her feet. As Darcy stood too, she suddenly rose to her tiptoes and gave him a quick kiss on his cheek. "Thank you," she said softly.

"And what did I do to deserve that?" he said with a smile. "For I shall be most diligent in doing it again."

"That was just for being you, for being so understanding, especially considering that I once thought you lost to all consideration for others. I have still so much to learn about you."

"Then here is one thing you should know, Miss Bennet," he said firmly. "The kiss you just gave me is your only free one. If you give me another, then I will definitely kiss you back."

"Truly, Mr. Darcy?" she said, with a gay laugh that warmed his heart.

"Truly, Miss Bennet," he growled at her.

Taking his arm, she gave him that wonderful smile he had once despaired of ever seeing directed his way. "Then I shall depend upon it, sir," she said before they opened the door to join the others.

As they entered the sitting room, Bingley and Jane sat with Fitzwilliam and Georgiana, and all were joined in general laughter as Fitzwilliam was obviously telling a joke. As Darcy watched Bingley, laughing with the others but glancing over at Jane and delighting in her laugh, he had to turn away suddenly.

"What now, William?" asked Elizabeth.

He looked aside for a moment, and then shrugged. Better to be straightforward, he thought, than to allow any more misconceptions between them.

"When I saw Bingley just now, I remembered a thought I had when I left his house on Sunday," he said sombrely. "I wondered at that time if I could have made a worse tangle of my affairs if I had actually set out with that as my objective."

It seemed as if so many things brought up some difficult recollection in this increasingly complex man, and that would require some study on her part, Elizabeth thought, but she had to laugh at this particular memory. "Come, come, Mr. Darcy. This will never do! If you will not accept my philosophy to remember the past only with pleasure, then you will simply have to stop remembering anything, especially if it is going to cause you to assume such disagreeable expressions."

"I am so pleased to have your assistance in telling him that, Elizabeth," said Georgiana suddenly, who had joined them in time to hear the last comment. "At times, William can be the most dour individual."

"I daresay," said Elizabeth gaily, turning to the younger girl. "It will surely take the two of us together to relieve such solemn spirits!"

Darcy winced as the two dearest persons in his life combined forces against him, but then he could not help but smile as his obvious discomfort made both of them erupt in new laughter. *It could have been so very much worse,* he thought in sudden contentment, as Elizabeth and Georgiana fell easily into cheerful conversation.

Chapter 17

Monday, April 20, 1812

D arcy was thoughtful as he sat with his sister in the parlour the next morning after breakfast, but she was quite cheerful, anticipating the coming visit by her new friends. Prior to their shopping excursion with Mrs. Gardiner, Jane and Elizabeth were to spend the morning with her in order that Elizabeth might see the house while he met with his solicitor. Obviously, any anxieties that Georgiana had previously entertained regarding his choice of wife had been relieved, and he smiled to hear her say how much she had enjoyed the previous evening.

"I believe that you approve of Elizabeth, dearest," he ventured.

"Oh, yes. She is so very nice." She coloured slightly. "I shall try to be more talkative this morning, but it is still difficult for me."

Darcy chuckled. "It is not so very much easier for me. Perhaps Elizabeth will help me as much as she helps you. We are both fortunate that I will not have to guide your entry into society without her aid."

Georgiana's good humour dimmed somewhat at the thought of her imminent coming out. "I am not looking toward that with any enthusiasm. I am not sure that I will be ready even a year from now."

He cocked an eyebrow at her. "I thought that, since you do not have to fear being guided by Miss Bingley, you would be filled with anticipation for that happy event," he teased.

"William, that is not funny," Georgiana said in exasperation. "The thought of being presented at court and then having to attend all the balls and parties is rather frightening—especially the dancing."

"Your dancing master says that you do quite excellently. He, at least, has no fear, and I have seen you myself."

She looked at him anxiously. "That was different. Those were at small parties of families and friends, and you and Richard are the only partners I have had. But what...what if no one else wants to dance with me?"

Darcy chuckled. "Georgie, the problem is not going to be dealing with an empty dance card but rather how to fit all the requests into a fixed number of spaces." He sighed in relief. "At least I will not have to try to weed out the fortune hunters all by myself. I daresay that Elizabeth could spot one as he entered the room every bit as fast as I could. Yes, I am indeed fortunate."

"That is another thing that distresses me. How can I tell? I know I am not beautiful like Elizabeth or Miss Bennet. If someone pays attention to me, how will I ever know whether he is after me or my fortune?"

Darcy patted her hand. "Do not talk like that, dearest, you are a lovely young woman already and will grow even more so. As for knowing a young man's intentions, I cannot say it will be easy. Just remember to take your time, listen to your own heart, and listen to Elizabeth and me—especially Elizabeth."

The sound of the knocker at the front door alerted him. "And now, I believe, your visitors have arrived."

As they waited for Elizabeth and Jane to be shown to the parlour, Darcy laid his hand on Georgiana's. "Georgiana," he said earnestly, "we have not spoken of this before, but do not feel that you are being forced into coming out next year. If you would prefer to wait, speak to me. I will not force you if you have reservations."

Her spirits much relieved, Georgiana quickly leaned forward to kiss his cheek. "Thank you."

ELIZABETH WAS CONSCIOUS OF A rising sense of excitement mixed with anxiety as the carriage rumbled through the streets on the way to Darcy's home. This would be her first glimpse of the house where she and William would live after they were married, and she was intensely curious.

William. She tasted that word in her mind, wondering at the newness of it and yet also wondering at how it seemed to suit him so very well. She had thought of him as 'Mr. Darcy' for so long that it seemed as if it ought to feel strange to call him anything else. Yet he already seemed so very much a 'William.' It was all very strange how so many things that would have seemed unthinkable just weeks ago were now becoming accepted and even expected in her own mind—such as living in the house she would be visiting today, of being mistress of Mr. Darcy's even larger estate in Derbyshire, of making her new home in those places and not returning to Longbourn except at some undefined time in the future when she would then be a visitor. Yet she was beginning to accept it, to expect it, and even to anticipate it. She felt a chill run down her spine at the intriguing thought of retiring each night to her own bedchamber where her husband might join her to claim his marital rights. She knew and accepted that such was only right and proper, but the thought of sharing her bed with another person, a man, and the mysterious things that they would do there was quite disconcerting.

And also quite exciting! She could not deny it despite her ignorance, and she felt yet another tingle run up and down her spine.

It was only a few minutes before their journey came to an end, and Elizabeth examined the exterior of the Darcys' house closely as she and Jane stepped down from the carriage. She had half feared that she would be living in a smaller version of Rosings, but that was not the case at all. Darcy House was one of several townhouses on the square, all appearing to have been built at the same time and of the same general fashion. It was larger than her uncle's house on Gracechurch Street, four stories in all, but not of especially elegant or ornate design. The outside was of fitted stone blocks, the windows were many and well sized. The door was made of heavy wood, carved but not elaborately so. It was impressive but not as impressive as she might have imagined.

The large metal knocker made a deep, reverberating sound and an older man in old-fashioned, formal dress opened the door and bowed to them as they entered.

"Good morning, ladies," he greeted them. "You are the Miss Bennets, I presume? Miss Georgiana is awaiting you in the parlour."

As he led them down the hall, Elizabeth took the opportunity to glance inside several rooms. One, obviously the library, had floor to ceiling shelves heavily laden with books, while another, dominated by a massive pianoforte, appeared to be dedicated to music. From what she was able to observe in passing, she could see that they were furnished with well-made and well-finished fixtures, and oriented more towards functionality and comfort than showy decoration.

Darcy was sitting with his sister when she and Jane were shown into the room, and both of them rose immediately. Georgiana preceded her brother, crossing to each girl to share a quick embrace and a kiss on the cheek, surprising Elizabeth with the warmth and familiarity of the greeting. Darcy waited for his sister to finish welcoming the guests, and when Elizabeth turned to him, she recognized the warmth and approval showing on his face. She could not tell, however, whether this was due to her own increased sensitivity and familiarity with him or whether he was simply expressing himself more openly in the familiar environs of his own home and family. Nonetheless, he welcomed her with a warm smile, bowing and raising her fingers to bestow the lightest of kisses on them. She smiled in return, cheered by his usual warmth and gallantry, and she could not help but wonder if this would be his normal reaction to her.

Surely, he will become more informal as we grow more accustomed to each other, she thought, *but in the meantime it is really quite nice to be treated in such a gallant manner.*

Life with this most complex and perplexing man promised many rewards as well as many challenges, and Elizabeth was certain that the coming months and years would be far from dull.

Darcy soon excused himself to keep his appointment with his solicitor, and the three ladies were left to themselves. After their conversation about music the previous night, Elizabeth was very interested in hearing Georgiana play and sing, but the younger girl suggested a tour of the house first and music later. Accordingly, the housekeeper, Mrs. Taylor, was summoned since Georgiana explained that her brother wanted Elizabeth to confer with her on any changes she might desire to make.

"I am very pleased to meet you both," the older woman responded with a curtsey before she turned to Elizabeth. "Miss Elizabeth, Mr. Darcy gave me explicit instructions to take the best care of you. He asked me to take special notice of any changes you might like to make in your own chambers."

"Thank you, Mrs. Taylor," Elizabeth responded with a smile, "I shall keep that in mind." But the taste and elegance of the few rooms she had seen was very much to her liking, and she expected the same from the rest, so she added, "I am not disposed to change for the sake of change, and since everything I have seen of the house thus far has been quite impressive, I believe that I shall take some time before I start recommending alterations."

Mrs. Taylor smiled back at the friendly young woman. She had worked for the Darcy family since she was a young girl, coming to the house after she married her Henry, then a very junior groom at Pemberley. She had been recognized over the years for her talents and sense, and after her husband's passing, she had become the housekeeper of Darcy's London house, a position of considerable prestige and trust. Confident of her position in the household, she nonetheless appreciated being treated with the dignity due that position. She also appreciated that Miss Elizabeth did not appear to be one of those elegant and fashionable ladies of society who treated the staff like serfs. Many of *those* ladies would have jumped at the opportunity to completely redecorate the house in order to put her own stamp on it.

Elizabeth was greatly interested as Georgiana showed them through the various public rooms of the house and then took them upstairs to show the private areas. Her first stop was the room intended to be Elizabeth's new sleeping chamber, and, as she had expected, it was very much to her liking.

"I understand that it has been little changed since my mother's death," Georgiana told them, "though I really cannot remember. I was only five when she died."

"It is perfectly delightful," said Elizabeth, and Jane echoed her sentiments. The walls were a light green, trimmed with wood and wallpaper that, when Elizabeth looked closer, appeared to be in much better condition than was likely for a room that had not been used in more than ten years. Mrs. Taylor smiled as she observed Elizabeth's close inspection, and she offered, "The rooms were cleaned up and readied for use earlier this year at the master's direction." She smiled at the other's quizzical expression. "When we received that unusual request, I suppose we should have realized that the master's attention had been captured by some young lady, but none of us at the time suspected anything."

Georgiana and Jane both smiled at Elizabeth's sudden blush, but she said nothing as she entered the dressing area. "It is not only more elegant, but also much larger than I had expected," she said to her sister. She pointed at the extensive closet, which was easily large enough to hold scores of dresses.

"I cannot imagine ever needing so much room."

"I suspect that you will need to purchase a good many more dresses than you know, Elizabeth," Georgiana said slyly from behind her. "And I volunteer to be your guide to make sure you know all the best shops!" The three ladies laughed gaily and continued their tour in good humour.

Mrs. Taylor was pleased by the ease and liveliness of the young Miss Elizabeth as she accompanied the ladies on their tour. She had obviously formed a bond of friendship with Miss Georgiana, and her sister was equally polite and pleasant. Her opinion of the future Mrs. Darcy, at least on first meeting, was favourable. The lady seemed to possess both sense and manners, though it would take more experience to make a full judgment. After receiving her instructions from Mr. Darcy that morning, she had been consumed with curiosity to meet the young lady who had attracted the master's interest and who would be the mistress of his household. Her character was also a matter of great interest among the staff though Mrs. Taylor was determined to ensure that interest never degraded into speculation and gossip. This was, after all, the *Darcy* household, and such unseemly behaviour was not countenanced.

When they had finished the tour of the house and released Mrs. Taylor to her other duties, Georgiana ordered tea sent to the music room. There she consented to play for Elizabeth and Jane, after which she successfully enticed the sisters to take their own turns, and the morning passed most pleasantly.

While Georgiana sat with Elizabeth at the pianoforte playing the parts of a duet for Jane's amusement, a knock sounded at the door and Colonel Fitzwilliam entered.

"Miss Bennet and Miss Elizabeth," he said, bowing to each lady, "we meet again and so soon. Stevens told me that Georgie had company, but I certainly did not know you both were here."

Turning back to Elizabeth and lowering his voice to a stage whisper so that all could hear, he said teasingly, "I hope you are making sure that Georgie is getting her full measure of practice, Miss Elizabeth. You *know* how Lady Catherine worries that she may slacken off, and she was *most* insistent that Darcy should ensure she practices every day!"

Georgiana giggled, "Richard, stop that! You have been using Lady Catherine to scare me for years, and I must admit that I thought her quite fearsome. But now that Elizabeth is here, that will no longer work; she has promised to protect me when my aunt next comes to visit."

"And so she shall, Cousin, for she is quite fearless," said Fitzwilliam, sitting down with the ladies. "I watched with considerable amusement as she would listen to Lady Catherine's many suggestions, so often offered without pause for hours on end, and then respond by offering a contrary point of view in a manner that quite disconcerted her ladyship. Darcy and I have for years simply listened to my aunt's many pronouncements without response, preferring avoidance rather than challenge, but Miss Elizabeth would have none of that!"

"Colonel Fitzwilliam!" Elizabeth laughed. "You make me sound positively formidable, and I have been trying to impress Georgiana with my amiability. You shall leave her quite confused, I am sure."

"But you *are* formidable," responded Fitzwilliam cheerfully. "Have you not shown yourself equally adept at dealing with Georgiana's most *impetuous* brother?" Georgiana giggled at this comment, which made Elizabeth glance at her curiously. Obviously, the cousins were sharing a private joke, but her curiosity was soon forgotten as Fitzwilliam's usual intelligent and amiable conversation quickly moved to other topics. He soon begged Elizabeth and Georgiana to play for him, lamenting that all too soon the both of them would be spirited off to the wilds of Derbyshire, leaving none to entertain a penniless and friendless colonel of the horse cavalry. Georgiana giggled again, and she and Elizabeth played several pieces for him, some together and others singly, all to effusive compliments from Fitzwilliam and more restrained, but no less admiring, praise from Jane. At last, as they finished a particularly difficult piece without any major errors, the general compliments were supplemented by a hearty round of applause from the doorway.

Twisting around on the bench, Georgiana and Elizabeth saw that Darcy and Bingley had come into the room while they were playing, observing silently from the doorway until they finished.

"Bravo! Well done indeed," said Darcy with one of his rare smiles that Elizabeth was coming to appreciate more, especially as they seemed mostly directed her way. She could not help but be pleased that she appeared to have such a beneficial effect on her future husband, as it promised much for the future. Bingley quickly crossed to Jane and seated himself by her while Darcy sat on the couch beside Colonel Fitzwilliam.

"It appears that your morning has passed agreeably," said Darcy, pleased and encouraged by the cheerfulness and lack of restraint he had already observed in his sister.

"Very much so, sir," said Elizabeth. "Your sister has been a most charming hostess. And you were quite right in your description of her talents. She has both skill and a feel for the music that makes her presentation a complete delight." Georgiana flushed slightly, pleased by the compliment but uncomfortable at being the centre of attention. Elizabeth noticed this and leaned over to clasp her hand. "Though we shall have to teach her to accept compliments with more grace, for she shall certainly be most effusively praised when more people have the opportunity to hear her!" This made Georgiana blush furiously, pleased and apprehensive at the same time, but Elizabeth gave her hand another squeeze, drawing at least a slight smile from the shy girl.

"And where have you taken yourself off to this fine morning, Darcy?" queried Fitzwilliam.

"Bingley and I visited my solicitor to consult on marriage agreements and the special license for myself and Elizabeth. Bingley shall soon be preparing for his own wedding, though he has more time at his disposal." Suddenly he realized that Fitzwilliam was ignorant of the problems with Elizabeth's father. "I believe that I have not informed you that a date has been settled on. We shall be married on this coming Saturday."

Fitzwilliam grinned hugely. "Capital, my good cousin, simply capital! Precipitate to the last, I see!"

Elizabeth was amazed to see Darcy blush a deep red. She looked curiously at him, but her attention was drawn to Fitzwilliam, who leaned forward to ask her slyly, "Perhaps you might like to take a walk with me in the garden while Darcy recovers, and I can play the part of a helpful cousin to give you some background on the *impulsive* Darcy family. It is information that you will very much need to know in the trying years to come!"

"Fitzwilliam!" growled Darcy, but his cousin's smile did not falter, and Darcy closed his eyes in exasperation.

"Will you relent, Cousin?" he asked, but the colonel only shook his head. "Very well, then," Darcy sighed. He had hoped to tell this to Elizabeth in a more confidential setting, but he could see that was not to be. Even Bingley and Jane were interested as he began, "You may have noticed, Elizabeth, that Richard quite enjoys teasing me. You have probably also noticed that both my sister and myself tend to be somewhat reticent. It might have been different if my mother had lived, but even then it might have turned out much the same. We Darcys," he smiled, "are not known to be great conversationalists."

"However," he said with a warning glance at Fitzwilliam, who appeared ready to interject a comment, "we Darcys are also known, at least among the family, to be somewhat...impulsive. My cousin enjoys relating the story of how my father courted my mother as an example of how...unconventional...the Darcy side can be, when in so many other respects we are the opposite."

Elizabeth coloured slightly but said nothing as Darcy sat back in his chair and continued. "My father first met my mother when he visited the home of a friend from Cambridge, the elder son of the Earl of Matlock and the present holder of that title. My father was a young man of five and twenty, but my mother was then only sixteen and not yet out in society. He immediately—"

"And impulsively!" interjected Fitzwilliam.

"—lost his heart to her, and after considering the matter for a few hours, determined to speak to her father that very day. That very daunting person was considerably shocked and more than a little affronted when my father informed him of his feelings and of his intention to offer marriage to his daughter at a future date when it would be acceptable. Then, since she was not to be presented for some two years, he further informed the earl that he was cognizant of the fact that any attentions on his part at the present time would be wholly unacceptable, therefore he would immediately remove himself from their home. The family was upset, and some thought was given to ordering their son to sever the acquaintance, but, since the Darcy family was wealthy and prominent, it was decided to let the matter lie and act as events unfolded.

"My father thus did not see my mother for two years. Then, on the day following her coming out, he again presented himself to the earl and confirmed his intention to seek my mother's hand in marriage. The earl, though considerably surprised by his most unconventional approach, was reluctantly impressed by his constancy and determination. At length he assented to allow him to plead his suit, but he informed my father that he would not yet allow my mother to respond, since she was only then starting her first season. Accordingly, he accompanied my father to his daughter's presence, where my father formally offered his hand and then went away unanswered as previously determined.

"My mother then enjoyed the various events attendant on a young girl's season, and my father had numerous occasions to see her in society, for he immersed himself in the social life which he normally avoided. My mother had several requests from young men to court her, and her family induced her to accept one particularly eligible gentleman. The courtship lasted for three months, when the man eventually made an offer, but she politely declined. She later told my father that she had already decided to accept his offer when he should be allowed to make it again. She evidently had no doubt of his dependability. Eventually, at the end of the season and with the other connection ended, my father was allowed to pursue her."

Darcy smiled as he glanced over at Elizabeth. "The courtship lasted a grand total of three days, at which time he again tendered his offer, she accepted, and the earl's consent was somewhat reluctantly given. It was, you see, a good but not a splendid match."

Elizabeth, interested but not sure how to interpret this information, at length was moved to a teasing mood. "I suppose, sir, that this history is offered as evidence of the eccentricities of the Darcy family?"

Darcy smiled at her. "It is rather offered as an example of the lengths to which we Darcys will go to achieve a desirable goal."

To this response, Elizabeth could not help but laugh, which was joined by the whole party, especially Colonel Fitzwilliam.

Chapter 18

Monday, April 20, 1812

Darcy had returned home the previous night to find a reply from Lord Matlock that he and his wife would be available at one o'clock the next afternoon. He spent the morning working his way through his back correspondence, and when the clock struck twelve, he sent word to Johnson that he would be leaving immediately. He then went in search of his cousin, finding him sitting in the rear garden with Georgiana and the two Miss Bennets, all of whom were laughing at one of his stories. Darcy was never able to determine to what degree his cousin mixed truth and fiction in the tales of his many and varied exploits in the service of his King, but he did know that he could not have survived to that date if even a quarter of them were to be believed.

"I am sorry to interrupt yet another sterling saga, Richard," he said as he entered the garden, "but I must borrow you immediately if we are to reach your parent's home by one."

"But Darcy, I was just getting to the climax! You cannot force me to leave the ladies in suspense, man!"

"Ladies," Darcy said firmly, "you must excuse us. I am sure he will finish his tale at another date. Of course, it is possible that his continuation will bear no resemblance to what he has related thus far, possibly because he makes it up as he goes along. But that you shall have to judge for yourself."

"William," Georgiana laughed, "do not speak so of our cousin. If he had not been a younger son and thus unable to buy more than a lieutenant's commission, he would undoubtedly be a general by now!"

"You see?" said Fitzwilliam, rising to his feet and preventing his sword from clattering with the instinctive motion of one who has worn the weapon daily for more than ten years. "At least one of the Darcy family appreciates my service to my sovereign!"

In truth, Darcy knew that Fitzwilliam's service had indeed been valuable, because he knew that his father, Lord Matlock, had actually offered to buy his son a majority at seventeen and a colonelcy at twenty, but Richard had refused, accepting only a lieutenant's commission. His subsequent promotions had been gained through merit, and he had seen a goodly share of action on the continent, in Spain and the Netherlands. But Fitzwilliam did not voice that aloud in gentle society, preferring to pose as a gentleman soldier rather than the experienced professional he was.

"Sweetling," Darcy leaned over to kiss Georgiana on the cheek, "enjoy yourself this afternoon. Remember, I am depending on you to make sure that Elizabeth purchases what is needed. If I am any judge of her character, I predict that she will protest that she surely does not need so much and will be quite reluctant to spend my money. I hope you will be able to convince her of the futility of such a course." Elizabeth looked at him in confusion, for his face was perfectly serious, and it was only the stifled giggle from Georgiana that let her know the unpredictable Darcy was teasing her.

"Mr. Darcy!" she exclaimed. "If you do not stop this immediately, we shall have to reveal to the world that you actually *do* have a sense of humour!" Georgiana laughed aloud, and Darcy gave a slow smile while Elizabeth considered him with her chin cupped in her hand and one finger tapping on her cheek. "It is a warped and droll sense of humour, to be sure, but I am sure you will not be allowed in any of your clubs once it is made generally known," she said with a solemnity equal to his own.

Darcy threw up his hands. "I surrender, madam! I should have known not to joust with you, and I yield the field to attend to family duties." He turned to Fitzwilliam, "Richard, we must be off before I decide that my chances with your parents would be improved if I left you behind."

Fitzwilliam laughed in good humour before both men bade the ladies farewell.

As DARCY AND HIS COUSIN entered the small sitting room where Lord and Lady Matlock sat at tea, he could only hope that this interview would go more favourably than his meeting with Mr. Bennet. During the drive, he had acquainted Fitzwilliam of that uncomfortable session, and his cousin had clucked in disapproval at Mr. Bennet's thoughtlessness.

But now Darcy had to deal with this interview, and as he greeted his uncle and aunt, he was unable to predict their reaction. Lord Matlock took seriously his position as head of the family, and he had often urged Darcy to have a care when choosing a wife, paying attention to both fortune and the connections of her family. He had at times remarked that Anne De Bourgh would fit those categories handsomely, but he had not urged her selection with any great fervency. His wife was more of a possible ally than her husband even though she herself came from a wealthy and landed family. Her good sense and optimistic nature had proved invaluable in raising the four Fitzwilliam brothers, three still living, and the single Fitzwilliam sister, all of them inheriting in full their father's decisive and dominant nature.

No wonder Richard has made a good soldier, thought Darcy, *and no wonder his brother Henry had made a considerable name for himself as a captain of one of His Majesty's frigates. Their competitive family life well prepared them for open warfare with the French.*

When both Darcy and Fitzwilliam had been served tea, Darcy addressed his uncle. "Sir, I have the honour to inform you that I am engaged to be married."

Lord Matlock paused with his cup part way to his mouth. "Indeed? I have heard nothing. This is rather surprising."

"What else could be expected?" murmured Fitzwilliam, and Darcy did not even let his irritation show. He had expected nothing else, and it was at least a relief that no part of the gossip in the paper had spread to Matlock.

"Who is the young lady?" asked his more practical aunt.

"She is Miss Elizabeth Bennet, the daughter of a landowner in Hertford-shire. I met her when I was visiting my friend Bingley last autumn."

"Oh, yes, I remember Mr. Bingley," said Lady Matlock. "A very cheery young man. I just read that he was also newly engaged; to who was it…" Her eyes widened as she made the connection.

"Yes, to Miss Jane Bennet, Elizabeth's sister."

"How extraordinary," said Lady Matlock, pouring herself another cup of tea.

Her husband frowned. "I do not know of this young lady, Darcy. But I remember that a friend remarked of the announcement of Bingley's engagement that his intended had no fortune and her family was completely unknown."

Darcy nodded. "That is true. Her father is a gentleman who owns a small estate, and Miss Elizabeth is essentially undowered."

"A fortune hunter, then," Lord Matlock stated firmly.

He was startled by the hoot of laughter from his son. "Hardly, Father." Fitzwilliam laughed. "I assure you, nothing could be further from the truth!"

The frown never left Lord Matlock's face as he turned his attention to his bewildering son. "I know of no way in which you could be sure, Richard," he said sternly. "I remember one of my friends at Cambridge was engaged to the most charming young lady, came from a good family, everything looked perfect. Only shortly before the marriage did it come out that her father had essentially gambled away the family fortune and that the daughter was desperately trying to secure my friend's wealth through marriage. But he would not believe it and married the lady, only to find out the truth when it was too late. An utter disaster—she sucked him dry."

"Father," his son said, leaning forward and fixing his lordship's gaze. "I cannot speak of the details, for it is a private matter, and you will have to take my word on this, but I know that such is not the case for Miss Elizabeth. I told Georgiana as much yesterday."

Lord Matlock looked at his son in consideration, but was disturbed by a soft laugh from his wife. "Give it up, James. If you had to pick a man to judge a woman's heart, you could do much worse than your son. And, in any case, it does not matter. Look at Darcy! Can you not see it in his eyes? After all these years, he has at last made a choice to marry. He is eight and twenty, after all. If he does not marry the woman of his choosing, he may well not marry at all."

"Of course, he will marry," said Lord Matlock. "He must, to secure an heir for the Darcy fortune."

"Georgiana could provide an heir as easily as I," said Darcy. "And I might submit that I need neither fortune nor name from the woman I marry, for I have a sufficiency of both. I will further offer that I would rather not marry than to marry without love, and Miss Elizabeth is the only young woman

I have ever loved or likely will."

"Believe him, father," offered Fitzwilliam. "I know the lady, and she is indeed a good match for him in the qualities that truly matter."

Lord Matlock looked at his son closely and he appeared to be completely serious, with none of his customary irony in his demeanour. At last, his lordship said, "Perhaps you are right, son. But even if you are, there still remains the matter of Anne. The assumption in the family has long been that only Anne's health prevented her marriage to Darcy. How will she take this?"

"She already knows, or at least has guessed," said Fitzwilliam.

Darcy nodded. "I assure you that Anne will not be hurt by this. She and I have spoken many times of Lady Catherine's fixed and oft-repeated determination that we marry, but that determination is my aunt's alone. Neither Anne nor I have ever desired a closer attachment than cousin, but we did not openly dispute it in order to avoid overt disagreement."

"A wise thought," murmured Fitzwilliam, "I could escape to Spain and have only Bonaparte's legions to deal with. Scotland would not be far enough for you to escape our aunt's wrath."

Lady Matlock had to stifle a smile, her amusement stirred by both her son's irreverence and her husband's predictable glare directed toward that same son.

"I have dispatched letters to my other relatives, including Lady Catherine," Darcy continued, "and the engagement will be announced in the *Times*. I have no doubt that my aunt will be upset, and I considered travelling to Rosings to inform her in person. I decided against it due to my belief that she would not refrain from openly abusing Elizabeth. This I absolutely will not tolerate, which would result in an open rupture of our relationship."

Lord Matlock made no response to this, because, while he loved his sister, he could not deceive himself about her temperament. She was so used to getting her own way that she would indeed do just as Darcy predicted. An open insult of that sort could not be ignored, and Darcy was likely correct in his estimation of the result.

For his part, Darcy had decided against mentioning either the gossip at Rosings that had prompted this chain of events or the published item in the *Chronicle*. He anticipated the announcement in the *Times* would be sufficient to kill any further interest in that disreputable organ.

"Uncle, I will be hosting a small dinner party tomorrow night for the

Miss Bennets, their family, and Bingley. I would be honoured if you and my aunt would attend."

Lord Matlock was reluctant to accede to this request. He knew nothing of the lady beyond his son's assurances, and he was desirous of a private talk with Richard before accepting an invitation that would be tantamount to official approval of the match. While he was trying to phrase his rejection, however, his wife disturbed his thoughts.

"James," she said softly, putting her hand on his arm and leaning closer. "Remember, it is Darcy's choice here—not ours."

"But Sophie, if we attend, it will be the same as saying that we approve of the match, and I am not sure I am ready to do so at this time."

His wife just looked at him, not saying anything, but thirty years of marriage enabled him to read her thoughts as clearly as if she had spoken them aloud. At length, he sighed in defeat. "Very well, Darcy, we would be pleased to attend."

"Thank you," said Darcy in relief. "Would seven o'clock be convenient?"

"Quite convenient. We will see you then. Richard, if you would be so good as to stay behind, I will provide transportation to return you to Darcy's house later."

"Certainly, Father," Fitzwilliam responded easily, turning his head to give Darcy a wink where his father could not see. "I will see you later in the evening, Cousin."

Darcy bid the three of them farewell, somewhat troubled knowing his uncle's purpose, but that matter would have to be left to Richard's discretion.

Mrs. Gardiner called on Darcy's townhouse shortly after the gentlemen left in order to assist Elizabeth in ordering a new gown for her wedding. She was doubtful that the task could be accomplished in the available time, but she suggested that they might go first to one of her own favourite shops. Georgiana was reluctant to contradict Mrs. Gardiner, but the older woman recognized that she had something to offer and was quick to solicit her opinion.

"I think I know a shop that might complete Elizabeth's gown in time," she said timidly. "I have had several dresses made there, and I know that others have commissioned dresses in very short periods of time."

When she named the shop, Mrs. Gardiner was familiar with it. "I have heard of them, but they are frightfully expensive for even the most ordinary items."

"My brother was adamant that Elizabeth should spend as much as she needed," offered Georgiana triumphantly. "And he said I should ignore her protests against it!"

Mrs. Gardiner laughed as Elizabeth turned red and looked away. "That does sound like Elizabeth. We must be careful to follow your brother's advice, Miss Darcy."

The owner of the shop recognized Georgiana immediately, and upon being informed that Elizabeth was to marry Mr. Darcy on Saturday and that a new gown was desired in time for the wedding, was most insistent that the task could be accomplished in time.

"If a suitable dress and fabric can be selected today," he told them, "I can have the gown ready for a first fitting on Wednesday evening and a final fitting on Thursday. We will have it delivered to your hands by no later than Friday afternoon."

Elizabeth started to ask how expensive this would be, but her aunt stopped her by laying her hand on her arm. Georgiana was obviously in her element when shopping for clothes, and she quickly arranged with the owner for a room to be set aside for the ladies and a variety of different styles and materials made available for their perusal. Georgiana also gave instructions that all bills were to be sent to her brother, and that all necessary accoutrements — stays, chemise, stockings, garters, and slippers — were to be included. The owner was solicitous and quickly escorted the ladies to a room with several couches and low tables where they made themselves comfortable while the various selections were prepared.

Soon, a procession of different dress styles and materials were presented for their inspection. Tea was served as the seemingly unending stream of choices left Elizabeth quickly bewildered by the variety. But Georgiana and Mrs. Gardiner made an alliance, recommending certain dresses and materials be left for examination while others were rejected as unsuitable. Elizabeth was inclined towards simplicity of style, and that was taken into account, but Georgiana proved an excellent judge of what was currently fashionable while Mrs. Gardiner proved an equally excellent judge of what styles would be most flattering on Elizabeth. Georgiana was unwavering that the cost of materials or sewing was of no significance for her new sister, and she would not even allow the subject to be brought up.

Soon a common ground between Georgiana's fashion-oriented suggestions and Elizabeth's desire for simplicity was found, and by four o'clock, an elegant gown to be made up in pale green silk had finally been selected. By five o'clock, all arrangements were complete, appointments made for fittings, and the carriage had been summoned. Before it was a quarter past the hour, the ladies were clattering back toward Darcy House, leaving Elizabeth feeling totally overwhelmed by the whole experience.

"I feel more exhausted than if I walked all the way back to Longbourn," she complained. "I only sat on a couch and sipped tea and watched other people bring in items for my inspection, and I am completely done in!"

Georgiana laughed. "It was rather a whirlwind, but at least our task is accomplished. Or, at least," she said slyly, "our main task, your wedding gown, is accomplished. Now we shall have to shop for the other things you will need to fill up your closet."

"Georgiana," Elizabeth pleaded, "have mercy! I am overwhelmed, and I demand that we do no more shopping for at least one day. Else I shall have to talk to your brother about Gretna Green!"

"But Elizabeth, you will need to shop for Pemberley also," Georgiana teased. "It gets very cold in Derbyshire, and you will need fur-lined gloves, boots, cloaks, and bonnets, as well as any number of evening gowns for the opera, the theatre, balls, and dinners."

"Gretna Green, Georgiana!" Elizabeth threatened, to general laughter in the carriage.

Chapter 19

Darcy arrived at Gracechurch Street on Tuesday at one o'clock to keep the appointment he had arranged with Mr. Gardiner to review the wedding agreements drafted by his solicitor. As he was shown in to Mr. Gardiner's study, Elizabeth was sitting with her uncle waiting for him, and as usual, he felt his heart turn over in his chest when she smiled at him in greeting. He was still so new to actually seeing a true light of welcome on her face that each new occasion gave him a thrill of excitement and a chill of disaster narrowly averted.

Mr. Gardiner sent for coffee for himself and Darcy as well as tea for Elizabeth before he turned to the rough draft of the wedding agreements that Darcy handed him. He went through the documents quickly while Darcy and Elizabeth waited quietly. He was impressed with the clarity of the documents, with Darcy's generosity, and with the completeness of his preparations, especially for a rough draft. Elizabeth's personal income—what his sister inelegantly referred to as 'pin money'—was quite generous, and provisions were made for the dowry of any daughters and the income of any sons prior to their majority. There were provisions for any children in the event of a death of either husband or wife and for the inheritance of the estate—to the eldest son, if there were sons, or to the management of the eldest daughter otherwise, to then be inherited by her eldest son. He continued through the documents, ticking off the items: income for Elizabeth after the estate was inherited, remarriage of either spouse after the death of the other, management of the estate if Darcy died before the heir was five and thirty. At length, Mr. Gardiner put the documents down and inspected the young man across from him with enhanced respect.

"This is very impressive, Mr. Darcy," he said earnestly. "Not only are the terms most generous to my niece, but, more importantly, they are quite complete. I must compliment you, sir. I have seen many families torn apart because the proper arrangements were not made in language clear enough to prevent misinterpretation." Darcy thanked him, and the three of them huddled around his desk as Mr. Gardiner set out to review the document with Elizabeth.

The first item he discussed was her dowry—her share of her mother's fortune of five thousand pounds when her father died. Darcy's documents made no mention of this dowry since Mr. Bennet had not mentioned it in his letters. Mr. Gardiner indicated that whether or not Elizabeth ever received it was completely at her father's discretion in his will. However, she was amazed at the income provided by Darcy.

"So much, William?" she asked in bewilderment. "Why should I ever need so much?"

He smiled. "It is not inappropriate to our station in life, Elizabeth. There will be expenses you have not considered, and it would not do for you to have to ask me for funds every time a new dress is needed. The solicitor set down the values"—he pointed out the section in the document—"and I can assure you that the sum for clothing alone is only slightly larger than what is available for Georgiana. I think your uncle understands the calculations."

Mr. Gardiner agreed. "It is generous, Lizzy, but it does not appear inappropriate for Mr. Darcy's fortune, which is, I would estimate," he said dryly, "to be rather more substantial than what is widely advertised."

"Please, sir," Darcy said with a wince. "What was bandied about was enough to have every mother in London busy pushing her daughters in my direction since I was of marriageable age!"

"I am sure." Mr. Gardiner smiled. Elizabeth looked at Darcy with wonderment. She was suddenly conscious of just how widely their spheres actually differed, and she was struck anew by the incongruity of his choosing her from all the many daughters who were dangled before him, every one of those daughters more than willing to accede to his every suggestion and to flatter him at every opportunity. How he could have rejected all those agreeable and acquiescent girls and chosen an impertinent creature like herself was a complete mystery.

As her uncle continued the review, she was further surprised by the complexity and the completeness of all the provisions. By the time he finished, she felt overwhelmed by all the detail. "I confess I had never considered all the possibilities that had to be provided for," she said. "It seems complete to me, but I must rely on your advice, Uncle. Are you satisfied?"

"With the general intent of the document, yes," he said seriously. "While I have some suggestions regarding specific language, the areas covered are as comprehensive as I think possible. To start, this statement could use a modest change to make sure there is no confusion. If I might suggest..."

The three spent half an hour discussing areas in which Mr. Gardiner and sometimes Elizabeth had questions, some of which occasioned an adjustment of language in order to make the intent perfectly clear and remove any ambiguity. At the end, Darcy thanked them and said that he would have his solicitor incorporate the revisions before returning the documents for Mr. Gardiner's signature.

Darcy was disinclined to leave immediately and toyed with the idea of asking Elizabeth to take a walk, but he had to have the draft documents back to his solicitor as soon as possible for the final copies to be drawn up. So reluctantly, he made his farewell to her uncle while Elizabeth accompanied him down the stairs to the front door. He turned around to tell her goodbye, standing on the floor by the door while she remained on the first step, and he was astonished as she leaned forward suddenly to give him a quick kiss on the cheek.

He looked at her while she looked back, merriment dancing in her eyes, and he smiled slowly. "I did warn you, Miss Bennet," he said softly as he reached out for her. She did not pull back as one arm slid around her waist and the other around her back as he pulled her close, though she did nervously lick her lips with the tip of her tongue. Even though she stood on the first step, he was still taller than she was, and she watched him as he lowered his mouth to hers.

At the first touch of the exquisite softness of her lips, Darcy felt the most sublime sense of completion come over him as his mouth claimed hers, and their kiss deepened as he pulled her fully against him. He felt her hands come up to grasp his lapels as his right hand explored the wonderful slimness of her waist, marvelling at the beautiful symmetry of her figure and the warmth and softness of her flesh under her dress. He felt her kiss him back, and a thrill went down his spine as dreams that he had despaired of ever seeing fulfilled were finally realized. He opened his mouth as he kissed her even deeper, pressing harder against her yielding lips, feeling her respond, and his left hand came up to the back of her slender neck to stroke his fingers along her velvety soft skin. She raised her arms and put them around his neck, pulling him down to her, urging him on, and he felt her shiver as his tongue slipped into her open mouth, caressing those yielding lips from the inside. At last, he lessened the pressure, gradually pulling back, though he still nibbled her lower lip with his own lips and tongue while he felt her quiver again. Finally, he drew back completely, seeing her eyes half-closed, and the thought that she could feel passion for him, when added to his own desire for her, made him suddenly long to explore all the hidden secrets of her body right there in her uncle's entry.

I can wait, he told himself firmly, pulling her close in an embrace, and tucking her head on his shoulder while his hand stroked the silky softness of her hair. He felt her quickened breath slow to its normal rate though his own breathing was far from even.

"Elizabeth," he murmured into her hair, drawing in the clean scent of her with just the slightest hint of perfume. *If she only knew how much I want to pull out her hairpins and let that mass of curls fall naturally to her shoulders, she would flee up the stairs this moment.*

"I almost believe that I am dreaming when I think that we shall be married in just four days," he said softly. "I am the most fortunate of men." The tickle of her warm breath on his neck was exhilarating, as was the feel of the slim line of her back as his hand moved slowly up and down its length from waist to shoulders. Finally, regretfully, he loosened his hold on her and stepped back to look into her eyes. They were no longer half-closed, they were wide open and sparkling, and the hint of a smile on her lovely face was such that Darcy determined that he must somehow capture that look in a portrait.

"I told you that I would depend on it, sir," she said lightly, and he laughed as he leaned forward to kiss her forehead.

"I must go, but I do thank you for your faith in my promise. I look forward to seeing you tonight."

"Yes, tonight." She suddenly looked worried.

"What is it? Surely you cannot be feeling any anxiety about meeting my uncle and aunt?"

"But your uncle *is* Lady Catherine's brother, is he not? I suppose I fear that he will be like her."

"He is not. Remember, *your* uncle is your mother's brother, and he is completely unlike *her*, is he not?"

"True, true." She sighed. "Poor Mama."

"Elizabeth, please do not take this badly, but I met your mother in the hallway at Longbourn after leaving my disastrous meeting with your father, and I found that mere silliness was a refreshing contrast and actually quite welcome."

"Yes." She sighed again. "Poor Papa. I thought that at least I could depend on him. Perhaps I should have sent a letter with you, but I confess I never anticipated the need."

"Nor did I." He chuckled. "And not a single prepared note anywhere on my person!"

She laughed lightly, and at that, he departed with one last look at her standing on the step, still with that delightful little smile on her face.

Dinner that night began most agreeably with Lord and Lady Matlock greeting their future niece and her relations with grace and civility. However, shortly after the parties sat down to table, that most decidedly changed. The first intimation came as Darcy heard the sound of raised voices clearly though the closed dining room door. He frowned, pausing with his soup spoon partway to his mouth as he listened

Soon the raised voices grew louder, obviously coming down the hall, and his concern was instantly replaced by alarm. Quickly putting his silverware down, he excused himself abruptly. A sharp rapping sound was clearly audible as he strode toward the door, but he was not yet halfway to it when it suddenly flew open. Every eye in the room turned to see Lady Catherine de Bourgh framed in the doorway with Darcy's butler visible behind her, almost wringing his hands in agitation.

Darcy stopped dead still, He realized the sharp sound in the hall had been her ladyship's walking stick slamming in anger against the wood floor. Displeasure was obvious in her face. Clearly, she was enraged beyond anything Darcy had ever seen, having pushed her way past Stevens, ignoring his attempts to waylay her until he could announce her arrival.

"Darcy!" Lady Catherine cried in a ringing, strident voice. "I have come to talk to you this instant, and I will not be gainsaid by that lackey at your door!"

"Lady Catherine," Darcy said coldly, trying to control his anger at her complete breach of decorum, "I have guests at table, and you will remember proper manners or you will leave."

But his aunt was past the point of remembering manners or being able to read the understated threat in his voice. "I will not be ordered about! I will talk with you immediately; do you hear? Immediately!" Her voice grew even higher and shriller. She suddenly saw Elizabeth still sitting at the table and pointed her stick. "And that woman! How could you? How could you forget yourself for that...that fortune hunter!"

Elizabeth was shocked by the cold fury evident on her face.

Can nothing between William and me ever be calm and simple, she wondered, but that was quickly followed by, *How could I ever have thought William was like this woman?*

At that point, Stevens had emerged from behind Lady Catherine. "I am sorry, sir. I told her ladyship that you were at dinner and asked her to wait in your study while I informed you of her arrival. But she demanded to see you at once and shoved her way past me. I was unable to dissuade her from interrupting your dinner."

"That is quite all right, Stevens. I do not expect that my staff should have to physically manhandle members of my family who appear to have forgotten all good manners. That will be all." Stevens bowed and vanished back through the door.

"And now, Lady Catherine," Darcy turned back with a glare, "we *will* proceed to my study instead of continuing this unseemly display in front of my guests." His voice made it clear that he would brook no dispute. Lady Catherine glared at him and then glared at Elizabeth, appearing as if she indeed intended to argue the point right there, but, after a moment, she nodded jerkily and left the room, her walking stick resuming its harsh clatter. Darcy followed, closing the door behind him.

Elizabeth looked around the table. Shock and mortification was universally displayed on the faces of the others. Lord Matlock's face was flushed dark red. "Disgraceful, just disgraceful," he mumbled in embarrassment since Lady Catherine was his own sister, after all. Georgiana was visibly upset, and Lady Matlock spoke quietly to her. The others were just sitting, looking down and saying nothing. The previously enjoyable conversation had been totally destroyed by the shocking display.

Elizabeth thought about Darcy confronting his angry aunt, and she suddenly knew where her place was—where she *had* to be. She rose and excused herself, though it was unlikely that anyone heard her. By that time, Bingley had come around the table and had knelt by Jane's chair, talking quietly, and everyone else was still too embarrassed to note her departure.

As she approached the study, she could hear the loud voices inside well before she reached the door. She did not knock; she simply opened the door and stepped inside. Lady Catherine was standing beside Darcy's desk, glaring at him as he addressed her, his words clipped and cold, "…most disgraceful episode it has ever been my displeasure to witness. In my own house and by my own aunt! Can you give me *one* reason, madam, why I should not ask you to leave my home immediately?"

At that moment, Lady Catherine became aware of Elizabeth as she closed the door. Pointing at her with her walking stick, she shrilled, "Her! Get her out of this house, Darcy! I will not have her in my presence!"

Darcy gave a quick glance at Elizabeth but his attention never left his aunt. "It is infinitely more likely that it will be you who departs my house rather than Elizabeth," he said icily.

Elizabeth came up beside Darcy and threaded her arm through his. He almost jumped at the touch. "You should not be here, Elizabeth," he said urgently. "This is between my aunt and me."

"No, William," she said calmly, "I am where I belong." She looked up at him firmly. "By your side."

Darcy felt a thrilling tingle down his spine at her firm declaration then nodded in agreement and turned back to his aunt. "Now, we were discussing why you should not be asked to leave my house after forcing your way past my butler and most impolitely disrupting my dinner party?"

"She knows," Lady Catherine said in fury, pointing again at Elizabeth. "She knows why I came!"

"Indeed, you are mistaken, madam," said Elizabeth coolly. "I cannot account for how I could have been the cause for such an appalling breach of good manners."

"Miss Bennet," responded her ladyship in a furious voice, "you ought to know that I am not to be trifled with! You may be as impudent as you please, but I shall be completely sober and frank. After your departure from Hunsford, I thought that I should never have to encounter your shameless behaviour again, but today I learned from this disgraceful announcement in the *Times* that you have not desisted from your nefarious plots!" She pulled a scrap of paper out of her reticule and waved it at Elizabeth. "I can only assume that you published these lies for the purpose of furthering your plan to connect yourself with my nephew! But it will not work, Miss Bennet! It will not work! I immediately resolved on visiting my nephew so that he could instantly contradict this infamous proclamation!"

"The announcement is perfectly true," replied Darcy in a controlled voice. "Indeed, I myself placed the announcement and wrote to inform you of this on Sunday."

Lady Catherine gaped in astonishment then turned her blazing eyes toward Elizabeth. "Then you *have* succeeded in your scheme to entrap my nephew! You are determined to ruin him! But it will not happen! I demand that you immediately and publicly contradict this report!"

"I will do nothing of the kind, your ladyship. Mr. Darcy made his proposal, I accepted him, and my father's consent has been given. We are engaged, and it was announced."

Lady Catherine rounded on Darcy. "How could you?" she shrilled. "How could you do this to your cousin Anne? Have you lost the use of your reason? I came here thinking that this shameless lady-bird had placed that announcement herself, trying to entrap you, but now I see that she is playing a deeper game! She has used her arts and allurements to catch you in a web of infatuation! Break free of it, Darcy! Break the engagement immediately! You are already engaged to Anne! Remember what you owe to yourself and all your family!"

"I am not and never have been engaged to Anne," Darcy said heatedly. "That has been your own delusion all these years. Though we love each other as cousins, Anne and I have never desired marriage. I know that this is her opinion, because we have spoken of it several times. We thought it best to avoid the subject, rather than to confront you openly in the matter.

But that was an error; I see that now. I should have flatly laughed in your face years ago."

Lady Catherine recoiled in horror. "This is not to be borne! From your infancy, you two have been intended for each other! Is this union to be prevented by a young woman of inferior birth, of no importance in the world, and wholly unallied to the family? It was the favourite wish of your mother! Will you deny the wishes your own mother, my sister, planned when you were in your cradle?"

"My mother never spoke to me of such an arrangement, madam," Darcy said in a low, angry voice. "Pray leave her out of any further argument, or this conversation will be at an end."

"Miss Bennet, you forget your place!" her ladyship cried, rounding on Elizabeth in fury, but the younger woman refused to be intimidated. Darcy started to step forward, but Elizabeth placed her hand on his arm, and he stayed back and stood silent. "Be warned! Even if you manage to succeed in attaching yourself to my nephew, do not think to benefit from it! You will be ignored by his family and friends, censured, slighted and despised by everyone connected with him! Your alliance will be a disgrace! Your name will never even be mentioned by any of us!"

Darcy was surprised at Elizabeth's sudden, impudent smile. "These are heavy misfortunes, madam," she replied cheerfully, "but even if all you foretold came to pass, I believe that Mr. Darcy and I will be quite happy and will, on the whole, have no cause to repine."

Lady Catherine erupted in fury at being mocked by the younger girl. "Obstinate, headstrong girl!" she shrieked. "I am ashamed of you! Is this your gratitude for my attentions to you last spring? Is nothing due to me on that score?"

"Your ladyship's behaviour," Elizabeth relied coldly, "has been such that I feel relieved from any obligations of gratitude that might have been warranted had you behaved in the manner of a true lady."

Lady Catherine recoiled as if she had been slapped, but Elizabeth continued coolly. "Allow me to say, Lady Catherine, that the arguments with which you have supported this extraordinary application have been as frivolous as the application was ill judged. You have widely mistaken my character if you think I can be worked on by such persuasions as these. And I cannot understand why you think you have the right to interfere in your nephew's life, nor do I think forcing your way into his home in such an unseemly manner will enable you to carry your point."

Her ladyship's eyes glinted with hatred as she leaned forward. "Insolent, selfish girl," she hissed, "if you were sensible of your own good, you would not wish to quit the sphere in which you have been brought up."

Elizabeth's chin rose in defiance. "In marrying Mr. Darcy, I shall not be quitting that sphere, madam. He is a gentleman. I am a gentleman's daughter. So far, we are equal."

"That may be, Miss Bennet, but who was your mother? Who are your uncles and aunts? Do not imagine me ignorant of their condition!"

"Whatever my connections may be," said Elizabeth with an impish glance at Darcy, "your nephew has told me that he has deemed them of no significance. If he does not object to them, they can be nothing to you."

"Correctly said, my dear," growled Darcy. "My patience is near exhaustion, Lady Catherine. I am still of a mind to have you ejected from my house."

"You would not dare," the older woman hissed.

"Do not push me, madam. I have been greatly provoked tonight."

"Provoked? Have I not been provoked by your taking this... this *fortune hunter* as your *Bird of Paradise* when you were visiting in my own household? In the same house as your cousin Anne? Will you pollute the shades of Pemberley with this scheming, selfish girl?"

Lady Catherine was shocked by Darcy's sudden burst of derisive laughter. "Fortune hunter? Madame, you are as ill-informed as you are witless! Do you not know that your own household was the source of these baseless rumours?" At the shocked look on her face, he leaned forward and snarled, "Yes, your own household! Have I not informed you for years of how the mistreatment and ill management of your staff would one day lead to disaster? And now it has occurred!" he concluded with a cold smile that had no mirth in it.

Leaning toward his still speechless aunt, Darcy growled, "And fortune hunter? Silly, foolish, woman! Do you think I could give credence to any such charge when Elizabeth refused my proposal that night at the Parsonage?"

Lady Catherine gaped in disbelief.

"Yes, refused! Turned me down flat! Try to spin that into a 'fortune hunter,' madam! Just try!"

Darcy regained a measure of control, conscious of Elizabeth's firm pressure on his arm, mindful of her courageous loyalty in the face of such hostility. "I had hopes that I might in time have persuaded her to accept me. But gossip from your dishonourable staff spread to London and even into the scandal sheets. So, to protect Miss Bennet's reputation, which is of the highest, madam, I was forced to renew my proposal before it was time, and she was likewise compelled to accept it before she would have otherwise wished." He smiled coldly at his aunt. "So you see, Lady Catherine, we would not be engaged at this moment if it were not for your inept management of your own household! Does it not console you to learn that you are the author of your own misfortune?"

Lady Catherine was staggered by this shocking information. "Darcy…" she began to plead.

"Silence!" he snapped. "I have had enough! I will not listen to any more foolish arguments, nor will I countenance any more lies about Elizabeth! You will leave this instant, or I will have you ejected!"

"Not just yet, if you please," came a voice from the doorway.

Darcy whirled to find Lord Matlock, as well as his cousin Fitzwilliam, standing just inside the door. "How long have you been there?" asked Darcy.

"Long enough, Darcy, long enough," said his lordship, as he and his son joined them in the study. He looked at Elizabeth with a twinkle in his eye. "I confess I would have made my presence known earlier, but I was enjoying the way your young lady faced down my much-feared sister." He chuckled. "It has been too long since anyone stood up to her in such a manner."

"James…" started Lady Catherine.

"Will you be quiet, Catherine?" Lord Matlock snapped. "Or do I let Darcy make good on his threat?"

Lady Catherine sagged back against the desk in dismay.

"Now let me tell you how it is going to be, Catherine. This is the most disgraceful exhibition you have ever displayed, and that covers some territory. It *will not* be repeated! Do I make myself clear?"

Lady Catherine could only nod, white-faced in shock and suppressed anger.

"I am the head of this family, and the instructions I am about to give you will be obeyed. Do you quite understand?"

Lady Catherine gave another jerky nod.

"Good. Now, Darcy did not ask for either my consent or my blessing on this marriage since he is head of his own house and did not need it. Nevertheless, as the head of this family, I hereby give both, unnecessary as they are. You will honour my wishes in every detail, or you will find every door in our family closed to *you*. Do you understand this?"

Lady Catherine moaned but nodded again.

"I do not know whether Darcy will ever again welcome you to his home, and I will not attempt to change his mind. Your daughter, Anne, may visit where she pleases, and you will not forbid her. She is of legal age and has her own income, even if she does not choose to use it. If you try to hinder her in any respect, my carriage will be at your door on the following day, and she will find sanctuary in my home." Lady Catherine stared at her brother in horror. She could not believe that he had just addressed her in such a manner, but she had not yet realized that her actions that night had finally pushed him beyond the limits of his own considerable tolerance.

"Now, you will cease your petulant rage and leave this house immediately. I trust your coach is still outside? Good. Then I wish you a safe return to Rosings, and I suggest you stay there for some time. I do not believe you will be invited to the wedding, but I assure you that Lady Matlock and I will be in attendance. Good evening, sister."

And Lady Catherine, white-faced in mortification and rage, had no choice but to exit the study. The tapping of her stick was heard until it was eclipsed by the solid slam of the front door.

Lord Matlock chuckled in good humour as he looked around at the others, who stood stunned by the manner in which the argument had been terminated. "Well, well, well. It is long past time that Catherine received her just deserts," he said with a smile. "I am afraid that we tolerated her tantrums for too long, including you also, Darcy, and we all just had to pay the price for that. But it is over and done. Now, if you will allow me to escort your courageous young woman back to the dining room, I believe we might finish the evening with at least a measure of good humour!"

Elizabeth could not help but feel cheered by Lord Matlock's words, and she willingly took his proffered arm with a dimpled smile, leaving the bemused Darcy staring at his cousin in perplexity.

"What came over your father, Richard? I have seen him tolerate so much from our aunt that I never thought to see him so forceful."

Fitzwilliam shook his head as they left the study to return to their interrupted meal. "I cannot give you a good answer, but I do know that I am exceedingly pleased that I did not miss it!"

Chapter 20

Wednesday, April 22, 1812

Elizabeth and Jane were surprised the next morning when they heard the voice of their mother from downstairs. The two sisters looked at each other in confusion. Elizabeth had written both her father and mother, informing them of the day of her wedding, but her letters could not have arrived so soon, so no one was expected for several days. But their mother burst into the room before either girl could take more than a step towards the door.

"Lizzy, Jane, my dear girls!" she exclaimed. "Good gracious! Lord bless me! Mr. Bingley and Mr. Darcy! Who would have thought it? What clever, clever girls you are to have caught yourselves such rich and grand husbands!"

Both sisters looked at each other in dismay, and they could only be grateful that they were alone as they were not engaged to go shopping with Georgiana until one o'clock. Mrs. Bennet first embraced Jane, "Oh my dear, dear Jane! I am so happy; I have hardly been able to sleep since you wrote your letter! I knew how it would be; I always said it must be so. I was sure you could not be so beautiful for nothing!

"And Lizzy!" she continued, embracing Elizabeth. "Mr. Darcy! Who would have thought it? Such a charming man! So handsome, so tall! Oh, my sweetest Lizzy, how rich and great you will be! What pin-money, what jewels, what carriages you will have! A house in town! Everything that is

181

charming! Ten thousand a year, and very likely more! 'Tis as good as a Lord! And married by a special license! Two daughters married! Oh, Lord! What will become of me? I shall go distracted!"

Mrs. Gardiner had come into the room by this time, and she and her sister exchanged greetings though Mrs. Gardiner was unable to interject more than a word or two into Mrs. Bennet's continuous commentary. They soon found out the occasion for her unexpected arrival—their father's desire for peace, for his wife had evidently complained loudly and continually about his failure to notice Elizabeth's wedding.

"I would not allow him to evade me," she proclaimed proudly, "and I even followed him into the library to inform him of my opinion. He dropped many hints and even demanded to be left alone, but I would not relent until he eventually allowed me the carriage for travel." Elizabeth easily could see how her father had been browbeaten into surrendering to achieve a modicum of peace, but it pained her greatly that he had to be forced into even that much. Meanwhile, her mother continued her ecstatic congratulations to her daughters at their skill in catching two such fine husbands.

Mrs. Bennet was quite loud in her condemnation of her husband for his treatment of Elizabeth and his denial of both the Longbourn chapel and of wedding clothes, though she was somewhat mollified by Elizabeth's information that she had already ordered a gown at Darcy's expense and that the church in the Gardiner's parish had been arranged for the wedding.

"It will be quite an easy journey for all the family," Mrs. Bennet said, "or at least for my sister Philips and the girls, but I am still most vexed at Mr. Bennet for his refusal to give you away, Lizzy! He tells me that he is quite angry with both you and Mr. Darcy, even though it is such an advantageous match, and he absolutely refuses to give me even a single reason for his refusal. But never mind," she said dismissively, "it is of no significance. Two daughters married! Why, when I informed Lady Lucas and Mrs. Long of the news, they both were quite unable at first to speak, they were so astonished by my family's good fortune. And your Aunt Philips sends her congratulations to you both. She is sure that your marriages will greatly benefit the other girls since they will often have the chance to meet other men of considerable wealth!"

Elizabeth looked at her sister helplessly as her mother lamented of the abuse suffered by her nerves and how she never would have been able to make the terrible journey had it not been her duty to assist her daughters in the many arrangements that must be made in the coming weeks. But when Elizabeth reminded her that her own wedding was scheduled in only three more days, she was dismissive. "On Saturday! What could you have been thinking of, child? That will not do at all! You must change the date, that is all there is to it. There are so many things to be done; two months at the least are needed to accomplish them all!"

"Nevertheless, Mama, it is already settled for Saturday. I will go to have my gown fitted this afternoon so that it will be ready by Saturday, and whatever is not done by the time of the wedding may be completed later. Mr. Darcy plans for us to stay in town for some weeks after we are married before we journey to Derbyshire."

"But Lizzy! You must come home to Longbourn before the wedding! I know all your friends will want to see you and offer their congratulations! And you can talk to your father; he listens to you much more than he does me, and surely you will manage to cool his anger."

Elizabeth smiled sadly. She knew that her mother dearly wanted to ferry her around to her friends in Hertfordshire to bask in the praise of such an excellent match for the Bennet family, but she no longer felt the need to try to change her father's mind. She had realized from the night she learned of his refusal of his blessing and even more during the confrontation with Lady Catherine where her loyalties must be planted, and that transition was already virtually complete in her own mind. She no longer considered Longbourn her home, and if her father suddenly relented and gave his blessing and the promise of the Longbourn chapel, she would not change a single arrangement already made. She was not yet a Darcy, but she was no longer a Bennet daughter, and the thought was certainly bittersweet. She embraced her mother fondly, telling her, "The arrangements are already made, Mama. It will all work for the best."

Mrs. Bennet was not satisfied, but Elizabeth changed the topic to Jane's wedding, and her mother soon was energetically dwelling on the many and myriad preparations that must be completed before her eldest daughter surrendered the title of Miss Bennet.

Mrs. Bennet accompanied her two daughters and her sister Gardiner that afternoon when they kept their appointment with Georgiana, and she was uncommonly restrained when Elizabeth performed the introductions. And, though she was so awed by Darcy himself that she was hardly able to say a word to him, she was less restrained when Georgiana showed her about the Darcy home. She was greatly impressed by its size and elegance, and she made numerous observations and suggestions to her daughters.

Darcy returned to his work in his study and thus saw and heard only snatches of the tour through the open door. He was again surprised to find the excesses of Mrs. Bennet more amusing than repelling though he realized his relations might not agree with him. But there was nothing he could do about that, so he tried to concentrate on his work until he heard the party preparing to depart on their shopping expedition.

For her part, Georgiana did observe Elizabeth's mother with some alarm, at least at first, but her concern receded somewhat when she glanced at her future sister, who only responded with a rueful smile and a shrug. Her concern was alleviated further when they were preparing to depart and she observed her brother's tolerant amusement as he came out to see them off. She was quite familiar with her brother's restrained demeanour and was better able to discern his feelings than those who were less familiar with him. So, if her brother was able to tolerate Elizabeth's mother, she was not going to worry about it, especially since she was too overjoyed with his choice of a wife. She had been mesmerized the previous evening after their guests departed and her cousin Fitzwilliam gleefully recited the events that took place in Darcy's study, placing special emphasis on the manner in which Elizabeth had refused to be intimidated by her ladyship. As she took Elizabeth's arm as they left the house, she looked at her future sister with an emotion very close to heroine worship. Never again would she be intimidated by her Aunt Catherine. Elizabeth would not allow it!

Darcy saw the party off with some regret since he would have preferred to spend the afternoon in Elizabeth's company. And when he returned to his work, he was further surprised to find the familiar silence of Darcy House far less comforting than previously.

SINCE ELIZABETH'S GOWN WOULD NOT be ready for its fitting until the evening, Mrs. Gardiner had earlier suggested visiting one of her own shops in order to look for a gown for Jane. While Georgiana continued to insist that much shopping for Elizabeth was needed, Elizabeth had been quick to agree with her aunt, since she would have preferred to visit with Georgiana and play the pianoforte in the Darcy home than to trek from warehouse to warehouse in search of apparel that she was convinced she did not need. She was only glad that she had not allowed herself to be talked into waiting longer to be married. She had hardly had any time alone with Darcy except that stolen moment in the entry when he had kissed her so delightfully, and she would not have minded a chance for a repetition. She had been most pleasantly surprised by her enjoyment of the impulsive kiss that she had brought on herself, and she again wondered how she could enjoy such an intimacy when her own feelings were more of contentment than a passionate regard. In any event, she had to admit that she was becoming quite comfortable with his company and would prefer more of it.

As well you ought, she told herself wryly, *since you agreed to marry the man!*

Elizabeth's avoidance of Georgiana's objective could not last longer than the several hours it took to settle on a suitable gown for Jane, aided by the advice of both Georgiana and Mrs. Gardiner and amid much embarrassing behaviour from Mrs. Bennet. But Georgiana refused to let herself be diverted from her goal of outfitting Elizabeth by her mother's flutterings, and she again advanced the proposition that the expedition should now concentrate on what Elizabeth needed since little time remained before the wedding.

Elizabeth tried to argue that, having already ordered her wedding dress and accessories, her own wardrobe did not need any additions until after she was married. But Mrs. Bennet was enthusiastic in pointing out that she needed, at the very least, several new gowns as well as gloves, bonnets, stockings, and shoes, especially as Mr. Darcy was paying the bills, and Georgiana was quick to weigh in on her side

"Elizabeth," Georgiana told her future sister firmly, "I assure you that you will need more than what you are considering. William told me this morning that he is surprised at the low cost of your gown and that he does not desire you to be quite that . . . economical."

"Georgiana," Elizabeth laughed, "you would not tell me the cost of my wedding gown, but it had to be beyond anything I ever dreamed. And I do not desire to require a caravan of wagons to carry my clothing when we travel to Pemberley! Surely there is plenty of time to expand my wardrobe as it becomes necessary."

But the argument was also taken up by her aunt. "Elizabeth," said Mrs.

Gardiner seriously, "you will be entertaining much more than you have any idea, and it would not be unusual to require several changes of clothing each day. It is a more visible world you will be entering, and many eyes will be on you to see how well you conduct yourself. You should listen to Georgiana in this matter."

Georgiana eagerly confirmed Mrs. Gardiner's opinion, pleased to have her assistance. Elizabeth was so much more confident and knowledgeable than herself in most areas, but on this subject, she felt that she might usefully instruct her future sister.

"We have not even started on what you will need just for summer in town," she said. "I know that William does not plan on entertaining extensively, but he will want to introduce you to his close circle before we leave for Pemberley. You will be hard-pressed to make do unless you have at least a dozen new gowns to start with in addition to what you will bring with you. And you should also remember that Pemberley is cooler than here, and you will need clothes that you will leave there. During the winter season, for one, you will require much warmer clothing than you are used to."

Since this might have been the longest single speech that she had heard from Georgiana so far, Elizabeth was forced to capitulate with whatever grace she could manage. "Perhaps I did not really understand what being the wife of Mr. Darcy would entail," she said with a rueful smile. "I am at your disposal, Georgiana."

Chapter 21

Caroline Bingley tried to suppress her considerable sense of agitation as she and her sister waited for their brother to call. He had sent a note earlier asking if they were free to meet with him privately, and Caroline had not even the slightest idea of what to expect from his visit. Normally, she would have been supremely confident in her ability to manipulate him but no longer — not since that disastrous morning a week ago Sunday when he had shown astonishing determination and forthrightness as he ordered the servants to pack her belongings, personally escorted her to his coach, and deposited her and her trunks before the Hurst townhouse. Since that time, he had neither called nor sent word until that morning, and she was so unsure of what to do to mollify his anger that she had done nothing. She had seen the announcements in the *Times* of his engagement to Jane Bennet and of Darcy's engagement to Elizabeth Bennet, but her explosion of rage on those occasions had no direction since even then Charles did not call.

When he was finally announced, Caroline at first attempted to act as if nothing whatever had occurred. "Charles," she said brightly. "It is so good of you to call. Louisa and I have been most anxious to offer our congratulations to you and to dearest Jane, but we were quite unable to call."

Charles's expression was unreadable as he stood looking at the two of them. At last, he said, "Had you called at my house, you would have been refused admittance. Had you called at the Gardiner house, they would have been more gracious, because your *dearest Jane* is much too well-bred to treat you as you have treated her."

Caroline was more shocked by this open expression of disdain than she had been by her banishment. She had never seen anything like it in all their life together. It appeared that, at least in the area of his future wife, her brother had become a completely different and much less amenable person.

"I came to inform you," he continued, "that Miss Bennet and I have set a wedding date for the second Saturday in June, the eighth. Whether either or both of you will be invited to attend is what I have come to speak of today."

Caroline looked at Charles in total surprise.

Not invited? Her mind reeled in confusion. *How could he not invite me? I am his sister!* She looked at her brother with real apprehension, and this first sign of her weakening seemed to discomfit him. Before Caroline could interpret the softening of his face and act on it, Bingley reached inside his coat and retrieved a folded piece of paper. After looking at it for a few seconds, his face resumed its previous unreadable expression that had made her so uncomfortable, and he folded the paper and returned it to his coat.

"Caroline," Bingley said, "if you have any desire to be invited back to be mistress of my household until I am wed, either in town or at Netherfield, or if either you or Louisa wish to be welcome in the future, you would do well to listen carefully to what I have to say. First" —he held up one finger and looked closely at his two sisters— "you will remember that I am the head of this family, and I expect your manner to reflect that from now on. Second, I will tolerate neither disrespect nor insincerity to Miss Bennet, either now or after we are married. Third, the same pertains to her sister, the future wife of Mr. Darcy." Caroline could only stare numbly at her brother after this unprecedented display of firmness.

"If either or both of you are unable to amend your condescending and insincere behaviour toward the Bennet sisters, then you will neither be invited to our wedding nor Mr. Darcy's, nor will you be welcome in either of our homes once we are married. Oh, yes," Bingley said, seeing the look on Caroline's face. "Mr. Darcy is well aware of my trip here today and even advised me on the manner in which to present the choices you face." Here he patted his coat pocket with the folded paper before he continued, "In your case, Caroline, if you are unable to accept my conditions, under the terms of our father's will, you will receive your inheritance when you turn thirty or when you marry. I will no longer provide an allowance. Until that time, I am sure the Hursts will at least offer you a room in which to sleep."

"But how will I live?" wailed Caroline.

"That is up to you, Caroline," he responded. "Change your manners, or you will not be invited to return."

Caroline was crushed by several mortifying realizations, not the least of which was that she would now be acquiring relations from Hertfordshire whether she willed it or not. Also, she would not, after all her effort, ever be mistress of Pemberley. But the most mortifying thought of all was the very real possibility that she would never again be able to manipulate her brother as she had done for years.

Seeing that she had no real options, Caroline lost little time in pledging that she would honour Charles's wishes, and her sister quickly did the same.

"Very well, then. But I warn you both, that I will accept nothing less than your full compliance with our agreement. If either of you renege, you will be banished from my home permanently." Neither of his sisters had any doubt of his sincerity since the brother talking to them in such a manner was not one that either had ever seen before.

And so, Caroline Bingley returned that afternoon and resumed her position as mistress of Charles's house, at least until his marriage in a month's time. She was uncomfortably aware that her future was not as rosy as she had previously thought, but the events of the morning had had a traumatizing effect on her. She now understood that she would never again be able to influence Charles as she had been wont to do previously, and that led to the dawning realization that events could have turned out worse—and could still do so if she did not change her ways. She vowed to herself that she *would* accept Jane, for Charles would stand for nothing less. In any case, Jane was really the most amiable girl, even if her relations were considerably below what she thought her brother deserved. The thought of doing the same with Elizabeth Bennet, however, was much more difficult to swallow since that simple country girl with the impertinent and self-sufficient attitude had gained what she had most wanted for herself.

She also knew that Mr. Darcy was harder than stone compared to her brother, and if she ever wanted to be welcomed to Pemberley again, she would have to be as cordial to Elizabeth as she was to Jane. The thought was humiliating in the extreme, but there it was; there was no way to change it, and she would just have to submit to the inevitable with as much grace as she could summon.

Her new resolution and that of her sister was put to the test on Thursday morning when the Miss Bennets came to visit at Bingley's request. Caroline and Mrs. Hurst received the two sisters in the most civil manner although Mrs. Hurst left virtually all the conversation to her sister, who was almost as effusive in offering her congratulations to Elizabeth on her engagement as she was to Jane. Elizabeth could see that Miss Bingley was not truly sincere, but she could also see how hard she was trying, so she said nothing and repaid civility with equal civility. As they had tea and cakes and later were conducted on a tour around the townhouse, the difference between Caroline's previous and present manner was so striking that both Elizabeth and Jane comprehended that some significant event must have occurred.

However, while Jane attributed the change to Caroline's realization of her fault in her previous behaviour and was thus endeavouring to make amends, Elizabeth somewhat more pragmatically believed that something had made Caroline recognize that she had pushed her brother too far and she would do well to make the best of the situation. Neither of them guessed that Mr. Darcy, during an afternoon in his study, had gifted Bingley with one final piece of advice, instructing and assisting him in preparing for his confrontation with his two sisters by committing his intentions to paper. Thus, the ever-affable Bingley was able to successfully confront his sisters regarding the conduct he expected towards his future bride. Though ignorant of the true reason for Caroline's change of manner, both Jane and Elizabeth were certainly pleased with the results.

The Bennet sisters and their mother, along with Mr. Darcy and Georgiana, dined that same night with the Bingleys. Mrs. Bennet was duly impressed by the townhouse, but she was nevertheless quite free with recommendations and suggestions to Jane as to what needed to be changed. Jane simply smiled and nodded to her mother before returning to her conversation with Bingley. Darcy and Georgiana sat with Elizabeth, and it was obvious to Caroline that both brother and sister had achieved a most intimate and comfortable level of amity with the future Mrs. Darcy. She saw the easy manner in which Elizabeth and Georgiana laughed with each other and the way in which Elizabeth's gentle teasing only made Mr. Darcy smile more fondly at her.

He is as besotted as the most lovesick character from a romantic novel, Caroline thought, with emotions owing as much to regret as to mortification and disgust.

With this realization, she began to see what she had cost herself in her single-minded pursuit of Mr. Darcy. Even though she had treated him with the utmost attentiveness and deference in the socially approved manner for a young lady of gentle birth seeking to attract a husband, she had not only been completely unsuccessful, but it was now clear that she had never had even the slightest chance of success. It was the common wisdom that a young lady must never be spirited, opinionated, and argumentative toward her chosen object, yet Darcy had ignored her, Caroline Bingley, a young lady of substantial fortune and social prominence, and had chosen a bride who displayed all these unfashionable behaviours. Given the complete adoration and approval that he at present showed toward Elizabeth, he was apparently one of the few men at his level of society who desired something different than what she had to offer. It was all so perplexing!

Clearly, her basic mistake had been to fix on Mr. Darcy in the first place, though she wondered how she could have perceived that he was not and would never be interested in a young lady who behaved in the socially approved manner that she had been taught. It had seemed so simple when she first selected him; he was a close friend of her brother, ensuring that she would often be in company with him, he was older than many other eligible young men, and he had control of his fortune and a sister who would need guidance when she was introduced to society. It had seemed so straightforward and clear, but it had instead been a waste of valuable time, during which she had not considered any other possible matches. If she was to secure a husband now, she would have not only to find one who was interested in what she had to offer, but she would have to search in areas other than she had heretofore searched. It had been years since she had thrown herself into a Season, and it was rather distasteful to consider it at her age and after the present evidence of her failure, but she knew of no better place to search.

For a moment, she had a mental vision of herself in ten years' time, an occasional visitor in the households managed by the two Bennet sisters, watching their children fill the house while she still searched with increasing desperation and decreasing hope for any chance of ever being mistress of her own establishment. The vision was chilling in the extreme, and her smile was brittle as she announced to her guests that dinner was now ready.

It was truly, truly vexing!

Chapter 22

Mrs. Bennet left for Longbourn on Friday morning, planning to return in the evening with her other daughters. She was well pleased at having done her duty to Elizabeth and having made a start on the more substantial task she had set herself for Jane's own wedding clothes. Since Mr. Bennet would not advance any money for Elizabeth's wardrobe, she was determined to spare no expense for her eldest daughter.

Jane had declined to return to Longbourn with her mother, desiring to stay with Elizabeth this last day before their lives changed forever. Every night since Elizabeth had returned from Kent, the two sisters had sat up late as they had done so many times in their lives thus far, but in just one more day, Elizabeth's home would be with Mr. Darcy, and these sisterly conferences would be a part of the past.

Jane was particularly distressed that Elizabeth, though she continued to proclaim her contentment with the situation, could not say that she loved Mr. Darcy. She felt uncomfortable at not being able to rid herself of the notion that Elizabeth might be sacrificing herself in order to ensure Jane's happiness, but whenever she expressed such an apprehension, Elizabeth would declare such considerations as nonsense and would often lean close to Jane, letting her eyes get wide, as she said in a low voice, "Jane, do you not realize that he has *ten thousand a year?*" This imitation of her mother

193

invariably reduced Jane to impotent giggling, but it could not totally quell her concern.

However, one subject did distress Elizabeth, and that was the fact that she had not received any communication from her father, despite the long letter she had written in which she explained in complete detail all that had happened and why, urging him to reconsider his ill will toward her future husband. She knew that her uncle had also written with equal lack of success. Mrs. Gardiner had shared with her, in the strictest confidence, that her husband had firmly chided Mr. Bennet for his uncharitable response to Mr. Darcy and had reaffirmed his own valuation of Darcy's worthy character. Despite their efforts, Mr. Bennet, never the best of correspondents, had not so much as acknowledged the receipt of either letter with even the briefest note.

After her mother left, Mrs. Gardiner took her two nieces on a private shopping expedition, just the three of them. In a secluded showing room, Elizabeth and Jane were shocked at what was brought to them at their aunt's request—nightwear items for their wedding night and afterwards.

Elizabeth's face was bright red as she held up a gown made of a fabric both filmy and revealing. Further, the cut and tailoring was exceedingly immodest, with a neckline that would reveal much of a young bride's bosom and even more of her back, not to speak of the way it would cling to her figure.

"I cannot even imagine wearing such a nightgown," she said in embarrassment. Jane's response was quieter than Elizabeth's, but her cheeks were equally red.

"There will be ample time to purchase more sensible nightwear in future years, Lizzy, but you will only be a young bride once in your life and for only one man." She smiled at her furiously blushing nieces and continued, "Your husbands will always remember and keep in their minds the memory of being freshly married to a beautiful bride in the full bloom of her youth, and as you grow old together, you will ever be in his eyes that same young girl. You both will want those memories in the years to come when you may have to face tragedies and trials that will make such shared memories more important than you can know at the present time."

"But Aunt Gardiner, what will Mr. Darcy think if he sees me wearing such a gown?" she asked in confusion, trying to balance her aunt's advice against the strict mores of her society.

"And Mr. Bingley!" said Jane, holding up another nightgown over her

194

dress. The front of it plunged dramatically, and the back even further. Her face was red all the way to her ears.

"Girls, are you afraid your husbands will think you wanton?" her aunt asked with a smile. Jane said nothing, but Elizabeth managed a small nod. Mrs. Gardiner laughed softly. "Have you considered that he will think of the compliment that you bestow by wearing such a nightgown for him and him only?" Elizabeth had to confess that she had not considered that.

Her aunt smiled again, "And Jane, have you considered what you will do if, or rather when, he removes that gown completely? Have you, Elizabeth?" Elizabeth gasped at the very thought, and Jane could only look at her aunt in shock. A sudden vision came to Elizabeth of William sliding this filmy nightgown up her leg, placing his hand on her bare skin that the nightgown had formerly concealed, and of that same hand continuing to slide even higher...

The very thought made her shiver, and she was grateful for the long sleeves of her dress, for she knew that she had just broken out in goose flesh all down her arms.

"The intimacies of marriage are far more precious and endearing than what your mother has likely informed you," their aunt continued, and both Jane and Elizabeth had to blush at this, for their mother had spoken more of enduring and closing their eyes than of anything precious and endearing. Elizabeth had believed that her mother could not be completely correct, but she had not been able to contradict one who had borne five daughters. "You and your husbands will know intimacies that only a husband and wife should know, and those intimacies are not only for the procreation of children but are also intended to strengthen and enhance the love you will share."

Elizabeth blushed again at this, for she had only to close her eyes to see William's eyes darken into that penetrating gaze meant only for her. She could hardly imagine with what intensity he might look at her if she wore the gown she now held before her, but the thought was oddly pleasurable. While she was still not completely comfortable with her aunt's advice, she was much more comforted than after the previous conversation with her mother, and she agreed to the purchases suggested by Mrs. Gardiner. Jane was equally anxious, but she was also agreeable to her aunt's suggestions though she remained unsure she could ever wear what she was buying.

THE REST OF THE DAY passed rapidly. Two new trunks had been delivered in the morning for Elizabeth's clothing purchases, though only a portion had yet been delivered. The purchases already at hand were packed by the two sisters, each item being carefully folded and placed in the trunks in such a way as to minimize creasing. Her wedding gown was delivered after noon, tried on, and carefully hung up along with her gloves, shoes, and bonnet in preparation for the next day. Elizabeth spent part of the afternoon visiting with Georgiana and Darcy at the Gardiner's home, and she could not complain about his attentiveness or courtesy. Nevertheless, the way in which he sometimes looked at her proved extremely disquieting, especially after the morning's conversation. She could only wonder at those times whether he was repressing an eagerness to take her to his home and his bed, and she had all the nervous anxiety of an innocent virgin — wanting to flee yet, at the same time, wishing that he could quickly succeed in his purpose. Meanwhile, Darcy was the soul of discretion, limiting his intimacies to holding her hand when they were occasionally alone and a discreet kiss to her forehead when he departed.

Elizabeth had grown to enjoy their time together over the past days and found that she missed his company when they were apart. She had examined and re-examined her feelings, believing that she ought to be developing a more tender regard for him as her enjoyment of his company increased, but she had no past measurement against which to compare her feelings. Therefore, she could not boast of stronger emotions than contentment for herself, concern for his well-being, and a distinct anxiety that she would not live up to his expectations as his wife. In this last, she was determined to do her best, and she little knew that Darcy himself was delighted at the pleasant and happy manner in which she conversed and jested with him.

Mrs. Bennet, Mary, Kitty, and Lydia arrived that evening, and it grieved Elizabeth anew that her father was not with them though by this time she no longer really expected his presence. She very much missed his wry smile and dry wit at this time, especially since she still had no convincing explanation for his distaste for her future husband, nor could she forgive his harsh response when she accepted him.

Darcy called again that evening after dinner while Elizabeth was upstairs reading to the children in the nursery. He apologized to the surprised Gardiners for the lack of warning and lateness of the hour, but Mrs. Bennet was instantly aware of the reason for his arrival by the box he held. Any doubt was erased in the next instant when he asked if he might borrow Mr. Gardiner's study again for a few moments alone with Elizabeth.

Elizabeth was sent for, and she could see that he was both excited and agitated as he ushered her into the study and closed the door. "I apologize for calling so unexpectedly, Elizabeth," he said as he handed her the box, "but I was beginning to worry that these would not be completed in time."

Elizabeth was as happy to receive a gift as any young lady, and she had been charmed by the way Darcy often called with flowers for her or small gifts for the Gardiner children. However, this was obviously something special, given the expression on his face. She seated herself and carefully untied the ribbon, gasping in surprise when she opened the box, for inside was a string of the most lustrous pearls that she had ever seen. All were carefully sized, with the largest in the middle gradually diminishing in size to the smallest. This was a gift that dwarfed in value everything that she had spent on wedding clothes.

"They are so beautiful," she whispered.

"They were only delivered tonight, and I wanted you to have them in case you wish to wear them with your wedding gown. Please do try them. Georgiana helped with the measurement to make sure they fit, but it is best to be sure."

Elizabeth carefully lifted them, unable to see a flaw in any of the gleaming orbs, then looked up at Darcy. "I am most appreciative, sir," she said with a warm smile, "but these are much too extravagant for a simple country lass."

Darcy laughed easily, for they had both come to grips with the many misjudgements and errors they had both made in their earlier association and were now able to view those events as a source of amusement rather than of mortification. He had even learned not to wince whenever she referred to something as "only tolerable," and she equally could laugh when he asked if he might read her some poetry.

"You were meant to wear these, Elizabeth, simple country lass or no," he commented softly after he fastened the pearls around her neck. Mr. Gardiner's study had no mirror, so she could not verify his compliment, but the look on his face told her all she needed to know.

"Thank you," she told him tenderly. "I am very, very fortunate. I shall certainly wear them tomorrow."

"Then let us show them to the rest of your family immediately, for it is later than I would have wished."

As he turned to lead the way out of the study, he was halted by the touch of Elizabeth's hand on his arm. When he turned around, she surprised him by putting her arm around his neck and pulling his face down to hers. When their lips touched, she raised up on her toes, tightening her arm around his neck while her other arm slipped around his waist under his coat. She shivered in delight at the exquisite sensation of his lips pressing into hers, her mouth opening slightly as his own kiss deepened. His arms went around her, and she had a sudden realization of his true strength and power as she felt his muscles tense as he fought against the urge to crush her fiercely to him. She was more prepared this time when his tongue probed at her lips, and she shivered again, then she felt him react as she tentatively reached her own tongue to touch his.

Instinctively, she pressed her body closer to him as their tongues darted and touched in a dance of exploration and discovery, arching herself upward while he pulled her even more firmly against him. His hands moved to the side of her waist, measuring its narrowness, and Elizabeth felt the heat from his touch, even through her clothes. His fingers moved, explored, and she sucked in a breath as she felt one hand slide to her hip and then to her bottom, but she did not pull away. She trembled. No one had ever touched her in such a way, and while some might think her behaviour shameless, she cared not. She kissed her future husband fiercely and nibbled at his lower lip with her small teeth while she moved her hips under the urging of his hand on her bottom.

Darcy opened his eyes to find hers open also, dark and dancing in delight under her half-closed lids. He lowered his lips to her throat, trailing soft kisses down to her shoulders while her hands moved up his back, exploring how his torso widened towards his shoulders. She dropped her head backward, opening the way for his lips to move to the hollow of her throat. A small moan escaped from her lips, and he felt her shiver again as he moved up her neck and nibbled at her delectable ear lobe. She thrust her hips forward into him as he slipped his tongue into her ear, then planted small kisses across her cheeks, her nose, her chin, and returning to her moist lips, kissing her deeply as his tongue danced and slid over her own.

When he lifted his mouth from hers, she was gasping for breath; her body almost limp in his grasp. His feelings as he held her close were conflicted. Certainly, he was pleased at the passion she had shown, but he also felt ashamed when he remembered his previous determination to control his urges. He should have simply kissed her back quickly, but instead he had taken advantage of her honest reaction to his gift to take liberties that...

Elizabeth, through half-closed eyes, saw the sudden look of self-disgust on Darcy's face, felt his hands leave her waist and her bottom, felt him start to pull away from her. She instinctively pulled him back against her, unwilling to be separated from the closeness of his embrace. As he started to speak, preparatory, she knew, to issuing the expected apologies for his unforgivable behaviour, she put one hand up to cover his mouth.

"No, William. I will not have it," she said softly but firmly. His eyes widened in surprise and confusion. "We are to be married on the morrow, sir," she continued softly, putting both arms back around his waist and clasping him to her, "and you did nothing that I did not want you to do. If you are going to castigate yourself for taking liberties, then I shall have to castigate myself for allowing you to take those liberties — for being wanton."

"You could never be wanton, Elizabeth," he groaned in despair.

"And you could never be less than a gentleman, Fitzwilliam Darcy," she told him firmly. "But even a gentleman cannot treat his wife like a Vestal Virgin, nor would she want it so. Especially not," her eyes sparkled with delight as she hugged him tightly, "when it felt so very lovely to me. Now, sir, I repeat: I will not have it."

Gradually, Darcy brought his emotions under control, and he could not help but be amused at the manner in which Elizabeth had completely reversed their roles, refusing to let him play the part of shamed and disgraced rascal.

"Well, perhaps you will at least admit that I was a little premature," he said with a smile.

"By less than a day, and I repeat, you did nothing that I did not want you to do. And I started it, and you *did* warn me!" He had to chuckle at that, and she joined him with her soft, delightful laugh. "Now," she continued, "I suggest that we join the others before they come looking for us. We do have a wedding to accomplish in less than twelve hours, after which we can resume this...*conversation*...in the privacy of our chambers!" Darcy had to laugh at the mischievousness dancing in her eyes and agreed to her proposal, contenting himself with a chaste kiss to her forehead and one last, quick embrace.

Quickly, Elizabeth tugged her clothes straight, and her hands went to her hair to capture a few errant curls and pin them back into place.

"My uncle does not seem to have a mirror in here. Does everything look correct?"

Darcy cocked his head in thought. "You look fine from this side, but please turn around." She turned around at his request, and then she jumped as he planted a kiss on the back of her neck.

"William!" she admonished him sternly, though the scolding might have carried more weight if she had been better able to suppress her smile.

"All correct, dearest," he told her. "The pearls are lovely, of course, but you are even lovelier."

"William!" she repeated, her cheeks colouring.

"I believe that you shall have to work harder at learning to receive a compliment, Elizabeth," he told her, "for you shall be receiving many of them." His face wore a look of innocence as he repeated her own admonition to Georgiana back to her, and she laughed lightly as she quickly rose to her toes to kiss his cheek.

"Thank you," she told him softly. "I shall indeed attempt to improve."

As they left the room to join the others, Elizabeth had no further doubts as to whether she could wear one of the daring nightgowns that her aunt had induced her to buy.

Chapter 23

Saturday, April 25, 1812

Fitzwilliam Darcy felt his heart lurch as Miss Elizabeth Bennet stepped through the doors of the church on the arm of her uncle. Her sister preceded her up the aisle to join the party at the front of the church, and Darcy did not have to look to see that Bingley's eyes were locked on his beloved Jane as he anticipated his own forthcoming wedding.

This, however, was Darcy's day, and Jane slipped through a gap in the onlookers to stand to the right side of the Reverend as she waited for her sister to take her place at Darcy's side. From his own family, Lord and Lady Matlock were in attendance along with two of their sons, Colonel Fitzwilliam and his brother, Henry, who had hurried north from his ship at anchor at Plymouth at his father's summons. Darcy did not know him well at all, and he could only attribute his presence to his uncle's determination to show his approval of this marriage since the earl's eldest son was unable to attend, being absent in Ireland while travelling to inspect the family properties. Bingley and his two sisters also attended, along with Bingley's brother, Mr. Hurst. On Elizabeth's side were her mother and her sisters, along with her Aunt and Uncle Philips, and, of course, her Aunt and Uncle Gardiner. Her friend, Charlotte Collins, had not come, likely because her husband had forbidden her at the command of Lady Catherine. Nor was Mr. Bennet in attendance, a fact that also was a source of irritation to him, at least for

Elizabeth's sake, though she would not speak of it, smoothly changing the subject whenever her father was mentioned by her mother or sisters.

Darcy's irritation was only momentary, since no negative emotion could cloud his mind once Mr. Gardiner led Elizabeth to his left side in front of Reverend Jackson. He felt his heart in his throat as Elizabeth looked up at him and smiled that lovely, impish smile that spoke of merriment and high spirits at a moment that reduced so many brides to tears. She was a vision of loveliness, to his eyes the most lovely and beautiful of women, and the pearls around her neck complemented her pale green dress exquisitely.

He had to force his eyes away from her as the reverend began the solemn ceremony, heard numerous times before, but which was wondrously new this day, for it was for them and them alone. Elizabeth, despite her earlier smile, was overcome by the fluttery sensation she had heard described as butterflies in the stomach. She was not reluctant, she told herself, not at all, and it was far too late for reservations, but these feelings were undoubtedly common at such a pivotal point in a woman's life, for from this moment on, she would be defined by her marriage to Fitzwilliam Darcy. She would be Mrs. Darcy, mistress of Pemberley, expected to live up to and perform as society expected from the wife of such a prominent man. How could this realization of such a profound change in her life not lead to the internal disquiet that was only increased by the words of dear Reverend Jackson?

"Dearly beloved, we are gathered together here in the sight of God, and in the face of this congregation, to join together this man and this woman in Holy matrimony; which is an honourable estate, instituted of God in the time of man's innocence, signifying unto us the mystical union that is betwixt Christ and his Church; which Holy estate Christ adorned and beautified with his presence, and first miracle that he wrought..."

The familiar words rang in her ears as if she had never heard them before, and Elizabeth could not stop herself from looking away from the reverend and focusing on her groom. She was surprised and pleased to see that the solemn words were evidently striking him in the same way, their familiarity in no way lessening their import. He listened in rapt fascination, his eyes fixed on the reverend. But something seemed to tell him of Elizabeth's gaze, and his head slowly swivelled until his dark eyes met hers. Elizabeth felt a thrill run down her spine at that moment, for the intensity of his stare was almost a physical thing, drawing her in, forging an invisible bond that none could see but was as strong as the links of an iron chain for all that. Neither knew how long the moment lasted, in which everything else in the world disappeared except the two of them, but they were finally drawn back to the awareness of the ceremony when Reverend Jackson addressed Darcy.

"Fitzwilliam Darcy, wilt thou have this Woman to thy wedded wife, to live together after God's ordinance in the holy estate of Matrimony? Wilt thou love her, comfort her, honour, and keep her in sickness and in health; and, forsaking all others, keep thee only unto her, so long as ye both shall live?"

Darcy's voice was firm and resolute. "I will."

And then it was her turn. "Elizabeth Bennet, wilt thou have this man to thy wedded husband, to live together after God's ordinance in the holy estate of Matrimony? Wilt thou obey him, and serve him, love, honour, and keep him in sickness and in health; and, forsaking all others, keep thee only unto him, so long as ye both shall live?

Elizabeth's clear voice was equally firm, though her eyes were again dancing in merriment. "I will."

"Who giveth this woman to be married to this man?"

"I do," said Mr. Gardiner, and, releasing her hand to the reverend, he stepped back to join the others standing around the bride and groom. Then, as they stood face to face, the reverend took Elizabeth's hand, placed it in Darcy's and instructed him to repeat:

"I, Fitzwilliam, take thee Elizabeth, to my wedded Wife, to have and to hold from this day forward, for better, for worse, for richer, for poorer, in sickness and in health, to love and to cherish, till death us do part, according to God's holy ordinance; and thereto I plight thee my troth."

Then the reverend took Darcy's right hand, giving it to Elizabeth to hold in her smaller hand, while he commanded her to say after him:

"I, Elizabeth, take thee Fitzwilliam, to my wedded Husband, to have and to hold from this day forward, for better, for worse, for richer, for poorer, in sickness and in health, to love, cherish, and to obey, till death us do part, according to God's holy ordinance; and thereto I give thee my troth."

Bingley placed the ring on the Bible held by Reverend Jackson, and the reverend gave the ring to Darcy, who lifted Elizabeth's left hand and slid it onto her fourth finger. Elizabeth shivered at the significance of the simple action, looking down at the gold band that signified so much. Darcy continued to hold the ring on her finger as he said, his eyes locked on new bride's and his voice husky with emotion, "With this ring, I thee wed, with my body I thee worship, and with all my worldly goods I thee endow. In the Name of the Father, and of the Son, and of the Holy Ghost. Amen."

Darcy released her hand, enthralled by the loveliness of her face and the expression in her eyes meant for him alone, as Reverend Jackson then said, "Let us pray. O eternal God, creator and preserver of all mankind, giver of all spiritual grace, the author of everlasting life; send thy blessing upon these thy servants, this man and this woman, whom we bless in thy Name; that, as Isaac and Rebecca lived faithfully together, so these persons may surely perform and keep the vow and covenant betwixt them made, and may ever remain in perfect love and peace together, and live according to thy laws; through Jesus Christ our Lord. Amen."

Reverend Jackson took the right hands of Elizabeth and Darcy, and looking out at the assembly of family and friends, said, "Those whom God hath joined together, let no man put asunder."

The reverend let go of their hands, though they remained clasped together, as he continued, "For as much as Fitzwilliam and Elizabeth have consented together in Holy wedlock, and have witnessed the same before God and this company, and thereto have given and pledged their troth either to the other, and have declared the same by giving and receiving of a Ring, and by joining of hands; I pronounce that they be Man and Wife together, in the Name of the Father, and of the Son, and of the Holy Ghost. Amen."

He concluded with the blessing, "God the Father, God the Son, God the Holy Ghost, bless, preserve, and keep you; the Lord mercifully with his favour look upon you; and so fill you with all spiritual benediction and grace, that ye may so live together in this life, that in the world to come ye may have life everlasting. Amen."

Then the assembly crowded closer, offering their congratulation and best wishes as Darcy raised Elizabeth's fingers to his lips, kissing them with all the tenderness and love that he felt before turning to greet the well-wishers. Georgiana pressed close, even crowding in front of Mrs. Bennet, as she embraced Elizabeth with tears of joy, and she bestowed a kiss on both of her cheeks before giving way to the bride's exuberant mother.

Most surprising of all was Caroline Bingley, who offered her congratulations to both Mr. and Mrs. Darcy in a manner that, if it held any insincerity, at least expressed none that could be discerned.

It was some while before the marriage party made their way to the vestry to sign their names in the parish registry. As Elizabeth signed 'Elizabeth Bennet,' for the very last time, she felt emotion rise in her throat, and she welcomed the strong arm of her husband that was instantly around her. After Darcy signed his name in the last of the formalities, the wedding party exited the church to board their carriages for the trip to the Gardiner's and the traditional marriage breakfast, though it was approaching noon. And, as Reverend Jackson closed up the church behind them, he did so with all the warmth in his heart for two souls joined in wedlock. He had believed, when first approached by Mr. Gardiner, that the haste of the ceremony betokened some violation of propriety, but after his observations of the couple, he believed that even if propriety had been breached, he had seldom united two souls who came to their union more willingly than did these. He was a well-contented man as he returned home to his own beloved wife and family.

As they pulled to a halt in front of his house, Darcy looked down at Elizabeth as she leaned against his side, having fallen asleep almost immediately after entering his coach for the short drive from the Gardiner home following the wedding breakfast. She had admitted to him that she had hardly slept at all the night before, succumbing most unexpectedly to an attack of bridal nerves. She had sought Jane out in her own chamber, and the two sisters sat together talking until almost dawn, she had said, both of them conscious that this was the very last time for such a shared experience.

She looks so beautiful, he thought, but then he smiled. He always thought she looked beautiful. *But she is especially beautiful now, because she is no longer Elizabeth Bennet, but is now Elizabeth Darcy.*

He leaned down and whispered in her ear, "Elizabeth." She murmured something under her breath and burrowed deeper into his chest. "Elizabeth," he said in a louder voice, "we have arrived."

Elizabeth opened her eyes and smiled up at him. *My husband*, she thought. *It is real, it has happened, for better or worse, in sickness and in health, and all the vows we exchanged.*

"We have arrived, Elizabeth," Darcy told her again, once she had her eyes fully open.

"Yes, I see," she replied as the footman opened the door and folded down the stair. When she sat up, she realized that her hair was fully down around her shoulders. "Mr. Darcy!" she exclaimed, reaching up to discover that her hairpins were completely missing.

Darcy was unrepentant as he held out his hand and opened his fist to disclose the missing pins. "I have wanted to do that for the longest time," he told her cheerfully.

"What am I going to do with you, sir?" she said sternly, though a smile tugged at her lips. She quickly and expertly wound up her hair in a passable fashion and secured it with the hairpins. Once she was tolerably presentable and had donned her bonnet, he descended and held out his hand to assist her in exiting the coach. Mrs. Taylor and Stevens stood in the open door, beaming as Elizabeth took Darcy's arm and climbed the entry steps.

"Welcome home, Mrs. Darcy," said Stevens, giving her a bow. Mrs. Taylor had what looked suspiciously like a tear in her eye as she curtseyed to her new mistress, and much of the rest of the staff was lined up inside the broad entry. Elizabeth was pleased that they all seemed quite happy to greet her as the new Mrs. Darcy, and Mrs. Taylor explained that she would arrange for her to meet the complete staff in the coming days.

The wedding breakfast had taken considerable time, and many toasts were drunk to the future happiness of the newly wedded couple. It was now approaching five o'clock, and Elizabeth wanted to change from her wedding gown to simpler attire before the evening meal. Darcy escorted her up the stairs to her room — *her room!* she thought, in amazement — as the staff dispersed to their duties. Once again, Elizabeth felt her stomach flutter when they came to her chamber door, and she thought again of just how much her life had changed. She would never go back to her dear bedroom at Longbourn; she would never curl up on Jane's bed as they shared confidences late into the night; she would not hear the amiable chaos of noise that characterized her previous home life at Longbourn. Darcy's home was quiet and efficient, and the change would be dramatic. She looked up at Darcy as they came to a stop to find him studying her worriedly, and she smiled at his continuing insecurity.

"I was just thinking of all the things that have changed so suddenly, and all the things that used to be a part of my life that will never again be the same," she said softly. "It is rather overwhelming to think of, but from the look on your face, I see that I must again remind you that I am not disposed to melancholy."

206

Darcy smiled ruefully. "I try to keep that in mind, but sometimes I cannot help worrying just a little."

"That was a *pensive* look on my face, William," she teased him. "It was not a *worried* look."

"I shall attempt to remember that. Now, if I just knew how to tell the difference…"

She smiled and squeezed his arm before entering her room. It looked the same as it had on her tour, she realized, but already it was different. As her mother had informed her, Sarah had indeed arrived from Longbourn, the only consideration that Mrs. Bennet had been able to wring from her husband, and the maid was busily emptying Elizabeth's trunks into the closets, humming softly to herself.

Sarah turned to her mistress, now her only mistress, and curtseyed. "Welcome home, Mrs. Darcy," she said with a smile. "Hot water is being brought up for your bath whenever you shall be ready for it."

"Thank you, Sarah." Waving at her trunks, Elizabeth said, "I would have thought these would already be unpacked since they were sent over last night."

"Oh, no, Mrs. Darcy!" exclaimed Sarah. "Mrs. Taylor was informed of my coming and very properly left that to my care. I only arrived two hours ago."

"Ah, I see," said Elizabeth, hearing the obvious pride in Sarah's voice. It would have been so easy, she realized, for Sarah to be slighted by the staff in a large, established household like this, the implication being that she could not possibly perform her new tasks, coming, as she did, from such a small estate as Longbourn. But Mrs. Taylor was obviously thoughtful and considerate enough to avoid this slight and had left Elizabeth's trunks to the care of her personal maid.

Supper was served in a small dining room that was just the size to serve four or five. Darcy said that it was the room where he commonly ate with Georgiana, who was spending the next week with her Aunt and Uncle Matlock. Not having partaken much at the wedding breakfast, Elizabeth ate with enthusiasm, but despite the tastiness of the meal, prepared with skill by Darcy's kitchen staff, she noticed that her husband only picked at his food.

"Are you not feeling well, William?" she asked with concern. While she had much to learn about her new husband, she knew enough to know that he was not a fussy eater.

"No, I thank you, Elizabeth. I am not ill, but I am not particularly hungry." As she looked closer, she could tell that Darcy seemed rather ill at ease. When she thought back to his playfulness in the coach, she had a sudden suspicion of what might be troubling him. Satisfied that she could deal with the problem, she finished her dinner and then smiled at her husband.

"It has been a momentous day, has it not, Mr. Darcy?" she asked him.

"Yes, it has been the happiest day of my life," he told her sincerely, but she could see he was still troubled.

"May I ask the time, Mr. Darcy?" she asked as her smile broadened. Darcy appeared surprised, but he fumbled for his watch.

"It is just past eight," he replied; then he stood quickly as Elizabeth arose from her chair.

"Might I suggest that we retire early since it *is* our wedding night? If you will give me a half-hour, you can come to me then."

There, she thought, *if it is as I suspect, he will start being the proper gentleman right about now.*

Darcy seemed to have a hard time speaking before he finally began, "Elizabeth, I do not want to force you into anything that you may not be prepared for." He was grave but earnest as he continued, "I am willing to wait if you need... that is, if you are not..."

Elizabeth put a finger to his lips. "Do not be foolish, William. What I *need* is a half-hour," and he stiffly extended his arm to escort her back to her bedchamber.

At the door, she looked up at her new husband and was amused to see that she had guessed correctly, for he appeared even more ill at ease than he had downstairs. "In a half-hour, then?" she said playfully, and, as he nodded formally, she rose to her toes to lightly brush her lips across his before entering her room.

Chapter 24

A half hour later, Elizabeth was brushing her hair after having dismissed Sarah for the evening. The girl she had known so long had been terribly excited and pleased to help Mrs. Darcy prepare for the first night of her marriage, and she had selected the most daring of the nightgowns that her Aunt Gardiner had helped her choose. The style was even bolder than she remembered, and the deep neckline displayed the pale skin of her bosom to maximum advantage, and she knew that her back was bare to her waist.

She was delighted at how the sheer fabric felt against her skin, and she could not help remembering Aunt Gardiner's comment the previous day. *This gown seems almost designed to be removed,* she thought, and she wondered if she might wake in the morning wearing her pearls and nothing else. She felt another of those delightful shivers that made her break out again into goose flesh. She wondered whether William would come to her or she would have to force the issue, and she decided that either prospect would prove quite entertaining.

At length, she decided she had waited long enough. She knocked gently on the door before opening it, stepping into his room to find him sitting with a brandy in hand, still fully dressed, on a small sofa before the fire.

Darcy had been trying to get up the courage to go to Elizabeth when the knock came. Surely he could not have misinterpreted her, but he did not want to do anything wrong on such a night. He was willing to wait until she overcame any doubts she might have before he attempted to consummate the marriage, but then she entered the room, and he suddenly found he could not breathe.

He saw that she had left her long, dark hair loose, just as he had dreamed of so many times, and she smiled as she walked across the room. The sight of her in that enticing nightdress was literally breathtaking, and the sheer fabric of the dressing gown she wore over it did nothing conceal the daring cut. The way the garment displayed the fullness of her lovely bosom and the sway of her hips under the clinging folds of fabric left him speechless. As she crossed to where he sat, he thought that he had never seen anything so beautiful in his life. He was touched that she still wore the pearls, but he could say nothing.

"Mr. Darcy," Elizabeth said wickedly, "I began to wonder if you would ever come."

Darcy found that he could not make his mouth move as she paused in front of him, and he was completely unaware that he had not stood when she entered the room.

"Are you not going to invite me to sit, sir?" she enquired with that same challenging smile. As he vaguely waved his hands, she gracefully sat down beside him with a rustle of fabric.

"I repeat myself, Mr. Darcy. Were you going to come to me, or was I to be left alone on my wedding night?"

Still he was dumbstruck.

Elizabeth leaned toward him teasingly, displaying even more of her bosom. "Sir, did you forget to write out your lines before this night? Shall I call for pen and paper?"

Darcy continued to stare at her. Her lovely face showed profound innocence, but the enticing pale skin of her bosom was even more visible beneath her neckline. Then he saw the merriment dancing in her eyes as she struggled to repress her smile. He started to chuckle, which made her smile openly, and then it became a low laugh that grew and grew. Unable to restrain himself, he soon was roaring, with Elizabeth joining him, and he clasped her to him with tears rolling down both their cheeks as they both laughed so hard their sides ached. Finally, the laughter began to subside, but even then, it only took a single giggle from Elizabeth or a chuckle from Darcy to set them off again. It was many minutes before they were finally able to achieve a level of calmness where they could talk. Darcy held Elizabeth's shoulders and moved her slightly away so that he could see her smiling face while she dried her tears.

"Minx," he said fondly, his heart swelling for love of this marvellous woman.

"I *told* you I was not unwilling."

"I was trying to work up the courage to knock on your door. But I was afraid to push you too fast."

Elizabeth smiled at him. He was really the dearest, most honourable man. "William, my friend Charlotte lectured me the night after you first proposed that I should not let my romantic impulses prevent me from marrying the man who would best make me happy. It is a sad state of affairs when *I* am forced to be the logical and rational one while *you* wallow in romantic sensibilities! How will we have children, sir, if you continue in this manner and never come to my bed?"

He smiled ruefully. "I kept having visions that I would be ravishing a virgin, Elizabeth, and I would rather wait, hard as it is, than to force you into anything before you are ready."

Her eyes got round as she said teasingly, leaning over in a way that again disclosed the swell of her breasts so enticingly.

"But I *am* a virgin! And if you do not ravish me, then my mother will have warned me all about the distasteful obligations of a dutiful wife for nothing!"

"Oh, Lord," he groaned, "I hesitate to ask what she said!"

"Well, there was repeated advice to just hold still and it would soon be over," Elizabeth said appraisingly, cupping her chin in thought. "And I believe that she tried to cheer me by saying that you would then leave me in peace for a while afterwards. And then there was the truly delightful part that, once you got me with child, I would be left alone until the child arrived and even some time afterward!" He laughed delightedly at her recitation while she looked up at him demurely, fluttering her eyelashes in affected modesty.

Finally, she said, in a voice that told Darcy she was now serious, "Will you not take me to your bed, William?"

He smiled down at her in love, full of joy, yet bittersweet, because she did not return his love. Still, he knew it was his good fortune to have finally won this most marvellous woman. "Indeed I will, Elizabeth Darcy. Indeed I will."

And, as he surged to his feet and picked her up as if she was a mere feather, she shrieked in delight as he whirled her about, and then she threw her arms around his neck as his mouth descended on hers. Elizabeth arched in his arms, tightening her hold around his neck as he walked toward the massive bed that waited with the covers already turned down for the night.

Darcy placed a knee on the bed in order to lift Elizabeth into the centre and placed her down carefully. As he stood up, preparatory to removing his waistcoat and shoes, she immediately reached out both arms to him beseechingly. Her need to have him close struck him with a warmth that made his eyes prickle with a surge of love, and he could no more have rejected her wordless plea or her half-closed eyes than he could have stopped breathing, so he simply lay down beside her and toed off his slippers. She murmured in contentment as he came within her reach, and her arms again went around his neck. He pulled her against him as they kissed long and slowly this time, knowing that the night was theirs and they had all the time in the world.

Elizabeth snuggled closer to him as they kissed, pressing her body against him, and his hand moved down her back to her waist and then lower, squeezing and caressing her through the thin fabric of her nightgown, then pulling and bunching the sheer material until his hand rested on the bare skin of her slender thigh, just as she had imagined it in the shop. A thrill of excitement ran up her spine at this fulfilment of her fantasy, and she shivered again as his hands explored her soft curves. She moved her own hand beneath his waistcoat as far as the tight garment would allow, feeling the muscles sliding in his back as he changed position to kiss her throat and then her ear, then her fingers moved around to the buttons. She fumbled with the unfamiliar fastenings, and Darcy assisted her, feeling a sense of wonder that she appeared to be enjoying herself as much as he. He was not inexperienced, but neither was he a rake with a list of conquests to his name, and he had not really known how Elizabeth would react when he took her to his bed. As their hands roamed, touching and exploring each other, he had never felt a warmer love for the wonderful woman in his arms who demonstrated her desire to bring him the same pleasure that he brought to her.

Inexperience was an impediment to them both, but Elizabeth's nightgown was a much simpler garment than Darcy's, so that his hand was soon moving over her bare skin, seeking out her most pleasurable areas to stroke and caress. Elizabeth's excitement mounted as new and heretofore unexpected desires woke within her, and urgency drove her own hands as she tugged his shirt from his breeches so she could run her hands up inside it, feeling the hard muscles beneath his warm skin. But Darcy had been more successful than she, and her nightgown was off her shoulder as well as pulled up around her waist, and she gave a soft cry of passion as his lips moved to her breast while his hand moved to her private place, the source of the throbbing warmth that kept her shivering. She clasped his head to her chest convulsively as his fingers stroked and slid over the incredible softness at her core. Suddenly, she pulled his head so hard against her breast that he was unable to continue to tease the sensitive flesh, and she arched upward as she reached her crest of pleasure, crying out in passion as she called his name repeatedly, softly but still urgently.

Elizabeth felt absolutely spent and drained, and the discoveries of this night had already indicated the superiority of her aunt's advice over her mother's. In the soft aftermath of her passion, she murmured deep in her throat in contentment, as Darcy began to kiss upward from her breast to her shoulder before moving to her neck and then her cheek. His tenderness and solicitude for her were more than merely heart-warming and comforting; they raised in her a feeling of attachment and affection that, if it were not love, was still more than she believed her own parents had ever shared. She made no attempt to restrain her soft laughter again as she thought of how her mother had advised her to lay back and endure the unpleasant duties of her wedding night!

She opened her eyes to find William looking down at her with a gratified smile. She smiled upward at him, conscious of her half-clad state as the cooler air of the bedroom swirled over her. But she made no move to cover herself with the bed coverings or to pull her nightgown back to its original position. She felt that same feeling of safety and security that she had felt the night he first held her, and she was suddenly certain that she could never have felt that with anyone else.

If that is not love, what is? she wondered languidly. She did not know, but she did not believe that she could have acted as she just had with another man.

"Mr. Darcy, sir," she murmured to him contentedly.

"Mrs. Darcy." He smiled in return, and she cocked her eyebrow at him in her calculating and impertinent manner.

"You will have to forgive me," she said archly, her face so close to his that she could feel his breath on her cheek, "and it may be due to my inexperience, but as delightful as it was, I cannot believe that is all that there is to experience of the marriage bed."

"No, not quite all," he agreed cheerfully, "but we did retire early. It will do for now, for we have the rest of the night."

"But you *will* show me more later?" she asked sweetly as she began to work on the buttons of his shirt again.

"Most assuredly," he answered her, looking down at her loveliness lying languidly on the bed, with one breast bare and with her gown up to her waist, and he felt the surge of arousal. *But there is time*, he told himself; *there is no need to rush…*

Elizabeth finished the last button of his shirt and spread it wide, viewing William's bare chest with considerable interest. She had no indication of the effect this had on her new husband, but Darcy had to bite back a growl as her hand moved up to his chest. She seemed to find the short hair there fascinating, for she kept stroking it before moving to other areas of his body to investigate.

"Elizabeth…" he groaned.

"Yes?" she said sweetly, raising her eyes to his with that delightfully mischievous smile.

"Do you know what you are doing to me?"

"No, I do not know what I am doing, but you are making me wait far too long before instructing me in the other intimacies of the marriage bed, so I am just exploring," she said teasingly, and her hands continued their examination.

"We have all night," he said, making one last attempt at restraint.

"I am impatient, sir." She smiled, noting with interest that her hands seemed to be provoking the same sensitive response as he had produced in her, and she had to laugh at a sudden thought.

"What?" Darcy asked helplessly.

"I was just thinking," she said saucily, smiling at him, "that you ought to remove those breeches. I am quite inexperienced, you know, but my investigation has given me some hints, and I do not believe that you can ravish me until you do so!"

Darcy's response was immediate. He sat up in bed and seized her by the shoulders to sit her up also. He took the hem of her nightgown and quickly pulled it upwards. Elizabeth assisted by raising her arms so that he could whisk it over her head and sail it off the bed. He slid his shirt off and likewise threw it away, and his breeches soon followed, while Elizabeth, sitting quite unclothed in bed, watched with interest. As he got back into bed beside her, she said to him slyly, "My aunt warned me this might happen."

"What?" he growled as he pulled her bare body down to his.

"That you would likely take the gown that she helped me choose completely off of me...ooh!" She ended with a gasp as his mouth came down on her breast again.

"I have always been quite impressed with your aunt's wisdom," Darcy said, his voice muffled, while Elizabeth crooned contentedly, cradling his head to her breast tenderly. But, as Darcy continued his attentions, their lovemaking lost its tender nature and became more urgent. His mouth at her breast was imperative, not soft, and it was not long before the urgency of Elizabeth's breathing and the strength of her hands on him told Darcy that she was ready. He rolled her over on her back before swinging himself over her, and she pulled his head down to her hungry mouth, her arms roaming over the broad planes of his back until she felt a tightness and a single small but sharp pain as he started to enter her.

Darcy raised his head, releasing her mouth. "This will hurt a bit, dearest Elizabeth," he said, and his new wife thrilled at the soft and caressing tone that she had first heard that night in the Hunsford Parsonage. She nodded her understanding, her arms around him firmly as he pushed deeper and harder. She cried out softly at the sharp pain inside her, and Darcy stopped in concern, only to be urged on by the strength of her arms as she pulled him against her. He waited momentarily as he looked closely at her lovely face, watching until the pinched expression relaxed as she accommodated herself to him.

At length, he asked tenderly, "Are you ready, dearest?" When she nodded, opening her eyes to watch him with a slight smile on her face, he began to move, slowly at first and then more rapidly as she began to take pleasure from the movement and urge him on. He lowered his mouth to hers, and her kisses in return grew hungrier and more demanding as their lovemaking continued. She began to respond, almost purring as she felt him inside her, awakening feelings that only a woman could feel. She knew her girlhood was gone forever, and she felt herself building to another crest of pleasure while Darcy began to move even more powerfully and deeply. She arched upward to meet him, instinctively opening to allow him complete entry, and she felt him surge powerfully inside her, pushing against her very limits while her own pleasure crested. She cried out in release, her cry smothered as Darcy's mouth clung to hers, and she felt a sudden flood of wetness deep, deep inside her. Darcy himself was almost frozen over her for long moments until he slowly slumped as his own passion ebbed from its peak. She pulled him to her, holding him close while she trembled and shook in response to those receding sensations that were almost too extreme to bear.

After a time, Darcy bestirred himself to pull the sheet up, shielding their unclothed bodies from the chilled air of the bedchamber. He rolled to the side and Elizabeth felt the delicious lassitude resulting from the release of passion and the equally delicious approach of sleep as a balm for exhaustion.

"Well, Mr. Darcy," she murmured sleepily, as she snuggled closer to him, "I do believe that I have now been ravished."

"Indeed you have, Mrs. Darcy," he said as he shifted position onto his back until Elizabeth lay cradled against him, her head on his shoulder and her arm over his chest while he clasped her hand in his. She moved her thigh up over his hips as she snuggled closer, and within minutes, she was fast asleep.

"Indeed you have, dearest, loveliest Elizabeth," he whispered, holding her precious body against his as he treasured the memory of the night. In a very few minutes, he was asleep beside her.

The hours of their bridal night passed as it usually does for those soul mates who are newly married. Periods of sleep alternated with periods of delicious exploration and turbulent activity. The candles had guttered out when Darcy first awoke in the dark to find Elizabeth nibbling at his ear while her hands caressed him intimately. Twice after that, Elizabeth was awakened by her new husband's hands sliding gently over her bare skin, seeking those sensitive areas that he had already learned brought her such sweet pleasure. The sun was peeking though the curtains as he collapsed over her for the final time while she clasped his sweating body to her own, gasping as the last throes of pleasure gradually ebbed away. Contentedly, Elizabeth Darcy let her husband roll her over on her side and tuck her against him, her back nestled against his chest. She pulled his hand up and clasped it to her bare breast, with her own hand over his as she fell into the most secure and comforting sleep she ever had known.

It was full daylight and the sun was high in the sky when Darcy next awoke to a tickling sensation. When he opened his eyes, he found Elizabeth lying fully on top of him, her slender body pressing him down in the bed. Her face was only inches from his own, and her eyes were wide-open, bright, and dancing with merriment as her long, dark hair cascaded over his upper chest. He discovered that the tickling sensation was her using a lock of that hair to sweep it gently in a slow, gentle motion that brushed over his nose and lips.

He looked up at her as she stared into his eyes, stopping when she saw that he was awake. He was conscious of her skin touching his from his shoulders to his knees, and he put his arms around her, stroking the silky softness and delighting in the firm muscles that lay beneath. She smiled, her eyes still bright as she moved against him in response to the pressure of his hands, and he felt himself becoming aroused once again. She levered herself higher up his body and lowered her face to his, kissing his nose gently then planting quick kisses over his cheeks and eyelids as the delicious curls of her hair surrounded both their faces.

Darcy felt emotion catch in his throat as her soft lips caressed his with the lightness of a butterfly's wings, as the full and true realization of his heart's desire swept through him. He now understood that even the affection that led to his proposal at Hunsford could not match the love he felt for the woman who lay atop him, kissing him with a tenderness beyond even his dreams. Perhaps those emotions had contained the seeds of love, but those seeds had grown and blossomed into something that transcended the pale and feeble feelings of bewitchment, fascination, and desire. He remembered the moment in the church when he and Elizabeth had locked eyes together, and he knew that he could never doubt her bond to him. It might not be love from her point of view, but they were now husband and wife for the remainder of their lives, and he had never been as certain of anything as he was of Elizabeth's total commitment to him and their marriage.

But now Elizabeth's kiss had grown deep and demanding, and her movement quickly brought him to full arousal even as her tongue danced over his, licking the inside of his lips as she pressed her mouth into his. He heard a delightful chuckle deep in her throat as she recognized the success of her actions, and she started to roll off him so that he might once more have his way with her. Darcy stopped her, holding her hips firmly astride his, then he lifted her up, pulling her forward so that she came to a sitting position on his belly with her legs on either side of his waist. He reached up to caress her breasts, and her breath caught in her throat. Then his fingers began to tantalize her, squeezing and stroking in the way he had learned that she loved.

He grinned wickedly up at her, marvelling at the figure that he had once disdained but now could not look on enough. He moved her hips downward gently, and, once she understood his intention, she began to assist him so that quickly he found her entrance. She gasped in pleasure, and he pulled her down again so that his mouth could claim her breast. It did not take her long to find a rhythm that matched his and resulted in the most delicious feelings inside her. That the motion was to Darcy's liking was clear from the expression on his face, and his mouth claimed hers as the tempo of their movements increased.

It was a new and thrilling feeling for Elizabeth to experiment, to find her own rhythm to excite and stimulate different areas inside her, and she was soon gasping as shuddering thrills began to build in her belly. As her pleasure mounted, her cries were again smothered by Darcy's mouth as she thrust herself downward and then went rigid as the molten pleasure inside her ebbed. When she finally managed to open her eyes, she found Darcy smiling up at her; then he suddenly rolled her onto her back as his own cadence resumed, while she moved against him to help him reach his own peak. Afterwards, she held him close as his rigid torso gradually slackened, and she held him atop her so that his weight pressed her deep into the bed.

Slowly, his eyes opened to meet hers. "Good morning, Mr. Darcy," she said wickedly, running her heels down the backs of his thighs. Before he could answer, Darcy's empty stomach gave a rumble that sounded like the growling of a dog.

Elizabeth looked down in amazement. "My goodness, sir," she said cheerfully, "you appear to have missed your breakfast."

"As well as most of my dinner and a good portion of my wedding breakfast. I am suddenly ravenous—at least for food. My *other* appetites have been quite fully satisfied," he said wickedly, and Elizabeth slapped him gently on his bottom as she smiled back at him. He made another move to slide off her, and again she restrained him.

"I am afraid I will hurt you," he said.

"I will not break," she said firmly, but then she relented. "But now that you mention food, I do believe that I might be interested in at least a nibble."

"Then let us ring for breakfast," Darcy said cheerfully, "or whatever meal is closest, since I have not the slightest idea of the time." He started to reach for the pull beside the bed, but Elizabeth put her arm on his.

"Perhaps I might put on a robe before we have a servant respond to your call?" she said sweetly but with a significant lift to her eyebrow.

"Yes, dearest," Darcy said with an embarrassed grin. "Perhaps you might pull the covers up, and I can close the bed curtains to provide the necessary privacy."

"And it might be advisable to collect some of the clothing that went goodness knows where in the night time," she suggested helpfully. "I believe that I should have asked my Aunt Gardiner many more questions before last night," she continued thoughtfully as Darcy swung out of bed.

"Your Aunt Gardiner has already become one of the most sensible women of my acquaintance," Darcy said cheerfully as he gathered up the various clothing items and threw them onto the bed before he went to his dressing room to retrieve a long robe. "You should talk to her often," he said over his shoulder.

Elizabeth watched his bare body move across the room, interested and intrigued by the way the muscles in his legs and buttocks moved beneath his skin. *So different from my own body,* she thought with interest. *This has been a most memorable day and night—so many new things that I had never before imagined.* She sighed as she thought what her mother's honeymoon must have been like to have caused her to give the advice that she had given; she was swept by a feeling of sorrow and loss to know that her mother had never experienced the warmth and delights that had marked her own wedding night.

Poor Mama, she thought for the thousandth time.

ELIZABETH LAY BACK IN THE bed with a sigh. "That was delicious," she said, as Darcy continued working on his own plate beside her. "Did you ever find out the time?"

"It was past one when I first got out of bed," Darcy said as he cut another large bite of ham. "It must be past two now."

"Much of the day is already gone, then," Elizabeth said thoughtfully. "Whatever can we do for the rest of it?"

Though she had put on her nightgown and tied her dressing gown around her, she saw the familiar expression come into Darcy's eyes as he looked at her.

"Besides that, sir," she said gaily, patting him on the arm. "Perhaps we might at least manage a trip down your stairs before returning to your bed."

Darcy reached over and clasped her small hand, raising her fingers to his lips to kiss them gently. "I am the most fortunate of men."

Elizabeth felt her cheeks colour slightly as she struggled to contain the embarrassment at receiving such a heartfelt compliment as she remembered all her mistakes during their acquaintance, mistakes due to her own pride and misjudgements.

"I do not deserve to be put on that lofty a pedestal," she said uncomfortably. "I have many defects to rectify, and I will be content if I can simply be a good wife to the most honourable man I know."

After some thought, he decided that he could no longer avoid the subject that still concerned him. "Elizabeth," he said carefully, "you must know how wonderful the past day has been. You have fulfilled and surpassed every desire and expectation that I ever could have entertained as my wife. But there is still…that is, I could not help but wonder…well, I was thinking…"

Elizabeth smiled and laid her hand along the stark curve of his jaw, feeling the stubble of his beard.

"You are wondering how I could behave so wantonly when I cannot say I love you as you love me."

"I did not mean…"

She laid her fingers again over his mouth. "William, you do not need to worry about my feelings. I *did* behave wantonly, and I would do so again and again to please my husband, for you deserve no less. I said that you are the most honourable man I know, and I know how much you would like to hear me say the words, 'I love you,' but I am quite confused as I wonder whether I really know what it is to love a man. Remember that less than two weeks ago I was totally ignorant of your regard for me. Already, my feelings for you have changed dramatically, and they are still changing. Is it love? I am too confused to answer; it is too soon. But this I know. In future years, I do not want our memories of this special time to be tainted because I withheld my affections in any way as a result of the rapidity of our courtship." She paused as the most delightful smile appeared on her face. "You do understand, William, that Richard will rise to new heights when he tells *our* courtship story to our children? Your comment about my being 'only tolerable' will be nothing compared to what your cousin will tell them!"

Darcy groaned as he considered it. "It was bad enough when he only had the story of my mother and father to tell. He will be simply insufferable now."

"Perhaps." Elizabeth smiled. "But one day the good colonel will provide some amusement for the rest of the family himself."

"Richard?" Darcy laughed. "Marry? Never! He will be a bachelor forever!"

"Perhaps," Elizabeth said with a slight smile.

Darcy looked at her quizzically, but she only looked back at him with a smile that hinted of secrecy. Dismissing the thought, he pulled Elizabeth more firmly to him. "Thank you, dearest. You have made me happier than I had any right to dream."

"For what," Elizabeth teased. "For being a dutiful wife?"

Darcy pulled her to him in sudden emotion, his throat choking and an unfamiliar burning in his eyes. "I do not deserve you, dearest, loveliest Elizabeth," he said huskily, and Elizabeth could not doubt the earnestness of the compliment, even though she was still uncomfortable at being described in such flattering terms. Not being able to put her discomposure into words, she reverted to a wife's most effective options in such a situation as she turned toward him and raised her lips to his own. Naturally, such a display of affection led to the inevitable consequence, and shortly afterward Elizabeth's gay laughter sounded from behind the bed curtains.

"It is just as my aunt said!" she chortled, as her nightgown again sailed out through the gap in the bed curtains.

Friday, May 1, 1812

THE REMAINDER OF THE WEEK passed in a similar fashion for the newly wedded couple. They rose when they pleased, ate when they were hungry, irrespective of the time, and made love when the urge struck them. Darcy ventured to the library and brought up several books in which Elizabeth had expressed an interest. Often, he would read to her while she nestled comfortably against him, her head on his shoulder, but much of their time, they simply talked, lying in his bed under the covers. They did go downstairs for supper on Wednesday evening but otherwise took all their meals in their rooms. The household staff had few duties other than to provide meals for the couple, and thus they were well aware that their master and mistress were enjoying a most successful honeymoon. All concerned were certain that this boded well for the future happiness of the family though Mrs. Taylor was forced to quell a considerable degree of good-natured speculation as to how soon a Darcy heir might be expected. To be sure, her attempts in that matter would have been more effective if she had been better able to suppress her own smile, for she was well pleased at the way her master and mistress got on together on the rare occasions during the week when she had seen them.

Georgiana returned to Darcy House late in the afternoon on Friday along with her Aunt and Uncle Matlock, accompanied by Colonel Fitzwilliam. She had quite enjoyed her visit, having entertained Jane several times, as well as accompanying her friend on several shopping expeditions and to the theatre for a performance of Shakespeare's "Julius Caesar" along with Mr. Bingley and the colonel. She was not as fond of the Bard's histories as she was his comedies, but it was still a pleasant diversion. It was made more pleasant by Colonel Fitzwilliam's whispered asides during the play that had kept all three of them in a constant struggle to contain their laughter. She particularly remembered one comment as Mark Antony alluded to Caesar's many victories when Richard had muttered to her, "Now I *know* old Will was making this stuff up. Could anything be more unlikely than an Italian general who not only *fought* a battle but *won* it? And more than once?"

Elizabeth and Darcy were just coming down the stairs as the family party entered the house. Georgiana was immediately struck by the changed aspect of her brother. She had known and been comfortable with his solemnity and seriousness for so long that she was quite taken aback by his cheerful expression and warm smile as he greeted them with Elizabeth on his arm. He was clearly filled with good cheer, and the look of pride as he showed off his new bride was a large part of his changed aspect.

As greetings were exchanged, Georgiana could see that her aunt and uncle were as amazed as she was. Richard, however, had a grin as large as Darcy's, and the light of mischief danced in his eyes. He was not, however, the first to comment on Darcy's demeanour. This was a Darcy whom none of his family had ever before seen, and Lord Matlock was even quicker than his son to weigh in on the subject.

"Marriage *does* seem to agree with you, Darcy," he said as they shook hands. "As well as looking like you have been sampling a new delivery of port to excess. You look incredibly self-satisfied, almost smug."

"I believe the word 'besotted' would be appropriate," offered Colonel Fitzwilliam, clasping hands with his cousin in turn.

"Like a cat that swallowed the canary," added Lady Matlock, as she embraced Elizabeth and gave her a kiss on the cheek. Darcy's smile only grew bigger if that were indeed possible. "You seem to have worked wonders on our nephew, dear," she told Elizabeth as Georgiana embraced her new sister. Then, taking Elizabeth's arm, she started down the hall. "We have decided to invite ourselves for supper, Darcy," she said over her shoulder as the others followed her toward the parlour. "We sent a note over earlier to enquire about it, but Mrs. Taylor replied that the master was 'indisposed' and was not to be disturbed." Darcy suddenly broke into a fit of coughing as he tried to choke back his laughter.

Colonel Fitzwilliam solicitously pounded his cousin on the back, inquiring blandly, "Did the canary go down the wrong branch, Cousin?"

"Have no fear, Mrs. Darcy," Colonel Fitzwilliam turned his attention to Elizabeth. "Tweaking my favourite cousin is a sport that is always in season, and this time Darcy has provided a wealth of material for years to come!"

"Richard!" Georgiana chided. "Have some sympathy for William, for someday he will have the chance to turn the tables on you!"

"Darcy?" Fitzwilliam laughed. "It could never happen, Georgie! All the impulsiveness lies on the Darcy side of the family. We Fitzwilliams are models of boring and staid behaviour. No material for him there!"

Georgiana made no reply, but Elizabeth noticed the look she gave her buoyant cousin and filed it away in her memory for later consideration.

"My dear niece, have you heard the story of how Darcy's father courted my sister?" asked Lord Matlock jovially. "It has become almost an epic tale in the family."

Elizabeth dimpled over her shoulder. "I did hear a version of it earlier from William, but if you think that you might be able to add more detail, I feel certain that I would be fascinated!"

Chapter 25

Saturday, May 2, 1812

Elizabeth was sitting with Darcy in his study the next morning, reviewing the multitude of cards that had been left by callers during the past week while her husband attended to his neglected correspondence. When the sound of the door knocker was heard, he looked up in mild irritation and pulled out his watch.

"It is too early for callers," he told Elizabeth, but in less than a minute, Stevens tapped on the door to his study and announced his aunt. Lady Matlock smiled at the confusion on Darcy's face as he and Elizabeth rose to greet her.

"I suspect that today will see any number of the curious come to call," she said, eyes sparkling with humour, "and I wanted to be the first."

"I believe you are correct, Lady Matlock." Elizabeth gestured to the silver tray mounded with cards on Darcy's desk. "If all of these friends and acquaintances of William come to call today, I am afraid we will be overwhelmed."

"Not all will call today," said Lady Matlock, speaking with the voice of experience. "But there will still be an impressive number. Are all of these people known to you, Darcy?"

"I have met most but not all," he growled, "and several of those whom I *do* know are persons I would much prefer to avoid."

"That is the way it is," Lady Matlock told him. "Ours is a prominent family, and there are many who wish to be acquainted with you and your new wife. There are also," she continued, her expression changing to one of distaste, "others who desire to see whether certain rumours can be stirred into something more entertaining. It is for this reason that you find me on your doorstep at such an early hour."

"I do thank you, Lady Matlock," Elizabeth said. "It is exceedingly thoughtful of you." Elizabeth indeed felt true appreciation, for by coming that morning to be with her when she received her first visitors as Mrs. Darcy, Lady Matlock would squelch any gossip cold in its tracks. A more overt gesture of approbation could not be imagined.

"Then let us take this tray of cards into the parlour, Elizabeth," said Darcy's aunt, "and we can sort it into various piles—those whom we wish to see, those who wish to see us, and those who shall not be allowed past the front door! That way"—she smiled— "my nephew might catch up on those duties he has surely been neglecting while keeping his new wife locked in his chambers!"

Darcy groaned in response while Elizabeth and Lady Matlock joined in cheerful laughter.

DARCY RELUCTANTLY QUITTED THE LIBRARY to join the ladies as the first of the callers knocked at the front entrance. When he entered the parlour, Lady Matlock was seated with Elizabeth on a sofa just large enough for the two of them, thus ensuring that they would not be separated. Darcy would normally have been amused at his aunt's skill in social manoeuvring, but he was distinctly out of sorts. Just the day before at that same hour, he had been reclining in bed with Elizabeth at his side, talking of Pemberley and its surrounding environs, always one of his favourite subjects. And he also recalled the way his discourse was interrupted when Elizabeth, in a sudden fluid, catlike motion, had somehow shifted from his side to completely on top of him. The way in which she smiled wickedly at him while she lazily moved her hips had—

He had to firmly squelch that line of thought as he came to sit in a chair beside Elizabeth. He looked over at Colonel Fitzwilliam, who was talking with Georgiana. "Not that I am not always glad to see you, Cousin, but it confounds me how you continually manage to just suddenly be here without any indication of your arrival."

Richard grinned cheerfully. "I rode Wellington in from the Dragoons and left him in the care of Johnson. I came in the back way."

"Ah," said Darcy noncommittally. Then he cocked his eye at his cousin. "Wellington? New horse?"

"No—same horse, new name. When Wellesley was made Earl of Wellington in February, I deemed it a good time to promote Arthur accordingly, thinking it might change his disposition. But alas, I fear that Wellington is as ill tempered as Arthur was. He barely missed taking off one of Henderson's fingers the other day."

"Perhaps a different animal might be advisable," suggested Darcy.

But Fitzwilliam was firm. "Not for any amount of money. Wellington is a mean, nasty animal, I grant you, but the sound of gunfire only makes him prick up his ears. And he will go all day and half the night without tiring. No, I think I will put up with his little foibles in return for a better chance of surviving the next encounter with that rabble Bonaparte calls cavalry."

"But if they are a rabble," asked Georgiana suddenly and somewhat sharply, "why do you need a beast like Wellington?"

"Because there are so blasted *many* of them, Georgie!" Fitzwilliam exclaimed airily.

"And you make *such* a lovely target with that red coat," Georgiana shot back in some spirit.

"Ah, yes, well I might agree with you there, Pigeon, but their lordships believe the colour provides the proper inspiration for the men. No one else dares to wear red, so when we see it, we know it is one of ours." He turned back to Darcy, "But my arrival was not pure coincidence, Darcy. It was at Mother's special request—I will have you know—so that I might assist her and your lovely bride in doing combat with the social mavens of our fair city. She specifically requested full dress uniform—including medals,"

"I did notice that you appeared even more awesome than usual," Darcy said dryly.

"She considered asking Father to also make an appearance, but she rather thought that might be deemed a trifle heavy-handed. Between the ladies and myself, I believe that we shall be able to cover your own social inadequacies quite brilliantly."

"No doubt," Darcy said. However, if Elizabeth felt any measure of uncertainty, it did not show, and she seemed perfectly at her ease as the door was opened for the first of their guests.

"Mr. and Mrs. Thomas Wallace," Stevens called out, as a heavy-set man whom Darcy recognized from one of his clubs entered with a much younger woman on his arm. Darcy was certain that he had never seen her before in his life. *Now it begins,* he thought wryly. *For what we are about to receive, let us give thanks...*

"Well, *that* went rather well!" exclaimed Colonel Fitzwilliam buoyantly as they heard the front door close after the last of their guests.

"Perhaps you feel so," groused Darcy as he sprawled in his chair. "But I, for one, am exhausted by inaction and feel an inordinate desire to indulge in some type of exuberant exercise by way of compensation. Perhaps you and your Wellington against me and my Ned? To Matlock and back, perhaps? For a guinea?"

"Darcy," his aunt said, "I believe the constabulary takes a decidedly dim view of gentlemen racing through town streets. It would be rather a scandal to have your name mentioned in the *Times* for being fined ten or twenty pounds for behaving like a common ruffian—especially after your wife's triumph this day. Elizabeth," she said, "I cannot imagine why I ever worried about your first contact with London society. You acquitted yourself marvellously; as a hostess, you charmed them out of their slippers."

"You are too kind, Lady Matlock," Elizabeth responded. "I noted several of our visitors who might have been positively fearsome had it not been for your presence by my side."

"Certainly, certainly, my dear, though I am confident you would have found a way to handle them. But a goodly number of them were like Mrs. Wallace, who may not be an intellectual giant but is certainly as good-hearted a young lady as you might ever meet."

"She very much reminds me of Jane," said Elizabeth with a smile, "and I plan to call on her next week. Mrs. Simmons was also of the same sort. She was curious, of course, but it was a simple, honest curiosity—not at all malicious."

Before the conversation could progress further, Colonel Fitzwilliam rose to his feet, having just glanced at his watch. "I just noticed the time, Mother, and I believe that we must hasten on our way," he said. "I am already late returning to the regiment, and did you not mention an appointment at two o'clock?"

"Oh, yes, and it is past one already. My goodness, I do need to hurry."

"I ordered your coach readied at the stables a half-hour ago when I saw the rush of visitors start to decline," said Darcy, also rising to his feet. "I will escort you there. I do thank you for your assistance this day though I also am certain that Elizabeth would have done splendidly in any event. But your thoughtfulness is much appreciated."

"Very much so," agreed Elizabeth. "But, if I might be excused, I believe that I will retire to my chambers. I feel a slight headache coming on." She came over to embrace her husband, stretching up on her toes to kiss his cheek with a gleam in her eye and a slightly wicked smile that only he could see.

Darcy struggled to keep his features immobile, but the futility of this was made clear by the flash of Colonel Fitzwilliam's teeth as he walked by Darcy's side to the stables, though he surprisingly made no comment. Darcy was more uncertain as to his aunt, but he was inclined to believe his feelings must be clear to everyone since even Georgiana had repressed a smile when she left the parlour for the music room.

AFTER SEEING HIS AUNT AND cousin on their way, Darcy headed briskly back to his bedroom and bounded up the stairs, taking them two and three at a time. As soon as he entered his room and closed the door, he came to a sudden halt, for the view was arresting. Elizabeth stood near the window, looking out at the sunlit street below, wearing one of those alluring night-gowns that he loved so much. The bright sunlight streamed through the filmy material, outlining her slender body in a manner that made Darcy's mouth go suddenly dry.

Elizabeth turned as she heard the door close to see her husband standing stock-still, staring at her as if mesmerized. It was still surprising to her that she could have that effect on him when he was such a masterful man in so many other areas.

Perhaps this reaction would fade in time, but it was really most flattering that she could cause such a response in so confident a man. If that was what love did to a person, then the warmth and attraction she felt for him could not be the same emotion that he felt. But perhaps, the love the poets waxed so eloquently about could not have the same expression on two such dissimilar creatures as she and her husband. Whether it were love or another emotion, there was no disguising the way she had come to want and even need to spend so much of her time with him.

"I see you lost little time in acting on my hint, Mr. Darcy," she told him wickedly as he seemed to shake off his bemusement.

"I would be daft not to respond to such a sensible suggestion, Mrs. Darcy," he said huskily, as he walked across the room, tugging on his cravat. He paused by his bed long enough to throw back the covers before turning to Elizabeth, removing his coat and tossing it over a chair as he crossed to her.

"I did worry a little that you might not have taken my meaning," she said, cocking her head in an inquisitive manner.

"There is little chance of that, madam, not until I have completely taken leave of my senses," he said, as he reached her and slipped his arms around her waist. Elizabeth had already tilted her head back as his arms pulled her close, and her eyes were half-closed as he lowered his mouth to hers. Even the familiarity of the past week could not dull the sweetness of her kiss as he felt her arch upward, kissing him back with an eagerness equal to his own. He drew back slightly as he felt her fingers at the buttons of his waistcoat, but then, realizing what she was about, he again lowered his mouth to hers. Her tongue darted and teased at his as he slipped it between her eager lips, and his hands explored the curves he found so exciting as she finished with the buttons of his waistcoat and began to tug it over his shoulders.

"I am glad you decided to wear trousers today, sir," Elizabeth said breathlessly, her fingers fumbling at the buttons at his waist. "I have decided that I much prefer them to . . . ooohhhh!" She gasped in delight as she felt the delightfully delicate touch of his tongue on her ear, and she tried to concentrate on unfastening the buttons of his trousers. That was especially difficult since she could feel his arousal through the fabric of the garment. Finally, she finished with the last of the buttons and pushed his trousers downward until they fell to his knees.

"It is fortunate . . . ohhhhhhh . . ." she leaned her head to the side as Darcy moved from her ear, pressing delicate kisses down the column of her neck. She tried to concentrate on the fastenings of his shirt as his hands roamed freely over her back, from her shoulders down to her bottom while his wonderful lips left a trail of tingling flesh down her shoulder to the upper slope of her breast. "It is fortunate," she managed to continue, as Darcy slipped one shoulder strap of her gown off her shoulder, "that I am not disposed to flee…ahhhhhh…for I fear you would be…oh, yes…rather hampered if you tried…if you tried to pursue me…oh, William, yes…" She finally managed to finish her sentence as Darcy's mouth found the tip of her breast. Meanwhile, she had finished with the last fastening of his shirt, and he aided her in removing the garment.

Suddenly, he bent at the waist and scooped her up, with one arm behind her back and the other under her knees. Awkwardly, he shuffled around in a turn, taking little baby steps toward his bed, hampered by his trousers still pooled around his ankles. Elizabeth smiled and then laughed aloud at the lurching motion that was all he was capable of as he carried her over to the bed, and Darcy grinned back at her in shared delight. Her arms circled his neck as he finally reached the bed, and she shrieked in sudden surprise as he held her out over the centre of the mattress and dropped her. She bounced as Darcy sat down and feverishly worked at his shoes and trousers until finally he ripped them off. Quickly, he rolled to his side to join Elizabeth.

She was smiling as she felt his hands at the hem of her nightgown, and she lifted her hips so that he could free her from it. Darcy managed the rest, as he lifted her shoulders to pull the nightgown completely over her head before launching it out into the room. As they embraced fully, their bodies melded together in that special way they had both learned to love so much, and Darcy was immediately aware that Elizabeth needed little preparation. Her hands on his hips urged him to move on top of her, and she was only too willing to help guide him as he entered her fully. She sighed in contentment at the wonderful feeling that resulted, both from the physical pleasure and from the incredible closeness she felt to him at this time. She began to match her movements to his own rhythm as she pulled his head down to hers, arching up to him to feel the glorious sensation of his bare skin on hers. Her kiss was hungry and eager, her tongue searching, and Darcy responded in kind as she quickly picked up and matched the now-familiar motion of their lovemaking.

Darcy took his time, but, though Elizabeth was willing and eager, he was not able at first to bring her to completion. Even so, her hands urged him on, drawing him into increasing the frequency and power of his movements until he felt her own begin to quicken. As he felt his peak building, her whispered endearments increased in fervency while her legs and hands implored him to continue until finally he hit the crest and plunged deep into her, arching his back as he tried to make their union as close as possible, while her own shuddering response told him that she had found her own pleasure.

Afterwards, Elizabeth held him close, and she would not let him move off her. Both of them were sweating from the exertion, but she did not mind. She just wanted Darcy to stay as he was though she did allow him to pull the sheet over them.

"I wish we could stay like this forever," she said softly, and Darcy felt his heart leap with the warmth and tenderness in her voice.

"I also," Darcy said huskily, "but I do fear that I will crush you."

"Nonsense, William," she said archly, "you have a most comfortable bed, and I told you before that I will not break."

At length, however, Elizabeth allowed him to roll aside, but he did not rise from bed, only changing position to pull her against him.

"But should we not rise and dress?" she asked. "What will Georgiana think?"

"Georgiana will have to learn to deal with a newly married brother sooner or later, and she will be well able to take care of herself, for Mrs. Annesley returns today. In any event, she will just mark it up to the Darcy *impulsiveness.*"

Elizabeth giggled softly and then snuggled contentedly into Darcy's side, for she did feel the most pleasant lassitude. Soon, Darcy felt her breathing slow and deepen. He fell into a light sleep himself but awoke within the hour, for he was not used to taking naps. He lay still, with Elizabeth's head on his shoulder and one of her arms across his chest while her leg was across his own.

Just as he was wondering whether he ought to wake her, for the sun was close to going down, he heard Elizabeth mumble something. He looked down, and though she was still obviously asleep, her lips were curved in a soft smile. Again, she murmured something, then her arm clamped around his chest as she pulled herself closer to him. Darcy leaned forward as much as he could, straining to hear what she said. He held that position for long minutes, listening as Elizabeth talked in her sleep, sometimes in low tones, other times more clearly, before she gave a long, drawn-out moan. Whether the moan was of satisfaction or of pain might have been difficult for an observer to determine, but after Elizabeth slipped back into deeper sleep, Fitzwilliam Darcy lay back himself on his pillow with a broad, happy smile on his face and a surging in his heart.

Chapter 26

Tuesday, May 19, 1812

Elizabeth peered anxiously out the window as the coach drew up before the well-remembered front steps of Netherfield. She had not seen Jane since the wedding though she had written telling her of their expected arrival time. Jane's reply suggested meeting at Bingley's house rather than Longbourn as their father was still not reconciled to Elizabeth's marriage and would not allow her name to be mentioned there.

By the time Darcy assisted Elizabeth and Georgiana out of the carriage, Bingley and his sister Caroline were already waiting for them at the top of the stairs to the front entry.

"Mrs. Darcy," Bingley exclaimed, bubbling with enthusiasm and good humour, "permit me to welcome you to Netherfield!" He welcomed Georgiana in a similar fashion before he turned to clasp hands firmly with her brother, welcoming him and clapping him on the shoulder. Even for Bingley, this was exuberant behaviour. However, Elizabeth was completely unprepared for his sister's greeting as Caroline Bingley stepped forward briskly.

"Welcome to Netherfield, Mrs. Darcy," she said before she embraced Elizabeth and then kissed her on each cheek. She turned to Georgiana and welcomed her in the same manner. Elizabeth looked at her husband in profound surprise at the warmth and unaffectedness of Miss Bingley's greeting, but he only shrugged. Obviously, he could no more explain her behaviour than could she. But she did catch a surreptitious wink that Bingley gave Darcy.

"Jane will arrive in about a half-hour," Caroline said as she ushered Elizabeth and Georgiana inside. "She and Mrs. Bennet were delayed at the chapel until then. Your trunks have already been taken up, and your maids have arrived to assist you in refreshing yourself. Tea will be served downstairs when Jane arrives, and I know you will have much to talk about..." Caroline continued to chatter on cheerfully as she escorted the three guests to their rooms. When Miss Bingley left her, Elizabeth lost no time in entering her husband's chambers.

"Just what has happened to Caroline Bingley?" she asked. "I saw that wink Bingley gave you, so I know that there is something you have not told me."

Darcy had already removed his coat and waistcoat and was untying his cravat. "I do not know for certain," he said cheerfully, "but if I were forced to speculate, I would hazard that Miss Bingley has seen the error of her ways and is determined to reform herself."

"William," Elizabeth told him firmly, "it is quite clear that something dramatic must have happened. What I want to know is what could have ever induced her to behave as she did today? And now that I think on it, she was absolutely civil at our wedding, too." Darcy unfastened the buttons to his shirt and pulled it off.

Darcy dropped his shirt to the floor and took Elizabeth by the shoulders, turning her around so she faced away from him. "Now, I know we have not been married a month," she persisted, as his fingers worked on the buttons of her dress, "but I can already detect that you are dancing around my question and hoping that I will forget what I asked. But it will not work, sir," she told him sternly. "Nor will I be distracted!" she tried again, but he had by now finished with her buttons and was sliding her dress off her shoulders and letting it fall about her ankles.

"I believe that Charles may have had a talk with Caroline about her future," Darcy said, unlacing her stays, which soon joined her dress about her ankles, leaving her clad only in her chemise and stockings.

"After he made his offer to your sister, Charles knew he needed to confront both his sisters back in London," Darcy continued, grinning hugely as her chemise followed her dress and stays to the floor. "He was, however, unsure that he was up to the task," he told her as he kissed her neck, moving down her back and all the way to the cleft of her buttocks. Elizabeth's breathing grew ragged as he kissed her all over while he removed her garters and then slid her stockings down her slender legs.

"And?" Elizabeth said with difficulty. Darcy was still kissing her bottom while he busied himself removing her shoes. Her hands were clenched into little fists at her side as the most delicious thrills radiated up her spine.

"And as a good friend, I could not help but think of how I achieved my own heart's desire, so I helped him prepare a set of notes..."

"You did not!" exclaimed Elizabeth delightedly, both from what he was saying but also from what he was doing as he had now removed her shoes and had turned her around. He remained on his knees while his hands claimed the roundness of her bottom even as he kissed her all over her belly. He chuckled as he felt her stomach muscles ripple beneath her skin in testament to the effect he was having on her.

"But I did, dearest. Then, armed with his script...Charles presented his ultimatum...knocked both Caroline and Louisa back on their heels...and never let up until he had secured their oath...that they would treat both Jane and you...with perfect civility."

He came to his feet and scooped Elizabeth up in his arms, carrying her over to the edge of the bed. Elizabeth shivered as Darcy's kisses moved up the insides of her thighs until he reached the juncture of her legs. When she felt the first touch of his lips there, she cried out at the throb of pleasure that radiated outward from his heated touch.

Darcy gloried in her reaction, in the way he could bring her pleasure, just as she delighted in doing the same for him.

"And you could tell all that with just a wink?" she said, gasping as Darcy's kisses and tongue flicked over the incredibly sensitive core of her femininity.

"Well, I must admit that I did receive a letter from Charles earlier in the week acquainting me with the particulars," he murmured, as he slipped a finger inside her to assist in stoking her passion.

"Oh, William...yes, yes...oh, please do not stop..."

As his tongue and his lips teased and licked her tingling flesh, Elizabeth began to tremble. She wanted to move her hips, the instinctive response to the warmth that was building inside her, but she most assuredly did not want to move away from the delightful touch of Darcy's lips and tongue. Her pleasure built and surged until she finally fell over the waterfall, putting her fist in her mouth to stifle her cries as she shuddered and arched upward even as he kept his mouth glued to her.

BY THE TIME THAT DARCY and Elizabeth came downstairs, Jane had arrived and was sitting with Bingley, Caroline, Georgiana, and Mrs. Hurst in the parlour. Elizabeth, certain that it must be obvious what had just transpired in their rooms, was relieved of the embarrassment she felt from coming downstairs late when Jane immediately ran to her and embraced her closely.

"Oh, Lizzy, it is so *very* good to see you!"

After that distraction, Elizabeth felt able to sit down with some equanimity.

"I hope your rooms are to your liking, Mrs. Darcy?" Caroline asked politely, and again Elizabeth was struck by the lack of sneering incivility that had previously marked Miss Bingley's conversation.

"They are perfectly comfortable, Miss Bingley," she said with a smile. *At least, I know that the bed is certainly comfortable!* she thought. *Especially considering how quickly I was in it!*

"But, as I explained to Georgiana earlier," she continued cheerfully, "if we are going to be sisters, we cannot continue to call each other 'Miss Bingley' and 'Mrs. Darcy.' I hope you will call me Elizabeth, or Lizzy, or even Eliza, or else people will think that we are quarrelling."

Caroline's smile was somewhat brittle, remembering all her previous sneers and innuendos about this upstart country miss, but she had resolved to amend her manners lest Charles carry out his threats, and she responded with acceptable civility.

"Then I shall call you Elizabeth, and you shall call me Caroline," she said firmly.

Elizabeth smiled in answer. There was a measure of watchfulness in her expression, to be sure, but the smile was genuine, and Caroline Bingley recognized it as such. She was well aware that a truce had just been offered and that she had accepted it. A truce was not quite the same as a peace treaty, but she had no interest in breaking the armistice just agreed on.

ELIZABETH WAS EAGER TO SPEAK privately with Jane about her father and the atmosphere at Longbourn, but she was not able to secure any time alone with her until the late afternoon. Finally, she enticed Jane into a walk in the Netherfield garden while her husband and Bingley contested at billiards and Caroline was engaged in writing letters.

She could hardly contain herself until she and Jane had turned the corner before she began. "Jane, I must know what is going on at home. I am guessing that father is no more amenable to understanding than he has been previously."

Though she knew it would be of special concern to Lizzy, Jane was very reluctant to discuss this topic as she was completely out of her depth in such a feud. Her love for her sister warred with the duty she owed her parent, and she wished for nothing more than that two of the dearest people in her life would find a way to mend their differences. But her every suggestion and question to her father had been rebuffed, for he absolutely refused to talk of it and would not hear of a resolution with his daughter. Finally, Jane heaved a sigh.

"I am quite sorry that I am forced to agree with you," she said sadly. "My father will simply not discuss it, either with me or with Mama. Even worse, though he refuses to speak of you, Lizzy, he will not cease speaking of Mr. Darcy in the most unflattering manner."

Elizabeth's lips pressed together in anger. "If that is Papa's reaction, then I cannot call at Longbourn. I will not abide such unwarranted abuse of my husband. If I have learned nothing else in the past month, I have at least learned that I have married an honourable man."

Jane was miserable as she was forced to agree with her sister. "I believe that Mama understands this, for she is planning to come here for supper tonight and to bring our sisters so they can see you before the wedding."

"It also means that we almost certainly cannot attend the wedding breakfast."

"I know," said Jane, unable to hold back the tears that gathered at the corners of her eyes.

"Why is Papa being like this?" Jane exclaimed in uncharacteristic agitation. "I would not have believed it if I had not seen it! When I tried to tell Papa of what Mr. Wickham has done to the Darcy family, he only said, 'Well, well, well, there are two sides to every story, and I daresay Wickham's report is every bit as likely to be true as any other.' I was so shocked that I was unable to speak further, and I had to run upstairs to my room."

Elizabeth was similarly affected, but she resolved to put aside her anger now that she had learned what she needed to know. "Let us not allow this to distress us further, Jane," she said, managing to summon a smile, "for tomorrow is to be your day, and I would not want my troubles to diminish your own joy."

Jane had one last thought to share on the subject of her father before she would allow a change of topic. "I hope that you understand why I did not ask you to stand up with me tomorrow. I was afraid of Papa's reaction, and it still pains me, for I had never dreamed of being married without you beside me."

"You made the correct choice. William and I will be close by, for Papa would never make a scene in public view. We will simply depart for Pemberley immediately afterwards. Now, let us leave this subject and talk of other things. Are you completely packed?"

"Yes," Jane said, but her smile was wan. "I remember how we talked before your marriage about how nothing would ever be as it was, but I must confess that I did not fully realize it until I came home to our room and all of your belongings were gone. It was even more striking when the time came time to pack up *my* things. I had to make choices about what to take and what to leave behind, and now I know how you felt when you mentioned never again returning to the room we shared."

She frowned suddenly. "Lydia was quite exasperating. She kept trying to talk me into giving her some of my new gowns even though they would not fit her, and she several times pulled folded dresses out of my trunk in order to look at them in the mirror to see how they would appear on her. I had spent considerable time folding those dresses correctly, and it irritated me to have to do it over again. And Mama simply would not make her stop."

"No, she would not," replied Elizabeth sadly, "for we both know that Lydia is her favourite daughter. I am sure that Lydia is unable to stand the fact that she is not the centre of everyone's attention, and she has said many times how much fun it would be to be married before any of her sisters. And now, with the two of us having made splendid matches, I believe she is feeling jealous."

"Perhaps so," said Jane doubtfully. "I will have to give way to your better understanding on this subject. But I know I would not be marrying if it were not for you, Lizzy. You have been the cause of much happiness for both of us." Now Jane smiled mischievously at her sister. "Or do I not interpret the signs correctly? I saw the way that you and Mr. Darcy looked at each other when you joined us, and you both appeared to be well pleased."

Elizabeth instantly blushed at this proof that she had not been as successful at disguising the reason that she and Darcy were so late coming downstairs as she had imagined. Jane laughed delightedly at her success at discomfiting her sister, and Elizabeth could not be angry with her on this day and soon joined in.

"I hoped you had not noticed." This drew another laugh from her sister. As they walked further through the garden in companionable silence, Elizabeth determined on a way to turn the tables.

"Have you given any thought to the advice that Aunt Gardiner gave us the day before my marriage?" she asked, giggling at Jane's sudden blush.

"I do recommend that you give careful consideration to that rather than what dear Mama tried to warn us of," Elizabeth continued cheerfully when Jane made no response.

The sisters walked on in silence for several minutes before Jane was able to venture any response to that remark.

"Truly?" she said, her voice so soft and tentative that Elizabeth barely heard her.

"Truly, dearest sister," smiled Elizabeth.

"You have worn one of those...those gowns for your...for Mr. Darcy?"

"Yes, Jane, I did, and on our very first night together," Elizabeth said cheerfully, "and on most nights since then. Though," she said with the most innocent expression, "our aunt was also correct in estimating my chances of keeping that gown on for very long."

"Oh," was all that Jane could say. They walked on further before she ventured, "I *would* like to wear one for Charles, but I do not know if it would please him. And," she confessed in a low voice, "I worry that I would be too embarrassed to even put one on, much less let Charles see me in it."

"I think you should trust Aunt Gardiner on this," Elizabeth encouraged her. "I believe it would please him, Jane; I truly do. And I would further advise you to wear the most daring of your nightgowns on the first night. I remember that one well, and you will look beautiful beyond compare in it."

Elizabeth's eyes danced mischievously as she looked over at her sister. "But I must repeat the warning that, no matter what you wear to your husband's bed, you will not wear it for long! Our mother is quite mistaken in this matter, and our Aunt Gardiner is correct. My husband has said several times that he has come to regard our aunt as one of the most sensible women of his acquaintance!"

Jane had to laugh, and Elizabeth continued, "Plus, there is the further consideration that Bingley has grown quite confident of late."

"And he did say that he was done with prudence!"

"There, you see?" said Elizabeth delightedly. "You would not want to give a *prudent* signal to a man who is determined to be quite *imprudent!* Trust our Aunt Gardiner, and trust what William says about her!"

Jane smiled and hoped that she could follow her sister's advice, for she dearly desired to see Charles look at her as Mr. Darcy had looked at Elizabeth earlier!

Wednesday, May 20, 1812

ELIZABETH AND DARCY ARRIVED WITH Georgiana at Longbourn Chapel early the next morning, for Elizabeth was anxious to avoid an open confrontation with her father. She had come to the belief that much of his intransigence was due to pride, in much the same way that her own pride had misled her in her evaluation of her husband prior to that memorable evening at the Hunsford Parsonage. Her father prided himself on his insight into other people even as she once had, and he would be even less likely to admit error than she had been, for he had for too long disengaged himself from the world outside his library.

Mr. and Mrs. Gardiner were the next to arrive, having travelled early that morning for the ceremony. Darcy immediately went over to Mr. Gardiner and drew him aside, for Darcy had suggested the previous evening that they invite the Gardiners and their children to Pemberley for Christmas. Elizabeth was pleased to see the easy manner between Darcy and her uncle, and she was easily able to see her uncle's pleased surprise when he received the invitation. Darcy returned to Elizabeth and Georgiana just as Bingley's two sisters entered and joined the others at the front of the chapel by the altar. The remainder of the guests arrived after that—Aunt and Uncle Philips, Sir William and Lady Lucas, the Longs, the Gouldings, and others, followed finally by Mrs. Bennet. Bingley, attended by his brother, Mr. Hurst, made their entrance from a side door and came to stand by Reverend Palmer.

Once all were present, the Bennet daughters entered singly. Lydia came first, giggling and irreverent as always, followed by Kitty and then Mary.

Finally, Mr. Bennet walked in with Jane on his arm, and Elizabeth saw Darcy's gaze immediately shift to Bingley. He had told her of the almost physical impact he felt when she entered on the arm of her uncle, and she knew Darcy recognized the same impact on his best friend; she was momentarily enraged that her father's displeasure had prevented her husband from standing up for him.

Darcy did indeed see and understand how Bingley saw Jane, for Elizabeth's elder sister truly looked beautiful. But even more, Darcy felt a profound sense of relief and thankfulness that he had been able to atone for his earlier mistakes in separating them. He could only be grateful that his friend would soon be joined in a union that was almost certainly more perfect than his own. For while Bingley and Jane were like two identical coins, laid one on the other in perfect symmetry, he and Elizabeth were like two parts of the same coin—they fitted together to make a whole, but both of them were different in so many ways from each other. He grimaced inwardly, wishing that he had possessed similar insight the previous fall; so much anguish could have been avoided. But then he felt Elizabeth's elbow dig into his ribs, and he realized that she must have read his mind—or his expression—and was reminding him of her advice: *Think only of the past as its remembrance gives you pleasure.* He smiled weakly down at her and put his hand over hers on his arm in acceptance of the rebuke.

Mr. Bennet never looked their way during the whole of the service. Elizabeth struggled to keep her distress over her father's snub from marring the joy she felt in Jane and Bingley achieving what was most assuredly the best of all outcomes, but she was only partially successful.

After the ceremony concluded, family and friends crowded around the newly married couple to congratulate them. Elizabeth was conscious of how her father had quickly withdrawn from the crush of people, so as not to be forced to even make a polite greeting to either of them.

The other guests departed to Longbourn for the wedding breakfast with the men, including Mr. Bennet, walking and the ladies taking the carriages. Meanwhile, Elizabeth and Darcy said their goodbyes to the remainder of her family, and Elizabeth believed that Jane, in the excitement, had noticed little of the manner in which her father had snubbed both Darcy and herself. She was certainly in good spirits as she embraced Elizabeth, bubbling with joy and clinging to the arm of her new husband. It was with sadness for what should have been, mixed with relief that it was completed, that Elizabeth made her goodbyes to her mother and sisters and Darcy made his to Bingley. Then, as Bingley and Jane boarded one carriage and her mother and sister boarded the remaining one for the short trip to Longbourn, Darcy handed Georgiana and Elizabeth into his own coach for the trip to Pemberley. It was with decidedly mixed feelings that they bid goodbye to Hertfordshire.

Chapter 27

"Look, Elizabeth, there is the entrance to Pemberley!" exclaimed Georgiana, leaning forward to point out the window. Elizabeth leaned over to see the lodge amid the trees of Pemberley Wood as the coach turned off the road.

"I cannot see anything but trees," Elizabeth said. "Where is the house itself?"

"It cannot be seen from here," answered Darcy. "We have to climb up to the rim of the valley to see across it to the other side where Pemberley House is located. I will have the driver stop there, for the view is excellent."

"The woods are certainly beautiful, William. I believe that I shall enjoy exploring them very much."

"I would suggest that you take provisions along if you are determined to walk rather than ride," teased Darcy. "And I would still suggest that you learn to ride, Mrs. Darcy."

"I am not a horsewoman, Mr. Darcy. If you desired a horsewoman for a wife, it is your own fault for choosing a simple country girl who is frightened of the beasts!" she teased him back. "I long ago agreed to a truce with my father's animals — they stay to the stables and the roadways while I stay to the woods and fields."

Georgiana was still trying to accustom herself to the way in which Elizabeth and her brother would sport with each other, but evidently, Elizabeth's lively nature was the tonic her brother needed, for he only chuckled and patted her hand in contentment.

The coach continued to climb for some time, with the extensive wood stretching out on either side of the road. Finally, after about half a mile, they reached the top of the ridge, and Darcy called to the driver to pull up. Leaning over to Georgiana's window and looking out, Elizabeth's eye was instantly caught by Pemberley House, situated on the opposite side of a valley. It was a large, handsome stone building, standing well on rising ground and backed by a ridge of high woody hills, and in front a stream of some natural importance was swelled into greater but without any artificial appearance. Its banks were neither formal nor falsely adorned.

"It is completely delightful, William," Elizabeth said, and Darcy could not hide the pleasure that he took from her artless and sincere compliment. "I am impressed by the way that nature has been left unchanged in everything I can see," she continued. "The house seems so well placed that it appears to be part of the valley, and I cannot remember ever having seen a place where nature so well complements what has been added."

"I have always felt more at home here at Pemberley than anywhere else, even in London," said Georgiana softly. "I know William feels the same way."

"However, I believe that we must move on, for our arrival appears to have been noticed," said Darcy, pointing across the valley where the household staff poured out of the entrance to gather on either side of the stair to the door.

"It is always amazing the way they seem to know when someone is approaching," smiled Georgiana. "It is almost as if they have some kind of signalling system like the semaphore towers that pass messages from the seaports to London."

Darcy called to the driver to resume, and the coach descended the hill, crossed the bridge, and drove to the door of Pemberley House. Elizabeth inspected the assembled servants in their various uniforms apprehensively then berated herself, for the staff at Pemberley must be equally as capable and welcoming as in town, and she could have no complaints about her reception there. But she could not help the nervousness she felt as Darcy assisted her down from the coach.

At the head of the assembly stood a respectable-looking elderly woman with a tall man of similar age beside her. Darcy led Elizabeth immediately over to them. "Elizabeth, I would like you to meet my housekeeper, Mrs.

Reynolds." The housekeeper curtseyed to her new mistress. "Welcome to Pemberley, Mrs. Darcy," she said in greeting.

"Thank you, Mrs. Reynolds." Elizabeth smiled, nodding her head in acknowledgement of the older woman's curtsey. "Mr. Darcy has sung your praises for much of the journey here, and I look forward to your assistance in learning what I need to know." Mrs. Reynolds curtseyed again, pleased at this first meeting with the young lady of whom Mrs. Taylor had written. She certainly seemed open and friendly, not at all like some ladies who were supposed to be much higher bred.

"And this is Reynolds, her husband," Darcy indicated the tall man beside the housekeeper. "He has been the butler here at Pemberley for most of my lifetime."

"Welcome to Pemberley, Mrs. Darcy," rumbled the tall, elderly man as he bowed to Elizabeth even as his wife welcomed Georgiana home with a warm embrace. He gave a signal with one hand, and a dozen servants immediately bolted for the carriage, unstrapping and passing down trunks and boxes. Their luggage disappeared up the stairs into the house, followed by the three travellers.

AFTER ELIZABETH REFRESHED HERSELF, SHE was quick to seek out Georgiana and accept her offer to tour the house. They were joined by Mrs. Reynolds, who was anxious to know the desires of her new mistress. Darcy was unable to join them since he had been immediately ensconced in his study with his steward to review the numerous items that needed his attention after several months of absence. The ladies' first stop was the dining-parlour, a large, well-proportioned room, handsomely furnished and fitted up. Elizabeth was quick to compliment its appearance but, after a brief appraisal, was drawn to a window. She was greatly impressed by the view of the hill across the valley, its distant crest crowned with the woods through which they had passed earlier. She was pleased by everything she saw, and every disposition of the ground was most agreeable. The whole scene, including the river, the trees scattered on its banks, and the winding of the valley, as far as she could trace it, was delightful.

"This is truly charming Georgiana!" she exclaimed with delight. "What a lovely view to accompany a meal."

As Georgiana led Elizabeth into other rooms, beauty was evident from every window. The rooms themselves were lofty and handsome, with furniture suitable to the Darcys' fortune, but Elizabeth was again impressed by the taste expressed in their selection, just as at Darcy's house in London.

"The furnishings are very much to my liking," she told Georgiana, "neither gaudy nor uselessly fine, and it shows more real elegance than is visible in the furniture of many other houses."

"Such as at Rosings." Georgiana giggled, drawing a smile of agreement from Elizabeth.

In one room, a small miniature, suspended along with several other miniatures over the fireplace, caught Elizabeth's eye. When she looked closer, she saw it was a likeness of Mr. Wickham. A quick sidelong glance told her that Georgiana had turned away, her face grim and pale. Meanwhile, the housekeeper came forward and gave a sniff of disdain.

"That is a picture of the son of my late master's steward. Mr. Darcy's father had him raised and schooled at his own expense." She sniffed disdainfully again. "He is now gone into the army, but I am afraid he has turned out very wild.'

"I am acquainted with Mr. Wickham," said Elizabeth, taking Georgiana's hand and squeezing it warmly, "and I can safely say that you have described his character completely."

"And that," said Mrs. Reynolds, pointing to another of the miniatures, "is my master—and your husband, Mrs. Darcy!—and very like him. It was drawn at the same time as the other—about eight years ago. I think it captures his handsome aspect quite well."

"I would agree with you on this point also, Mrs. Reynolds," Elizabeth said with a smile.

"In the gallery upstairs is a finer, larger picture of him than this one. This room was my late master's favourite room, and these miniatures are just as they used to be then. He was very fond of them. And this," she continued, indicating another picture, "is one of Miss Darcy, drawn when she was only eight years old."

"And even more handsome than her brother, would you not agree?" said Elizabeth.

"Elizabeth!" said Georgiana as her cheeks turned pink.

"Dear Georgiana, did your brother not say that you shall have to learn to receive a compliment, for you shall receive many of them?" teased Elizabeth.

Mrs. Reynolds was quick to warm to one of her favourite subjects. "You are absolutely correct, for Miss Darcy is certainly the handsomest young lady that ever was seen. And she is so accomplished! She plays and sings all the day long."

"I well know." Elizabeth smiled, still holding the hand of a blushing Georgiana. "I have heard her perform with great pleasure, and she plays and sings like an angel."

"Indeed you have it right. Just like an angel!"

Georgiana was finally emboldened to say, "Now stop it you two. You are making me blush!" She was answered with the laughter of the two ladies, well satisfied in their endeavours.

Georgiana then led Elizabeth to the spacious lobby above and into a very pretty sitting room, lately fitted up with greater elegance and lightness than the apartments below.

"Oh, it looks wonderful!" Georgiana exclaimed.

"Mr. Darcy gave us complete instructions on how to decorate it just for you, Miss Darcy, since you took a liking to it when you were last home."

"He is certainly a good brother," said Elizabeth, as she walked towards one of the windows to once again enjoy the glorious view.

"That he is. He will be pleased to learn how delighted Miss Darcy was when she saw her room. And that is always the way with him. Whatever can give his sister any pleasure is sure to be done in a moment. There is nothing he would not do for her."

"Of that, I am sure," said Elizabeth, linking her arm with Georgiana's.

Next was the gallery. As Georgiana and the housekeeper commented on and identified the many family members, Elizabeth found little to interest her, for she was searching out the only face whose features would be known to her. At last, as Georgiana led her to a portrait of her brother, Elizabeth halted to examine it. The portrait was finely done, and it bore a striking resemblance to the subject. The artist had captured that smile she had seen so often when he looked at her and which she had at first so completely misinterpreted. She stood several minutes before the picture in earnest contemplation, and she saluted the competence of the painter, for he had captured her husband perfectly. He had already told her that he very much desired to have her likeness painted and to place it beside his own, but Elizabeth suddenly decided to insist that the portrait be painted of both of them instead. That would look more appropriate, for she had no place in this fine house apart from her husband.

After the tour of the house, Elizabeth expressed a desire to see the grounds, so Mrs. Reynolds turned back to her work while Georgiana remained with her. As they walked across the lawn towards the river, Elizabeth turned back to look again at the stately aspect of the house.

"It is rather overwhelming," Elizabeth said, waving at the house and the surrounding grounds. "I find the thought of being Mistress of Pemberley to be slightly terrifying." She noticed that Georgiana seemed withdrawn, and she took her arm and tucked it into hers.

Georgiana," she said as they resumed walking toward the river, "you must put your experiences with Mr. Wickham behind you."

Georgiana stopped in shock, "How... how do you know..."

Elizabeth pulled her back into motion as she continued walking. "Because you are not the only young lady he has deceived, dear sister. He did a most effective job of deceiving *me* about William, and I am still mortified when I think of how credulous I was in believing his lies. But William was also correct when he said that Mr. Wickham is most successful when the object does not possess the cynicism and suspicion to detect his treachery. Would you not say that describes both of us?"

Georgiana was shocked that her brother had spoken of her troubles, even to Elizabeth, and she said as much.

"Georgiana," Elizabeth sighed, "you should probably know this since Colonel Fitzwilliam is aware of it, but when your brother first proposed marriage to me, I was so incensed at his purported mistreatment of Mr. Wickham that I was very firm in rejecting his offer. We spent several hours talking out my objections to him, and after he explained the truth about Mr. Wickham and, even worse, his offences against you, I was possibly the most mortified girl in all of England."

Georgiana stared at Elizabeth with wide eyes. "So *that* is what Richard meant when he said that he knew you were not a fortune hunter!"

"Yes," she said, smiling, "I am innocent of being a fortune hunter but guilty of being a very foolish girl who almost threw away her chance of happiness. So, you see, you shall have to give up this embarrassment about last summer lest you make me inclined to dwell on my own transgressions against good sense!"

"But Elizabeth, you did not almost elope with Mr. Wickham! That is what causes me to feel such uncertainty and worry. I almost destroyed my whole life and possibly William's as well!"

Elizabeth stopped and put her hands on Georgiana's shoulders. "I cannot allow even that to stand. I *knew* that Mr. Wickham could have no serious intentions since I had no money. But what if I had ten thousand pounds like poor Miss King in Meryton? Can I say with certainty that I would not have been swayed by his charms? We both know that I cannot guarantee that. No, Georgiana, we must be thankful that neither of us was forced to pay the full price of our foolishness, and we must go on with our lives without allowing that experience to be a burden on our future happiness."

"That is what William says." Georgiana attempted a smile.

"You should listen to your brother," said Elizabeth gaily. "He is almost as wise as my Aunt Gardiner!"

"In what way is your aunt so wise, Elizabeth?"

"Oh…well…never mind…perhaps I will tell you another time."

Georgiana continued her walk with her friend and sister, but she was quite curious at what could have caused Elizabeth to suddenly blush so scarlet.

It was mid-afternoon before Darcy finally finished with his steward and went in search of his wife and sister. He found Georgiana studiously practicing at the pianoforte, and he was not surprised to find Elizabeth in the library; indeed, it was the first place he looked after the music room. She was on the far wall, halfway up the movable ladder, inspecting some volumes that were beyond her reach from the floor. Silently closing the door, Darcy took great care to cross the room without a sound, aided by the thick carpet. The first inkling that Elizabeth had of his presence was the touch of his hands as they slid under her petticoats. She could not prevent her sharp cry or her start of surprise, and she tried to look severe as she peered down at her husband.

"Mr. Darcy," she said in the sternest voice she could manage, "if you are going to creep up on your wife like that, you may sometime have to deal with a fainting female in mid-air."

"It is no matter, Mrs. Darcy," Darcy responded, not moved even a jot by her scolding, "for you are as light as a summer breeze, and it would be no burden to pluck you out of the air."

Elizabeth closed her eyes and held tightly to the ladder as his hands moved up her thighs to the bare skin above her garters. "Perhaps I should come down," she said shakily as she felt his fingers dancing over her hips and her bare bottom.

"It would be best," her husband responded with a definite smirk on his face. "Now that my business with my steward is resolved, I had thought to give you a more intimate welcome to Pemberley. I intended to conduct this welcome in my chambers, but it might be a refreshing change to do so on a library ladder."

"The ladder is much too unstable for such exploits. I will come down immediately." She replaced the book she had been examining on the shelf. Darcy smiled and offered his hand and arm to stabilize her as she descended.

When she reached the floor, he raised her fingers to his lips. "Dearest Elizabeth, will you accompany me to my chambers, where it is my firm intention to welcome you to Pemberley by ravishing you though you are no longer a virgin?"

"Indeed I am not, Mr. Darcy," said Elizabeth, smiling back in her turn, taking his offered arm, "and it would be most delightful to accompany you to your chambers and be ravished once again. But I must tell you, sir, that I do begin to fear that you may be insatiable, considering that you ravished me twice last evening at the inn and seem completely unsatisfied today."

"I shall never get enough of you," Darcy said fervently, and Elizabeth laughed gaily as that familiar look came over his face.

"I shall depend on *that*," she told him firmly, squeezing his arm as they left the library.

At the top of the stairs, they came upon Mrs. Reynolds talking with two maids, but they passed with just a quick word and a nod. With Elizabeth on his arm, Darcy briskly continued on to the door of his bedroom and disappeared within.

Mrs. Reynolds smiled to note that Mr. Darcy did not even bother with the pretence of escorting his wife to her own chambers while he went to his own. Then, though the bedroom door was quite heavy, the three women heard the sound of Elizabeth's gay laughter and the master's answering merriment. They all tried to hide their smiles, for they had heard tales of the impulsiveness of Darcy's good father, and it appeared his son was cut from the same cloth.

"Please inform the staff that the master is not to be disturbed until he rings," said Mrs. Reynolds, struggling to contain her smile. Certainly, the master and his wife were on the most friendly terms just as Mrs. Taylor had intimated in her discreet letter.

"Yes, ma'am," chorused the giggling maids.

"And no tales!" cautioned Mrs. Reynolds, and the two maids quickly gave their agreement before they departed.

"Though much good it will do," said Mrs. Reynolds softly to herself, allowing herself to show a broad smile of contentment for the first time. It was *good* to have the master home and so well settled!

WHEN ELIZABETH AWOKE, THE ROOM was dim, and a quick glance outside showed that the sun was nearly at the horizon. Quickly, she shook Darcy awake. "William, we have overslept. It is almost dusk."

Darcy rubbed the sleep from his eyes and smiled up at her. "There is no rush, Elizabeth." He reached out his arms for her, and she allowed herself to be drawn back down to his embrace.

She snuggled comfortably into his side. "It shall be as you wish, Master of Pemberley. However, I *do* seem to remember that you told your sister that we would dine at six o'clock, and it *is* rather past that time."

Darcy's eyes opened wide at that, and his only comment was, "Oh." After a few minutes, he sighed. "Well, there is nothing for it, dearest. We shall have to hurry and dress for dinner."

After another few minutes, they reluctantly arose and adjourned to their separate rooms. Quickly, Darcy summoned Jennings, and Elizabeth rang for Sarah with the result that they were descending the stairs in little over a half-hour.

They found Georgiana in the library engrossed in a book, and the three of them went to the small family dining room with a small table sized perfectly for their party. Within moments of their seating themselves, the servants began to bring out the steaming bowls of soup.

"What were you reading?" asked Darcy.

"Shakespeare," she replied. "'Julius Caesar.'"

Darcy raised his eyebrows in surprise. "I thought that you preferred the Comedies."

"I do. But I had the opportunity to see 'Julius Caesar' while I stayed

250

with my aunt and uncle, and I was interested in actually reading the play. Especially since I had so much time available with nothing to do," she said innocently, her eyes on her soup.

Darcy looked at her sharply, but he was not able to read her expression. "Well," he said hesitantly, "I am sorry about making you wait, Sweetling. I quite lost track of time."

"I daresay," Georgiana said in the same tone as before. "But I truly expected no different, given the *impulsiveness* of the Darcy family."

Darcy was immediately seized by a fit of coughing, choking on his soup when he swallowed convulsively at her unexpected tartness.

"Georgiana, you must not sport with your brother like that," admonished Elizabeth dryly as Darcy took a sip of wine to clear his throat. "I am too newly married a wife to become a widow!" Georgiana was completely unaffected by her comment, wearing a wide smile at her success in discomfiting her brother.

"Have you been giving my sister lessons in impertinence, Mrs. Darcy," he said accusingly, though the sharpness of his question was belied by the smile on his face.

"I have not, Mr. Darcy," responded Elizabeth gaily, "I daresay she has a natural talent for it!" Both ladies laughed in delight as Darcy tried to assume his stony visage, but he quickly desisted and joined them. In truth, he was mightily encouraged that Georgiana seemed to be emerging from the shell she had retreated into after last summer—even if it meant that he might be the recipient of such jibes from the two dearest individuals in his life.

Chapter 28

Elizabeth opened her eyes sleepily to see the light of dawn just beginning to filter through the curtains. She felt her husband behind her and she nestled against him, her back to his front, holding his free hand with both of hers, clasping it to her bare breast in the way that she found so comforting and secure.

She dreamily faded back into a half-sleep, thinking about the previous evening, and she knew her nightgown was somewhere on the floor of the bedroom. She smiled as she remembered the almost boyish glee that he seemed to derive from peeling it off and lofting it out into the darkness. She would have to keep a warm robe near to the bed once winter came. But how pleasant it was to lie there in William's arms, right where she was, and to be held in such a way. She was truly contented with her life as his wife—more content than she had ever dreamed to be.

As Elizabeth continued to drowsily think on how happy she had become over the past weeks, of how confident she was of William's love, of her pleasure in their conversations and walks, a realisation penetrated to her consciousness that what she felt was more than contentment—much, much more. She opened her eyes completely now, suddenly wide-awake as she searched thoughts and emotions that she had only become aware of in her dreamy state. At that moment, Elizabeth clearly saw what had been murky before, and she realized that she was happier than she had ever been in her life. She clutched his hand fiercely as she suddenly, with a flash of insight, understood that what she felt was *love*. She knew now—not just suspected but absolutely knew—that she had fallen completely in love with her husband. It had occurred so gradually that she had not seen the change, wrongly putting down her feelings to comfort and contentment and affection. She had been unaware of it until that very moment!

Elizabeth twisted around, feeling a sudden stab of emotion in her heart as she looked at William's handsome, well-known, and yet somehow freshly new features. The sudden realization of how very dear he was to her was almost frightening in its intensity. As she inspected the face that had become so familiar to her in the past weeks, she thought back on the twisted road that had led to that moment. When she considered the many obstacles that could have caused them to lose their way, she was deeply thankful to have successfully arrived at such a state.

She could not restrain herself, for the surging in her chest was completely new to her.

"Wake up, William," she said, putting her hand to his cheek.

Darcy's eyes opened to find her face close to his own, and he smiled at her tenderly. "Good morning."

Elizabeth put both of her hands on his cheeks and said intently, "I could not wait for you to wake up, dearest. I want you to know that I *love* you."

Darcy smiled and pulled her close. "I know," he said softly into her ear.

Elizabeth sat up suddenly, only to be pulled back down by his strong arms. "What do you mean, you know?" she said in confusion. "I did not know myself until just a few minutes ago! How could you know?"

Darcy's smile grew, and he kissed her forehead tenderly. "Because you talk in your sleep."

"I do not talk in my sleep!" Elizabeth said firmly, but Darcy just continued to smile at her.

Eventually, she whispered, "I do?"

"Yes, dearest Elizabeth," Darcy said softly. "For weeks now, usually in the hours just before dawn, I have awakened to hear you murmuring things like, "I love you, William," or "Yes, love, yes," or "Love me, William.""

Elizabeth blushed as she realized that she must have been dreaming of their lovemaking, but her discomposure only made Darcy kiss her again.

"Then I should make myself perfectly clear," Elizabeth persisted, breaking off the kiss. "Now that I am awake and finally know myself. I do love you, Fitzwilliam Darcy, and it has made me the happiest woman in the world to be your wife."

Darcy smiled as the last piece to the puzzle of his own happiness snapped into place, and he kissed her tenderly. "I would have waited a lifetime to hear those words, Elizabeth, and, as gratified as I have been, I am now the happiest man in the world to be your husband."

Then Elizabeth grinned wickedly. "Then, since you have heard these words before, let me repeat them." She looked deeply into his dark eyes. "Love me, William. Love me and make me your wife in every last particular."

"Your wish is my command, dearest," he said, as his hand moved to her bottom and pulled her hips firmly against his while his other hand went to the back of her neck.

As his lips touched hers, Elizabeth almost gasped at the heat. It had to be her imagination, but his lips seemed almost on fire as he kissed her. Her passion was fuelled by the emotions surging through her, and she kissed him back fiercely, her tongue reaching deeply into his mouth to dance against his own. She arched herself against him, trying to force her bare skin inside his own in the strength of her need to bring him close to her, and Darcy felt a sharp pain as her fingernails dug into his back.

Their lovemaking was as fierce as her surging passions. Elizabeth lowered her head to Darcy's chest and her teeth delicately nipped at his flesh to send sharp thrills through him. She clutched him with her small hands in the way she knew he loved, bringing him to an arousal that matched her own before her hands moved to his hips so that he felt her fingernails again sinking into his skin as she urgently pulled him against her. She did not need any preparation; her only desire was to feel him inside her, and she writhed as she begged him, "Please, William...please, I need you...oh, hurry, darling...please hurry..."

As he finally entered her, Elizabeth arched herself to meet him, her hands urging him to penetrate her deeper. She opened herself fully for him, her legs capturing his as he moved inside her, and her legs joined her hands in signalling her desire for him to move faster and deeper. He was caught in her need, and surrendered to a rhythm as old as humanity and as new as the morning. Elizabeth gasped as she pulled him down to her so that her sharp little teeth could nibble at his ear lobe: "Oh, yes, dearest…oh, my love, do not stop…William…oh, William, oh, William…yeeeessss!!"

Darcy's mouth smothered her cries as she was wracked by a wave of pleasure and fulfilment almost too intense to bear. She shuddered and quivered as Darcy continued his rhythm, and he brought her to another crest of pleasure even as he reached his own. She pulled him downward against her as she arched upward toward him, and the blissfulness of completion was an emotional sweetness as intense as her physical release.

Darcy was sweating from the exertion, but Elizabeth was gasping and slippery from an even greater effort, continuing to stroke him from his shoulders to his bottom while she murmured endearments into his ear. He felt her need to atone for the weeks past, and he knew that she did not want him to move from atop her. Despite his instinctive wish to take his weight off her, he had learned that she desired that feeling in the aftermath of their lovemaking. *Especially such an occasion as this,* he thought.

At length, Elizabeth allowed him to roll off her and tuck her into his side. She was still murmuring as she fell into a deep sleep. She was, at last, truly and completely, Mrs. Fitzwilliam Darcy.

She slept.

It was late when Darcy and Elizabeth finally arose, for Elizabeth was insatiable that morning, and it was well after noon before they finally left their room. Georgiana came upon them in the hallway at the bottom of the stairs, Elizabeth's arm tucked through her brother's and both of them laughing softly at a shared moment. She halted at the look of radiance that her brother and his wife wore. They had always appeared comfortable with each other, but this morning was…different. But their eyes lit up when they saw her, and they were quickly upon her, clasping her arms and sweeping her down the hall, almost dragging her along with them as they laughed gaily. Georgiana's heart swelled at the growing love between her brother and Elizabeth. It made her only more firm in her resolve that she would settle for nothing less.

Chapter 29

Elizabeth hummed as she knocked on the door to Darcy's study. He gave her a quick smile before returning to work while she sat in what had become her chair beside his desk, where she often helped him sort through and arrange the mountains of correspondence he received. She never could have imagined the range of matters that claimed his attention, from letters on estate business and tenant issues to social letters that could either be invitations to social events or correspondence from friends such as Bingley—though that gentleman, never the best of correspondents, had gone simply silent since marrying Jane.

Elizabeth was not offended by the scratching of Darcy's pen as he concentrated on his letter. She had learned during the three months of their marriage how disciplined her husband was in the discharge of his duties. So she sat quietly beside his desk while he finished, enjoying his look of intense absorption. *It is so typical of him,* she thought fondly, *to throw his total concentration into whatever he does.*

Darcy was not long in finishing, and after quickly sanding and sealing the letter, he turned to Elizabeth with a warm smile that made her heart lurch. Despite what she had told him, she did not think he even yet comprehended how very dear he had become to her, and besides, she was almost bubbling over with good spirits that day. For not only did she anticipate the arrival of her Aunt and Uncle Gardiner later with her sister Kitty, but she also had some news to share.

"I have just come from a conversation with Mrs. Reynolds and Mrs. Stenson," Elizabeth said, as soon as her husband had put down his pen. "You are certainly familiar with a woman's time of month, both from your sister and from me."

"Indeed I am," Darcy said seriously. "And I also remember Mrs. Taylor's advice, when I consulted her the first time you experienced that event, and I have been very careful what I did and said on that occasion."

Elizabeth coloured lightly, but she laughed also before continuing, "And have you noticed, dear husband, that there has been no recurrence of such an event since then?"

Darcy sat up straighter at the implication of her comment, and she laughed and put her hand over his. "And both Mrs. Reynolds and I believe that it is now safe to say that our activities have borne their usual fruit, William, and I am now with child."

Darcy sat for a moment in stunned silence. Then his face came alive, and a slow smile stretched ear to ear in sublime glee. "Truly, my love?" he said, taking her hand in both of his.

"Truly, William," she smiled back. "Mrs. Stenson estimates that we may anticipate a child around the end of February or the first part of March."

Darcy came to his feet and pulled Elizabeth to him, enfolding her in his arms. "This is truly wonderful news," he told her softly. "Already I have been so very happy, and now there will be a child at Pemberley for the first time in more than sixteen years!" He smiled as he remembered something.

"Stevens will be happy," he told Elizabeth. "When I told him that I was to marry, he congratulated me and then said that it would be wonderful to see children again in Darcy House."

He put his hands on her shoulders and looked her in the face. "Should you see a physician, Elizabeth? I do not believe there is a really good physician here in the country."

"Mrs. Stenson says there is nothing to worry about. She acts as midwife for the staff here at Pemberley as well as most of the tenant farmers. She also said that a young surgeon has been travelling through the nearby villages for the past year and that she has heard he is very good. She has sent word to Lambton to have him call on me when he arrives next week. And there are several other experienced midwives nearby if Mrs. Stenson is unavailable, so we will be well served when my time comes."

Darcy looked somewhat concerned. "Perhaps I should ask Doctor Peterson to make the journey from London to examine you," he said worriedly.

"William, stop worrying! I come of good physical stock—no matter how silly some of them are—for my mother had five girls with not a single problem. I was five years old when Lydia was born, and I clearly remember that Mama continued her usual endeavours up to the point when the midwife was summoned."

"Her usual endeavours, was it?" Darcy said with a teasing smile. "Was she even then searching the neighbourhood for suitable husbands for her daughters?"

"Stop that!" Elizabeth laughed. "Jane was only seven at the time. It was *at least* three or four years before she started plotting!"

"I daresay." Darcy smiled, pulling her to him. Then, suddenly fearful that he might be squeezing her too hard, he loosened his grip.

"There will be none of that, Mr. Darcy," growled Elizabeth. "I have told you many times, I will not break, and I do dearly like being held!"

Darcy pulled her close again. "As you wish, dearest, as you wish."

Elizabeth looked up at him carefully, and she saw a slight trace of worry remaining. "And I will not have you going all gentlemanly on me," she said firmly. "I am convinced that such tales recommending that husbands and wives separate during this time are completely without basis."

"Whatever you say, dearest." Darcy grinned.

"Well, I am glad we got *that* settled," she said archly, "for I do not think my aunt and uncle will arrive until well after luncheon."

She could not have said anything better contrived to drive away any last lingering hints of worry, and Darcy lost no time in escorting his wife from the study and up the stairs to the privacy of his chambers.

ELIZABETH AND DARCY WERE SITTING in the music room listening to Georgiana when Mr. Reynolds knocked at the door.

"Beg pardon, sir," he rumbled, "but Tad tells me that a carriage has just pulled in by the Lodge. I expect it is your visitors."

Darcy looked up at the older man quizzically. "You would not consider sharing with me how the news could arrive here so quickly, would you,

258

Reynolds?"

The butler simply smiled. "Pemberley has a most excellent staff, sir."

"I still have no idea how they do it," Darcy said to Elizabeth as Reynolds left. "It is uncanny."

Having thus been warned well in advance, a small force of servants was already assembled when Darcy and Elizabeth walked outside with Georgiana to await the arrival of their guests. Elizabeth recognized her uncle's carriage just coming into sight around the curve of the road. In less than five minutes, the driver halted before the entrance to Pemberley.

After the travellers were settled in their rooms and had refreshed themselves, Elizabeth and Georgiana offered to take their guests on a quick tour of the house and garden before supper. Mrs. Gardiner and Kitty were eager to see the grand house, while Mr. Gardiner accepted Darcy's offer of a game of billiards. As Elizabeth led them through the public areas downstairs, Kitty gawked in wide-eyed wonder at the loftiness of the rooms and the richness of the panelling. Mrs. Gardiner, however, was more impressed with the subdued elegance of what she observed.

"It is very grand, to be sure, Lizzy," she said, "but it is not so imposing and ornate that it loses the sense of being a home where people live. Pemberley has a, well, a *lived-in* appearance, if you know what I mean. I do not mean to be critical," she said quickly, glancing at Georgiana, who only smiled.

"I do indeed know what you mean." Elizabeth smiled. "And I had the same thought when Georgiana first showed it to me. More true elegance and less useless finery. As she told me when I first arrived, Pemberley is where she has always felt most at home."

She pointed to the windows. "What I most love, I believe, is the delightful prospect that can be found at almost every window. When I sit and read or just sew, it is so pleasing to look out on such pleasant and comforting scenes."

"But what she *really* loves is to go walking for miles and miles through the paths and woods," offered Georgiana. "William says she should learn to ride so that she could see more, but Elizabeth is adamant that she would never make a horsewoman."

"How could I enjoy the charming views if I was sitting up on some huge beast, afraid that every moment might be my last?" Elizabeth asked with a smile. "I am much happier walking."

Next was the music room, and Elizabeth pointed out the imposing pianoforte that was the centrepiece.

"This was just recently delivered, a gift from William to Georgiana. You will have to hear her play on it; it is a wonderful instrument, and she is truly able to draw the best from it."

"Do not let Elizabeth raise your expectations too high, Mrs. Gardiner," said Georgiana. "She is always determined to sing my praises, but she is more than competent in her own right." She looked at her new sister. "We shall play a duet, Elizabeth," she said firmly.

"As you wish," Elizabeth said. "Of course, we shall both have to sing," she teased, but she was pleased to see that Georgiana did not shrink from her challenge, as she would have done only a month earlier. It was rewarding to see the younger girl's steadily increasing confidence.

Elizabeth led the way through the remaining downstairs rooms and then up into the upstairs lobby and the gallery. But the party did not tarry long, for the sun was close to the horizon and the outside gardens awaited. As they left the house to see the grounds, Georgiana turned to Mrs. Gardiner as a sudden thought occurred to her.

"Did you have a chance to see Mrs. Bingley when you stayed at Longbourn?" she asked. "Her letters have been quite cheerful, but I would dearly love to see her again."

"We did have the chance to dine with them at Longbourn on the evening that we stayed, and Jane gave me several letters to both you and Elizabeth. They are in my trunk, which was just being unpacked when we came downstairs."

"I trust Jane is adapting well to married life," said Elizabeth. "Her letters have always been cheerful, but they now seem to, well, *bubble!*"

Mrs. Gardiner laughed in delight. "A better word could not have been chosen, Lizzy! Yes, she is blossoming more and more every day. She and Bingley have always been well matched in temperament, and it continues, for Mr. Bingley is as amiable as ever, but he has also become quite accomplished at managing an estate. He is only leasing Netherfield, so he does not wish to make major improvements until he decides whether he should keep it or search for another that is better situated."

Elizabeth smiled, understanding her aunt's intimation, for it was readily apparent from Jane's letters that she had begun to deduce that Netherfield was *much* too near Longbourn. Jane had been able to keep her mother away for the first week of her marriage only with difficulty and had not had any success in that regard since. It seemed that Mama was wont to call at least once a day with predictable consequences to the composure of both her daughter and her son-in-law. She made a mental note to talk with Darcy about it. Perhaps he might know of an estate better situated for his friend.

"I do want to thank you for the wise advice you gave both Jane and me in London," Elizabeth said quietly. "The adjustment to being married would have been more...ah...*interesting*...without your observations." They were slightly ahead of Georgiana and Kitty, who seemed to be enjoying each other's company and had lagged behind as they toured the garden.

"I am very glad to have been helpful. You appear very well settled, as well as being very pleased with your husband."

"Very pleased, Aunt. Very pleased. He is the best and most honourable man I have ever known," said Elizabeth earnestly, and Mrs. Gardiner's mental eyebrows rose. She had known that Elizabeth held Darcy in esteem before the couple had left London, but this was high praise indeed, especially coming from Elizabeth.

They walked further before Mrs. Gardiner decided to give Elizabeth a subtle prompt to see if she had any announcement to share. "Yes, you look very much the young wife," Mrs. Gardiner said slyly. "Marriage obviously becomes you; the change is very apparent."

"Ah," was Elizabeth's only comment, though her ears did redden slightly. Then she regained her composure and said blandly, "You might be interested to know that my husband has come to believe you one of the most sensible women of his acquaintance."

"Really?" said Mrs. Gardiner with a suppressed smile. "That is most flattering, especially since Jane said that *her* husband had said much the same thing. Yes, that is most flattering, indeed, to have one's advice taken to heart by one's two favourite nieces."

Elizabeth decided that this conversation ought to go no further lest her decidedly deductive aunt gain too much information with which to tease her.

Chapter 30

The next morning following breakfast, Kitty and Georgiana took a walk in the gardens, taking pleasure in the company of someone closer to her own age than the rest of the party. Georgiana enjoyed Kitty's high spirits though she was slightly disconcerted at her obsession with the entertainments of society and of young men, especially officers. Since she was not yet out in society, her own associations were limited to those of family and close family friends, and that was more than enough for her at present. She did not look forward to coming out though she knew it was expected of her in the next few years, but Kitty obviously was not of a similar opinion.

"It was really quite unfair," Kitty lamented as they walked, "that my sister Lydia was allowed to accompany Mrs. Forster, and I was forced to stay at home. Lydia has been at Brighton, much in the company of officers since the end of May while life at Longbourn has become dreadfully boring."

"Please excuse me," Georgiana asked tentatively, "but who is Mrs. Forster?"

"Colonel Forster's wife. He commands the regiment of soldiers that spent the winter near Meryton. The officers provided many opportunities for diversion for the neighbourhood, balls and dinners and such, but now the regiment has gone to Brighton, and Lydia has gone with her friend, leaving me almost to myself at home."

"The only officer I have ever known is my cousin. He is a colonel also."

"Really?" asked Kitty in interest. "Where is he located? I know he was not part of Colonel Forster's regiment; I knew all the officers. Do you not think that a red coat is the most delightful attire for a young man?"

"I have never really thought about it," Georgiana confessed. "It is just the way my cousin has always dressed. He commands a regiment of cavalry near to London though he has been to the continent several times. I think it must have been dangerous, but he never talks of it."

"I should quite like to meet your cousin," Kitty said enthusiastically, failing to notice the look of distress that came over Georgiana's face suddenly and then disappeared just as quickly.

"But surely you are enjoying your travels with your aunt and uncle?" Georgiana changed the subject.

"It seemed better than staying at home with the regiment gone, but it has turned out to be so tedious. We visited any number of large estates on our journey, but they soon began to look much the same. I had thought earlier that we would be going to the Lakes, but my uncle's business would not allow it."

"The Lakes are very beautiful, Kitty. William took me there two summers ago."

"Perhaps, but there are no parties or balls. Will you not be having any parties while we are here?"

Georgiana smiled. "I am afraid that our life here might seem rather dull if parties and balls are what you measure by. We have some celebrations in the autumn after the harvest is in and then a larger celebration at Christmas. But right now, all the tenants are exceedingly busy in the fields."

"Is there not an Assembly hall in Lambton?" Kitty asked.

"I believe there is, but I have never attended. I do not believe that William has attended either; he is not much interested in such activities though Elizabeth has mentioned that we might host a ball now and then, once I am out."

"It is really most vexing!" Kitty exclaimed. "Especially since Lydia is so much enjoying her time in Brighton. Her last letter was especially annoying since she said that one of the most popular officers in the regiment has become her particular favourite and has even gone so far as to talk of marriage."

"Then he has proposed to her? Oh, how exciting that must be!" exclaimed Georgiana.

"Well, he has not actually proposed yet from what I can tell from Lydia's letter. But she is sure that he will at some time or the other, and it is really difficult to swallow how she keeps going on and on about 'dearest, dearest Wickham.'"

Kitty did not see Georgiana blanch, but she did notice that the other girl stopped walking suddenly. She turned around and could not help but observe that her friend looked most distressed, pale and trembling as she clenched her hands into fists at her side.

"Why, Georgiana, whatever is wrong?"

Georgiana could not talk at first, but at last she got out tremulously, "What... who was that you talked about?"

Kitty frowned in confusion. "Lydia? Or was it Mr. Wickham? He is an officer in the militia that she has become quite fond of."

Georgiana finally forced herself to ask, "What... what is his Christian name?"

"Why, it is George. George Wickham. Are you acquainted with him? Is he not the most handsome and amiable young man?"

Kitty was thus completely unprepared as Georgiana broke down, bursting into tears and turning to flee, stumbling and tripping, toward the house. Kitty chased after her friend, calling her name.

Elizabeth and Darcy had just left the house, planning to walk some of the yet unexplored paths of Pemberley when Georgiana burst around the hedge and ran past them, sobbing and crying as she fled into the house. Kitty came up at just that time, asking in concern, "What is wrong with Georgiana? We were walking when she suddenly started crying and ran into the house. She would not even answer when I called her."

Darcy turned around quickly to follow his sister, pausing only to say, "I will find Georgiana, Elizabeth, if you will speak to Kitty to see if we can find out what could have caused such distress."

Elizabeth instantly pulled Kitty aside to sit on one of the benches to discover what they were talking of when Georgiana became so upset.

"I have not an idea, Lizzy," said Kitty, wringing her hands. "I was telling her about how bored I have been since the regiment went to Brighton, when she ran off."

"The regiment has left? That is good news to me though you and Lydia might not find it so," said Elizabeth.

"Well, at least Lydia got to go to Brighton. I have been forced to stay at home with no officers, no parties, and no one except Mary for company."

"Lydia went to Brighton?" Elizabeth asked in shock. "And father allowed her to go? By herself?"

"She went as the special guest of the colonel's wife, Mrs. Forster. Mama tried to get Papa to take us all there, but he would not hear of it."

"But he allowed Lydia to go? That is deplorable!" Then she remembered what she was trying to determine, and came back to her object. "But why should that distress Georgiana? She knows nothing of this, and she only met Lydia briefly at my wedding."

Kitty wrinkled her brow, trying to remember exactly what she had said. "I was talking about how Lydia was becoming quite attached to one of the officers when she suddenly stopped dead still and asked me his full name. After that, she ran off."

"Who was this officer?"

"Why, you know him, Lizzy! Mr. Wickham was quite your favourite for a while, was he not?" Kitty said with a smile.

"Wickham!" exclaimed Elizabeth with a look on her face that made Kitty's smile disappear instantly. "Quick"—she grabbed Kitty fiercely by her shoulders—"tell me *exactly* what you said to Georgiana."

"Lizzy, you are hurting me!"

"Tell me, Kitty!" commanded Elizabeth sternly though she did release her grip.

"Well," said Kitty, rubbing her arms, "I told her that Lydia had written that Mr. Wickham had become her particular favourite and that Lydia was sure that they were going to be married. Georgiana asked if he had proposed, and I told her not yet, and then I mentioned his name, which I guess is when she fled into the house."

"Married!" Elizabeth exclaimed, grabbing Kitty again. "Lydia said Mr. Wickham was going to marry her?"

"She said that she was sure that they were going to be married at some time or the other," Kitty said, and Elizabeth instantly recognized that Kitty was holding something back.

"Kitty," she commanded, "you are hiding something. You know that I can always tell. Tell me what you are not saying!"

"Lizzy, please!" pleaded Kitty, but seeing the determination on her sister's face, she eventually admitted, "Lydia did say that Wickham had some business problems to take care of and that it would be much less expensive if they went to Gretna Green. She said it did not matter to her, as long as she could sign her name, 'Lydia Wickham.'"

Elizabeth released her sister and sat back in dismay. "Wickham! Will we never be free of that man?"

"Why do you speak so?" asked Kitty in confusion, rubbing her arms again. "You always thought well of him, did you not? He is certainly the most handsome and amiable officer in the regiment."

"Wickham will never marry Lydia," Elizabeth told her sister in irritation. "He must marry a woman with money since he has none of his own. Do you not remember Miss King? And he is, in addition, a most wicked man. Did my father not warn you of him?"

"Father? Certainly not! He spoke quite well of Mr. Wickham, and I remember at the party before the regiment went away, Mr. Wickham told father that Mr. Darcy would soon make you rue the day that you ever married him, that his cold manner and pride would soon make you dreadfully unhappy."

"He said that?" Elizabeth asked, shaken again. "And did my father say anything in my defence to this outlandish statement?"

Kitty only shook her head miserably. "He only said that bad results come when daughters refuse to heed their father's advice."

"Do I look unhappy to you?" asked Elizabeth in exasperation. "Does Uncle Gardiner think my husband a cold and proud man? Does Aunt Gardiner? Cannot you see that he is truly the best of men? Oh, how silly can you be? Do you not have the wit to see anything other than officers and red coats? Oh, you and Lydia are the two most foolish girls in the world!"

With that, Elizabeth jumped up and ran into the house, heedless of Kitty, who promptly burst into tears at her sister's harsh words.

ELIZABETH MET DARCY COMING DOWN the stairs, and the look on his face told her that Georgiana had informed him of what Kitty had said, and they quickly compared notes

"We must talk, Elizabeth. I would suggest that you ask your aunt and uncle to join us in my study. I value their advice and sense, and they are more familiar with your family than I am, though I am far more familiar with the character of George Wickham than I desire to be!"

Quickly, Elizabeth found them, and she and Darcy informed the Gardiners of what they had learned.

"Mr. Wickham?" asked Mrs. Gardiner in confusion. "I would no more wish Lydia to marry him than I did you, Elizabeth, but the reaction of both of you tells me that there is much that you know that your uncle and I do not."

Elizabeth realized that she had never related even a part of the story that Darcy had told her in Kent of his history with Wickham, and she looked at her husband questioningly, seeking to know how much she should reveal.

"We must tell them everything, Elizabeth," said Darcy. "I have tried to keep the details quiet to spare Georgiana, but I now believe that was a mistake. I should have made his character known years back. It might have saved much trouble."

Between Elizabeth and Darcy, Mr. and Mrs. Gardiner were soon made aware of the history and background of George Wickham. Both were shocked at learning the full tally of the man's iniquities, and this knowledge made their concern for their niece much greater. Lydia had never been one of their favourites, but they had no desire to see the family scandalized by a possible elopement. However, Darcy was quick to dissuade them of that thought.

"I assure you that the idea of having Wickham as my brother is enough to make me ill, but please believe me when I tell you that there is no fear of that happening. Wickham will never marry a girl like Lydia Bennet because he must marry for money in order to solve his problems. I believe that he has probably run out his string at the regiment and must soon disappear as he has done before in order to evade his debts and avoid debtor's prison. I know that, for I have paid off his creditors twice before both in Lambton and at Cambridge. Despite his pleasing manner, the man has no trade, no source of income, and is always in search of a match with a woman such as this Miss King that Elizabeth mentioned."

He looked soberly at the other three, wondering whether he should mention his suspicion, and decided there should be no more concealment.

"I must make you understand what I truly fear. I believe that Wickham is preparing to disappear again, and when he does, he may well take Lydia Bennet with him for... for idle diversion."

Elizabeth and Mrs. Gardiner gasped in shock, but Mr. Gardiner's expression only became graver; he had been working toward the same conclusion though he had not the same experience with the man as Darcy.

"He will deceive her into thinking that they will be married, he will take his pleasure with her, and one morning, she will wake up to find him gone.

Then she will just be one more young girl, alone and friendless and without funds, left ruined and hopeless in a situation that will lead to only one result: she will be forced to use her only possession, herself, merely in order to eat."

Elizabeth tried not to cry, for she was so offended by Lydia's foolishness, but the tears that flowed down her cheeks could not be stopped. They would have been the same as occasioned by any young girl caught in a similar situation by a single, foolish mistake. At least, that was what she told herself…

Mr. Gardiner at last broke the brooding silence. "I believe you have the truth of it, Mr. Darcy. I would suggest that we immediately dispatch an express to inform my brother of what we have concluded. He can then immediately travel to Brighton and bring her home."

"I do not believe my father is likely to act quickly enough in this matter," Elizabeth said regretfully, "for I fear that he will not take our warning with the seriousness that is required. From what Kitty said, he is inclined to regard Wickham favourably in order to maintain his disapproval of Mr. Darcy. There is also this—despite our warnings, he allowed Lydia to accompany the regiment to Brighton in the first place, and if he had taken us seriously, it would make the foolishness of that decision crystal clear. But not only did he ignore these warnings, it is obvious that he never cautioned my sisters to beware of Mr. Wickham. That is assuming he ever read my letters; certainly, he has never answered any of them."

Mr. Gardiner was unhappily forced to agree with her. "Certainly, my experience has been little different than yours since none of my letters have received the courtesy of a reply," he said slowly. "For these reasons, I fear you are correct, and my brother might ignore our warning altogether."

"Still, we *must* send word, for Lydia *is* his daughter," Elizabeth said. "But is there not something else that can be done? An express to Colonel Forster, perhaps?"

"I have another idea," said Darcy. "I think an express to my cousin Fitzwilliam might bring more immediate results. He is with his regiment near London, and he can be in Brighton the same day after receiving it."

"But will he be willing to simply go immediately to Brighton?" asked Mr. Gardiner. "And would he be able to do anything once he arrived? Lydia is not even a particularly close relation, and she certainly will not listen to his advice."

"As I told you, my cousin is very well acquainted with Wickham's transgressions with regard to my sister. I assure you that, once Colonel Fitzwilliam reaches Brighton, Lydia might do any number of things, but she will *not* do them with George Wickham. My cousin will make sure that any attempt by Wickham to flee before we arrive, with or without Lydia, will result in his urgent need for a surgeon. My cousin, you see" — he smiled grimly — "is not a particularly forgiving man, and it took considerable effort on my part to convince him to allow George Wickham to continue breathing our air after the affair at Ramsgate. I am not disposed to go to that effort again."

"Before we arrive?" Elizabeth asked. "What do you mean by that?"

"Our first task, of course, is to notify Mr. Bennet and my cousin immediately. Fitzwilliam will be on his way within the hour of receiving his letter. He can talk to Colonel Forster as a fellow officer and thus ensure that Wickham makes no sudden departures. As for ourselves..." He looked at Mr. Gardiner. "The express will not arrive at either destination until tomorrow evening. If we leave within the half-hour and push hard, we can be in Brighton early on the day following. Even if Mr. Bennet acts immediately, he could not be there sooner."

"I agree, Mr. Darcy. It is exactly this kind of bold, forceful move that could possibly thwart Wickham's plans, and I am gratified that you would involve yourself to save the honour of my family."

"My family now also," returned Darcy, and Elizabeth's uncle nodded gravely in agreement.

"I will go as well," said Elizabeth. "I will be needed for Lydia. She will be hard enough to handle even for the two of us."

"It will be a hard trip, Elizabeth," warned Darcy. "It might be better if you stayed to attend to your sister and Georgiana."

"But sir," answered Elizabeth impudently. "What is fifty miles of good road? And is not the Darcy coach up to the task?"

"Touché," said Darcy with the hint of a smile curling his lips. "Though in this case, it is closer to two hundred miles than fifty." He paused then smiled in defeat. "I shall have to be more careful of what I say in the future, my dear," and he and his wife shared a look of both humour and understanding.

"Very well, Elizabeth," he continued decisively, "it shall be as you wish. In a half-hour, then?" he suggested, and the travelling party nodded agreement. Seeing that all minds were in accordance, he rang for servants to prepare his coach and to pack a travelling kit of clothing and provisions for the three of them.

Chapter 31

Thursday, July 30, 1812

It was somewhat beyond the half-hour before the travelling kits, provisions, blankets, and cloaks were stowed into the coach and the travellers were ready to begin their journey, but it was a testament to the efficiency of Pemberley's staff that all was accomplished as soon as it was. After saying their goodbyes to a still-pale Georgiana, a tearful Kitty, and Mrs. Gardiner, they boarded the coach.

"Heigh-up, Stephens," called Darcy, and the coach rattled off down the road, attended by the stares of the three ladies in the rear courtyard. They watched silently until the coach drew out of sight, and then, equally silently, turned and entered the house, made so much quieter by the departure of the rest of their party.

IN THE COACH, THE TRAVELLERS tried to make themselves as comfortable as possible. Though the coach was well sprung, Darcy had ordered a pace that would maximize their speed with changes of drivers and teams arranged accordingly along the way. Thus, even the springs of his coach were not equal to the task of smoothing all the bumps and jerks of the road.

Though their bags were tied out of the way on the top of the coach, Darcy had kept one satchel with him. Elizabeth said nothing as he opened it to disclose a brace of pistols, inspecting each one in turn to make sure they were loaded and primed but not cocked. Elizabeth did not know Wickham to be a dangerous man or prone to violence, but if it came to a choice between his life and the infinitely more precious life of her husband, she would much prefer Darcy to be armed than otherwise.

When he finished checking the pistols and secured the satchel in a pouch on the door, Darcy put his left arm around his wife and drew her close. He looked over to see the smile on Mr. Gardiner's face as she rested her head on his chest and closed her eyes, and he smiled back, both men joined in their love and concern for her. Darcy knew that Elizabeth had planned to tell her aunt and uncle of her pregnancy, but with the events of the day, there had not been time. The paternal look of affection on her uncle's face, however, made Darcy believe that Mr. Gardiner, or perhaps his wife, had already surmised her condition. He held her tightly as he felt her breathing slow and deepen, and he prayed for her safety, wondering anew if he should have allowed her to come.

As if you were going to stop her, his common sense told him dryly, and he smiled at that as he closed his own eyes. On a trip like this, he knew, it was advisable to sleep when possible before the accumulation of aches and pains made it impossible.

The long miles passed slowly. Darcy passed out food from the baskets— bread and cheese and fruit, washed down with warm wine in thick mugs. About every two hours, the coach stopped to change teams, and the passengers were able to get out, stretch out the kinks, and relieve and refresh themselves before climbing back in to return to the bouncing journey. Elizabeth napped off and on well into the night, waking once to find the others asleep. It was dark in the coach though the moon was bright, lighting the roads and passing fields so that the driver was able to guide the coach easily. They were travelling more slowly than they had done during the day, which was only sensible, and she could occasionally hear the voices of the driver and his assistant. She knew that her uncle and husband had kept their own conversation to a minimum so that she could sleep, so she sat silently and watched the moonlit fields pass by until they stopped at the next coaching inn.

So the long journey continued with the passengers conversing when they were awake, discussing what might be done at Brighton or moving on to lighter topics such as the theatre or books they had read. When Darcy and her uncle fell to discussing the war news from the continent, Elizabeth listened with interest though she could contribute little. Dawn broke, and the day stretched on, but the unending monotony continued as the miles crept past. It was after dusk when the coach finally clattered into the courtyard of Darcy House, where lanterns were lit and the staff was prepared to assist them. The hot baths awaiting them were a particular delight after the dust of the journey had worked its way into every part of their clothing and skin. When she was clean, Elizabeth joined Darcy in his bed and fell asleep instantly in his arms, only to be roused while it was still dark for the last leg of their journey.

The coach rattled through London and onto the road to Brighton as the sun began to come up, and the routine of the day before continued. It was just short of noon when the driver called, "Mr. Darcy, sir! Brighton ahead!" The passengers became more alert at the signal that their excruciating journey was nearing an end. But shortly afterward, the driver called out again, this time with a note of urgency in his voice. "Mr. Darcy! There be a red-coat up ahead, a'wavin' to us! Do we stop or ride on?"

Darcy reached into the satchel on the door and pulled one of the pistols out then leaned out the window to take a look. "Pull up!" he called suddenly, replacing the pistol as the coach came to a halt. "It is Sergeant Henderson, my cousin's man. He must have been sent out here to intercept us."

He opened the door, jumped down without bothering to lower the step, and strode quickly out of sight. He came back with a uniformed soldier Elizabeth remembered seeing at Rosings.

"Sergeant Henderson, may I introduce my wife, Mrs. Darcy, and her uncle, Mr. Gardiner. Sergeant Henderson has been with my cousin for at least ten years."

"Ever since he was but a lieutenant, sir. He sent me out here to look for ye, so that ye din't go clatterin' into town and alert the rascal."

"Very good. I assume that means he has not yet flown away."

"Aye, sir. The colonel has had words with this Colonel Forster, and a watch has been set on Wickham and on the young lady."

"Excellent. Then we are in time. How does my cousin want us to proceed?"

"If yer coach will follow me, I'll take ye to the stables and then lead ye to the colonel."

"Very good! Lead on, Sergeant."

Sergeant Henderson led them around to the other side of town before he then took them through a number of winding streets until they came to a large courtyard. Two red-coated soldiers swung the heavy gates open at their arrival and quickly guided the coach inside.

The door was opened immediately and the step swung down. Darcy took the satchel with the pistols with him before he helped Elizabeth out.

She grimaced as her feet hit the ground. "I do not believe I have ever hurt so much before," she told Darcy, trying to stretch the kinks out of her back.

"But, Elizabeth," Darcy said with an innocent expression, "what is two hundred miles…"

"…of good road! Yes, yes, I know, and you *did* warn me, sir. But I still hurt." Darcy only smiled at her and leaned forward to kiss her forehead.

"If ye could follow me, sir, I'll take ye to Colonel Fitzwilliam."

The three followed Sergeant Henderson into a building and then out the side door, going down an alley for several minutes before coming to a whitewashed house. The sergeant knocked on the door — three quick raps followed by one more. The door opened a crack as the person inside verified who desired entry then was opened by another red-coated soldier. They were led down the hallway to the front of the house, where Colonel Fitzwilliam sat at a table looking out the window.

"Darcy!" he exclaimed, jumping up. "You made excellent time!"

"And every joint in my body aches from every rut and hole on the road between here and Derbyshire," Darcy said, clasping Fitzwilliam's hand.

"And I see you brought your courageous wife with you! And her uncle! Mrs. Darcy, Mr. Gardiner, it is grand to see you both, though I wish the circumstances were different."

"It is always a pleasure to see old friends, Colonel," said Elizabeth, smiling, "especially when they are showing their worth as you are doing."

"It is the least I could do, considering you have now given me the opportunity to see Wickham locked up good and proper!"

"Locked up?" said Darcy. "Can that be accomplished? I aimed to prevent him from ruining Elizabeth's sister, most probably by removing her to Longbourn, but I was unsure of what we could do beyond that."

"Henderson and I arrived last night and made sure our friend had not disappeared. Once we had him located, the good sergeant did a little nosing about among the local tradesmen. Show my cousin what you found, Sergeant."

"Aye, sir." Sergeant Henderson pulled out a folded piece of paper from his tunic. "This be a list of at least some of his debts, Mr. Darcy. He owes near every tradesman in town, and they been starting to make noise about it, so the lads tell me. Almost a thousand pounds, sir, or possibly more. That should be good enough for a spell in debtor's prison, and Wickham without a friend to get him out."

Sergeant Henderson's smile was that of a hungry predator. He had spent his professional life serving a true gentleman, both a good soldier and a good man, and he well knew the strengths and weaknesses of the class. What disturbed him more than Wickham's offences against *his* gentleman, was Wickham's pretences to such a distinction himself when he was not prepared to meet the obligations that went with the title. Thus, the sergeant was only too happy to lead the pack to pull the impostor down.

"And Colonel Forster was only too pleased to help," said Fitzwilliam. "When I told him of what we suspected, he took a closer look into Wickham's affairs. He found out about the debts, of course, and he also discovered that Wickham has hired a chaise for tonight and was evidently planning to disappear since he does not seem to have requested leave. This is desertion since Wickham is a serving officer, and for good reason, the army really, truly frowns on desertion. Capital offence, at least in some situations, though probably not, unfortunately, this one. Anyway, once the good colonel understood Wickham's intentions, he became quite offended with our old friend. A good part is due to the intent to desert, of course, but, even worse, Wickham's plan involved a friend of his wife who was under his personal protection. It was he who suggested that we catch him in the act rather than simply thwarting his plan by arresting him now. That will allow him to be held on any number of charges, from desertion to dereliction to conduct unbecoming." Fitzwilliam's teeth gleamed behind his hungry smile. "It does appear that friend Wickham has well and truly stepped into the smelly stuff *this* time, old sport."

Darcy's mouth curled into a slow, cold smile, and he and his cousin again clasped hands fiercely.

"Mrs. Darcy," Colonel Fitzwilliam turned to Elizabeth. "Sergeant Henderson has arranged a room upstairs for you. There is hot water, but even he was not able to provide a bath, though he did ensure that it has a clean bed. If you would like to refresh yourself and perhaps catch up on a little sleep, now would be a good time. Wickham is in the pub across the street, but nothing is expected until after sundown."

"That sounds heavenly," said Elizabeth, conscious of her dishevelled appearance and the grit in her hair, on her skin, and under her clothing. "I will certainly take advantage of your kind offer, and thank you."

"It be the room at the top of the stair, Mrs. Darcy," said Henderson. "All the lads are down here, so ye will have yer privacy." Elizabeth thanked him, but, as she started to leave, she saw a look of regret in Darcy's eyes and knew that he would have liked to come up with her and share the bed. But they both knew that she needed to sleep and recover from the rigours of the journey, both for herself and the new life growing within her.

But she could not ignore that look, so she first went over to give him a kiss on the cheek before she left, taking the opportunity to whisper into his ear, "Wait until Netherfield, William." He nodded in agreement, but his eyes followed her as she quickly embraced her uncle before leaving the room.

Saturday, August 1, 1812

ELIZABETH WOKE TO THE TOUCH of a hand on her shoulder. "Elizabeth," whispered Darcy, "it is almost dusk. Ready yourself, but we do not want to show a light to avoid even the possibility of alerting Wickham."

"I understand," she whispered back. "Give me a few minutes, and I shall be down to join you." She saw his teeth flash whitely in the gathering gloom, and she felt a quick kiss on her forehead and a squeeze of her shoulder, then he was gone.

When she descended the stairs about fifteen minutes later, it was almost full dark, and she had to feel her way down. The men in the room were mere shadows, and she was only able to discern her husband by his height.

"There be a seat over here for ye, Mrs. Darcy," whispered the voice of Sergeant Henderson. She took his arm as he guided her over to a chair beside Colonel Fitzwilliam. Thanking her escort, she gratefully sat down. Even after her nap, her joints and muscles ached from the journey, and it felt good to be off her feet. Darcy came to stand behind her, and when she felt his hand on her shoulder, she reached up to squeeze it, comforted by his presence and protection.

The hours slipped by, and still they waited. Traffic continued into and out of the establishment across the street, but Wickham did not show himself.

"Are you sure he is even in there?" she whispered.

"He was still there a quarter hour ago, Mrs. Darcy," whispered Sergeant Henderson. "It be an establishment for officers, not common soldiers as it were, so I just poked me head in and saw him there a'drinkin' with his cronies. There were only one other door, and a pair of the lads are watchin' it."

Eventually, the hour grew late, and clusters of officers and other customers began to leave. One of the last was Wickham with several other officers; Elizabeth recognized Denny among them but none of the others. The group stood talking for a short time; then Wickham's companions went away up the street, leaving him alone. He turned and sauntered off in the other direction as if he had not a care in the world. If the drink had affected him, it did not show in his walk.

After he disappeared around the corner, the men in the room rose and began to leave by the front door. Darcy held her arm to guide her as they exited into the street. She saw the sudden flash of a lantern from a doorway, and Fitzwilliam said softly, "There is the signal from Private Smith. It is safe to follow now. Others are tracking Wickham and will show the way.

In this manner the group followed Wickham through the darkened streets of the town, always just out of sight and around the corner so there was no chance that he might hear the sound of their muffled footsteps on the cobblestones.

Eventually, they came to one last corner where all the streets of the town came together in an open, paved area. Looking carefully around the corner, Elizabeth saw Wickham talking to the driver of a chaise. After several minutes, they evidently reached an agreement, for Wickham handed up several coins then walked to the far side of the square.

Elizabeth missed a signal, but she heard the sharp sigh of satisfaction from Colonel Fitzwilliam.

"Right," he whispered. "He has gone to Forster's house." She did not miss the next—the long flash of a lantern from an upstairs window, followed by two more quick flashes. "He is on his way back, lads," continued Fitzwilliam, "and he has a companion. Stand by but be prepared to step lively at my command."

There were shuffling footsteps all around Elizabeth as she stood beside Colonel Fitzwilliam with Darcy standing behind her, his hands on her shoulders. They waited in the darkness of a covered entry right at the corner, invisible from more than a few feet away. She heard the sound of boots on cobblestones before she saw Wickham, and when he appeared, Elizabeth easily recognized the exuberant bouncing of Lydia in the moonlight next to him.

Wickham had just handed Lydia up into the chaise when Colonel Fitzwilliam called out, "Now, lads! Surround them!"

Four soldiers bolted from behind Elizabeth and covered the thirty paces to the chaise in no more than a few seconds. Wickham stood frozen in confusion as one man went to the front of the team and seized the reins while another pointed a pistol at the driver's head, harshly commanding him to stand easy or eat a pistol ball. The other two positioned themselves a dozen feet away from Wickham, blocking his escape.

Fitzwilliam, followed by Darcy and Elizabeth, ran to the chaise. By the time they reached it, Wickham had recovered his composure.

"Well, well, it is Colonel Fitzwilliam, is it not? What brings you to the seashore, Colonel?" he asked in a voice as amiable as it ever had been. Elizabeth could not believe that he showed no sign of shame or mortification at being caught in the act.

At that moment, Colonel Forster made an appearance from the direction that Wickham had come. As Wickham saw him, the first indications of panic showed in his face, and Elizabeth heard the sudden rasp of steel on leather as Colonel Fitzwilliam drew his sword with the smoothness and speed of a striking cobra. Before she was even aware of the motion, the sword was out and extended, the tip mere inches from Wickham's throat.

"Do resist arrest, Wickham," said Fitzwilliam pleasantly. "I would be highly obliged to you if you would."

The barely controlled hunger in Fitzwilliam's voice made Elizabeth shiver as she looked at him, and she hardly heard Lydia's shriek of outrage and fear. His sword was pointed at Wickham's throat, his body turned into a fencer's stance, right elbow slightly crooked, wrist firm, and right knee flexed and ready to thrust. She realized that she was looking on a man who had had seen fierce action against Bonaparte on the continent, who had killed in the name of his King and dearly wished to act right now on his own behalf. She remembered what Darcy had told her of Colonel Fitzwilliam's service—that he was a fair-spoken man and a gentleman, but that he was also a seasoned professional who performed his duty with ruthless efficiency.

Wickham also knew Fitzwilliam's history, and he saw his death in the shadowed eyes of the man across from him. He could see the white gleam of Fitzwilliam's teeth and knew one wrong move on his part would result in that sword buried to the hilt in his throat or chest. Though Wickham also wore a sword and was not inexperienced in its use, he made not a single move as Colonel Forster angrily placed him under arrest and ordered guards to take him away and lock him up. Wickham's eyes remained on Fitzwilliam, and he did not resist as his own weapon was unbuckled from his waist. The sudden noise of metal and boots sounded as four musket-bearing soldiers came clattering into the square to march him away.

Lydia had screamed when she saw her Wickham threatened, and she cried out again as he was marched away, claiming that she absolutely would not leave the chaise until her precious Wickham was released. It took two soldiers to pry her from the vehicle.

Mr. Gardiner stepped forward to Colonel Forster and introduced himself.

"I am the young lady's uncle. I want to thank you for your help in thwarting Mr. Wickham and preserving my niece's reputation."

"It was my pleasure, Mr. Gardiner," said Colonel Forster. "I am only sorry it took this long to discover his true colours. It is highly mortifying that such a man was in my regiment in any case, but I can assure you that Ensign Wickham will face a court martial within the week. And, while I have no doubt as to the outcome of the court, I shall see that his debts are brought to the attention of the civil authorities, which should land him in debtor's prison as sure as sunrise."

Darcy had always been opposed to the concept of debtor's prison in principle, but, in Wickham's case, he was inclined to make an exception.

"I also thank you, Colonel," Darcy said, offering his hand. "It was certainly smartly done."

"My pleasure, Mr. Darcy," answered Colonel Forster, shaking Darcy's hand, angry but also embarrassed. Wickham had been most effective in destroying Darcy's character, and Colonel Forster felt more than a little foolish for having believed him.

"We have a coach, Colonel Forster," continued Mr. Gardiner, "and we plan to bring Miss Lydia to her father's house as soon as her belongings may be packed."

"Certainly, sir," agreed the colonel.

Within the hour, Lydia and her trunks were loaded in the coach, and all preparations were complete for the journey to Longbourn. Before they left, Darcy and Elizabeth thanked Colonel Fitzwilliam for his help, but he declined all their gratitude.

"I should thank you for the chance to finally see him meet his just fate," he responded. He took Darcy's extended hand and held it firmly.

"I wanted to kill him, you know," he said thoughtfully, and Darcy nodded. "Hardest thing I have ever done," he continued. "Wickham has no idea just how close he came."

"I think he did, Colonel," said Elizabeth. "I saw his eyes. I saw him just crumple into himself. He must have always been a hollow man with only his pleasing manners and amiable exterior to disguise that fact from the world. I truly believe, even if he were not on his way to prison, he would have difficulty now in ever again assuming a convincing attitude. That kind of disguise requires a great deal of confidence, and Wickham just had his confidence shattered. I do not think he shall easily recover it."

Fitzwilliam looked at Elizabeth closely, then nodded. "Perhaps you are correct. I admit I was so focused on not giving in to my impulses that I did not look. But, in any case, it is done and done well."

Darcy turned to Sergeant Henderson and extended his hand. "You have done my family an inestimable service tonight, Sergeant. If you ever have reason to take off the King's uniform, rest assured that there will be a place for you at Pemberley."

Sergeant Henderson shuffled and ducked his head in embarrassment, thanking Darcy for his offer. "I have me heart set on serving a general before I takes the coat off, sir. But I shall certainly remember the offer; indeed I shall."

Both Fitzwilliam and Darcy laughed agreeably, then Fitzwilliam shook hands once more with his cousin and Mr. Gardiner, and the coach rattled away into the night.

Chapter 32

Early morning hours, Sunday, August 2, 1812

"How could you allow such beastly treatment of poor Wickham, Uncle?" Lydia whined, as Darcy's coach started out of town. She had ceased her shouting, at least, but her complaining had begun immediately and had not stopped. She sat beside Mr. Gardiner while Darcy and Elizabeth sat on the other side of the coach. Elizabeth was not at all pleased that the singular events of the night had apparently not affected her sister in the slightest. She remained the same wild, unrestrained, and fearless creature that she had always been, and she appeared to be completely unconcerned with the consequences of her actions.

"I am sure I have never seen such ungentlemanly behaviour in my entire life," Lydia continued, "and I am of a mind to report it to the authorities."

"Lydia, hush!" her uncle commanded. "It is the authorities who have taken Wickham into custody and saved you from ruin! You have put all of us to a great deal of trouble by your thoughtless actions. How could you have considered going off with that man? Did you not even think of how the embarrassment would affect your father and the rest of your family?"

"Oh, I care nothing for what Papa says," Lydia said carelessly. "If he had brought us all to Brighton, I might listen to him. But all he ever does is talk, talk, talk, and then he disappears into his library."

"Your father has raised you and protected you and provided for you for your whole life! You owe him a debt of gratitude for what he has done, and you are under the obligation to behave as a proper daughter!" Mr. Gardiner said sternly. Though he tried to keep his anger under control, he was unable to prevent his voice from growing louder and angrier as he continued, "You do *not,* for example, simply accept the casual assurances of a penniless opportunist and plan to run away without even a word to your father! Had you even given a thought to how that man was going to support you? Or how your elopement would adversely affect your sisters? Now be silent, Lydia, for your rescuers need their rest!"

"I will not be silent!" retorted Lydia angrily. "And I hardly needed to be rescued! It is your fault!" she cried, pointing to Darcy, who sat beside Elizabeth, arms folded, looking on expressionlessly at the disgraceful exhibition. "You will not leave him alone! You stole his inheritance and hounded him out of town, and now you get your cronies to lock up an innocent man! Will you never cease your vendetta, Mr. Darcy? Will you never stop persecuting a man who should be like a brother to you?"

"Lydia, stop it!" Elizabeth said sternly. "Mr. Darcy just saved you from being ruined by that . . . *that scoundrel!* You owe him a debt of gratitude that you cannot comprehend!"

"Him? Gratitude? That is a joke!" Lydia spat. "He kept me from marrying the man I love! And who loves me! Your husband did to me just what he has done to Wickham when he denied him his legacy. I could never feel gratitude to such a despicable blackguard!"

"Mr. Wickham was never going to marry you, Lydia," said Elizabeth coldly. "He never loved you; he just wanted an ignorant, innocent young girl to keep him warm at night. There never would have been a marriage, and one morning you would have awakened to find him gone!"

"What do you know of it, Lizzy?" cried Lydia. "You are jealous because he chose me instead of you! And love? What do you know of love? I wanted to marry the man I love while you married a cold and revolting man simply for his money!"

Elizabeth turned white with outrage and suppressed fury, though Lydia could not see it in the dark coach. But Darcy felt the rigidity of her body and leaned over to whisper words of consolation in her ear.

"Lydia, for the last time, be quiet!" commanded Mr. Gardiner at the very limit of his control

"You cannot make me stop telling the truth!" she hissed. "And it *is* true that Lizzy married only for money and then only after Mr. Darcy ruined her! Yes! It is true, he ruined you, Lizzy, and you know it! And then you made him marry you somehow, but Papa would not bless the marriage, no matter what Mama said to him! He knows your husband is a rake and a scoundrel, and you are surely not the first girl that he has—"

The sound of flesh striking flesh was like a pistol shot in the coach as Elizabeth leaned forward and slapped Lydia as hard as she possibly could. The sting of the blow ran up Elizabeth's arm, and Lydia's head was turned halfway around by the impact. She was shocked into sudden momentary silence before she burst into tears and wild cries of pain and mortification.

"Lydia, be quiet immediately!" Elizabeth hissed in fury, but Lydia's wails only increased.

The repetition of the sharp *'smack'* of an open palm hitting her cheek was repeated, and this second slap finally shocked Lydia into a partial compliance with her sister's command, whether from astonished disbelief or the sudden fear of being struck again could not be determined.

"If you *ever* again dare to insult my husband, Lydia Bennet, I will not hesitate to strike you again!" Elizabeth told her sister icily. "You will treat him with the utmost politeness and respect at all times, or you will have to deal with me! And do not let me hear *even a rumour* of your speaking ill of him to others. You may not respect anything else in this world, but you should fear *me*, for I will not tolerate such behaviour from you ever again!"

Lydia could only listen without speaking, trying to choke back her sobs, and she turned to her uncle for solace. Mr. Gardiner would have none of it, however.

"Elizabeth only did what I was on the edge of doing," he said sternly. "My brother should have done it years ago rather than allowing you to grow up to be such a wild and foolish child without any sense of restraint or propriety."

It soon was quiet in the coach with only the sound of Lydia's quiet sobs and involuntary hiccupping as she tried to stifle them, and slowly Mr. Gardiner and Darcy relaxed. Darcy put his arm around Elizabeth, pulling her to him, and only then did he become aware that she was quietly crying, her bonnet pulled over her face and her handkerchief pressed against her mouth to muffle the sound.

"Elizabeth," he whispered to her, "do not be distressed over having to slap your sister. It had to be done."

He bent down as she lifted her head, and she whispered back, between sobs, "I am not...crying...because of...Lydia. It is because of...the casual cruelty...that my father would show to speak of you in such a manner...before his family...and possibly others."

Darcy had no reply to this, and he could only hold her close until her crying eased and she drifted into exhausted slumber.

It was an hour past dawn when the coach rattled to a stop before the front door of Longbourn. Mr. Gardiner exited the coach first and immediately—and energetically—knocked at the door, but it was more than a minute before the door was opened by Hill, who looked at Mr. Gardiner worriedly.

"I must see my brother Bennet immediately," he said tersely.

The housekeeper peered past him to see Elizabeth stepping down from the coach and helping her sister out. Clearly, something was amiss involving Miss Lydia.

"I will inform the master at once," she told Mr. Gardiner, curtseying and opening the door to allow him entrance.

Mr. Gardiner stepped into the entry, soon joined by Elizabeth and Lydia, while Darcy stopped at the doorway. Lydia stayed as far away from Elizabeth as possible, but her first impulse to flee up the stairs was halted by her sister's imperious gaze.

It was about ten minutes before Mr. Bennet descended the stairs, showing evidence of having dressed in a considerable hurry.

"Good morning, brother," Mr. Gardiner greeted him, though he was having trouble remaining civil. "It appears that you did not take our express seriously enough to do anything about it, but we have managed to prevent what you would not. Here is your child, who we managed to keep from going off with that villain Wickham, but only by the action of your daughter's husband."

By this time, Mrs. Bennet had also descended the stairs, but she could not understand the meaning of what her brother had said, and she cried out as she saw Lydia looking so ragged and forlorn.

"Lydia! But what has happened to you? My poor girl! Tell me who did this to you!"

"Lydia was caught in the act of what she thought was an elopement with Mr. Wickham," Mr. Gardiner told her. "But it was not an elopement, madam, not at all. Only the swift work of Mr. Darcy and his cousin Colonel Fitzwilliam prevented Wickham from carrying Lydia off to London—and to her ruin!"

"I sent an express to Colonel Forster," Mr. Bennet was finally able to offer. "I have not yet received a reply."

"Had you left immediately, Brother, you might—might!—have been in time to save your daughter," said Mr. Gardiner coldly, rapidly running out of sympathy for his sister's husband. "Sending an express was a useless and indolent act; Wickham and Lydia would already be in London by now. But we were able to catch them just in time."

"But Wickham said he was going to marry me!" wailed Lydia, in the arms of her mother.

"Be quiet, girl!" retorted her uncle sternly. "Any beliefs you had in that regard were foolish and uninformed. The man had no money, no trade, and had he successfully managed to desert his regiment and been caught, he would have been lucky to escape the noose. You would have wound up walking the streets of London, selling yourself for the price of a meal like many other foolish girls before you!"

Mrs. Bennet wailed at the crudity expressed by her brother, but this sordid scenario finally impressed her with the seriousness of what Lydia had done, and she took her youngest daughter into another room, scolding her fiercely as she went. Mrs. Bennet might complain about the exertions she was forced into by the demands of society, but the prospect of losing her position in that society was suddenly much more important than her inclination to spoil her child.

"Wickham is now under guard, charged with attempted desertion and other offences, and he is bound for debtor's prison after the militia is through with him, for he had creditors aplenty in Brighton," continued Mr. Gardiner. "I am sure it is the same in Meryton or even worse since the regiment was quartered here longer."

This last made Mr. Bennet start, and he looked up to meet Darcy's cold gaze, remembering what he had been told that day in the library.

"I...thank you, Brother," he managed in a halting voice. "And...and my thanks to you too, Mr. Darcy, for saving my daughter." Both men nodded in return then turned to leave, planning to stop at Netherfield to seek the hospitality of the Bingleys before they returned to Pemberley in a considerably more leisurely fashion than they had left.

"Uncle, William, would you wait for me in the coach, please?" Elizabeth asked. "I would like to have a word with my father."

Darcy nodded and left the doorway, and Elizabeth followed her father into the library. Unseen by her, Mr. Gardiner lingered in the hallway while she closed the door.

Mr. Bennet had not even seated himself before Elizabeth burst out furiously, "I would like to know, sir, by what right you openly denigrate my husband before your family?"

Her voice was as cold as ice, and she was remorseless as she continued. "I would like to know just what makes you believe that you can call him a rake and a scoundrel, such that Lydia would throw those terms back in his teeth after he had just come to her rescue? For your information, Father, this man whom you denigrate and mock has travelled over two hundred miles in less than two days in order to save *your* daughter from her own foolishness — foolishness that never should have been given expression had you performed your duty as a father! You *knew* that she was too young and foolish to be sent into such temptation, yet you allowed her to go anyway! Have you an explanation, sir, for *any* of this reprehensible and unforgivable behaviour?"

Mr. Bennet had frozen halfway into his chair, shocked at being spoken to in such a manner by his daughter. His mouth was open as he gazed at her in amazement.

"Well, sir?"

"I did not...that is, I..." Mr. Bennet struggled to begin, but Elizabeth interrupted him.

"I could not at first understand the manner in which my sister dared to insult the man who was the means of her salvation, but then she informed me that she only quoted her father. I could not believe it, but then she repeated it, and I could no longer evade the truth. In the end, I had to slap her full across the face, not once but *twice,* before she would desist!"

Mr. Bennet stared at his favourite daughter in complete shock. Every word she said hit home in his conscience like a hammer-blow of fire and sparks, and still he could say nothing. He was too ashamed to admit his fault and too proud to display his shame, so he said nothing as she continued, her cheeks blazing red in agitation and anger.

"But slapping Lydia will do no good; both you and I know it, Father. If you could have troubled yourself earlier in her life to perform the same discipline on her, she might not have grown up to be such a foolish and wild child. She is silly, undisciplined, totally bereft of any sense of propriety, and is so completely without fear of consequences that she sees no reason to restrain her most irresponsible impulses.

"In addition to being insulted on behalf of my husband, who is the *very best man I have ever known*, I am also insulted for *myself!* That your opinion of *me* is such that you would even for a moment consider that I could marry such a man as you have described is beyond belief, whether threatened by scandal or not." She paused to take a few quick breaths. She was feeling decidedly dizzy, but she was determined to finish what she had to say.

"After the manner in which you have treated Mr. Darcy, I have my doubts whether you would ever be welcome in his home. But make no mistake, Father—if you *ever* again fail in politeness to *my* husband, you will never be welcome in *mine!* Nor, in that event, will I ever set foot again in *yours!* I wish you good day, sir!"

Mr. Bennet was stung and angered by this treatment from his favourite daughter. He was shocked as it finally hit home just how badly relations between them had deteriorated, for he had never believed their estrangement would be permanent. He had been certain that Lizzy would sooner or later desist in trying to change his mind and would write to ask his forgiveness, often thinking on how he would play the part of offended but forgiving father, willing to welcome his erring daughter back into his good graces and even to tolerate the rogue that he had been forced to allow her to marry.

But he now knew how wrong he had been on that point, even if he was not yet able to consider whether the rest of what Lizzy had said could possibly be true. When she spun on her heel and left the room, he realized that he might never see her again. The pain in his heart at the thought of being forever estranged from his darling daughter was like a spear of ice. He had assumed that Elizabeth would bend to his will and refuse to marry without his blessing. He had assumed that she would not choose another man over her own father, and he had been angered by her defiance when she did just that. Now he understood his monumental error as he realized that Elizabeth had stormed out of his library and out of his house without his having said one single word to her.

Mr. Gardiner had overheard much of what Elizabeth said and he was still in the hall as she ran past, white-faced with anger and with tears running down her cheeks.

He opened the library door to see the older man look up in sudden hope and then sink back in despair as he saw that it was his brother who had entered and not his daughter.

"Brother," he said softly, "I must tell you that you have been as wrong in this matter of Elizabeth and Mr. Darcy as a man could possibly be. Your opinion of him is completely a delusion of your anger, and your opinion of Elizabeth scarcely less. After the manner in which you have affronted them in every way, I do not know whether a reconciliation is even possible. You, sir, have counted on the fierce loyalty that Elizabeth has for her family. What you have *not* calculated is that Mr. Darcy is now her family, and the loyalty that you relied on is now being exerted on *his* behalf.

"And there is another thing to consider, Brother," said Mr. Gardiner softly. "I would not spend an excessive amount of time contemplating what you might do, because Madeline has told me that she believes Elizabeth is with child. If you desire to see your grandchild before he is full grown, I would suggest consulting what the gospel says on the matter of humility and the asking of forgiveness. Your daughter and her husband have nothing for which to ask forgiveness while you have almost everything. Now, we are all excessively tired, so I will wish you a good day."

The sound of the library door closing rang in Mr. Bennet's ears like the final blow of a gigantic hammer that had earlier struck such fire and sparks.

Chapter 33

M
r. Bennet, already discomfited by the morning's developments, was even further disturbed when an express arrived in the afternoon, in which Colonel Forster confirmed in great detail the story he had earlier heard. Confronted with this further evidence of his mistaken judgment of Wickham, Mr. Bennet summoned Lydia to the library.

When Lydia was seated before his desk along with her mother, Mr. Bennet turned a cold eye on her. "It is past time that we had a talk, child. I have allowed you to be out in society and to go and do as you willed because of your mother's pleas that your liveliness not be stifled, but look what has come of it!"

"What do you mean, Papa?" said Lydia sulkily. "I have done nothing wrong."

"Nothing wrong? What do you call agreeing to an elopement with Mr. Wickham? Somehow, you seem to have formed the idea that a sixteen-year-old girl can marry without her father's permission! Even Lizzy would not do that, though I disapproved of her choice of husband."

Lydia was shrill as she pounced on this last statement by her father.

"Well, at least my Wickham is not a rogue like Mr. Darcy!" she exclaimed. "You have said that yourself, Papa, many times!"

"And I am now beginning to believe that I may have been completely mistaken about both men," said Mr. Bennet slowly and contritely. "For example, I have just received this rather long express from Colonel Forster. He informs me that he has been investigating Wickham since his arrest. *He* will not talk, but his drinking companions are singing like canaries. Captain Denny, for example, says that Wickham stated several times that he had not the slightest intention of marrying you—ever. But Wickham was not as forthright with Denny as he was with Lieutenant Jerremy from another regiment. He did not tell Denny that he was planning to desert and never return, for example. This Jerremy says that Wickham confided in him just the previous day that he must disappear, for some of the Brighton merchants were becoming quite pushy about the money they were owed. He also said that the guest of the colonel's wife would do quite well to warm his bed during the cold nights. When Jerremy asked Wickham how he could justify deceiving this 'bed-warmer,' Wickham only laughed and said that he had never committed himself to anything, and in any event, since it was all her own choice, that she should be able to make do quite well in London after he moved on."

If Lydia's eyes had been getting wider in disbelief as her father read this account, it was nothing compared to her mother's reaction.

"My brother had the right of it!" Mrs. Bennet shrieked in sudden anger, grabbing her daughter by the arm and shaking her fiercely. "You would have been left to be just another 'bit of fluff' on the London streets! Foolish, thoughtless child! You would have ruined yourself, as well as Kitty and Mary, for who would ever marry them after the scandal you would have brought about?"

Her father's words and her mother's scolding finally broke Lydia down. She might not be able to fully recognize the truth just yet—her faith in her Wickham was not yet completely destroyed—but she was at last able to recognize how her actions would be interpreted by everyone else. And, for the first time in her life, she was frightened.

After Mrs. Bennet calmed herself, Mr. Bennet was able to get the rest of the story out of Lydia. It took considerable time and much repeated questioning before his daughter finally admitted that Wickham had never explicitly proposed marriage. Even after admitting that, it took still further inquiry before she reluctantly acknowledged that her belief that he would marry her had been a product of her own imagination. It was not that Lydia was still trying to protect Wickham or even herself; it was that she had not previously been able to see the events in which she had been a participant as anything more than a huge and diverting game. It was not until her father's probing questions forced her to give answers she did not want to give, that she was unwillingly compelled to at least *consider* how foolish her actions had been.

While Mr. Bennet regarded Lydia as quite as silly as her mother, he did not believe that her silliness deserved so harsh a fate as what she had barely evaded. Now, finally, he had been able to make her partially aware of the narrowness of her escape. Then, while she was struggling with the heretofore never experienced emotion of mortification, he then sent her into another paroxysm of tears when he pronounced her punishment.

"I have at last learned to be cautious, daughter!" he thundered. "Your brief period of being out in society is ended! I would not trust you even to take a walk to Meryton without your mother! Further, and this is final, no officer is ever to enter my house again! In fact, they are not even to pass through the village! Balls will be absolutely prohibited unless you stand up with Kitty or Mary! And you are never to stir out of doors till you can prove that you have spent ten minutes of every day in a rational manner!"

Lydia moaned and wept at the imposition, but her mother stifled her incipient protests when she considered what her daughter had almost cost all of them. No, it would be better—much better—for everyone, including Lydia herself, if she stayed at home and learned to keep her mother company. As Lydia continued to cry, terrified of her father and deserted by her mother, Mr. Bennet added, not at all helpfully,

"Well, well, well, do not make yourself too unhappy, child. If you are a good girl for the next ten years, I will take you to a review at the end of them."

After this, Lydia, now wailing inconsolably, was finally allowed to seek the sanctuary of her room. But even though he thought that he had made his point as well as he could, Mr. Bennet did not delude himself that Lydia was truly any wiser as she left the library than when she entered. But he at least felt confident that she would not make *that* particular mistake again.

The rest of the evening was spent in even more unpleasant thought, and in the morning, Mr. Bennet reluctantly ordered his horse to be saddled for a ride to Netherfield. He did not at all look forward to what he had to do, and as a result, when he was left waiting in the entry while a servant went in search of Mr. Darcy, he was tempted to bolt for his horse and return to his library. But even as he rejected this tempting thought, he saw Darcy enter the hall, arm in arm with Elizabeth, and obviously enjoying an entertaining conversation.

When they saw him waiting in the entry, they paused momentarily, and both their faces instantly lost all expression. Mr. Bennet felt an icy dagger in his heart; his brother was completely right, and he was completely wrong. Elizabeth and her husband were obviously united, connected by the strongest of bonds, and they were of one mind in their opinion of him. He had not only offended his dearest daughter in his thoughtless desire to bend her to his will, he had furthermore insulted her husband in the most offensive manner.

The men exchanged cold and wary greetings, and Mr. Bennet then asked whether he might have a few minutes of Darcy's time.

"Of course, sir," Darcy responded coolly, "but I will ask my wife to join us." He did not ask Mr. Bennet's agreement or permission, he simply stated how it was going to be, an unalterable condition to which the older man could only silently accede. So saying, Darcy led the way to Bingley's library with Elizabeth on his arm and closed the door behind them.

Mr. Bennet was understandably reluctant to begin, as he did not believe that he had ever faced as humiliating an interview as what he faced now. He had no assurance whether or not he would even be successful at making his apologies, but he had never been quite as wrong before as he had been in this matter. In the dead of night, he had finally resolved what he must do, hard though it was to begin when actually face-to-face with his daughter and her husband. Taking a deep breath, he forced himself to start, even though he could not meet their eyes.

"Mr. Darcy," he began, "I have come to properly tender my thanks for your efforts to succour my youngest daughter." Darcy gravely inclined his head, making no comment. "In addition, I have come to apologize and beg your forgiveness for the manner in which I have deluded myself as to your character and thus insulted you in the most unforgivable manner. Both my daughter and my brother have taken me to task quite severely, and I received an express from Colonel Forster yesterday that confirms your account in every detail. I have also confronted Lydia and at length forced the true story from her. All these things have convinced me that I have been wrong in every regard, and I would like to attempt a reconciliation between our houses, at least to the extent that is possible given my many errors."

The silence that followed this admission was complete, and Mr. Bennet imagined that the beating of his heart must be audible to everyone in the room, so loud did it sound in his ears. At last, Darcy stirred himself.

"On my behalf, sir, your apology is accepted and your request for forgiveness can only be granted as is commanded of all Christians. But if this matter is truly to be put to rest, something more is required. You must make your peace with your daughter. And I believe that purpose will be best served if I leave you two together in private. Good day, sir," he said simply then left the room.

For several moments, neither Mr. Bennet nor Elizabeth said a word. Mr. Bennet was loath to begin, and Elizabeth was not willing to make it easier for him.

"Lizzy," Mr. Bennet finally said, "I am —"

"How could you?" Elizabeth interrupted abruptly. "How could you say what you did about William? And about me?" Mr. Bennet seemed to shrink from the fire of Elizabeth's anger and could not at first answer. At length, he sighed, and his shoulders slumped.

"I will be completely honest, daughter, though it pains me greatly. But I have thought long on this during the night, and I believe that it was my pride that blinded me to the truth."

"Well, that, at least, I can certainly understand," Elizabeth acknowledged. "I almost let my own pride blind me to the merits of the man who made his proposal to me in the most civil manner I ever could have imagined. But I explained all that in my letters, as did William when he visited and my Uncle Gardiner when he wrote. Why did you not listen to us? To *any* of us?"

Mr. Bennet drew a deep breath. "Because of *my* pride, Lizzy. I was so certain I was right that I was blinded to any other testimony. And I was certain, as only a lifetime with a child can make a foolish father certain, that you would accede to my will and beg my forgiveness for going against my wishes."

"That I might have done — if only for peace between our families — if you had not maligned my husband as you did. You do not *know* him, Father, just as I did not know him when he first proposed. But I, at least, did not deny him the chance to change my opinion."

"And I did deny him that when I refused to give my blessing to your marriage," her father admitted morosely. "I cannot understand how I could have been so blind, but I was. I have asked your husband's forgiveness, Elizabeth, and now I ask yours. I beseech you, do not allow my foolishness to be the point that divides us forever!"

"If I did, then I would be allowing my own pride to seek vengeance for the hurt I suffered, and that I refuse to do. For that would be an offence against my husband and my family." She looked at her father. "And I do not want to set an example to my child of the price that pride can cause one to pay."

Mr. Bennet could only nod miserably.

"I did not have a chance to make an announcement to anyone except William before this crisis broke over us, but it is true. You will have a grandchild no later than March. And yes, Father, you do have my forgiveness."

And as she crossed the room to embrace her father, Mr. Bennet was unable to stop what he had not done since he was a child. He wept.

At length, he regained his composure, and Elizabeth guided him toward the door to the library. "Come, let us join the others so that I can make my announcement. Then I must go to Longbourn and tell my mother."

"Of course, dear Lizzy," her father said, as he wiped his eyes with his handkerchief and offered his arm.

When Elizabeth entered the parlour on the arm of her father, she saw the sudden burst of joy on Jane's face and the look of relief that Mr. Gardiner gave, both happy that father and daughter had managed to effect a healing of their breach. She was glad for their sake, yet saddened by the knowledge that nothing could ever make things the way they had been before. She was learning that not every dispute could be fully resolved, but she also knew that, for the sake of her family and for the life growing within her, the attempt must be made.

But as she looked into the smiling eyes of her husband as he crossed to her and accepted her arm from her father, she knew that some of the distance that would forever lie between her and her father would have occurred in any case. Her first loyalty now was to William and their family—Georgiana and Colonel Fitzwilliam now, and their children to come. As her husband leaned down to kiss her forehead, she allowed herself to be enfolded in his arms while she heard her father awkwardly open a conversation with her sister and Bingley. With her face against Darcy's chest and his chin on top of her head, Elizabeth Darcy knew with absolute certainty that within these strong arms was where she belonged.

Epilogue

Pemberley, Christmas, 1857

Fitzwilliam Darcy looked down the long table and smiled at Elizabeth at the other end. Sitting at this table and the several tables surrounding it for Christmas celebration was the Darcy extended family—Darcys, Bingleys, and Fitzwilliams—twelve children, thirty-one grandchildren, and eleven great-grandchildren.

It makes an impressive array, Darcy thought, *but how many more Christmas seasons can we gather together?* He was starting to feel his seventy-three years—that winter seemed worse than he remembered, making his joints ache and throb—and though he still rode daily when the weather permitted, riding was increasingly painful, especially in his knees and lower back. Elizabeth, thankfully, was less affected, and she still took her daily walks through the Pemberley grounds that she loved more than ever. And as it had been ever since that first night forty-five years earlier, they still retired every night to his bed.

I could not have wished for a better life, he thought, looking down the table at his wife. As always, Elizabeth seemed able to sense the direction of his thoughts, both the satisfaction and the melancholy, and she accepted one and rejected the other, sending him a lovely smile that was meant for him alone. It was the same one she had first given him on that April day when they were married, and the sight of it dispelled his gloom as it always did.

Georgiana smiled as she caught the exchange, and she leaned over to whisper in her husband's ear. Darcy could only shake his head as Richard snorted in laughter.

General Richard Fitzwilliam was resplendent in full scarlet dress uniform for the occasion, but, like many of his fellow officers, he had had little employment in his trade since Bonaparte had been sent into exile over forty years before. It was on that occasion when, after returning from the continent and despite his military training, he had been taken completely by surprise when he visited the Darcy home after the remnants of his regiment returned from Waterloo. There, while he still limped from a wound received in that last battle, he had been most sternly taken to task by his young cousin at the dinner table. Before Darcy and Elizabeth, she told him firmly that it was long past time that he stopped rambling about Europe making a scarlet target of himself, that it was time that he settled down to married life, and that the month of September would do most splendidly for their wedding.

He had looked at his other cousin in shock, only to hear Darcy respond calmly as he continued eating, "Do not look to me for support in this matter, Richard. We Darcys—as you have said so many times—are rather impulsive."

Fitzwilliam never recovered from his initial stunned amazement, easily succumbing to Georgiana's well planned campaign, and he was to that day uncertain whether he had ever formally proposed. Nevertheless, he was present along with friends and family as Darcy escorted a beaming Georgiana to his side in the Pemberley chapel and his bachelorhood came to an end. Between Georgiana's fortune, his half-pay, and various gifts from his father and Darcy, the newlyweds had purchased a modest house in town and settled down to bear and rear three children, eleven grandchildren, and one great-grandchild.

Elizabeth well understood her husband's thoughts as his eyes swept the large room, taking in all the various sons and daughters and their offspring, sitting either at the large table or at one of the other tables set up for the occasion. She knew the pleasure he took in the presence of all their family in this sacred season, and she also knew the reason for the bittersweet expression that accompanied his look of satisfaction. She knew that their long married life was in its closing stages, but the thought did not rouse her to melancholy, for she knew how unlikely their happiness must have appeared to so many others all those long years ago. And she was cheered that her smile at him blew the winds of sadness from his face, as he could not help returning her own smile. And she had to laugh at Richard's oft-repeated comment on the Darcy 'impulsiveness,' especially since he had fallen victim to a version of it himself.

Not, she thought to herself with an inner smile, *that he ever seems to have regretted the manner in which Georgiana had out-manoeuvred him!*

Elizabeth looked around the room herself, seeing not only those in attendance but also those who were missing, including her parents. After her father's apology to both Darcy and herself, she had eventually been able to again enjoy his company even though he and Darcy had never been truly comfortable with each other. But at least both her mother and father had lived long enough to see four of their five grandchildren born.

At least Mama was spared much of the pain of seeing Longbourn possessed by Mr. Collins, she thought, *though little good it did him.* Lady Catherine, who had never reconciled with her nephew, had released Mr. Collins from her service six months after Mr. Bennet's death, and that foolish man had tried to assume the role of landed gentleman. He had taken a chill while trying to make a show of inspecting his new estate and had never recovered, passing on within two months of taking possession of Longbourn. The entail had also died with him, and Longbourn had passed to the management of his wife, Charlotte, who accomplished that task even better than her own father before passing it on to her eldest son.

After her mother's passing, Elizabeth had brought Mary to Pemberley, and Mary still remained, though she seldom left her room these days. Her reading remained as avid as ever, though her tastes had changed as the years passed and as her need for thick spectacles and bright daylight increased. At her own request, she sat that night at a corner table with the youngest of the children, for in her later years, she had developed an affinity for the children she had never borne. Elizabeth had to smile as she watched the young children swarm around her sister while Mary told them the Christmas Story, answering all their questions about Bethlehem and the Christmas Star and Wise Men and all the other facets of that happy season.

Elizabeth looked fondly at her other sister as Jane sat with her beloved Bingley. She did not think the couple had ever had a single serious dispute in their many years of marriage. She and Jane had sat and talked long into the morning hours the previous night, and Elizabeth now mentally smiled in remembrance of that talk, with both herself and Jane sitting on her seldom-used bed. It had been like a return to their time before their marriages, and their talk had ranged the years and the experiences, the loss of loved ones and the birth of children, so many events of happiness and some of sadness. They were both conscious of the aging of their husbands, Bingley even more than Darcy, though he was seven years Darcy's junior. As they sat in their thick robes and warm, woollen nightgowns against the chill that even the bright fire could not wholly dispel, Elizabeth and Jane had laughed in remembrance as they compared the sensible garments they now wore to the daring and revealing nightgowns they had first worn for the delight of their new husbands — nightgowns recommended and urged on them by their eminently sensible Aunt Gardiner.

Dear Aunt Gardiner, Elizabeth thought with fond recollection. Her Aunt and Uncle Gardiner had spent much time with Darcy and herself, either in town or at Pemberley, and Darcy had loved the couple dearly. She remembered his tears of grief as they laid Mr. Gardiner to rest at Pemberley, for they had brought her aunt and uncle to live with them as Mr. Gardiner's health failed. Aunt Gardiner, who was ten years younger than her husband, had lived on with them, content but no longer complete without her husband, and her passing two years ago had not brought the tears that her husband's passing had occasioned. It was clear to both Elizabeth and her husband that Mrs. Gardiner had not minded her approaching end and was more than ready to be re-united with her husband. She was buried beside him behind the Pemberley chapel, and Elizabeth often came upon Darcy as he stood silently before the white headstones that were not far from those of his own parents.

Elizabeth's thoughts were not as cheerful as she thought of Lydia and Kitty. Kitty had died in childbirth thirty years earlier, and Lydia had disappeared to America, embittered by her experience with Wickham and estranged from Elizabeth and Jane by her continued refusal to treat Darcy with respect — even after Mr. Bennet recanted his objections. Kitty's death had been tragic, but at least she had prospered under the care of Jane and Elizabeth, eventually marrying a respectable man and bearing two sons before her untimely death. Afterwards, her husband had brought up their two surviving sons to be fine men, who even now sat at one of the side tables with their families.

But Lydia was simply a waste, Elizabeth thought sadly, and she had not heard from her youngest sister since she had turned one and twenty. On coming of age, Lydia had received a fifth share of their mother's fortune and had disappeared to America after sending Elizabeth a venomous letter blaming her for all her misfortunes. In all that time, Lydia had never again communicated with any of her family, and Elizabeth had no idea what had become of her youngest sister.

As for Wickham, he had never again surfaced in their life though he had at length been released from prison some seven years after she and Darcy were married. But Elizabeth had certain suspicions about Mr. Wickham, for Major General Fitzwilliam had suddenly left his wife two weeks before Wickham was released. He had departed in company with former Colour Sergeant Henderson, who had finally taken off his uniform to enter service with the Fitzwilliam family in town, and the two men had not returned for some three weeks. After their return, neither man would ever answer a direct question as to where they had gone or what they had done. But Elizabeth had noted that her husband had never evidenced any curiosity about Fitzwilliam's disappearance even though such an apparent desertion of his sister ought to have aroused Darcy's protective instincts. Nor had Georgiana, in her turn, ever shown any curiosity about where her husband had disappeared. In any event, Elizabeth had asked no questions of Darcy since she had her own suspicions of what Major General Fitzwilliam and Colour Sergeant Henderson had been doing during their sabbatical. She suspected that Wickham had been confronted with Fitzwilliam and Henderson upon his release from prison, and those two men had given him a choice of leaving England immediately and forever or else meeting Fitzwilliam on the field of honour. It was also possible that Fitzwilliam had simply cut down the other man in cold blood, but she assigned that a rather low level of probability given what she knew of Fitzwilliam's character. Whatever the actual facts were, it was noticeable that, when Fitzwilliam returned, both brother and sister were curiously uncurious. This fact was so singular that Elizabeth was convinced further enquiries into what had actually transpired during that absence were unnecessary, and her opinion proved correct since *that man* never plagued the happiness of her family again.

Lady Catherine had also never again plagued her family though she knew that Darcy had been unhappy when his attempts at healing the breach had been spurned. But Lord Matlock had consoled Darcy, telling him, '*At least you tried your best, nephew. It is not your fault that Catherine continues to reject your peace offerings. At least we gave Anne some comfort and happiness before the end.*' Lord and Lady Matlock had brought Anne to live with them some months after Darcy and Elizabeth had married, and there the frail woman had stayed though her health had continued to decline until her death five years later.

Most interesting was Bingley's sister, Caroline, as she sat beside Jane and Bingley that night while she held and rocked Elaine Bingley, Jane's great-grandchild, on her lap. Caroline had rather surprisingly married a Scottish doctor of modest means about three years after her brother's marriage, but she had been so devastated at his death from the influenza after only five years of marriage that Elizabeth and Jane had been forced to literally take her under their care. That formerly haughty and supercilious lady had been in a state of shock and breakdown after her husband's funeral, for she appeared to have loved Andrew McGrath quite deeply and had become almost another member of the Bingley family. The couple never had children, for Caroline had miscarried twice, and it took many months after her husband's passing before she could even attempt a smile. For so many years, Caroline McGrath had been such a true friend that Elizabeth had a difficult time recalling the arrogant and deceitful woman who Bingley had once banished from his house.

Elizabeth looked toward the head of the table as her husband rose to his feet and cleared his throat in preparation for the traditional toast at the Christmas season. Silence began to spread outwards as more and more of the family became aware of Darcy's intention. The children's tables were the last to become quiet, and Mary had to chide several of the children before they were stilled.

When the room was sufficiently quiet, Darcy began. "For my whole life, our family has gathered at Pemberley to celebrate this sacred season. I can remember my father standing here in this same position, and I remember wishing that he would hurry up so we could exchange presents and light the Yule log." A ripple of laughter swept the room, louder in the sections where the younger people sat.

"But my father would always remind us that we should honour the most important things in our lives and would do so in their proper order: God, Family, and Country. So I will begin by speaking of this Christmas season and the reason for its celebration, which is the birth of our Saviour. I will not offer a toast, for we shall share communion with Reverend Mayfair at the Pemberley Chapel on the morrow, but I will just ask that all of us keep the reason for this celebration in our hearts as we enjoy the festivities."

Darcy was silent for a few moments, his head bowed in either prayer or contemplation before he continued. "Now I shall offer the first toast to our family, who are gathered together in unprecedented numbers," he said, raising his head to sweep the room. "These numbers are especially extraordinary since it seems we have finally found the limits of Pemberley," he said, drawing another round of laughter, since the guests had filled the house to bursting and beyond, so that some of the late arrivals had been put up at one of the inns in Lambton. "But nevertheless, we are all gathered together on this most special evening, and it is overwhelming to look out on all those who are most dear to us. I speak of my brother, Charles Bingley, who was my good friend before he was my brother. I speak of my sister, Jane Bingley, who was my wife's sister before she became my own. I speak of my first sister, Georgiana Fitzwilliam, and her husband, General Richard Fitzwilliam, who was my cousin before he so *impulsively* became my brother."

The laughter this time was loud and long, and Richard was among those who laughed loudest. One young voice called from the back of the room, "Control yourselves, please, cousins! Else we shall again hear the story of his courtship!" This comment only made the laughter swell.

When the laughter died out, Darcy continued, "I speak of all our children, grandchildren and even great-grandchildren. And now I ask you to join me in a toast to all the members of our family on the occasion of this Christmas season. To our family!" he exclaimed, raising his glass of wine before draining its contents.

When all had lowered their glasses, Darcy continued, "And now, I shall ask my brother, General Richard Fitzwilliam, to offer a toast to our country."

Turning to Fitzwilliam, he commented slyly, "And I would suggest that you keep this short, Richard." The laughter was light amid the clinking of decanters against the rims of wine glasses as General Fitzwilliam rose to his feet.

"Friends and family," he said, raising his glass, "I am honoured to give the toast to our beloved country, whose uniform I have worn my whole life. I give you England, Scotland, Ireland, Wales, and the British Empire, on which the sun never sets, and its sovereign, Victoria, by the grace of God, Queen and Empress. Ladies and Gentlemen, God Save the Queen!"

"God Save the Queen!"

Fitzwilliam took his seat after draining his glass, and Georgiana put her arm through his and leaned over to kiss his cheek fondly.

Darcy once again stood at the head of the table — to the surprise of everyone since the toast to Country was the traditional final toast at these yearly gatherings.

"Friends and family, Ladies and Gentlemen," he said, "I ask your indulgence to make an additional toast this year, a toast to the most extraordinary woman I have ever known, who has made my life a delight since we exchanged vows on a bright April day that seems like it was only yesterday. The woman who has borne my children and shared my life and who has been an unequalled mistress of Pemberley. I do not deserve her, and I came unbearably close to never winning her, and I thank God every day for my good fortune!"

"Tell us about *your* courtship!" one of the guests called out, but Darcy only smiled.

"So now I propose that we drink to my wife these last 45 years." He raised his glass toward the foot of the table, while tears stung at the corners of his eyes.

"I drink to you, dearest, loveliest Elizabeth. Ladies and Gentlemen, I give you Mrs. Elizabeth Darcy!"

"Mrs. Elizabeth Darcy!" came the thundering response.

End

CPSIA information can be obtained
at www.ICGtesting.com
Printed in the USA
BVHW04s1115010618
517967BV00001B/36/P